ETERNAL SHADOWS

GODS OF THE NIGHT

NINA BANGS

Please Note

This is a work of fiction. Names, characters, places, and incidents either are the product of the author's imagination or are used fictitiously, and any resemblance to actual persons, living or dead, business establishments, events or locales is entirely coincidental.

Cover Design and Interior Format

DEDICATION

Eternal thanks to critique partners Gerry Bartlett and Donna Maloy for their patient suffering—most of the time—as I whined, made excuses, and promised that, yes, I would finish this book during my lifetime. I'm certain they had their doubts.

ACKNOWLEDGEMENTS

Sending mega thanks to Jenah Yuah for contributing the title, *Eternal Shadows*. Love it! If anyone lives in the shadows, it's Rap, or is he Adam?

I also want to thank the many readers who have waited far too long for this. Every time I heard from one of you, it gave me the incentive to keep going.

CHAPTER ONE

December 2012

"YOU *FIRED* ME." SELENE SPAT the offending word, trying to get rid of its sour taste. "In a *text* message." She waved her phone in front of the seven men lined up in front of her. "You cowardly scum."

All seven men wore the same terrified expressions. In fact, they were identical in every way. Tall with long dark red hair that sparkled where the sunlight shining in from the hotel window touched it. Beautiful faces with swirling blue-green eyes. Gorgeous wrappings to cover up big fat lumps of coal for souls.

"Here, let me read your exact words." Selene pulled up the message.

"Relieved of duty." She glanced at the man on the far right. He shattered, pieces of him littering the floor like a broken plastic toy.

"Not emotionally suited to job." She glared at the next man in line. His head disappeared, leaving his body still standing.

"Will find someone more useful." She waved at the third man. He was gone in a cloud of purple smoke.

She slammed the phone down on the desk. "What the hell does that mean? You've only got six of us left. Fin took out the rest. That's why you hired me to plug one of the holes. Do you really think someone else will have better luck at infiltrating Fin's forces?" She sneered at the complete ludicrousness of the thought.

The next man in line whimpered.

"Just because I refused to order my recruits into that one building, you're getting rid of me? Well, let me tell you something, you slimy snake. I don't destroy anything without a good tactical reason. We wouldn't have gained one thing by turning those demons loose on everyone. It would've thrown San Diego into a panic, and we're not ready for that yet. The authorities couldn't have ignored that many deaths, and cable news would've spent 24/7 dissecting the reports of nonhuman involvement." Besides, kids had been eating with their parents in the cafeteria, and there'd been a box of newborn kittens in one of the offices. Not that the kids or kittens had anything to do with her decision. She wasn't sentimental about young things. Selene shut the door on any opposing thoughts.

"You'll regret your words. I don't need you. And I always finish a job. Now, I have some shopping to do." *Pop. Pop. Pop. Pop.* They all disappeared in a haze of multicolored smoke. Selene did so enjoy dramatic displays of her power.

She took a moment to retrieve the scattered bits of her essence before grabbing her phone and heading for the door. Selene couldn't stay in this hotel. She'd have to find her own place.

Behind her, a woman turned from where she'd been staring out the window. "Well, you certainly told *them*."

Selene didn't miss the sardonic tone. She paused with her hand on the knob to look   back . . . at her own face, except the other woman had no scars and better hair. "I did, didn't I?"

The woman frowned. "Why seven of him?"

"Because I get more satisfaction from yelling at a

crowd." Just before she closed the door, Selene glanced at the woman again. "Pack and meet me at the car, Meg." She slammed the door. A childish gesture, but it felt good. She paused. Not the elevator. Selene needed something physical to take the edge off her fury. The stairs. But before she could move, a boy raced down the hall toward her. He stopped, panting, a few feet away.

"Don't do anything stupid, Selene." He swept dyed black hair away from his face exposing pale green eyes darkened with worry.

She sighed. "Why're you here, Ace?"

"I know what Zero did to you."

She responded automatically. "Don't call him Zero. You know he hates that name." Ace called the boss Zero whenever he was ticked off and wanted to annoy Frost. Selene had no idea how Ace got away with that. No one else dared call Frost by the name Fin had given him.

He shrugged. "Hey, calling him by a name he hates and surviving seems to be my only power." Bitterness laced his voice. "That's me, Super-Gnat. Annoying to the end."

On second thought, Frost was a jerk. Why was she worried about his thin skin? "Forget what I said. Call him Zero all you want. It's a great name."

"Are you going to give up the search now that he's cut you loose?" Ace shifted from foot to foot, unable to control all his energy.

"What do you think?" Selene would miss the boy. He looked around seventeen, but she didn't have a clue about his actual age. Maybe he really was that young. He acted the part.

His smile was sly. "You never give up. So, are you going to search for Fin's men today?" He took her silence for a yes. "Take me with you."

"Can't do. Frost might be done with me, but you're special to him. He'd stomp me into mush if I put you in danger." She often wondered why Frost kept him around.

Ace wasn't related to anyone, and he had no powers. Frost wasn't someone who tolerated anyone who didn't benefit him in some way.

"He doesn't have to know. And I'll stay out of trouble." Ace leaned forward. He set the hook. "Besides, I have some interesting info I might be willing to share." He reeled her in. "I know where two of Fin's men will be today."

Damn. Selene weighed the pros and cons. She needed any help she could get. She didn't have a clue where Fin and his men were holed up. On the other hand, Frost would make short work of her if something happened to Ace.

She took a deep breath and then decided. "What do you have?"

To Ace's credit, he didn't gloat. "I got this the old-fashioned way. I listened at Frost's door. He was talking to Crow."

Selene curled her lip. "When did *he* reach town? And please tell me he isn't my replacement."

Ace frowned. "Do you think he could manage your job?"

She did a mental eye-roll. "He's a one-dimensional predator. No creativity." Crow's considerable power was only equaled by his ruthlessness. He didn't need a reason to slaughter. The whole destroying process put him in his happy place. It made his day to take his big-ass bird form and then rip off someone's head. "I wonder what he's up to."

Ace shrugged. "Bet he's not trying to infiltrate. He just wants to kill everything that moves. Anyway, Frost told him a vampire contact said two of Fin's guys would be at the zoo today."

Selene nodded. "Guess we'll be going to the zoo. You, me, Meg, Crow, and Fin's men." She smiled. "It'll be fun."

He grinned back. "Going to take your demon recruits?"

"Frost fired me, so I suppose they're not my recruits anymore." Her smile widened. "It doesn't matter. I have my own army on call."

CHAPTER TWO

———

"**T**HEY KNOW WHAT WE ARE." Just saying the words made Rap feel good. The scent of their fear washed over him, that heart-stopping explosion of adrenaline that jump-started his motor, made him feel alive and ready for the hunt. He liked the fear. Okay, so at least two of him did.

He forced his expression to remain neutral, though. No smiling. A show of teeth would scare all the little kids eating candy and staring at the animals. Funny thing, he and his brother were the most dangerous predators in the zoo today, but the humans flowing past didn't even glance their way. How had the species not gone extinct long ago? It was a mystery.

"Who? Where?" Tor whirled from the fence to face the streaming crowd, searching faces for that spark of horrified recognition.

Excited anticipation widened Tor's eyes. His breathing quickened, and Rap knew his brother was only seconds away from changing. Something in Rap really wanted to see that happen, to feel the terror rippling through the humans as they got their first look at his brother's soul. But then Fin would get involved. The boss would end the fun way too soon.

"Not the people." Rap nodded to the bottom of the hill. "Them."

Tor's breathing returned to normal as he followed his brother's gaze. "The tigers?"

"Look at how they're watching us. Ears flat, teeth bared, eyes narrowed to slits, tails down—every one of them is scared shitless. They recognize us." One part of him longed to release his soul and become the mindless hunter he once was. The tigers would be worthy prey. To kill, to feed, to sleep, to mate. Life was a lot simpler then. Tor closed his eyes and sniffed. "You're right. I can smell their fear." He smiled. But then he remembered his brother's words. He opened his eyes. His smile faded. "Jeez, don't do that to me again." He exhaled deeply as his tension drained. "I almost lost it. Then what would've happened?"

"Bloody death." Rap forgot not to smile. Two older women who had stopped beside Greer to stare at the tigers glanced at Rap. He met their gazes. His smile widened. They hurried away. He seemed to have that effect on humans lately. "Just like the old days. Good times."

Tor shook his head. "I don't know, Rap. You worry me. We're supposed to blend in, not cause riots." He glanced at his watch. "Time for lunch. What do you want to eat?" He looked over at Greer to include him in the discussion, but their driver was too focused on the tigers to notice.

Rap stretched. "I don't know. I haven't decided who I am today. Am I Adam?" He watched a young couple walk past. "Warm blood makes a great pick-me-upper." He pointed at the tigers. "Or am I the beast? We could find a deer enclosure, and I could slip into my true form. Venison for lunch. Rare. Just the way I like it." A glance assured him that Tor was only a few seconds from sending out a mental call for help from Fin, so Rap put his brother out of his misery. "Nah, no sport in killing penned deer, and I always get blood stains on my shirt. Besides, I'm feeling really human today. Guess I'm Rap.

Let's get out of here and find that Italian place we passed on our way in."

Tor nodded. He didn't try to hide his relief as he followed Rap away from the Tiger Trail. "I've had all of the zoo I can take. This isn't getting us anywhere." Greer lagged behind, trying to get a last glimpse of the tigers.

Rap agreed. Sure, the hill overlooking a view of tigers padding across rocks and along the stream below was spectacular. A beautiful setting—lots of greenery. The mist from the waterfall that arched over the trail actually chilled him, though. Thankfully, the December weather was cool enough for his hoodie not to look strange.

The San Diego Zoo was too freaking big. They'd done the Safari Park, ridden the Skyfari Aerial Tram, and suffered through the Kangaroo Express Bus as they hopped off at different places to sit and stare at a bunch of happy families. The whole experience depressed him. What did he know about happy families? Why did he even care? He focused on his brother, shoving the questions out of his mind.

Tor was just warming up. "I wish just once our legendary leader would lay things out in plain-speak. Fin could've said, 'Yo, I had a vision a gazillion years ago showing these two babes walking past the tiger exhibit at noon this Friday. One of them will save our butts from the Big Bad.' And here we'd be, ready to invite them to a meeting with Fin. Instead, it's like, 'Um, I see two women. Look like twins. Blond hair. One of them has a scar on her face. The woman with the scar is holding a piece of metal, and she's standing in front of something with bars like a cage. Feels like the zoo.' *Feels* like the zoo? He's kidding, right? Besides, his visions only show the ultimate butt-saving moment. These women could be anywhere now. What? Does he expect us to sit around the zoo every day until December twenty-first?"

"Probably. But we aren't the only ones. Other guys are

out there searching the city, too." Rap didn't elaborate. He was too busy juggling his multiple personalities to think hard thoughts about Fin.

"Hey, any chance I could watch the tigers a little longer before we leave?" Greer had caught up to them.

Rap's first instinct was to say no. He didn't want to spend another useless minute here looking at captive animals, even if their captivity looked comfortable, even luxurious compared to what he remembered of his own . . . He shook his head. Wouldn't think about that now.

Tor spoke for him. "Really? We've just spent a half hour staring at them."

Greer didn't answer, but Rap sensed his disappointment. Rap understood. To the rest of the world, Greer was a small man who created miracles in the kitchen. His exterior was all they saw. Inside, though, their chef and temporary driver had the soul of a tiger. He was otherkin—a tiger trapped in a man's body, never able to shift, never able to physically express his true form.

Rap knew the feeling of not belonging to a group, of being a little of this and a little of that, but never a whole of anything. He took a deep breath. *Get over yourself.* No use regretting what he couldn't change.

"Why not. Do it. You can never have enough tigers." Rap grinned at Greer. "Don't stay too long, though. I'm starving. We'll wait in the car."

Greer paused before turning away. "You sure you don't need me to stay close?"

Rap glanced around. There were other humans walking the trail. They acted as a shield. The enemy could only sense Rap and the rest of Fin's Eleven when no humans were nearby. Not a problem here. "No, go look at your tigers."

Tor seemed about to complain, but then he just shrugged.

Rap dodged the direct sunlight all the way to the exit.

It wouldn't turn him to ash, but it irritated his skin. He was so busy searching out the next shady spot that he didn't realize Tor had stopped until his brother shoved him in the back.

"Look." Tor pointed.

They were standing in the parking lot. No shade, lots of sun. He pulled his hood further over his head. Rap forgot about his discomfort, though, as he realized what Tor had seen. Three people leaned over the really flat tire of a nearby car—two women and a man, no, boy. He looked about seventeen or eighteen. Rap moved a little closer, narrowing his gaze on the three. Fin hadn't mentioned a teen, but his vision would only have involved the person responsible for taking out Six. The two women looked right, though. Blond. One was scarred. The vision, only not.

Rap hoped not. They didn't need to deal with a third person. Maybe the kid was just trying to help with the tire. Had they gotten lucky? Were these the women Fin wanted? No matter how much of a pain this was, he knew better than to doubt his leader's visions.

Then, as though they could sense his stare, the women turned to look his way. Instant impressions: twins, twenties, blond hair, one beautiful, one . . . interesting. The interesting one caught his attention. She had the same face as her sister, but different. A scar cut a jagged path across one cheek to disappear into her hairline near her ear. But his interest went deeper than that. There was something about her gaze . . .

Rap didn't have a chance to carry that thought further before the teen put his hand on the arm of the unscarred twin and pointed at the tire. She smiled as she patted his hand but didn't take her attention from Tor and him. Her hand-patting seemed a little too familiar for the kid to be merely a passerby. When the boy realized her attention was elsewhere, he turned to look.

"Damn. Do you think he's with them?"

Tor's frustration mirrored his own. "Afraid so." What had Fin gotten them into? They were supposed to chat up the women, make a connection, and then call in Fin to seal the deal. The boy would screw everything up. "Looks young. Late teens." Maybe a brother or friend. Rap hoped for the best. "Not a boyfriend." But whatever his connection to the women, he was tall and looked as though he could take care of himself.

Tor raked his fingers through his hair. "What now? We can't stand here staring at each other."

"Right." Time to make a move before things got awkward. "You're the charming one. You go first. I'd scare them off." Only a short time ago things were different. Rap had looked exactly like his brothers. Blond hair, blue eyes, smiled a lot—identical triplets. Human women loved his face. They didn't have a clue that behind it lurked the soul of an ancient predator. But then everything had changed. "I'll get the jack and the lug wrench. Then I'll just stand behind you and glower."

His brother frowned. "Not funny." But he obeyed.

Rap walked the short distance to their car, opened the trunk, and pulled out what he needed. While he was at it, he mentally instant-messaged Fin. *We found the two women, but there's a problem. They have a boy with them.* He didn't need to say anything more. Fin knew where they were and would be monitoring them. Their leader could see through Rap's eyes if he chose. Rap wasn't happy with that part of Fin's power. Fin always made him feel less than totally in control of his mind. He closed the trunk and left his concerns about Fin's power locked inside for the time being.

When Rap reached Tor's side, he was in time to find the unscarred sister smiling at his brother. "I love the big cats, but I'm always glad to have a fence between us."

She was all long blond hair, big blue eyes, and dimples.

Rap sneered. He could almost see his brother melting under the force of her smile. He knew he should keep his mouth shut, but he was in a crappy mood. "Bet there are a lot more dangerous predators on your side of the fence." What a dumb thing to say. He didn't need to put ideas in people's heads.

The teen grinned at him. "Now she'll be looking behind every bush for a serial killer." He shook his head. "We come from a small town in Kansas. The only crime there is when Sheriff Lawson has to haul Waylon Trapp in for stealing chickens. Meg's convinced the whole state of California is one big crime scene."

Rap relaxed a little. The kid seemed friendly, not dangerous. He had shaggy black hair, pale green eyes with no hidden depths, and no suspicious tells that Rap could see. But . . . Just for a moment, Rap sensed something familiar about him. Then the feeling was gone. Rap let it go. He had other things to worry about. His love-struck brother for example. Meg blushed and Tor's eyes glazed over. Just great.

The scarred woman stared at Tor. She didn't look impressed. Then she shifted her attention to Rap. "You're here to help with the tire?" She didn't sound grateful.

There was nothing friendly about her eyes. They were hard and assessing. And just in case hair like her sister's might fool him into thinking her soft in any way, she'd had hers chopped short. Too bad it framed her face in a way he thought was sexy. He'd bet that's not what she'd intended.

Rap went for casual. He shrugged. "Just being neighborly." He tried for a smile, but he knew it came off twisted and cynical. "You know, so we can retrieve California's reputation from the swamp."

"How much will changing the tire cost, *neighbor*?" She gave him an almost-smile, but the brief quirk of her lips never even came close to the remote stillness of those eyes. Her gaze said she'd grind him into the dirt beneath her heel if he annoyed her. He reached out with his beast's senses, testing the shimmer of threatened violence he felt in her. The beast decided she'd be a worthy opponent.

Rap said what he thought before running it past his brain. "You're an interesting woman. Oh, and not everyone wants payment for doing someone a favor."

She didn't smile, she didn't blink, and her gaze turned icier, if possible. "Interesting? I can't imagine why you'd think that. And everyone wants something."

The kid laughed. "That's our Selene, always making friends wherever she goes." His voice had an edge to it.

Rap would think about what that meant later. But now he had to find a way to keep these people here until Fin showed up. Selene wasn't going to make it easy. "No problem. I'll just take care of your tire." He was looking at the bad-tempered twin, but it was the unscarred one who answered.

"You're a life-saver. None of us has any idea how to fix it." She offered her hand. "I'm Meg." She turned to smile at the boy. "This is Ace. And you are?"

He almost said Rap, but then thought better of it. He was wearing someone else's face and body, so he'd do well to maintain that identity. If it got back to his people that he was calling himself Rap, they'd want an explanation. One he wasn't ready to give right now.

"I'm Adam." He shook her hand as he nodded toward his brother. "This is Tor." Just then Greer hurried up. He was breathing hard. Fin had probably filled him in. "And this is Greer." He glanced at their driver. Greer gave him a thumbs up. Fin was on his way. And not a moment too soon. Once he fixed their tire, he'd have no reason to keep them there.

Tor leaped into the sudden silence. "So, are you just visiting the city?"

Rap left his brother to make conversation while he

took care of the tire. Tor never ran out of words, especially when there was a beautiful woman hanging onto each one. He half listened to Meg's and Ace's answers as he worked. "No. Here to stay. Blah, blah, blah." Jeez, whoever had tightened these lug nuts had never meant for them to come off. But they hadn't counted on his unscrewing power. As he removed the last one, he glanced up. And met Selene's gaze.

She was bent over watching everything he did. Her face was so close he could've reached out to sweep away strands of her hair that had fallen over her eyes. And what eyes. A clear brilliant blue that should've held no secrets. But he didn't believe that for a moment. Rap allowed his gaze to slip to her lips. Sensual. *Not* smiling. He blinked. Right. Back to the tire.

Selene forced her attention away from his face, but she'd seen enough. A strong jaw, knife-edge cheekbones, and amber eyes with a touch of cruelty in them. She could grow to like that face, so she'd make sure not to look at it any more than necessary. Humans were not for her. He'd fix their tire and then they'd leave.

She could feel his stare. Maybe she should explain why she'd been hanging over him. "I want to know how to change a tire so I can do it myself next time." The fact that she couldn't made her mad. Damn it, she was a warrior. She'd fought with armies. It was an insult that this stranger could do something she couldn't do.

Ace joined them, leaving Meg and the other man, Tor, alone with their heads together. Surprised, Selene realized that she resented Ace's presence.

He leaned in close to murmur, "Any Fin vibes?"

Selene shook her head. Both men were human. She would've sensed if . . . Or maybe not. Could they shield themselves from her in the same way Frost made sure all of his people were shielded? Something to think about.

But she didn't get a chance to do anymore thinking.

Suddenly, the ground shook and a rumbling sound rolled through the zoo.

Ace yelped, "Earthquake."

Adam shook his head. "No. Something else." He stood, listened for a moment, and then took a step toward the zoo.

Something else indeed. Crow. Selene could feel his destructive power crashing in waves from inside the zoo. She silently cursed him. What did he think he was doing?

She found out soon enough. First came the pounding of footsteps. Then a mob of people broke into view. The screaming rose to a roar. They pushed and fought their way through the exit and broke for their cars.

"No way!"

Adam had nailed it. Because behind the panicked flood of people ran and bounded the big cats—lions, tigers, along with a few bears. That idiot had freed the animals. Selene couldn't believe even Crow would be that stupid.

Tor turned wide eyes on Adam. "Tell me those aren't wolves in the back?"

Selene knew better. Not just wolves. Those monsters were Crow's recruits, at least twenty werewolves. She didn't believe Frost had given his okay for this. But then, she hadn't believed that he'd get rid of her for refusing to destroy that building either. Maybe he'd decided to begin the apocalypse early.

The first wave of humans raced past them, frantically trying to reach the safety of their cars. Selene could see they weren't going to make it. Already the animals were catching up to the stragglers. They were lucky the big cats seemed focused on escaping the wolves rather than chewing up the zoo-goers. Smart cats.

"This is crazy. We can't let this happen. It'll be a slaughter." Ace clenched his fists as he turned frantic eyes on her.

She froze. What to do? Interfere? Mind her own business? She watched Adam and Tor arguing. There was lots of shouting and hand-waving. But with all the noise the mob and animals were making, she couldn't hear what they were saying.

While she was still waffling, the two men seemed to finally agree. Adam and Tor turned to face the approaching wolves.

Selene finally moved. No, she wouldn't allow them to do whatever stupidly courageous thing they probably intended. They had to get into the car before the wolves reached them. Not that the metal would stop the werewolves, but the creatures would bypass them for easier prey. She ran toward the men even as she saw Ace opening the car door. "Get into the car!"

Adam turned to stare at her. He smiled. "Pray for the wolves."

CHAPTER THREE

T HEN BOTH MEN *CHANGED*.
Selene gasped. She stared at them from wide, unblinking eyes.

She'd found Fin's men.

"Oh." Meg had nothing more to offer.

"They're ..." Ace's voice trailed off into shocked silence.

"Utahraptors. Weight, 2,200 pounds. Height, six feet tall at the hip. Length, twenty-three feet. Biggest raptors ever to walk the earth. Hunted in packs." Frost had made all of them memorize that stuff so they'd recognize Fin's men. Tor. Of course. The other one was either Utah or Rap. Then where did the Adam name come from?

Selene didn't have time to think about that. The violence had ramped up. The big cats were too busy fleeing the werewolves and Crow to think about attacking any humans. Some of the wolves, though, had stopped to dine. Blood formed pools that the humans slipped and slid through in their panic. Its copper scent mixed with the bitter animal smell of fear. Screams blended with roars, growls, and the sounds of death. Carnage. And behind the wolves flew Crow.

He was monstrous in his bird form. A crow with the wingspan of a small plane, his huge shadow threw the terrified humans into that final night before death swooped down to tear them apart. His caw shook the trees, whipping them into a frenzy. And around him flew hundreds of ordinary crows, small satellites orbiting their big, stupid, jerk of a leader.

Fury knotted Selene's stomach. She clenched her hands into fists, wishing the idiot was in front of her so she could rearrange his ugly face. What the hell was he doing?

Selene was a warrior. She killed armed enemies, not helpless people out for a day at the zoo. For the first time, she questioned Frost's final solution. Is this what he envisioned?

What to do? If she helped the raptors, she'd make a deadly enemy of Crow, not to mention Frost. She could claim helping Fin's men was her way of fooling them into believing she was on their side. Frost wanted someone on the inside, and if he believed her story, he would reinstate her as his warrior. But would her pride allow her to walk back to him?

She lost her train of thought as she watched the raptors attack. They circled and cut off individual wolves in coordinated assaults honed over a lifetime of hunting with each other. Then they made short work of the wolves with powerful jaws and the deadly talons on their back feet. There was beauty in their primitive savagery. They were creatures like no human had ever seen except in movies. Their reality was so much *more*. Too bad the people flooding past her couldn't pause to enjoy the moment.

The rest of the wolf pack didn't seem anxious to engage the raptors. They had much easier prey in the form of the fleeing humans.

The raptors wouldn't be enough to stop the slaughter, though. There were too many large predators loose, and Crow was about to enter the battle. She had to make a decision *now*.

Ace was at her side. Meg had retreated to the car. Ace

leaned forward, eagerness for the fight gleaming in his eyes.

"I'm going to help the raptors." He took a step forward.

"No." She gripped his shoulder to hold him back. "Frost can't know you're here. Once Crow sees you, he'll tell Frost you fought with Fin's men." Ace didn't look as though he cared, so she added, "Besides, Frost will blame me for involving you. Do you really want to get me into that much trouble?"

Ace bit his lip in indecision. Finally, he huffed his disappointment. "Fine. I'll stay in the car. But if you get into trouble, I'll be here for you."

Selene watched as he climbed into the car. Looking grumpy, he slouched next to Meg. He locked the doors. She sighed her relief.

She reached deep, touched her essence, and felt it rise—hungry and ready. Then she sent it out to do its thing. Suddenly, there were ten more raptors killing wolves and herding the big cats back toward the zoo grounds. Fin's raptors looked startled for a moment, but as soon as they realized they weren't under attack, they returned to the battle.

An outraged caw drew her attention from her creations. Crow dived toward her, and at the last moment took human form. He landed in front of her, all tall cadaverous body, thin face with cruel eyes, and glossy black crows' feathers instead of hair. He wore a black cloak that swirled around him.

Selene smiled at him. "A black cloak? Don't you think you're overdoing the harbinger-of-death thing?" She watched his eyes narrow; his thin lips tighten.

"Does Frost know you've betrayed him?"

His voice made her shudder, a nails-raked-across-blackboard sound that sent chills squiggling down her spine. She raised one brow. "Me?" Selene swept her arm out to encompass the bloody battleground. "Did Frost order this?" *Please say no.* She still wanted to believe in him.

Crow made a sound that expressed exactly what he thought of Frost. "He's wasting time. Why does the slaughter have to wait for a certain date? Start the killing now." His smile was a mere baring of his teeth. "This is the beginning. The human population will panic. And in their terror, they'll lash out blindly. Frost won't be able to wait. He'll order their end." His eyes gleamed with blood lust. "Too bad you won't be part of it."

Was he threatening her? He was. "Bring it, bird turd. Before you can blink, I'll call up ten copies of you, all with your power. You'll be nothing but a grease spot on the ground when they finish with you."

Crow blinked. Selene's smile widened. When was the last time anyone stood up to this bully? She waited to see if he'd have the guts to challenge her.

She'd never know, because sudden and complete silence swung her attention back to the fight. Everything had frozen—humans, animals including her raptors, even the trees had stopped swaying. The air stilled. Wait, Fin's two raptors were still moving. They were staring at something behind Selene. She turned to follow their gazes. Crow did the same. Crap. He could move. Too bad.

Someone stood a few yards behind her, a tall someone who towered over Crow and her. Silver hair fell past his shoulders. The strands actually sparkled in the sunlight. His eyes were a metallic silver rimmed in black. Right now, purple bled into the silver. He had a beautiful face, but it was cold enough to generate its own blizzard. She shivered. Selene didn't need Crow's reaction to know who she faced. Frost had described him often enough.

Crow backed away, his body folding into itself. She barely had time to blink before he returned to his bird form and took flight. No one stopped him as he and his entourage rose into the air and were gone. The cowards.

She returned her attention to the leader of the Eleven.

What now? Unless she was unlucky enough to be Fin's number Six, she was safe from destruction although probably not from lots of bodily harm. Selene didn't have a clue who had written the rules of engagement for this war, but they seemed pretty random to her.

Frost couldn't kill humans directly, so he'd had to hire mercenaries like Crow.

Fin and his Eleven weren't any better off. They had to toss those closest to Frost from the planet one at a time according to some order only Fin knew. Lucky for them, the rest of Frost's fighters were fair game.

Was that any way to run a war? Nope. But she had more important things to worry about right now.

Selene met Fin's gaze. She took a deep breath and squared her shoulders. Frost had made sure they all realized how powerful Fin was. No doubt, even as she stared at him, he was probing her thoughts.

"Of course, I am. And such interesting thoughts they are." His expression didn't change. His eyes didn't warm.

Anger pushed her budding fear aside. "Get out of my head, Fin."

Fin ignored her to look at Adam who had returned to human form. Tor, still a raptor, guarded what remained of the motionless humans, wolves, and big cats. Fin glanced at the dead people and animals scattered over the ground. "We have a situation here."

Everything about him radiated cold. His voice was flat, emotionless. No anger at her, at Crow, at the wolves. No sadness for the dead. Just . . . nothing. He was the most terrifying being she'd ever met. Frost might have chosen a winter name, but he was a gentle summer breeze compared to Mr. Icy here.

So, she did what she always did when confronted by a challenge. She attacked. "No kidding. I hear sirens headed this way. The authorities will be all over this. What will you do, big man?"

Adam had moved up beside her. Selene glanced at him. He was looming, trying to intimidate her with his dark presence. Well, she'd been loomed over by the best. She cocked her head to stare up at him. "What?"

He nodded at Fin. "Not a good idea to irritate him when he's this mad."

She looked back at Fin. No change. Same stony expression. "How can you tell?'

"His eyes. The more purple, the stronger the emotion." Adam leaned down to whisper in her ear. "Trust me, he's totally pissed right now."

Selene took a moment for a little inner dialogue. *"Time to man up and deal with Fin. You've got this."* Maybe. She sneered up at Adam. "I don't need a warning. I've faced ticked off males before. They don't scare me." *Liar.*

Fin conveyed contempt for her without moving one facial muscle. "Faced? I don't think so. You're never on the front lines. You always send your clones in to do the dirty work."

His voice was smoothly sensual. You'd never know if he was insulting you or trying to seduce you. But she recognized this put-down and reacted to it. She couldn't help herself. No one dissed her power, not even the almighty Fin. "Wrong." She pointed at her frozen raptors. "Those are all *me*. No clones involved. Made flesh and blood from my essence, with the knowledge to do what I would do, but with enough sense of self to have individual personalities." Top *that* Mr. Oh-So-Powerful.

She felt Adam's hand on her shoulder, trying to steer her away from his boss. Selene attempted to shrug him off, but it didn't work. Maybe she should turn and punch him in that sexy mouth. Before she could decide, Fin looked away.

"We'll talk later, Selene. Right now, I have work to do. Oh, and you might want to get rid of those raptors before I start."

Selene didn't know what he intended to do, but she didn't waste any time in reclaiming her creations. They disappeared even as their energy returned to her. She watched as Fin strode to the epicenter of the disaster and then turned slowly in a circle. As he turned, all of the frozen wolves disappeared, along with the dead bodies. Even the blood was gone. Then he returned to where they waited.

"We need to leave. The police are close. They'll find panicked humans and loose animals. That's all. I've left the people with memories of the big cats and some sort of explosion, but nothing else. As soon as I release them, the animals will go back to their enclosures. Hopefully that will keep them from being killed by the authorities." He looked at Selene. "You'll come with us."

"Whoa! You might've tidied everything up, but someone's going to miss those dead people."

Fin offered her a fake puzzled expression. "What dead people? Every person at the zoo will go home with an exciting story to tell." His expression said that everything was settled.

Fin wanted her to ask how. She wouldn't give him the satisfaction. Selene glared at him and then turned her head to include Adam in her bad temper. Adam wasn't like his boss. He scowled at her. Good. It was nice to get a rise out of someone here.

She intended to go with them, but she didn't want to make it too easy. She didn't take orders from the enemy. "I have a car. My sister is with me. I'll follow you." She glanced at her car in the hopes that Ace had done the logical thing and left before Fin saw him. Selene sighed her disappointment. He was still there, staring at them through the windshield.

Adam spoke up. "She has a flat tire. I'll finish fixing it and then drive them to wherever you choose in her car. Tor and Greer can take our car."

Fin watched Tor return to human shape and join them. "I have a better idea. I'll drive Selene and you to our favorite restaurant where we can have a nice quiet talk. Tor can finish changing the tire and then Greer will drive your sister . . ." Fin glanced at the car and then did his version of an angry tirade, in other words he frowned. He stared at Ace and Ace grinned back. Then Fin speared Selene with a hard stare. "Who is he?"

She would kill Ace when she got him alone. This was difficult enough without her having to make up a fictitious identity for him. "He's just a friend who wanted to visit the zoo with us. I can drive my own car. I'll drop him off where he can catch a bus home." She threw up her strongest shields to try to keep Fin out of her mind. It was a long shot, but she had to try.

"I don't think so. He can join us for lunch." Fin's tone said the decision was made. "I've chosen to drive you and have Greer drive your sister and your friend because I wouldn't want you running off as soon as you got behind the wheel." He paused to give his next line extra emphasis. "You're still the enemy."

Of course, she was. Selene decided not to make a big deal about it. She hoped by the time lunch was over she would have convinced the Ice King that she would make a great ally.

Tor didn't look happy about having to finish changing the tire, but Adam knew his brother wouldn't mind spending time with the beautiful but not overly interesting Meg. Luckily, Greer would be with them to make sure his brother didn't lose his focus. Adam gave Ace a long look. Hopefully too young to pose any danger.

Selene tapped one foot as she cast Fin a death stare. "You're a hard man to like. Do you know that?"

For the first time since Fin had arrived, he smiled. "Thank you. I've worked hard to become that man." The smile disappeared. "Time to leave. The police are here."

Fin turned to the still-frozen humans and animals. Adam felt Fin's power as a hard shove against his chest. He was ready for it. Selene wasn't. She staggered. He put his arm across her shoulders to steady her.

For a moment he felt her body, warm and pliant against his side. He liked the feeling. But then she stiffened and jerked away.

"I'm fine. You don't have to hold me up." She didn't meet his gaze.

He was ready to throw out a comment about letting her fall on her butt next time, but he lost his train of thought as the humans and animals came alive around him. Tor went over to change the tire as Fin led Selene and him to where the boss had parked his car.

She climbed into the back seat of the luxury sedan before Adam had a chance to hold the door for her. Not that he wanted to hold anything for her. It didn't take many brain cells to figure out she was a dangerous woman. No way would he want to get mixed up with someone who worked for Zero. He ignored his whispered inner voice that reminded him of how exciting dangerous women could be.

Just to be a pain in the ass, Adam climbed into the back with her. She turned her face to the window and ignored him.

They drove away from the zoo just as the police were pouring in. Adam hoped he'd never see the place again.

Then Fin spoke. "Selene, why did Zero kick you out?"

Startled, Adam turned to stare at her.

She leaned back against the seat and closed her eyes. "I refused to turn my recruits loose to slaughter everyone in a building."

Adam frowned. "Wait. What? Did I miss something?" Then he remembered. No mind was safe from Fin. "Okay, I got it. You rooted around in her head." He looked at Selene. "Not one of his more loveable characteristics."

Selene didn't smile. "He actually has some?" She sounded serious.

Fin ignored the insult. "Why were you at the zoo today?"

Adam didn't see what that had to do with anything. Although it *was* a coincidence that she'd be there at the same time he . . . Coincidence? He didn't believe in them. He waited for her answer.

"A vampire contact told the boss that two of your men would be at the zoo." She shrugged. "I have no connections to anyone in this world. It made sense that I should search out the only other beings who understood what was happening and could use my skills."

"Not very loyal, are you?" Maybe he was being a little harsh, but loyalty was a big deal with Adam.

Selene didn't try to hide her scorn. "Loyalty goes both ways. He kicked me to the curb. That makes me a free agent in my book." Her expression dared him to argue her point.

Fin interrupted. "Speaking of loyalty, one of your vampires is a spy, Rap. You'll have to take care of that problem."

"Rap?" She frowned. "I get the Utah, Rap, Tor thing. But where did Adam come from?"

She seemed sincerely interested in his answer, so he bit back his snarky reply. "I don't use Rap around strangers. Makes it too easy for enemies to find me." He wasn't about to tell someone he didn't trust the real story behind his name.

Selene nodded. "Makes sense." A line appeared between her eyes as she thought. "You said the vampire who clued the boss in was a spy. That implies the vampires work for you. I thought they were independent."

Adam—he had to always be Adam even in his thoughts from now on, otherwise he might make a fatal mistake with the wrong person—decided that her expression was kind of cute. Not that he liked her, because he didn't. But cute was cute.

Fin answered her. "They *are* independent."

They weren't. Adam had them firmly under his thumb. Except for the spy.

Fin continued. "But we have to eliminate any vampires who choose to abandon their neutrality and work for your ex-boss." He met her gaze in the mirror. "You must understand that as a warrior."

"Sure. War is war."

Adam tried not to read too much into the slight bitterness he heard in her voice. Just to get a feel for her, he tossed a test balloon into the conversation. "Sometimes war isn't about what we thought it was about when we volunteered." He shrugged. "It's complicated."

For the first time, he saw her coldness thaw a little. It wasn't exactly a heatwave, but it was a beginning.

"No kidding. But that doesn't have to change who we are inside. We have to look at the circumstances and make our decisions based on our personal code of ethics." She looked away from him.

"I didn't think Zero's people had any." Fine, so he was a jerk. Fin obviously wanted to turn her from the dark side, and Adam wasn't helping. He should be mouthing warm fuzzy platitudes. Way to go, butthead.

Her eyes narrowed. "You'd be surprised."

"I hate to interrupt, but we have more important things to discuss." Fin had stopped for a light. He met Selene's gaze in the mirror.

Adam watched her tense. Did she think Fin would boot her from the car? She had no idea how important she was, but he had a feeling she was about to find out.

"I have a dilemma, Selene." The light changed and Fin turned his attention back to the road. "You're a very recent member of Team Zero. We've spent a great deal of effort finding and sending your colleagues back into the cosmos before they can usher in the next great extinction. Humanity."

"I realize that." She might be wary, but she didn't sound afraid.

"Now here's the thing." Fin paused as though gathering his thoughts. "Millions of years ago, I had a series of visions. Every vision showed me an image of the woman—it was always a woman—who could banish each of you from Earth before you could trigger the apocalypse."

Selene nodded her understanding. Adam didn't think she'd be so calm by the time Fin finished.

"The woman I saw in one of my visions was you, Selene."

Adam heard her indrawn breath and watched as she leaned forward. "That's impossible."

"It gets even more impossible. I've given each of Zero's people numbers. Adam can tell you I'm obsessed with numbers. They're immutable and never lie. I like that about them."

Selene braced herself with both hands on the seat. Adam figured she must be starting to get the picture.

"The next one to be banished is Six." Fin once again met her gaze in the mirror. "The universe is always up for a joke. So, what if Six is you, Selene?"

"I'm not Six." She didn't sound as certain as her words indicated.

"Perhaps not." Fin turned his attention back to the road. "But you could be."

"I'm *not*." She was more emphatic this time.

Fin chose to ignore her comment. "Now you see the problem. You might be in the unenviable position of having to banish yourself from Earth." He smiled.

CHAPTER FOUR

SELENE TOOK A DEEP BREATH. The predators in the room were sucking up all the air. Why were they even here? She had thought Fin would take her somewhere private where they could chat without a cast of thousands listening in. She'd been wrong.

She sat at a long, intricately carved table in the elegant room of a restaurant with a closed-for-renovation sign outside. The table was rapidly filling up with large, lethal looking men. They didn't seem friendly. Selene assumed these were the Eleven Frost was always ranting about.

Fear? Yes, she admitted to a little. Very little. If they all decided to attack her at once, her own army would only last until one of the Eleven managed to stomp on her, or tear her to bloody bits, or... *Stop.* She wouldn't allow negative thoughts to defeat her before the battle even began. She was immortal. Her temporary end might be painful, but she'd simply pull herself together and soldier on. Okay, so maybe not always. But Fin needed her, so she was safe for the moment.

While they waited for Greer to arrive with Tor, Ace, and Meg, Selene decided to ask a few questions. Ignoring the suspicious stare from Adam who sat across from her, Selene turned to the man on her right. He was a stark contrast to all the other men in the room who were dressed in killer-casual. Tall and sleek, he looked as though he belonged in a corner office with CEO on the door. Perfectly styled brown hair, a suit that screamed custom made, and if she took the time to look down, she was sure his shoes would match the rest of his expensive package.

"Hi, I'm Selene." She tried on her sweetest smile. Not as syrupy as Meg could manage, but it was the best she could do.

He nodded, casting her a dismissive glance before starting to turn away. Okay, so sweet didn't impress him. Time to give him a taste of the real her. "Here's where you tell me your name and maybe say something about the weather. You know, just to be polite."

He raised one brow. He didn't smile. "Lio. It stands for Liopleurodon."

Lio what? She didn't remember this one. He must have interpreted her blank stare correctly, because he leaned toward her, giving her a close up of cold dark eyes.

"Liopleurodon. Very large marine reptile. Eighty feet long even though some of your scientists claim I'm only thirty. But what's a few feet when you have eight-inch teeth, hmm?" He finally smiled. "Don't go swimming in strange places, little girl."

Selene only took one thing away from his speech. Little girl? She returned his smile. She hoped it looked suitably shark-like. "I'll swim where I choose. Attack me and get your eight-inch teeth handed to you one at a time."

She turned from Lio's startled expression to face Adam's narrowed gaze. He didn't seem impressed with her takedown of Lio.

"Why're you here, Selene? Fin should have locked you up somewhere until he needed you. I bet as soon as you get some useful info on us, you'll run back to Zero to report. I don't believe that crap about him firing you." Adam's gold eyes actually glowed.

Interesting. She didn't think glowing gold eyes were common among Fin's men. "See me crying because you don't believe me. By the way, why does Fin call Frost Zero?"

He blinked at her change of subject. "Because Fin is obsessed with numbers. He didn't know the names of Zero's people, so he gave you numbers. The perfect solution for him. Zero is an insult. He's nothing. As opposed to Infinity, which is everything." He muttered the next sentence. "I think he'd give us numbers too if he wasn't so proud of his play on our dino names."

"Frost and Fin both gave themselves temporary names while they were on this planet. I get that Fin is short for Infinity. A little pretentious if you ask me." Selene thought about that. Frost had always ignored her questions about his name. "I wonder why they don't use their real ones?"

"Maybe they don't remember them." He shrugged. "I don't. After a few million years, names aren't important. Besides, Fin loves the one he has now. Infinity is forever. It's more than any number we can count. He likes that concept."

Selena disagreed. "Names have power."

"What's *your* real name, Selene?" He smiled, daring her to part with it.

His smile was all hot predator. Selene took a moment to be impressed. Adam's smile would definitely count as a moment to remember in her scrapbook of amazing men. Too bad that overlaying his spectacular maleness was her mental picture of the Utahraptor. She could never forget his ancient predator alter ego. And neither version of Adam was her friend.

Selene was ready to refuse his request—because her name had to remain her secret—when Meg and the others arrived.

Fin sat at the head of the table. Of course, he did. The leader of the Eleven waved Ace to the empty seat on his right.

Meg took the seat to Selene's left. She was flushed and beautiful as she smiled across at Tor who had plopped down next to Adam. Selene leaned close to Meg. "Don't get attached. I don't know how long we'll be here."

Meg turned pouty. "Then I'll enjoy him while I have the chance. Maybe you should get over yourself, Sis. Ditch the warrior-queen image long enough to have some fun." She shifted her gaze back to Tor.

Selene's rage flared. Where did Meg get off telling her what to do? Meg wasn't the one with all the responsibilities. "You forget who you are."

When Meg glanced at her, Selene didn't miss the fear in her eyes.

Guilt replaced Selene's anger. "Forget it." She tried to rub away the tension between her eyes. "I'm a little worried right now. I shouldn't take it out on you."

Meg relaxed and offered her a weak smile. "Sure."

She returned her attention to Tor, leaving Selene to once again wrestle with the conflict she felt about Meg. Thank heaven Fin stood, putting an end to her newest crisis of conscience.

"We have some important issues to address today." Fin's silver hair glittered under the crystal chandelier hanging above the table. His silver eyes shone with a metallic gleam. "First, allow me to introduce our guests."

On, no. He wouldn't.

He gestured in her direction. "This is Selene and her sister, Meg. Selene might be number Six, or perhaps not. Unfortunately for her, Zero fired her today. Fortunately for me, she is considering joining us."

He would.

As one, the Eleven turned to glare at her. If Fin asked her to stand and say a few words, she'd beat him to death with a dozen copies of himself. Beside her, Lio almost vibrated with suppressed fury. Across from her, Adam expressed his feelings by peeling his lips back from impressive fangs. Fangs? In their mortal forms, none of the Eleven had anything but normal human teeth. She didn't have time to think about this, though. The combined outrage of the Eleven shook the chandelier until the crystal drops jingled.

Fin continued, "And here,"—he pointed at Ace— "is a mystery." He smiled at her friend.

She hoped Ace was smart enough not to accept that smile as an offer of friendship.

"Ace says he isn't one of Zero's immortals. I don't sense any power from him." Fin narrowed his eyes. "Which is puzzling, because Zero doesn't keep people around who aren't useful. So, who are you?"

Ace shifted and glanced away. "I do odd jobs for him. Working in the office, stuff like that."

Fin dug deeper. "And Zero keeps you out of the goodness of his heart?"

Ace glanced down. "Yeah. He's been kind to me."

Fin laughed. From the expressions on the faces around Selene, that didn't happen often.

"Ace, believe me, Zero is not a kind person. He has some other use for you." Fin's gaze grew distant. "Interesting."

At the other end of the table from Fin, one of the men leaped to his feet. He looked exactly like Tor except for his longer hair. His face was tight with fury.

"Why are they here at our table? Why haven't you locked them away so they can't do any more damage until we can toss their butts back into the cosmos?"

Fin's stare was glacial. "Because one of their butts belongs to the woman I saw in my vision, Utah, the one who will get rid of Six."

Angry mutterings and murmurings filled the room.

Utah subsided. Beside Selene, Lio voiced the obvious. "Then I guess she can't be Six."

Fin nodded. "A logical conclusion. But visions can be deceiving." He speared Selene with his icy stare. "Who is number Six?" His attention slid to Meg. "Is it you? Because you were also in my vision. But Selene was the one preparing to strike some sort of bar with a pipe."

Meg laughed. "Oh, no. If you really knew me, you'd understand how funny that is."

Keep your mouth shut, Meg. Selene spoke up before Fin could ask Meg to explain why it was so funny. "It's obviously Crow." Or one of the others who fought for Frost. She didn't care who Six was so long as Fin didn't target Meg or Ace.

Fin considered her suggestion. "Are there any other of Zero's people in town right now?"

"Not that I know of, but then Crow just got here, so more could be on their way." She shrugged. Who knew what Frost was planning? Everything was on a need-to-know basis with him.

Fin seemed to accept her comment because he switched his attention to his men. "I've been meaning to have this meeting for a while. Now seems the best time, when we have three guests from the dark side among us."

Selene wasn't amused even if Fin's comment drew a few smiles from his men. She glanced at Adam. At least he didn't think it was funny.

Fin continued, "Ty, Utah, and Al, your wives saw a little of what your lives were like before the age of dinosaurs. Now it's time that you all know what you once were."

It was as though he'd set a bomb off among his men. There were shouted questions, roars as some of them fought to keep from changing right there, and then there was Adam. He didn't move, didn't make a sound, just sat and waited. But death lived in those eyes. Selene was an apex hunter. She recognized another like her when she saw him. She decided that, other than Fin, he was the most dangerous being in this room.

Of course, she already knew what they once were—before this time, before they walked the earth as dinosaurs. Frost had filled her in. Then the rest of what Fin had said registered. Wait. They had wives? What woman would have the guts to mate with these men? She looked at Adam. He gazed back, all coiled energy and aggression. His flat stare promised an instant end to her if she even breathed the wrong way. The light from the chandelier threw the planes of his face into sharp relief. Shadows gathered beneath cheekbones and along his jaw, emphasizing the promise of power and ruthlessness she had seen on display back at the zoo. His long black hair framed all that predatory darkness. He didn't blink as she studied him.

She looked away as she realized Fin was watching her.

Fin's stare was chipped ice. His expression gave nothing away. "Selene, you'll find this of particular interest."

Adam stood. He glanced at the others. "Can you shut up for a moment?"

Surprisingly, they did.

He turned back to glare at his leader. "First, why didn't you tell us about this a long time ago? Second..."—he glanced at Selene, Meg, and Ace—"why're they still here?"

Fin's voice remained calm, nothing threatening in it, but Selene shivered.

"You were too close to your ancient predator lives to handle emotionally what I'll be showing you."

Adam tensed. "Who are you to decide what we should or shouldn't know?"

There was a sharp intake of breath from the other men as they waited for Fin's reaction. Then the room shook. Paintings fell from the walls and the chandelier swung. Adam cursed as it came loose from the ceiling and crashed to the table scattering glass shards and pieces of the ceiling. He stood amid the destruction as the others shoved back their chairs then clambered to their feet. Only Selene remained where she was. She watched him from those blue eyes—assessing, judging.

Tor leaned across the table to hiss a warning. "Don't move. Don't speak."

Adam froze as he gazed at his leader. Fin shone with a cold white light that hurt Adam's eyes. He blinked. Fin watched Adam through narrowed eyes that no longer had silver pupils. His eyes were purple. Power flowed from him in waves, touching all of them, making Adam itch with a need to turn to Tor and beat him to a pulp before he moved on to the others in the room. Being around Fin always had this effect on them. But this was a thousand times worse. If Fin didn't stop the flow, all of them would lose themselves to the bloodlust, not able to tell friend from foe.

Fin seemed to realize this. He spoke. "Sit." His voice echoed as though he spoke from a great distance away.

Everyone quietly obeyed. Except for Adam. Call it stupid pride, but Adam wouldn't allow Fin to believe he was cowed. Even though Fin had scared the crap out of him.

Fin's tight smile didn't reach his eyes. But at least some of the purple had bled from them. When he finally spoke, the weirdness had gone from his voice.

"The attacker had cut your throat, Adam. He was getting ready to fling your corpse onto the pile waiting to be burned when I took your soul."

Fin spoke calmly, quietly, and it was absolutely terrifying. Adam almost forgot to breathe.

Fin shifted his attention to Lio. "They'd thrown you from the top floor of a fifty-story building. I took your soul just as you hit the ground."

Methodically, Fin worked his way around the table, explaining in gruesome detail how each of them had died, and how he had been there to take their souls. Then Fin turned back to Adam.

"That is why I have every *fucking* right to decide when to tell you the details." Fin said the word gently, precisely. Then he smiled. "Now can we continue?"

Adam had pushed Fin as far as he could. He wasn't stupid. As Adam's temper cooled, he gave Fin credit where credit was due. Fin had saved all of them.

"Sure." Adam sat.

Selene caught his eye. She smiled and mouthed, "Awesome."

He frowned and looked away. Adam didn't want her damn approval.

Fin took up where he'd left off before Adam's interruption. "I'm going to show you the last hours of your civilization." He nodded at Selene and the other two. "Yes, I want you to stay." His gaze lingered on Selene. "I have a feeling you're going to be an important part of our future."

Adam braced himself. He knew from experience that Fin's show-and-tells didn't involve the usual screen and DVR. He glanced at Selene. She looked relaxed, but he didn't miss her quickened breathing, her restlessness as she shifted in her seat, and the way her gaze searched out the three exits. Adam almost wished she'd make a break for it. He needed a release from the tension building in him, the need to chase down *something*.

But he stopped thinking about Selene as the room suddenly darkened. Adam had a sense of falling, an elevator ride to hell. He resisted the urge to hurl. Then it was over. Before he could even draw a relieved breath, everything around him changed.

He was somewhere else, somewhere far from the safety of that restaurant and the rest of the Eleven. Night had fallen on the city. Familiar . . . yet not. He gazed up at buildings that defied gravity, flowing and soaring into a sky filled with fire and death. Explosions shook the ground and hovering aircraft fell to the street where they burst into flames and flying debris. People screamed, rushing from imploding buildings to join panicked mobs with nowhere to run.

Adam could only stand and stare while cold dread filled him. They were all dead—his parents, his grandparents, his sisters, his brother's wife and their unborn child. Their faces filled his memory, faint, etched with remembered pain. Beside him, someone spoke.

"We're trapped. They have the city surrounded."

Male. He spoke in a language Adam shouldn't under-stand but did. Adam turned to look. His brother. There should be another one, but he was gone, separated from them by a collapsing building.

He looked exactly like Adam, like the brother they'd lost. Triplets. Too tall to be from the present, with a larger than normal head, an elongated torso, and eyes that almost filled his face. Adam opened his mouth to reply and then closed it on the realization that he didn't remember his brother's name. *Why* couldn't he remember?

"Let's go." His brother shoved him, and they ran.

They ran until they couldn't run anymore, then paused at a corner to catch their breaths. A mistake. An explo-sion deafened Adam, tossing him against a building. He slid down its side, dizzy and confused. He closed his eyes. When he opened them again, he saw a jagged chasm fill-ing the whole street. His brother stood on the other side.

Adam met his gaze. The distance was too wide to jump. No way to go around it. His brother cast him a panicked glance. No. Adam wouldn't accept what that gap meant.

His brother shouted across the gaping hole. "Go. I'll find you."

Even as his brother shouted, Adam could see shadows creeping from ruined doorways and around corners. *They* had found him. The invaders. They'd come from a pirate planet that searched out peaceful and defenseless civilizations and then destroyed the population. His people had grown too comfortable, too complacent. Now they were paying for it.

Adam took one last look at his brother and then fled. But not far. A few blocks away from the crater, one of those shadows caught him. It reached out from a darkened doorway and grabbed him, yanking him inside.

Adam didn't get a chance to fight before a knife was at his throat. The hooded figure whispered into his ear.

"So soft and useless. We could destroy you without ever landing our ships, but I like the personal touch. I want to get my hands bloody."

Adam had one last thought. If he was ever given another life, he would be strong and merciless. *He* would be the destroyer. Then the slashing knife, the pain, the blood, and nothing.

Awareness returned as Adam fought to calm his pounding heart and slow his gasping breaths. Damn, he hated Fin's little presentations. The boss was big on involving all the senses. His adrenaline spike slowly receded. He looked around. From the expressions on the faces of the rest of the Eleven, he had no doubt they had each experienced their own end.

Then he realized that not all of the visuals had disappeared. One still hung in midair above Fin's head. Shocked, Adam recognized himself along with his killer. And for the first time he saw the male's face. He had human features, ones that would allow him to walk the streets of San Diego with no one staring. The man's narrow face stretched into lines of harsh cruelty. He was smiling, enjoying his killing moment. Adam clenched his teeth around his hate. He wanted to rip the man into tiny bite-sized pieces. His predator stirred. *Stay calm.* No one would appreciate his raptor making an appearance.

But Adam's rage only found another target. Why was

Fin showing this? That memory was personal. He had no right to put it out there for everyone to gawk at. Adam couldn't stay quiet. "Why am I up there?"

Wait. Everyone was focused on Selene, not him. What the . . .?

She sat frozen; her eyes wide with horror as she stared at the scene. Meg wore the same expression. Adam didn't get a chance to decide if it was empathy for his death he was seeing on their faces before Fin spoke.

"Is there something you'd like to tell us, Selene?" He cocked his head to take a closer look at Adam's killer. His puzzled expression was fake Fin at his best. "Hmm, I do see a resemblance . . ." He offered her a wide-eyed look of even phonier shock. "Could it be?"

"You bastard." Her voice shook with loathing. "You knew before you showed us those scenes."

Fin raised his hands in a self-deprecating gesture. "That moment was tough to forget. Besides, I can recall in detail everything I've experienced during my life." His voice softened as his gaze grew unfocused. "I've never been sure if that was a gift or a curse."

"Why reveal it now?" Ice coated each word she spoke.

"Because we need to know exactly what we're dealing with." He paused to scan all of them. "Before we become partners." Fin's words were as cold as hers. "Will you do the honors, or should I?"

She dropped her gaze from Fin before turning to stare at Adam. Selene didn't blink, didn't seem to be aware of everyone's attention. Some emotion he couldn't ID moved in her eyes and then was gone. She lifted her chin before taking a deep breath.

Adam knew it would be bad. He just wasn't sure how bad.

"That's my father. My father killed you."

CHAPTER FIVE

CURSES AND SHOUTS ERUPTED AROUND Selene. She drew in a ragged breath. Damn. She should've called up a pack of Galenian Soul Crunchers to protect all three of them before making that admission. But the shock of seeing her father's face after so many years had caught her unprepared. All the emotions, all the anger and recriminations flooded back. She pushed them away. Survival came first. Question. Could she make her move before Adam leaped across the table to rip off her head?

Keeping part of her attention on Adam, she glanced at Fin. He was the one who would control the situation. Why would he go to all the trouble of bringing her here just to see her killed by his men? She chanced a quick peek at Adam's expression. Bad news. He was definitely readying his raptor for a revenge strike. Fury sharpened his features. She could see the predator in his narrowed eyes. Her enemy.

The thought saddened her. Not an emotion she understood. After all, she'd been raised in a society that courted hatred from other races, other worlds. One more person who despised her shouldn't make any difference.

Wait. Adam wasn't looking at her. He stumbled to his feet, his eyes filled with rage and horror. All aimed at Fin. Everyone quieted.

"I just saw myself die in living color. How could I *forget* that? What the hell did you do to us?" He leaned forward, bracing his hands on the table. Hands that were now talons gauging grooves into the wood.

Uh oh. Selene got ready to flee with Meg and Ace if he changed. But Utah called a warning first.

"Don't, Rap. Control it." Utah started to rise but subsided as his brother's claws disappeared.

Adam pressed his palms hard against his temples, and Selene could hear his rasping breaths. Against all reason, she wanted to reach across the table to help him.

"Who am I? Am I that alien-looking guy who just had his throat cut? Am I Rap, a human with the soul of a dinosaur? Or maybe I'm Adam, vampire lord. Who will I be next week?" His glare should've incinerated Fin where he stood.

Vampire lord? Selene forgot to breathe. Now she understood the fangs. But she didn't have time to process any of it before Adam backed away from the table, knocking his chair to the floor.

His voice rose. "Now you want me to relive my death for a highlight?" He gestured at the scene still hovering above Fin's head. "Hell, no!"

Fin tensed, his eyes narrowing to purple slits. But he didn't reply or make a move toward Adam.

Tor stood, too. He tried to put his hand on his brother's shoulder.

Adam shrugged him off. "I need air." He strode toward the door but paused long enough to look at Selene. "Later you can explain how the daughter of my killer just *happened* to show up in Zero's merry band of mass murderers."

And then Adam was gone. Selene winced as he slammed the door behind him.

Fin exhaled wearily as he finally sat. "That went well." The scene of Adam dying faded away.

Tor glanced at Selene. "He'll be okay. He's strong. My brother has had a lot more to deal with than the rest of us." Then he followed Adam out the door.

Next to her, Lio stirred. "Rap, or Adam, or whoever the hell he is right now—I can't keep track of this crap—said what all of us were thinking, if a bit more emotionally. Why mess with our memories so we wouldn't remember any of this until now? And why bring us together to turn our personal nightmares loose in front of our enemies?" He turned his gaze on Selene. "No offense." His hard stare said he meant all the offense she could imagine.

A low rumble of anger rippled around the table. A few claws appeared.

Lio looked back at Fin. "Here's what I want to know. Who are you, and how did you happen to be there to remember each of our deaths?" He frowned. "And why didn't I ever ask you any questions like that before now?"

Silence fell. Suspicion lived in that stillness. Selene wanted to know the answers too. Because Frost was the same kind of Big Mysterious as Fin. If she understood the thinking process of one, maybe she could figure out the other. It was a thought at least.

Fin leaned back in his chair. His body language said relaxed, but his eyes said something else entirely. He met each person's stare with his icy gaze. He skipped over Meg. But then Selene figured since her sister wasn't one of his people and didn't have any useful powers, she probably wasn't important in his view. Fin lingered longer on Selene and Ace. Was he monitoring their thoughts? She didn't think so. His mind would be busy with more important things right now.

Fin finally spoke. "Why did I wait so long to tell you about your roots?" He shook his head. "Imagine. I tore your souls from your dying bodies millions of years ago. Then I placed them in ancient predators. When Zero caused the dinosaur's extinction, I ripped out your souls once again. I tucked them away in places of power around the world waiting for the moment when Zero would return to eliminate this planet's next apex predators. Finally, when the time was right, I put your souls into human bodies." He paused so they could think about that. "Suppose I hadn't taken your memories. You would've remembered the horror of your deaths in that long gone time as well as the savagery of your life as a beast. Could you have handled that along with the stress of adapting to your human identities?" He shook his head. "I couldn't take the chance of your minds shattering. Too much was at stake." He paused. "And you never questioned me because I redirected your thoughts whenever you grew too curious."

Selene heard an indrawn breath behind her. She turned her head to find that Adam had returned while she sat riveted by Fin's tale. Tor stood next to his brother. Both looked grim.

Lio wasn't placated. "We'll talk about the redirecting thing later. You still haven't told us who you are and why you were there the day her father helped to destroy our civilization." He glanced at Selene to make sure she understood who "her" was.

"I was an ordinary tourist caught in Zero's plan to obliterate your people."

Fin didn't move, didn't blink, but the aura of danger surrounding him spread sending the temperature in the room plummeting. Selene shivered. She didn't believe him. He'd never be mistaken for an "ordinary" tourist.

Adam spoke. "Then how did you survive when everyone else died?" He placed his hands on the back of her chair.

Selene felt his nearness, and for just a moment she wanted to lean back into all that warmth and strength. She caught herself in time. No way did she need his strength. Selene had strength to spare. And she could generate her own warmth, thank you very much. Besides, the only thing he probably wanted to do with those hands was to reach out and break her neck.

"I had . . . skills that you and your people didn't have." He shrugged. "I couldn't save everyone, so I looked for the most powerful essences I could find. Yours are the souls I took." He gestured at the Eleven.

"One more question, and then I'm leaving." Fin stood. He glanced at his three guests. "You should know that Zero and I might not come to physical blows, but we're always battering at each other's minds. Your boss has just realized you're missing. He's making an extra effort to break through my mental shields. I have to return home to isolate myself so I can give him my full attention."

Selene tucked that bit of info away. Frost had never told her that he had a mental battle going on with Fin. She had a million questions, but she didn't get a chance to ask them. Fin pointed at a big dark-haired man.

Tor leaned toward Selene to murmur, "That's Ty, short for tyrannosaurus Rex."

Selene took notice. Frost had mentioned him a few times.

Ty didn't waste words. "You had no right to mess with our minds. But now's not the time to start a war among ourselves. We still have to eliminate Zero. How do we kill his ass instead of just kicking him back out into the cosmos so he can continue to destroy civilizations?"

Fin sighed. "All of you together couldn't kill him."

Selene refused to remain quiet any longer. "Could *you* destroy him?"

The silence dragged on for so long she thought he wouldn't answer. Then he shrugged. "Maybe. But it wouldn't matter because someone else would just be sent to replace him."

Horrified silence followed Fin's words. Adam spoke for everyone.

"You mean he's not the boss? There's a higher power than Zero calling the shots?"

Adam's grip on the back of her chair tightened. It wouldn't have shocked her if he chucked it at the wall with her still in it.

"There always a higher power." Fin turned to leave amid a babble of yelled curses and questions. He waved toward the door. "Time to go. We've stayed here long enough. I've shielded this place, but I still don't want to take the chance of Zero sensing us. Besides, you've spent too much time near me already. Soon you'll be kicking each other's butts around the room." He glanced at Selene. "I'd like to see you, Meg, and Ace outside for a moment." He nodded at Adam and Tor. "Both of you too."

Selene didn't waste any time following Fin out of the restaurant. She figured it was only a matter of minutes before frustration made the men turn on the perceived enemies in their midst.

Fin paused outside to watch his people storm past. They offered their leader sullen looks promising that this wasn't over. None of them took a shot at him, though. She wondered why. Then Selene glanced at Fin. Wow. Icicles should be hanging from his glacial expression. Okay, so she wouldn't attack him either. Not with ice-storm clouds circling his head.

Adam stopped beside her. He practically vibrated with his need to kill something. Selene refused to move away from him. She needed a small victory right now. Something to bolster her belief that she was strong enough to survive this insanity.

Fin waited until everyone had disappeared except for his chosen ones. He focused on Selene, Meg, and Ace. "Selene, you'll be partnering with Adam. Meg, you'll be—"

"Wait. What?" No. Absolutely not. "I can't partner with

him. He hates me. Besides, I want to stay with Meg and Ace." She looked up at Adam. Yep, hated her.

"Whatever warped idea you have, Fin, forget it. It won't work. Tor is my partner. She's . . ." Adam searched for the right words. "a potential threat."

Selene figured his thoughts were a little more graphic. Probably included phrases like "a murdering bitch." She hoped his words swayed Fin.

Fin raked his fingers through his hair, his only sign of impatience. "I saw Selene and Meg in my vision. Selene was banishing Six. She's important to us. Deal with it. I've already called for a human driver who can make sure you both keep the peace."

Adam made a rude noise. "It will take more than a human to do that."

Selene broke in. "When did you call for a driver?"

Fin's smile was barely there. "When I made my decision. That would be about twenty minutes ago." He tapped his temple. "Mental messaging."

Tor interrupted. "Yo, what about me? I don't want a new partner."

"Meg will be your partner." Fin didn't take his attention from Adam.

Selene figured he knew where the biggest danger lay.

Tor glanced at Meg. She smiled at him. He turned back to Fin. "Yeah, maybe we can make it work."

Selene glared at Meg. She didn't need to encourage Tor. Meg refused to look at her.

Fin fixed his gaze on Ace. "Do you still want to join us?"

Ace studied his boots. "I won't leave Selene and Meg. They need someone in their corner." He looked up to meet Fin's stare. "Some of the things Frost's people are doing bother me. So, yeah, I'll stay. But I won't betray Frost."

"Why not?" Fin sounded mildly interested.

Selene didn't believe Fin was ever mildly anything. She silently begged Ace to speak carefully.

Ace shrugged. "I never knew my mother. She gave me to an old woman to raise right after I was born. The people in my world were mostly similar to the human species, so I didn't feel out of place growing up. Shulsa did her best, but she died when I was twelve. She wasn't even dead an hour when some men kicked in our door and stuck a needle in me. I was in stasis for millions of years before I was brought out of it."

"That's awful!" Frost would've hated Selene's outburst. Expressing sympathy was a weakness, and he wanted his people to be emotionless killing machines. Guess she was one of his failures.

Tor frowned. "Why would they put a stranger into stasis?"

"Wars were common on my planet. Men were always needed to fight. So, the government paid a bounty for every homeless or unprotected person captured to be stored away for a future army." Ace didn't sound outraged.

Well, Selene was outraged enough for both of them. "You were forced to fight as soon as you came out of stasis? Your planet was ruled by a bunch of barbaric animals."

Ace forced a smile. "No. Frost woke me, not the government. He offered me a home and safety. He's cared for me for five years now. I owe him for that. But I won't betray you either unless you hurt Meg or Selene."

Selene's heart sank. The kid looked impossibly young. She had gotten him involved in this. If Fin hurt Ace, she'd find a way to end him. A random thought: why had Frost chosen a twelve-year-old stranger to befriend?

Fin nodded. "Fair enough. You'll come with me. We'll see what we can do with you."

Just then a red SUV pulled up to the curb and idled. Waiting.

"Here we are. Your ride." Relief lived in Fin's words.

Selene thought her head would explode. "Whoa. All of my stuff is in my car." Fin was purposely rushing her into this, not giving her time to think.

"Tor and Meg will be taking your car. Greer will drive them for now until I can find another human driver. They'll drop your things off on the way to their apartments." Fin glanced at his watch. "I have things to do. Ace, come with me." He started to walk away. "Selene, Adam will answer all of your questions."

Selene caught Adam's sarcastic, "Good times."

She paused to think. She had two options. Walk away, which meant she was a failure. Fin probably wouldn't leave her with memories of this meeting if she bailed. So, no hot info to wave in Frost's face. Not that she'd go crawling back to him. She had her pride. Or she could go with Adam and see what shook out. She'd never been afraid of the unknown, so she'd go with option two. Only one question left. "Will Meg and Ace be safe?"

Fin looked offended that she'd ask. "Of course." He continued walking, throwing a last command over his shoulder. "Oh, and no more Frost. He's Zero to everyone on our team."

Sounded a little petty to Selene, but she nodded before striding to the SUV waiting for them. She climbed into the back seat without looking to see if Adam was following. A mistake. She should have followed him into the car so she could sit where he didn't. Was it too much to hope that he'd sit in the front with the driver?

It was, because he slid in beside her. Then he ignored her. Answer all her questions, huh? Fat chance. She chose instead to lean forward to speak with the driver.

"I'm Selene. I'm afraid that Fin didn't tell us your name." From what she could see, he looked like Mr. Ordinary American Guy. Nothing special—about thirty, pleasant if unremarkable face, short brown hair, average height as far as she could tell with him sitting down, and the eyes that looked back at her from the rearview mirror looked normal. No evidence of a serial killer in them. She sighed. With all the killing machines sitting here already, she supposed their driver could afford to be ordinary.

He smiled. "I'm Dave."

Adam spoke. "Anything we should know about you, Dave?"

Dave's eyes widened. "Nope. I just drive. Oh, and I know about you." His gaze in the mirror fixed on Adam. "Dinosaurs are crazy cool. I've done research. Do you have feathers?"

Selene swallowed her laughter. Feathers? She sneaked a peak at Adam. Was that a flush? It was.

"A few. Very few." His voice was cold.

That didn't stop Dave. "Chickens are your descendants, aren't they?"

Adam had heard enough. "I have no *chickens* in my family tree." His tone said the discussion was over.

Dave must've gotten the message because he subsided to focus on his driving.

Selene couldn't hold it in any longer. She laughed. "A chicken? You're just a big chicken."

He fixed her with a baleful glare before looking away.

Okay, time to change the subject. "Fin said you'd answer questions. Tell me about you as vampire lord." Maybe he'd refuse to answer, but she had to at least try to pry more information from him while he was trapped beside her.

She felt his indecision—to tell her or to keep quiet. Selene put in a word for her side. "I'm certain Fin will strip my memory if I try to pass on the information."

Adam looked at her. Maybe she was only imagining a slight thawing in his expression, but that didn't mean his eyes weren't still filled with suspicion.

"Your dad must be proud of his little girl."

That was unexpected. Now it was her turn to send him a frosty stare. "I haven't seen my father since I was sixteen earth-years old. He was *never* proud of me. I'm sure that hasn't changed."

Selene waited for him to press her for details. She was relieved when he didn't.

He nodded. "Vampires ambushed me in my human form. I died. Fin took my soul and stored it near a vortex in Sedona, Arizona. Adam was the leader of all the vampires in North America. When Adam chose to align himself with Zero, Fin killed him. Then he put my soul in Adam's body." He shrugged. "Only a few vampire friends know the original Adam is gone. Being the vampire leader is a pain in the butt, but it gives us the advantage of a strong ally."

Fascinating. "So, how does it feel being someone new again?"

He gave a smile laced with bitterness. "Like I'm buried in filth. Adam slaughtered his way to the top, but he had lots of power from his centuries as a vampire. I try to absorb the power without getting slimed by his personality. My raptor is pure savage. It lives for the hunt, for the kill. I have to keep it caged in a corner of my mind. I keep the worst of old Adam in a cage right next to the beast. The part of me that's still human is in a constant fight for supremacy with the other two."

She wondered how strong he had to be to keep from going crazy? "You don't have to drink blood or be dead all day?"

"No. Not that a pint of blood doesn't taste good after a hard night spent rending and slaughtering."

Selene didn't have to respond to that because Dave pulled into a spot behind an apartment building.

He parked then turned to look at them. "We're here. I'm in number 12A if you need me. You guys are in 10A or 9A. Take your pick." Dave handed each of them a set of keys. Then he climbed from the car and walked into the building.

Selene glanced at her keys. "Guess I'm in 9A." She didn't know how she felt being so close to him. Adam had a far-ranging aura of violence and—okay, admit it— sexual pull. No way did she ever want to get sucked into that. "I hope someone has stocked the fridge." Night was falling, and he loomed over her in the growing darkness, all shadowy danger and tempting puzzle. Nope, wouldn't try to solve him. It couldn't end well. "I guess I'll see you in the morning?"

His smile was a flash of white teeth as he smiled. It wasn't a comforting smile.

"Not even close. Take a short time to look at the apartment and then be ready to go as soon as it's completely dark. You're my partner. You go where I go. And I'm due in vampire court tonight. It'll give you a peek into how the creatures of the night live. We can grab something to eat afterwards."

She wanted to do a whiny, "Do I have to?" But that would be weak. Selene needed to show Fin she was able to help him, that she was a plus in his weapons column. "Sure. Give me a half hour to wind down and I'll be good to go." If the gods smiled on her tonight, there would be food in the fridge, because Fin hadn't delivered on his lunch promise.

She didn't give him a chance to argue with her time frame. Turning, she strode into the apartment building. Selene couldn't hear him walking behind her—sneaky vampire—but she knew he was there. She reached her apartment door and was almost inside when a question occurred to her. She looked at where Adam was opening his door to the next apartment. "What do you do at court? Just hang around and look important?"

His soft chuckle told her what he thought of that

stupidity. "I'm a working vampire. I'm the judge and exe-cutioner."

"Executioner?"

He closed his door without answering.

Selene sighed as she entered the dark apartment. Just what she needed, a fun night out on the town with the Night Court judge and a Bloody Mary.

CHAPTER SIX

SELENE WAS A PUZZLE. HOW did she manage to tick him off no matter what she did? And why did he even care? They sat side by side again as Dave drove them to vampire headquarters. Adam was angry at the thought of having to take her along, but Fin had said to keep her under surveillance until they knew they could trust her. Adam had figured she'd never shut up. Now, halfway there, he was annoyed because she hadn't said a word. *Just ignore her.* He was good at blocking things that bothered him. Adam slid a quick sideways glance. She sure didn't have any trouble ignoring *him*. A puzzle. His smile was slow with sly anticipation. He liked puzzles.

He broke the silence. "Why wouldn't your dad be proud of you?" Adam knew the question was none of his business, but he didn't give a crap. She didn't answer for a long time.

"I wanted to be a warrior, not part of a plague of locusts that descended on a helpless planet and stripped it clean."

"Did your mom agree with you?" He wondered how personal his questions would have to become before she lost her temper.

She scowled. "Don't have a clue. She left us when I was still young." Her expression warned him away from further questioning.

Warnings rarely stopped him. One more question. "Do

you think Zero will get your dad to help him again this time?" Her gaze seared a smoking hole in him.

"Did Fin tell you to pump me for information?"

"Nope, just naturally curious, I guess." His questions had nothing to do with wanting to know more about her. It was just . . . smart to find out as much as possible about your enemy. He refused to examine any other motives.

"Last answer. First, I don't even know if my father is alive or was destroyed by something bigger and badder than him. Besides, Frost—no, it's Zero now—will only call in outside help if things go south for his big uprising on the twenty-first. He doesn't like to admit he can't do it all." She held up her hand to stop his next question. "It's my turn now."

Dave interrupted. "We're here." Pulling into an underground garage, he parked and then turned to look at Adam. "Your boss said something about vampires, so I brought a few weapons—a cross, holy water, and a big-ass sword to cut off heads."

Adam tried to keep the smile from his face. "Won't need any of those, Dave." The only thing that would scare a vampire was the sword. "You're in my car. To any vampire, that means you belong to me. No one touches what's mine."

Dave nodded. "I'll wait here for you. Text if you need rescuing." He didn't smile when he said it.

Selene looked around. "Where are we? I don't know San Diego well enough to recognize this part of the city."

Good. The less she knew the better. "We're at the original Adam's condo. He might have put up with living underground when he was traveling, but at home he liked his luxury." She followed him to the private elevator that would take them directly to the penthouse suite. What was it about the old and powerful and their condos? Fin always had to have one, too. "Does Zero live in a condo?"

She shrugged as she watched him use the keyed access to open the elevator door. "Who knows? He's never invited me to his place."

Adam concentrated on her rather than the claustrophobic, windowless box as it whizzed them to the top of the building. Raptors were meant to roam free, but she was a great distraction. Those clear blue eyes promised she'd deliver on her promise to kick butt if butt needed kicking. Her lips were full and sensual. But she didn't try to use them with false puckering or I'm-available smiles. She was straightforward in her despising of him. His gaze slid lower. A nice, rounded bottom in that sexy little dress. He wondered if she could run in those heels, though. He glanced up. She met his gaze with narrowed eyes. He smiled. She didn't smile back.

The elevator doors slid open. Jude was there to meet him in the foyer that separated the elevator from the condo entrance. The vampire glanced at him before his attention shifted to Selene. He gave her a long assessing look and then smiled at her. His smile was patented seduction with a show of fang.

Adam frowned. They didn't have time for this. "Selene, this is Jude. He's an ally." Adam knew the glare he sent Jude's way didn't say ally. He liked the guy, but he needed to keep his smiles to himself when they had business to take care of. "Jude, this is Selene. She's my new partner." That's all Jude had to know right now. "So how do things look tonight?"

Jude shrugged. "Same old same old. A full docket. A bunch of lowlifes doing lowlife stuff."

Jude threw Selene a quick glance but didn't ask the questions Adam knew he was dying to ask. All right then. "Let's get to it."

Selene smiled at Jude. "Explain."

Adam ground his teeth. He didn't want them standing there while Jude explained things to her. "We don't have time to—"

Her smile disappeared when she looked at Adam. "Sure we do. I'm certain Jude can keep it brief."

Jude jumped in, obviously not wanting to have the attention shifted from him. "Once a month, the vampire lord—aka Adam—holds court to judge vampires who have disobeyed his laws. Those found guilty are punished. Those found innocent—there aren't many of those—hightail it out of the building before their lord can change his mind.

Evidently that satisfied her, because she headed for the condo door. Jude slipped in front of her to unlock it. It opened into a huge open-concept area dominated by a glass wall that looked out over San Diego. At one end of the room where the dining table usually rested was a massive throne. Adam the First never claimed to be humble. A mob of vampires stood in groups talking.

"Good thing it's dark." Selene stated the obvious.

Jude didn't give Adam a chance to answer. "Blackout shades automatically lower right before dawn and raise when night falls."

Adam tried not to care, but he was kinda wanting to kick Jude's ass. Not that *he'd* wanted to explain the shades, but she was his partner after all.

Jude reluctantly turned from Selene. He looked at Adam. What he saw there made him step away. "I'll announce you."

"You do that." Adam took a deep breath and tried to switch his focus to the suddenly silent crowd of vampires.

"Adam, lord of all North American vampires, has arrived. Be seated."

As the vampires silently found chairs, Adam and Selene followed Jude to the throne. Adam sat and then spoke to his subjects. "Before we begin tonight's court, I want to introduce you to Selene." He gestured to where she stood beside him looking cranky. She probably wanted her own throne. "She's mine. Any who touch her will not wake to another night."

"You've got to be kidding. Like hell I'm yours." Selene's outrage was merely a murmur in recognition that vampires had very good hearing.

Adam waved at Jude. "Explain it to her." He would have loved to do it himself, just to watch her glower and narrow those big eyes, but he had to give his full attention to his audience. And while Jude made it clear—in a whisper—that since Selene wasn't a vampire, she'd have to be Adam's lover in order to keep the rest of the vampires from trying to snack on her, he began the night's festivities.

Adam tried to look as though he cared. He leaned forward, propping his elbows on the arms of his throne and steepling his fingers under his chin. He glanced around the room lined with shiny-eyed vampires. They'd given up their nightly hunts along with favorite TV shows for this. He'd better make it worth their while.

Jude had finished laying out the facts of vampire life to Selene and now announced to the room, "Bring forth the first accused."

A huge vampire with greasy brown hair and small close-set eyes who looked as though he could take down a T. rex all by himself shoved the first victim forward.

As Adam waited for the accused to kneel in front of him, he allowed his attention to wander past those eager gazes to the condo's wall of windows. San Diego's lights, the darkness, and his need to be free of everything vampire beckoned.

He glanced away, only to meet Selene's hard stare. She looked as though she wanted to crack open his head, scoop out his brain, and riffle through his thoughts. Then she must've remembered she was supposed to be pretending to be his lover. Her gaze softened. She tipped back her head, lowered her lids, and then slid her tongue across her lower lip. He fixated on the wet sheen of it, and lost his entire train of thought.

"We're ready, lord." Jude's voice was sharp enough to bring Adam's train chugging back into the station.

He forced his attention to the accused. "So . . ." What was this one's name? Damn. *Concentrate.* He glanced at Jude.

Jude leaned close. "Kevin." And then murmured a list of the scum's sins.

Adam narrowed his eyes. "Children?"

Jude nodded. "Children."

Adam smiled coldly at the child killer. "So, Kevin. The word is that you've been draining people and leaving their bodies to be found by the police." Dumbass vampire.

Kevin managed to look defiant even kneeling in front of him. "Only humans. Who cares if someone found them? They're food."

"A lot of them were children."

Kevin shrugged. "They're easier to catch."

Do not tear is head off yet. "Children. Humans notice dead kids." Adam wondered how many ways he could find to describe this piece of crap. *Don't lose your temper.* "See, this is the thing, Kevin. I value discretion. You left a woman's body in front of a restaurant. That's not good for the dining experience. Although I will admit it did have a certain amusing irony. It made me smile." Not. He wanted to free his beast and then rip Kevin-the-child-killer apart.

But the vampires watching this would expect their leader not to care who they drained. Old Adam would've applauded Kevin. Adam took a deep calming breath. What he felt were his *human* emotions. He couldn't do anything to make his subjects suspect that their real leader had left the building.

Kevin looked smug.

"Only a small smile, and it didn't last long. Especially when the story cropped up on the news. We can't allow this to go on, Kevin. You understand, don't you?" He wrapped his disgust and rage in what Adam hoped was a regretful expression.

Kevin's eyes turned completely black as he peeled his lip back to expose his fangs. "The immortals you teamed us up with don't care how many humans we kill. They're going to destroy all of them anyway in a few weeks. What's the big deal?"

The idiot didn't even know enough to be terrified. Adam faked a sigh. "I've told everyone several times that we're no longer 'teamed up' with the immortals. And the big deal is that you defied me. *No one* disobeys me, Kevin."

Nothing else to say. Adam felt anticipation thrumming through the room. Blood-thirsty bunch of night-crawlers. He smiled at Kevin. *Showtime.* No twinges of conscience over this guy. He remembered too well what those other vampires had done to his first human body back in Philly.

Presentation was everything for the vampires watching him. Adam didn't move. Didn't have to. He had long-distance skills. He pictured Kevin's end in his mind, and his beast screamed its approval.

With no warning, Kevin's body split from neck to groin. Amid the spill of guts and other things, an invisible hand reached in and yanked out his still-beating heart. And crushed it. Kevin didn't even have time to scream. He died his final death amid a spray of blood and wearing an expression of shocked disbelief. Adam admitted that the original owner of his body had collected some cool powers over the centuries.

Adam allowed the silence to build as the vampires

stared at the bloody remains of what had once been Kevin-the-brainless. Okay, so to be accurate, he still had his brain—almost new with hardly any mileage on it.

He chanced a quick glance at Selene. Adam didn't know what he expected to see, but it wasn't her expression of calm thoughtfulness.

She acknowledged his gaze with a nod. "There are times when a public act of savagery saves many lives down the road. Besides, he deserved it."

He turned away, not sure what to make of her comment, or her. Was she thinking about her father? If so, she was way off the mark. Her father's public act of savagery had saved no one.

After Adam had allowed them the requisite five minutes of gawking followed by cleanup time, he leaned back in his throne. Then he turned his attention to the remaining line of vampires waiting judgment. He smiled. They shuddered. No need to tell them his craving for bloody death had been sated for the night.

Finally, the ordeal was over and the room empty. Adam stood. Damn, that felt good. "Jeez, I hate that throne. Feels like I'm sitting on the bones of good old Adam's enemies."

"Probably are." Jude's mutter was almost lost as he glanced around the empty room.

"Only a megalomaniac would get a rush from this kind of show." *Oh, wait, that must be me.* Adam kept forgetting. "Time to wrap this up and go home. I've done the creating-terror-and-visiting-lordly-wrath-upon-my-subjects duty for the month." Good thing this only rolled around every thirty days. He yawned, fighting the need for sleep as dawn approached. Not that he died at dawn like the others, but he still felt a pull to close his eyes and check out until dusk.

Jude grinned. "That's why they love you, O Great Vampire Lord."

Selene made a rude noise to express her opinion of that.

Adam scowled. "I don't think love was the exact emotion they were feeling. And I wish at least one of them had stood up and challenged me. I hate executions." Although Kevin's had felt pretty great. Usually, he was all about the hunt where the prey had a fighting chance. Assuming they ran fast enough.

"You did what you had to do," Selene said.

Surprised, Adam looked at her. Was that actual approval in her eyes? If so, it was a first.

Jude had stopped grinning. "By the way, you need to start living here. This was Adam's home. They'll only buy into the story that you've moved to an undisclosed location because of the report of a traitor among them for so long."

"It reeks of vampires." Adam chose to ignore the truth that he was now vampire, too. Talk about inner conflict. "I get that Adam wanted a home befitting his awesomeness, but I'm not loving this place." He waved his hand to stop Jude from commenting. "I know, I know. Adam demanded penthouse luxury. Fin, too."

Jude looked ticked. "Vampires smell great." He seemed to think about that. "Well, at least *I* smell amazing."

Adam searched for the right way to explain what he meant. "I'll reword that. This place reminds me of the vampires who ripped apart my original human body. And, yeah, I'm still bitter." Did that make him weak? Again, he glanced at Selene. Not that what she thought of him mattered. Her expression told him nothing. "Besides, this place will always smell of blood from the ones I've slaughtered here." His vampire and beast might enjoy the scent. His human? Not so much.

"I get that. But the clans expect cruelty from you, and it's wise to give them exactly what they expect. Get over it and move on." Jude didn't look overly sympathetic.

"Look, Adam, we have to—"

Selene interrupted. "How many have you killed in your raptor form? I'd think you'd be used to it by now." She raised one brow.

If this was payback for poking into her personal life, it was a good one. "Sure, my beast has killed. But that wasn't me, the human." *But that wasn't me.* The revelation punched him right between the eyes. Adam didn't look at her as he spoke. He gazed out that wall of windows into the night and saw the truth he'd finally faced. The raptor caged inside him wasn't *him*, not anymore. He thought of himself as human—not vampire, not Utahraptor. They rented space in his head, but the *human* Rap—not Adam—owned the building. "I wonder if my soul is becoming human?" Would he lose his power to change?

Jude interrupted his musing. "I don't care if it becomes a hot-air balloon. If any of your 'subjects' ever suspect the 'real' Adam is gone, they'll tear both of us apart."

Adam allowed himself a slow anticipatory smile. "They could try."

"It's not all about you, raptor. Your boss needs the vampire clans to fight by his side. That won't happen if they find out Fin destroyed their leader and hijacked his body. Besides, I don't want to end up as a footstool for the throne."

"There's that." Jude was right. Too much was at stake. But both his raptor soul and vampire instinct agreed busting loose and battling something that fought back would be a great stress reliever. "How's the assassin list look tonight?"

Jude pulled a paper from his coat pocket. "Only one. He's waiting for you in the parking garage."

Adam ignored his stab of disappointment. "What, Wednesday is a slow night?"

"Must be." Jude frowned. "This one is problematic."

"They're all problematic. They want to kick my butt for stuff I didn't do."

"You don't have to handle them yourself. Adam never did. He had an army of bodyguards. He never put himself in harm's way if he could help it." Left unsaid was that this was one more difference that could lead to discovery and death.

"I *want* to handle it myself." His predator screamed its need for a battle with someone who could fight back. Not an execution. Adam yanked open the throne room's door and headed for the elevator. "Have I mentioned how much I really don't like elevators?"

Selene kept pace with Adam. He glanced into her eyes and saw the same excitement he knew shone in his. They had this in common.

"Not in the last ten minutes." Jude followed them out, slamming the door behind him. "The attitude is getting old. You claimed Adam's body, so you own his lifestyle along with his sins. I haven't said much because you've only been on the job a short time, but—"

"You've said plenty." A headache was forming behind Adam's eyes. A human headache. Raptors and vampires never got the pounding pain that made him want to rip off his head.

"Not about the assassination attempts. Everyone hated Adam, but they feared him more. That's because he crushed anyone who crossed him. You've let the assassins from the last three nights live."

"They didn't deserve to die." As opposed to the old Adam, who had earned death over and over again. *But you wanted to kill them. You wanted to free your soul and tear them apart, watch their blood fill the sidewalk cracks, coat yourself in death.* Adam turned his face away from Jude. He didn't want the other vampire to see the bloodlust shining in his eyes, didn't want Jude to see how close he was to losing it. Adam took pride in his control. Someone in his family had to.

"That's not the point. By allowing them to live, you'll appear weak to the vampire clans. Perspective is everything. Luckily, I was there to wipe the assassins' memories. If not, you'd have challengers lined up around the block.

"Good. One of *them* can have this job." The elevator door slid open. He stepped inside and Selene followed him. Adam held out his hand to stop Jude from entering. "No. You still have stuff to do here before dawn. I have a partner. We can take care of tonight's assassin." Adam knew Jude wanted to go with them, but he didn't need a babysitter for this job.

"You don't understand, Adam. This guy is—"

Adam hit the down button, and the door slid shut on whatever Jude had been about to say.

"Aren't you afraid I'll stab you in the back while you're fighting the assassin, raptor?" Selene sounded indifferent, as though his answer meant nothing to her.

He didn't believe it. "No. There's too much at stake. You try to kill me, and you've burned your bridges with Fin. I think you want that connection too much." Adam hoped he was right.

She said nothing else until the door slid open. They stepped out. He led the way as they walked toward where Dave would be waiting in the SUV. Adam thought about what they might be facing. He spoke before thinking. "Maybe you should wait in the car. This could get messy." Then he remembered what she'd done at the zoo. She wasn't a wait-in-the-car type.

Selene didn't hide her outrage. "Absolutely not. I'm your partner. We'll take care of business together. Of course, feel free to wait in the car yourself. No need to get those great boots scuffed."

Adam almost smiled. Now *that* was an attitude he could get behind. His smile faded. If she wasn't working for the enemy.

Then everything fled Adam's mind as he saw the man waiting beside his SUV. He wasn't what Adam had expected. No shine of bloodlust in his eyes, no knife or sword ready to cut out his heart or lop off his head, just . . . nothing.

Tall, slender, with pale hair that fell almost to his waist, he watched them from cold ice-blue eyes. His emotionless stare was just creepy.

Selene leaned close. "He's a member of the Fae. I don't know which group. If he's from the Seelie court we're probably okay. They're friendly to humans. Usually."

Adam came up blank. His soul had been in timeout when Fin and his buddies met their first fairy. "How do you know all this stuff?"

"Frost filled everyone in on every possible entity we might meet. Just keep walking. I'll explain later. All you have to know is that the power you've inherited from the old Adam won't work on him. He's a lot higher on the food chain than vampires. If it comes down to a killing situation, you'll have to free your raptor and hope for the best." She didn't mention what she'd be doing during the battle.

Adam perked up. Now *this* sounded interesting. "Let's see what he wants." He prayed for a fight to clear his mind of the night's court proceedings. Adam glanced at the SUV. No Dave. He didn't know whether to be relieved or not.

Adam stopped walking about twenty feet from the fairy. Selene backed away, blending into the shadows behind him. He didn't have time to worry about what she was doing. "You wanted to talk?" Adam tensed, ready to act if talking wasn't on the agenda.

A brief expression of contempt crossed the fairy's face

and was gone. "I am Drajak, the messenger of Tatiana, queen of the Seelie court." He paused as if expecting a reaction.

Adam gave none. "And?"

"My queen has decided it would amuse her to aid Frost's immortals in their destruction of humanity on December 21."

"The Seelie court?" Adam frowned. "I thought you guys liked humans."

The fairy's lip curled in disgust. "We've never 'liked' humans." The lip-curl became a sneer. "They provide entertainment, especially the women." He shrugged. "We have permitted their existence. But in recent years they have become too powerful, developing weapons that might pose a danger to us. It is time for them to go."

"Not up to a human challenge, huh?" Adam filled his voice with all kinds of disrespect.

Drajak's eyes narrowed, but he didn't rise to the insult. "Our queen has spoken with Frost. He indicated that the vampires were his allies. She wants to assure herself we can still depend on your support." He didn't phrase it as a question.

The assumption was that Adam wouldn't dare turn away from the alliance. Adam allowed himself a semi-smile. "Well, the problem is the last time I did what Frost wanted and tangled with Fin's crowd I got my ass kicked. Lost a lot of my best fighters. So, I guess my answer is . . ." He enjoyed dragging out the moment. "Uh, no. You and your queen will have to muddle along without me." He waited for the expected rage, the threats of reprisal.

Drajak's expression never changed. "That is unfortunate."

"Why?" Adam decided that no pleasant expression would ever crack the cold perfection of Drajak's face.

"My queen tolerates no enemies. I will destroy you and

then return to my court." Drajak spoke with cold indifference and absolute confidence.

Adam scanned the area. They were alone. No one to see what would happen next. He didn't turn his head to speak to Selene. He wanted to make sure the fairy heard him. "This guy is as empty as they get. We need to find him a soul and maybe a heart to go along with it." He smiled. A smile his brothers would recognize and back away from. "While we're at it, he might need some balls to go along with his big talk."

Anger flared in Drajak's eyes; the first strong emotion Adam had seen there. Good. A mad fairy might mean a careless one. He crouched, ready to free his soul from its cage.

Adam welcomed the explosion of joy that came with the thought of battle. The zoo had not been enough. He had too much need locked inside him. He took deep breaths, trying to control the desire for savagery. The reasoning part of him, the *human* part, receded as the primitive force that was his soul fought toward the surface.

A gleaming sword materialized in Drajak's hand. Not metal? Didn't matter. Adam saw it as a declaration of war.

"This won't end well," Selene warned.

"Thanks for the vote of confidence." He didn't try to hide his sarcasm. Adam had thought she was as eager as he was for this confrontation.

Adam was beyond caring. Time for a preemptive strike. Just so no one could accuse him of not being versatile, he gathered all of old Adam's considerable power and flung it at Drajak. But instead of pulverizing the fairy, it bounced off an invisible shield. Selene had been right. Adam winced at the resulting thunder-like clap and flash of light. Damn. That would attract attention.

Drajak smiled.

Adam didn't intend to stand there waiting for the fairy

to take his turn. And he sure didn't see Selene joining him in battle. His human body could be destroyed, and this time Fin wouldn't be there to scoop up his soul. Adam's beast was almost indestructible. This was a no brainer.

He freed his beast.

CHAPTER SEVEN

———

"NO!" SELENE'S CRY CAME A second too late. Adam's raptor screamed its challenge at the fairy. Males. They were so focused on each other that they didn't hear the voices. Lots of voices—laughing, talking, and coming toward them. Wouldn't the humans be surprised when instead of their cars they found a Utahraptor and a sword-waving messenger of Tatiana?

She didn't have time to formulate any fancy plans. All she knew was that Adam wouldn't listen to her now. He was lost to his beast. He would need a more powerful authority figure to get his attention. Selene went with the first idea that popped into her mind.

"Stop. Now."

The man's voice was deep, commanding, as he strode out of the shadows. He was tall, with dark red hair that hung past his shoulders and glittered in the near darkness of the garage. Chiseled features dominated by eyes that swirled with color before settling into a startling blue-green completed the package. Damn, she was good.

"Frost. I was not expecting to see you here." The fairy stepped back, lowered his sword, and bowed his head. "My Queen sent me to make certain we could count on the vampires' help. This is their lord, who does not seem quite what he should be." He took a moment to glare at the raptor. "We would have heard if he was a shifter. I would ask where the real Adam is?"

Selene took advantage of Adam's momentary confusion to edge close enough for him to hear her. "Return to human form. Now." The beast's head with its predator's gaze and way too many sharp teeth turned toward her. "Trust me."

She held her breath. Would he take *her* head as a consolation prize for not getting the one he wanted? Would he ignore her and try to attack Frost? Selene exhaled as the raptor became vampire Adam once again, his eyes wild with battle lust.

"Where did Zero come from? I don't have the power to defeat him, but I sure can put a hurting on him. Look, my cover with the vampires is blown anyway. Not much to lose. My raptor can keep him busy long enough for you to escape." He glanced back to where Frost had paused in his conversation with the fairy to make a casual gesture in their direction.

"Don't you dare insult me like that. I don't run." She leaned closer to whisper. "You've forgotten that I have talents, too. Frost is mine, and he just froze us. Now look as though you can't move." Thank heaven he didn't argue with her, just made like a statue. Because he didn't need to know how much effort it took to maintain the fake Frost and argue with him at the same time.

Frost shifted his attention to the fairy. "Return to Queen Tatiana. Tell her the vampires will be ready to support her." He looked over at Adam. "I'll take care of this situation. The real Adam is absolutely ready to join with us. I spoke with him right before I came here. This was merely a poor attempt by Fin to sow discord among us."

The fairy's expression said he wanted to "take care" of the situation himself. But then he heard the approaching people. He aimed a last disappointed scowl at Adam before disappearing. Luckily, he didn't pause to ask how Frost had just happened to turn up at this particular moment. Relieved, Selene retrieved her essence and Frost disappeared.

They waited to make sure the fairy was really gone, and then Adam pulled her deeper into the shadows. They watched the laughing group of people troop past them on their way to their vehicles. A few minutes later, they drove away.

As her tension eased, Selene realized her back was pressed against Adam. He'd wrapped his arm around her, holding her in place. With adrenaline still surging through her, every one of her senses crested. A wave of emotion followed.

His heat warmed her. Everywhere. Even in places where his body didn't touch. She leaned into him, burrowing deeper, craving *something*, reveling in his quickened heartbeat. He had spread his legs, and she settled against the bulge that announced he'd stopped thinking about the fairy. She resisted the urge to turn, to wrap her arms around . . . *Not here. Not now. Not ever.* She needed to remember who he was. *Who she was.*

Selene stepped away before daring to face him. And if she felt a little shaky, it was just the reaction setting in from having averted disaster. This wasn't her. Selene didn't lose control around males. Even the thought angered her. She turned that anger on him. "You don't have to worry about becoming human. Your reaction was pure beast—strike now and damn the consequences." Part of her fury was because he had never even considered that she might be able to handle the situation—hadn't even asked her—before turning his dino loose.

Selene forced her breathing back to normal even as she tried to ignore the flash of hurt in his eyes. She did *not* feel guilty. "Let's get out of here."

"You've forgotten something." Ice coated his words.

"What? I—" She remembered. "Dave. Where is he?"

Adam's smile was no smile at all. "I'm sure he would be flattered to know you would've driven off without giving him a thought."

"We just escaped death, so maybe I'm a little distracted." That sounded lame. "Besides, I'm not used to having a driver." Even lamer. She turned to gaze into the darkness. "I'll search the upper levels. You can head down."

Before either of them could move, though, they heard the sound of someone running. Adam started to shove her behind him. Then he stopped. He said nothing as she stepped to his side. Selene decided there might be hope for this partnership after all.

She watched Adam relax as Dave ran into sight. Their driver slowed to a walk when he saw them. Selene breathed a silent sigh of relief. The vampires hadn't gotten him. Then she noticed the sword Dave carried. Blood dripped from it. This wasn't a good thing.

Dave didn't wait to reach them before he spoke. "Jeez, am I glad to see you. I got bored sitting in the car, so I took a walk around. Two vampires caught me on the top level. They were jabbering about showing the lord they could kill anyone they wanted, where they wanted, and when they wanted." He sidestepped them to open the driver-side door and pull out a cloth. He cleaned the blood from his sword as he talked. "After I took their heads, I started worrying about you guys. What if there were more idiots looking to drain people? I mean, you two would probably make a gourmet meal. But look at you, all safe. Good thing. I'm a little out of shape. Those two had me huffing and puffing at the end."

Selene and Adam simply stared at him. Adam broke the silence. "Who are you?"

Exactly what she wanted to know. Dave cocked his head as he considered the question.

"I'm who I need to be. And right now, that's your driver. Hop in."

She wondered. Had Fin vetted this man before hiring him? Not that she wasn't grateful that he had skills. But she hated mysteries, and Dave definitely didn't want to talk about himself.

Adam didn't press for an answer. "Wait in the car. We have to check out the vampires you killed."

Dave nodded before climbing behind the wheel. Selene followed Adam to the top level of the garage. It didn't take them long to find the vampires. Pieces of them were scattered all over the place.

Adam crouched to study the face of each vampire. "These two were up with us tonight. I remember them because they laughed when I took their buddy's heart. Cold. I guess they thought draining a human this close to my home would be like spitting in my face. After the kill, they could disappear and I'd never know who did it." He stood. "I bet this wiped the smiles off their faces."

Adam pulled out his phone. Distracted, she listened as he called Jude to tell him that he had a cleanup on aisle four.

She waited until he finished before speaking. "Dave didn't have any blood on him. The only blood was on his sword."

He nodded. "Can't imagine a human able to move that fast, faster than two vampires. No blood means he wasn't close to his kills, or he moved too fast to get spattered." Adam shook his head. "I'm going to have a long talk with our driver. All those body parts. That was massive overkill. I'd say Dave has anger issues."

Dave wasn't the only one. Selene studied Adam. They'd been partners for only a short time, but she'd bet the anger he had bottled inside gave *him* lots of emotional heartburn. She gestured at the scattered pieces. "Don't you feel anything? They were yours."

He turned his hard gaze on her. "They were never mine. I'm playing a part here. That's it. Other than Jude and Utah's mate Lia, I have no vampire friends."

So, his brother had mated with a vampire? Interesting.

Adam leaned in close. "How about you? Do you feel anything for your father? What if Zero calls on him again? Will you be able to fight against him?"

Selene chose not to answer that. He just wanted to make her uncomfortable because she'd asked him an awkward question. Besides, she didn't know the answer, probably wouldn't know it until she was face to face with her father.

Adam shrugged at her silence. Evidently, he was the only one who was expected to answer challenging questions. He led them back to the SUV. When they climbed into the car, Dave turned to look at them.

"Fin called. He wants to talk to both of you. He'll meet you at your apartment." He nodded at Adam. "He didn't say what he wanted to chat about." Then Dave drove them home.

It was quiet on the drive back to the apartment building. Selene pulled her phone from her purse and tried to make a few calls—probably trying to reach her sister and Ace—but couldn't connect. She looked worried. Adam tried to break the silence with a question for Dave. "You diced and sliced those vampires up pretty good. I assume you have lots of experience fighting them."

"Yep."

Okay, that had been an epic fail as a dialogue starter. "Where did you learn to fight?"

"Here and there."

Now Adam was getting mad. "You're not going to tell me anything, are you?"

"Nope. Answering questions isn't in my contract."

Adam retreated into angry silence. Both Selene and Dave were not only closed books, but they'd padlocked them to keep him out. He was the only one whose book had frayed pages from everyone flipping through his life's history. But his brothers could tell the two of them that he was stubborn. He'd get the answers to his questions. And if an annoying inner voice tried to point out that just a short while ago he'd sworn he didn't want to know anything about Selene, well, he chose to ignore it.

Once in the apartment's parking lot, Adam didn't have to search far for Fin's car. His boss's new luxury sedan diminished every other car there. Fin didn't even need a vehicle to get around, but he wanted to save his energy for important stuff like his ongoing mental battle with Zero.

Inside, Dave went his own way while Selene followed Adam into his apartment. She wore her stoic expression, the one he was beginning to recognize as her go-to face for things she didn't want to do but couldn't get out of. He felt the same way, except he chose not to hide his temper.

The light beside his one comfortable chair was on, and Fin looked relaxed sitting in it. Of course, he did. The owner of that car outside would always take the best seat. Adam tried to shake off his grumpiness. Fin didn't cause his bad mood. Adam always came away from his monthly vampire court meetings wanting to drive to the nearest wilderness area where he could turn his raptor loose on something big that wanted to mix it up with him. A grizzly would work. Too bad they weren't native to San Diego.

Selene moved up beside him. She placed her hand over his fist. "Unclench."

The unexpectedness of her touch took his breath away. "Relax."

Her voice was softer than any she'd used on him during their brief acquaintance. He could tell her that his continuing tension now had nothing to do with Fin and everything to do with the heat of her skin against his. He didn't tell her. Adam was finding it tough to maintain his glower in the face of her disturbing closeness and tempting scent of sexy woman. But he did uncurl his fingers, flexing them to get rid of their stiffness.

She didn't seem aware of her effect on him as she continued, "Today has been tough on everyone. You most of all. Don't worry, Fin won't have time to hassle you because he'll be too busy answering questions about Meg and Ace."

"*He* is sitting right here." Fin motioned to the couch. "Sit."

Adam thought about refusing but decided he was too tired to make a statement. He dropped onto the couch and stretched his legs out in front of him. Selene sat, too, but left space between them. She had removed her hand. His hand mourned the loss. She crossed her legs. The short, little black dress she'd worn to impress the vampires rode up on her smooth thighs. Adam tried not to notice the amazing length of her legs. And he definitely refused to imagine the feel of his hand gliding up and up and . . . *Remember. Possible enemy.* He took a deep breath and focused every bit of his attention on Fin. "What did you want to discuss?"

Selene didn't give Fin a chance to answer. "Where is my sister? What did you do with Ace? I want to talk to them."

"They're both fine. You can talk to them when we finish here."

She narrowed her eyes. "No. I talk to them now. I tried to call earlier but got nothing. Was that your doing?"

Fin looked faintly bored. "Fine. And yes, I blocked all their calls temporarily. I didn't want to make it too easy for Zero to contact them." He held up his hand to stop her from speaking. "And before you ask, I didn't block you because I trust you're strong enough to not wilt under the Dark Lord's displeasure."

"Dark Lord?" Adam laughed. "That's new. I like it."

Selene didn't like it. "Funny. Unblock them. We'll talk after I make sure they're okay."

Fin turned serious. "You don't really believe I'd hurt them, do you?"

She looked uncertain for a moment before shaking her head. "No. You need us. Manipulation, though, that's a different story."

Fin didn't even blink. "Manipulation is a time-honored strategy. Call them."

Selene nodded. She headed for the door with her phone. "I'll call from my apartment. I want privacy." She closed the door quietly behind her.

Fin didn't try to stop her. Adam was still reeling from the truth that she'd willingly touched him. She'd tried to comfort him. Where had all her hate gone? Or had it really gone? Was this just a ploy to confuse him? If so, it was working. His boss interrupted his thoughts.

"We'll have to keep an eye on the Sidhe. If Tatiana really means to fight on Zero's side, she'll make a formidable enemy. I'm bringing in Kione to join you and Selene. Tatiana's fairies will think twice before attacking you with him riding shotgun."

"Kione?" The name sounded familiar, but he couldn't remember . . .

"You never met him. Your soul was resting in Sedona when he arrived. He's a dark fairy, a prince of the Unseelie court. He has a violent history. And his powers are unusual." Fin smiled. "I think I'll allow him to explain them to you."

Adam didn't like that smile. Fin could have a sadistic streak sometimes. "The rest of the guys just have an ordinary human driver and their usual partner. I'm collecting a freaking army—a driver who can cut vampires into little cubes, a partner who may or may not be on our side, and now a dark fairy with unnamed powers." He glanced at the door to make sure Selene wasn't returning. "Want to explain?"

Fin leaned back in his chair and closed his eyes. "Zero's been extra annoying today. I have a killer migraine. Meds are just starting to kick in." He opened his eyes to slits. "Explain? Hmm. Don't you think Zero allowed Selene to escape a little too easily?"

Adam controlled his impatience. Fin was an expert at leading questioners off onto bumpy side roads. "He purposely looked the other way?"

"Makes sense." Fin shrugged. "Zero isn't careless. He could've stopped them at any moment until they met us."

Adam heard admiration in Fin's voice. Maybe that wasn't so strange, since Zero was the only being able to match Fin in power. But still . . . "Why would he do that? Are you sure Selene isn't a spy?" His stab of disappointment at that thought surprised Adam. After all, he'd never really trusted her, had he?

"I've been in her mind. She's telling the truth."

"Then what—"

Selene flung the door open, stalked across the room, and dropped onto the couch. Then she glared at Fin. "Meg thinks Tor is hot, and Ace thinks you're cool. I think you'd better stop manipulating them. Both of them are impressionable. If they grow attached, it will hurt them when they have to leave."

Fin raised one brow. "Thinking of leaving, Selene?"

"Of course not." She dropped her gaze.

Adam heard the lie in her voice. And as much as he still didn't trust her, the part of him that was starting to like her in spite of that distrust, wanted to convince her to stay. His first step would be to get her away from any more of Fin's probing questions. "It's been a long night.

I want to unwind. Is there anything else you need to tell us?"

Fin's glance was filled with secret knowledge. "I'll leave it to you to tell Selene about Kione. One other thing. I think Zero will recall his remaining immortals from around the world before the winter solstice. We know that Crow is already here. We pose the biggest threat to him. He'll want to whittle our numbers down before the big day. Besides, he already has his nonhuman armies in place ready to overthrow humanity. If things go as Zero's planned, he and his immortals will be ready to leave Earth once their job is done."

Selene bit her lip, her expression worried. "What can we do in a couple of weeks to stop them?"

"You and Adam are my greatest hope. Adam has the power of the vampires behind him, and you'll recognize Zero's remaining immortals. His nonhuman recruiters are still sweeping up new fighters in the city. I need you to find their headquarters and neutralize as many of them as you can."

Adam didn't like the picture that was forming. "You don't expect to stop him, do you?"

Fin didn't say anything for so long that Adam thought he wouldn't answer.

"Stop him? No. But I intend to cripple his operation enough that humanity will have a chance to survive. I'm sending most of the Eleven to major population centers to lead the resistance forces I've gathered."

"Resistance forces?" Adam wanted to go ballistic on Fin for being so secretive about what he'd been doing. "Were you ever going to tell us about this stuff?"

Fin didn't apologize. "You had your plates full already. I decided everything should be on a need–to–know basis."

"Sure you did." Adam raked his fingers through his hair. "So just a few of us will be defending San Diego."

Fin rose. He stretched as he headed for the door. "I'll

be giving you all the help I can. Going back to your original question, that's why you'll have Dave and Kione onboard."

Adam called after Fin. "Great. Thanks for keeping me in the loop. Make sure that Tor and Utah stay in San Diego." Sarcasm was wasted on his leader.

"I'll consider it." He left without looking back.

Adam stared at the closed door. He refused to lose his brothers again. They were pack.

Selene stood. "I'll head over to my apartment. Ignore any loud noises you hear. I'll have to unwind after tonight before I can sleep."

He turned to her as an idea took shape in his head. "We can talk about Kione later. Unwinding is good, but not in your apartment. I need to hunt. Want to join me?" Where had those words come from? Now came the justification. She was his partner. It was wise to keep a potential enemy close to you. Yeah, yeah, and that was a bunch of crap. Admit it. He wanted to spend more time with her.

She hesitated. "I don't know."

Adam plunged on. "I'm calling Utah and Tor. We hunt together." She was probably still worried about her sister and the boy. "Meg and Ace might want to come, too." What? Now he was expanding his lunacy to include a hunting party of thousands? He waited for her answer.

Then she smiled. "Sounds like what I need."

Right then, Adam decided her smile was her greatest power. Because damned if it didn't make him forget everything about this rotten day. He tried to renew his suspicions, his dislike for her, but it didn't work. So, for tonight, he'd let all the negative stuff go and just enjoy the hunt with a beautiful woman.

CHAPTER EIGHT

———

SELENE WAS ALMOST LIGHTHEARTED. OR as lighthearted as she could get while balancing on a blade's edge. Things would be a lot easier if she could jettison her conscience. She could have kept her doubts about Zero's plans to annihilate the human race to herself. Right now, she would be hanging somewhere with Crow enjoying a drink and talking about the fun they'd have in the coming apocalypse. Without her conscience, she wouldn't be feeling guilt about dragging Meg and Ace into her troubles.

The worst part? She still wasn't sure why she was here with Fin's group. Was she really just trying to prove to Zero that she could successfully infiltrate the enemy in the hope he'd take her back? Or was it her conscience again whispering the old "If you're not with us, you're against us" mantra. In other words, if she didn't agree with Zero, she had to try to stop him.

Don't think about all that. Enjoy the moment. The SUV was full. Utah had brought his wife, Lia. Tor and Meg were cozied up in the back seat. She was sitting next to Adam. No cozying going on. But at least the dark cloud dripping on his head all night had seemed to lift. Dave was driving. He'd had nothing to say the whole way. Probably contemplating the beheading of his next crop of vampires.

Ace had opted out. He claimed Fin was teaching him how to fight. That worried her. It wasn't wise to think any of these people were his friends. Fin would use Ace against Zero and not worry about any dents he put in his tool.

They'd been traveling for a while, headed for some wilderness area. Thankfully, no one expected Selene to be chatty. The guys were excited about the hunt, talking about the chance of having fresh venison to eat. Selene was pragmatic. She'd brought some protein bars to stave off starvation.

They had bumped along a dirt road for the last half hour. Finally, they stopped. Selene climbed out and looked around. From what she could see in the darkness, scrub, rocks, and the silhouettes of distant peaks surrounded them. She sensed no humans nearby. Good. They didn't need people racing to the press with screams of, "There be monsters in them hills." Worse yet was the chance of ending up on YouTube.

It felt great to be in comfortable clothes again—jeans, boots, t-shirt, and a jacket. She took a deep breath of clean, cold air. Lia and Meg joined her.

Lia grinned. "Feels great, doesn't it?" She rubbed her hands together. "I'm looking forward to stretching my legs."

Selene got her first good look at Utah's mate—curly blond hair and blue eyes. Cute. She said the first thing that popped into her mind. "You don't look much like a big bad vampire." Selene smiled to show she was joking. She wasn't.

Lia returned her smile. "And you don't look much like an evil minion of Zero."

Selene laughed. "Fair enough."

Meg didn't say anything. She was too busy following every move Tor made. Selene decided she'd have to talk to her sister. Soon. Before things got out of hand.

Adam joined them. "You and Meg won't be able to keep up with us, Selene. Lia is vampire, so she has enhanced strength and speed. You can ride me as long as you can hang on. You won't slow me down much." He looked a little embarrassed by his offer. "Tor won't mind carrying Meg."

Selene controlled her urge to laugh. *You can ride me.* He had no idea what mental images that conjured—tangled sheets, a night breeze cooling their sweat-sheened bodies, and him lying beneath her, all of that naked muscular yumminess open for her to explore. Selene blinked and was back from whatever weird rabbit hole she'd just fallen down.

"That's okay. Meg and I will stay here and watch." *While I give you the hunt of your long lives.* She made a shooing motion. "Go ahead. Have fun."

Adam looked disappointed as he turned away to join the others. Lia followed him.

Meg offered her a rebellious glare. "Maybe once in a while you should let me speak for myself. I have opinions, you know."

Selene sighed. "I know. I'm sorry. I didn't want you to go with them because in a few minutes Tor will need all of his strength and speed to stay alive. At least that's what he'll think." She knew her smile oozed evil intent. "He wouldn't be able to maneuver with you on his back."

Selene ignored Meg's sulky frown as she closed her eyes, pulled up a memory, and then flung it into reality powered by her essence. She opened her eyes to panicked shouts.

The creature emerging from the darkness was as much a nightmare now as the first time she had seen it. Selene had only visited its home planet once, but it was one time too many. Predatory monsters filled a lot of worlds, but this was one of the worst. She'd never forgotten a single detail of it.

Meg shrieked. "Where did you get that?"

"From somewhere far far away." More than sixty feet long, it wasn't heavy and ponderous. The creature was lean with a muscular back end made for leaping and a long, spiked tail made for whipping. Its arms were longer than the tiny T. rex ones, and each arm ended with foot-long talons. It could grab and hold its prey while it tore it apart. The monster had what looked like wings, but Selene knew better. She finally reached the head. On the end of a sinuous neck, the head was monstrous—six eyes to see in any direction along with a mouth that unhinged to gape open wide enough to swallow a careless Utah-raptor. Its teeth would make a T. rex cry.

Within seconds, the men had released their souls. Selene sat down and then leaned back against a boulder to watch. She motioned a nervous Meg to join her. Then she focused on guiding her monster in its battle dance. She could do this. Since landing on Earth, Selene had kept her skills sharp by practicing on video games.

The raptors were beautiful examples of pack mentality. They each seemed to know exactly what their pack mates were going to do next. But even though the three raptors looked alike, she knew Adam. He attacked with the same cold ferocity she'd witnessed at the zoo. He was tuned in and focused, the perfect killing machine. She admired that about him. Selene had her hands full keeping her creation out of his jaws.

And then there was Lia. She flowed through the darkness with a speed and agility that Selene wished she had.

Dave had abandoned his vehicle to join the battle. He was a whirling dervish of knives and his decapitator sword. Humans just didn't move like that. Selene wondered about his origin.

To keep it realistic, she knocked the raptors on their butts a few times. But she limited the damage the monster's teeth did to harmless snaps and the crushing of a few boulders Lia had flung at it. The creature let loose with roars that probably woke a few people miles away in San Diego.

The highlight of the whole fight was when her creature opened what looked like its wings. Surprise, surprise, they weren't wings at all. They were bony, hinged-type protuberances that extended yards out in both directions and were lined with deadly needles. The monster could twirl those babies like a majorette's baton. Yes! That made the raptors back off to catch their breaths. She laughed out loud with the joy of the battle

Almost a half hour into the fight, she decided to end it when Adam returned to his vampire form. He drew a circle in the dirt with a stick. Uh oh. She knew the original Adam had magic skills. At a guess, she'd say he was about to either summon help or banish her monster to places unknown. She couldn't afford to lose that much essence.

Selene sent her creation leaping back into the darkness never to be seen again. She felt the familiar jolt as her energy returned to her. Adam's two brothers along with Dave and Lia searched for it with screams of triumph from the raptors and whoops of excitement from the other two.

Adam didn't join them. Selene stopped laughing as he abandoned his circle to stride toward her. She poked Meg. "Maybe you should wait for us in the car." Whatever Adam was bringing, it wouldn't be joy and good cheer. She stood. Adam wasn't the type of man you met sitting down when he was ticked off.

He reached her as Meg disappeared into the SUV. She met his gaze. "Yes?"

Adam radiated anger. She expected to see lightning spark from his fingers and flames erupt from the top of his head.

She nodded toward the circle. "You didn't finish your magic."

He made a dismissive gesture. "I wasn't doing magic. The circle was just to convince you it was time to recall your toy." He clenched his fists. "You could've killed one of us with that thing." He showed fang.

Impressive. "I'm very good at what I do. If I'd wanted you dead, you'd be dead." She forced herself not to step back. "When did you know?"

"About ten minutes in. Something that lethal would've killed at least one of us by then. Besides, even Zero couldn't have kept a creature that massive under wraps just to make it appear here."

"So why didn't you cry foul?" He drew closer, invading her space. Her breathing quickened, but not from fear.

The anger slowly drained from his eyes. "Everyone was having too much fun. Even though it's been millions of years since we hunted as raptors, we only woke to this life months ago. Fin tried to stuff our heads with every bit of info we'd need to survive in this human world, but our predator existence seems like it happened yesterday. If we don't give in to our instincts once in a while, we'll go crazy."

She smiled. "Well, there you go. You're welcome." Selene glanced into the darkness. She could still hear the sounds of the hunters. "Do you think the others knew?"

He shrugged. "Probably. They're not stupid." Adam's gaze narrowed. "Why did Zero allow someone with your kind of power to escape him?"

There it was. The suspicion that always lurked behind everything he said. She sighed. "I've explained this before. He *fired* me. Zero didn't believe I was emotionally suited to annihilation warfare. I'm not my father." She felt she had to add that last just in case he still didn't believe it. Not that saying it a dozen times would change his mind.

He exhaled deeply. "Look, I've got to wind down."

Something moved in his eyes. "Want to go for a ride?" He clarified. "On my back. I flatten out when I run, so you can ride me like a horse."

What? "I thought you were mad at me."

Adam brushed aside his windblown hair. "Yeah, I was." He shrugged. "But now I'm not. No damage, and we all had fun." He speared her with a hard stare. "Even you?"

She didn't try to hide her grin. "I loved being the power behind the monster. I got to experience everything vicariously."

"Don't you miss being a part of the action instead of the manipulator?"

Since he put it that way, "Sometimes. But on the battlefield, I'm usually guiding more than one fighter. I'm constantly engaged. I don't have time to feel bored. Each of us has strengths. This is mine." Selene cast him a challenging stare. "In case you think I'm a pushover without my creations, my father taught me to fight with weapons and to hold my own in a hand-to-hand battle." About the only positive in a toxic relationship.

He finally smiled. "You can do it all."

She nodded emphatically. "Damn right I can."

"So, ride with me." In the space of an indrawn breath, he became raptor.

Just like the first time she'd seen him, he took her breath away. Over twenty feet long from head to massive tail, and weighing close to a ton, he rose above her on powerful hind legs armed with over nine-inch-long sickle claws. And his arms ending in deadly claws weren't made for hugging.

She should be terrified. Selene wasn't. No deep thinking went into her decision. She wanted this. He crouched, and she scrambled onto his back. Then she hung on— clamping her legs to his sides and wrapping her arms around his neck. She only had time to stroke his neck once. Smooth. Feathers. Evidence to fuel future teasing.

They flew. At least that's what it felt like. There was only silence now except for his footfalls over the deserted landscape. Wind whipped her hair into tangles as she lifted her face to the night sky and laughed. She hadn't felt this free since Zero had brought her to the planet. The dark peaks surrounded them, enclosing them in their own mini world. "Faster, faster." Selene urged him on. If this could only last.

Without warning, he stopped, gave a small buck, and then rose almost upright. She shouted her outrage before sliding down his back to land in a patch of scrub bushes.

Selene rolled over, scrambled to her feet, and then let him have it. "You prehistoric jerk. What was that about? I'll . . ."

Even as she tried to come up with a fitting revenge, he became Adam again. Selene stalked toward him. He stood waiting for her. Just before she got within swinging distance of him, he threw back his head and laughed at her.

His laughter stopped her dead. That laugh transformed his dangerous-predator face into the face of a sensual and warm man, one she wanted to touch. She tried to recapture her anger, but it kept slithering away into the shadows.

Adam's laughter died as he covered the distance between them. Definitely within her personal space. But her mind was too scrambled to react to the invasion. She could only repeat her question. "What was that about?"

"Your monster knocked me on my butt a few times. That was payback." He reached out to pick a few twigs out of her hair.

She held her breath. Adam dropped the twigs, but before moving his hand away, he slid his fingers lightly across her jaw. Every nerve in her body came alive at his touch. He blinked. Selene didn't think he'd planned that last move.

"You had dirt on your face." He glanced away as he stepped back.

Lie. She might have had dirt other places, but there was none on her face. That had been impulse contact. Part of her thought body parts touching would lead to nothing good. That was her thinking self. But every one of her senses clamored for more, lots more. Bad senses.

They stood staring at each other while the night seemed to hold its breath, waiting. For what? She wasn't sure. Selene felt the invisible barrier rising between them, could almost see it. She knew if she poked it with her finger, it would be cold and hard, made from all of their suspicions and the things they didn't know or understand about each other. No matter how much her senses wanted it down, she knew it wouldn't happen tonight.

More disappointed than she wanted to admit, she watched him head back toward the SUV. She could see the others emerging from the darkness. The moment was over. But she had discovered something tonight. Proving her worth to Zero and helping Fin save humanity were no longer her only motivations. She wanted to be a great partner for Adam out of more than professional pride. Selene wouldn't think beyond that.

She purposely allowed him to get a little ahead before she started to follow. She had only taken a step when someone whispered her name. Someone close. She froze. The voice had come from behind a nearby outcrop. Adam kept walking. He hadn't heard it.

Selene's first instinct was to shout for the others. But there was something about the whisper, a familiarity. Someone from her past. Quickly, she pulled one of her earrings free and then dropped it just as Adam turned toward her.

"Are you coming?"

"In a minute. I dropped an earring." She held her breath for a moment as he hesitated.

"Need help?" He started to stride back.

She waved him off. "No. I'm fine. It'll only take me a few minutes to find it."

He nodded before continuing back to the SUV.

As soon as she was sure no one was watching, she made her way to the outcrop, bending down now and then to make it look as though she was searching for her earring. Once there, she stepped into its shadow. She waited.

Someone emerged from the darkness. Someone tall wearing a long coat with a hood. The hood was up, leaving his face hidden. Selene could only see his eyes shining, but she knew those eyes.

He spoke. "Hello, Selenetaya."

Every nerve in her body screamed a shrieking denial. "Just Selene here."

He nodded.

"Hello, Father."

CHAPTER NINE

⎯⎯◆⎯⎯

HE SLIPPED THE HOOD OFF. Selene expected to see a shriveled old man. But no, her father looked just as he had all those millennia ago on the day she left home—a tall man of about forty with short blond hair and blue eyes that looked black in the darkness. Evidently evil was a great preservative. "How did you find me?"

He offered her a wounded expression. "What, no words of joyous greeting for your long-lost father?"

Selene knew fake when she saw it. "No."

His sigh said she was a cruel daughter. "And after I crossed the universe to find you."

"You didn't cross anything for me. I just happened to be here when you arrived." Selene didn't fool herself. Her father harbored no soft feelings for his family. "How did you find me?"

He shrugged. "Frost thought he might need my services again. While we spoke, he mentioned that you had worked for him, but he had to dismiss you." He shook his head sadly. "You weren't emotionally suited to the task. Our ancestors shed bitter tears of shame."

Selene did a few mental eye-rolls. Her father had always been the king of drama. She had forgotten how annoying that was. "You needn't mourn for me." Not that he ever would. "I've found other work. Now, answer my question."

"I will always be able to find you, daughter. Blood calls to blood."

"Uh huh." She made a gesture for him to continue. "How did you *really* find me?"

He grinned, and she was reminded of how charming he could be when he chose.

"I set my best tracker on you. Do you remember Gastor? No? A small man with a nose that never forgets a scent, ears that hear even the tiniest sound, and eyes that see all." Her father raised his hands in praise of the wondrous Gastor. "I put him on you the moment you left for the zoo."

Selene narrowed her eyes. "What do you want?" She hoped he didn't see how shaken she was knowing she'd had a tail all that time. Precautions would have to be taken from now on.

"I want you to work for me. I could use your talent when Frost launches his attack on the humans." He rocked back on his heels, his smile widening. "And isn't it convenient that you're living in the midst of the enemy, trusted by all?"

"No."

"No?" He blinked.

"No, I will never work for you." She couldn't forget the scene of him killing Adam in that time long past. As she turned away from her father, she heard Adam calling.

"I found the earring. I'm coming," she shouted back. Selene started to walk away.

"'No' sounds so final, Selenetaya. But I don't think your 'no' will be the last word at all." Behind her, his soft laughter oozed wicked intent. "I'm certain I can find a way to convince you that 'yes' is a much happier word."

She forced herself to not turn on him, to not fling all of the hurt and rage she'd hoarded since she'd run from him so long ago. Taking a deep breath, Selene put her earring back on as she continued toward Adam and the others.

She had a lot to think about once she was alone, not the least of which was how to neutralize the amazing Gastor.

She didn't reach the SUV. A movement in the shadows froze her. Something approached, darker than the night surrounding it. Closer, she identified it. A massive black jaguar. It studied her from unblinking golden eyes—predatory, dangerous, and a real pain in the neck. "Balan. What brings you here?" She glanced to make sure the others weren't watching her.

"Where else would I find you, your father, and a collection of the Eleven in one spot? I couldn't resist."

His voice in her head was a slide of silken savagery. "Yes, well, nothing much happening here, so you're wasting your time."

The jaguar yawned, expressing his complete contempt for all those beneath him, which was pretty much everyone in his opinion. *"Still, it is my purpose to observe and report. Even if no words of importance are spoken. My masters find use for even the most mundane conversations. It never ceases to amaze me."*

She had to cut this short before Adam and the others wondered where she was. But there was one question she needed to ask. "I've seen you reporting to Zero, but you just mentioned masters. Plural." Time to toss some praise his way. Balan would merely believe it was his due. "I know the rest of Zero's team isn't in your league. None of them could ever be your master. So, is there someone at the top of the food chain I've missed?" She hoped he'd throw a hint her way.

Balan made a grunting sound she suspected was laughter. *"You lack subtlety, woman. But I admire your audacity. I'll favor you with one last piece of advice. The answer to some questions might prove fatal."*

And then he was gone, leaving her seething with no new information about the leadership of Zero's band of planet-killers. She hurried back to the vehicle.

They were all waiting. Utah, Lia, and Dave had never seen her in action. Dave didn't comment as he climbed behind the wheel. But Utah didn't hold back.

"Holy Monster Maker, lady! Tor told me what you could do, but I had to see to believe. You scared the crap out of me with that big guy. When no one died, I figured out he was yours, but I would never have guessed anyone could create that kind of reality on such a huge scale. And it was real, not an illusion. Hey, all kinds of respect to you."

Lia grinned. "I'm glad you're on our side. I wouldn't want to face anything like that creature if you really wanted to destroy us."

Selene warmed with the praise. How long had it been since she'd wielded her talent just for fun? She glanced at Adam for his reaction.

He didn't smile as he glanced away. A cold breeze stole all that warmth away. Selene didn't say anything as everyone piled into the SUV. Meg and Tor took up their cuddling where they'd left off while Utah and Lia laughed as they reviewed everything that had happened tonight. No one seemed to notice the silence stretching between Adam and her.

She allowed the quiet to build its wall between them moment by moment on the long ride back to their apartments. But once Dave dropped them off, she didn't even wait to go inside. The parking lot was as good a place as any to clear the air. "Let's hear it."

He didn't pretend to misunderstand her. "Who were you talking to?"

Selene winced. Adam had loaded all of his mistrust into those five words. They were back to the beginning again. "You heard?"

"I'd turned around to help you search when I realized you were talking to someone. A man. Someone you knew because you sure didn't call for help." His smile was a mere baring of his teeth. "Raptors and vampires have excellent hearing."

So, he might've heard their voices, but not what they'd said. And he'd heard a man's voice. Not Balan. That, at least, was a break. She had a decision to make. Tell him the truth or not? She hadn't inherited her father's talent for lying, so she opted for the truth. "That was my father. He's here to help Zero, if needed. He used a tracker to find me. He wants me to work for him."

"Your answer was?" His expression said he couldn't care less if she stayed or went.

Did it matter what he thought? Absolutely not. And two could play at the couldn't-care-less game. She shrugged. "I already have a job. It would be too much of a hassle to switch to someone new now. But, you know, I thought about it. I mean, it was good old Dad asking me. Besides, nothing is holding me here. Still, I think I'll stay." Maybe good old Dad *had* passed on some of his lying genes.

He shrugged. "Your choice." Adam started to turn away and then paused. "So, what kind of tracker does he have?"

"Gastor, a virtual god of trackers, is following me." She had one more question. "Will you tell Fin?"

"Sure." His expression said it was a stupid question. Then he smiled. It didn't reach his eyes. "But don't worry. Your job is safe. Fin needs you."

Selene watched him enter the building before following. "I get all warm and fuzzy knowing how many people want to use me," she commented to the stunted bush growing by the door. The bush had no opinion.

Once inside her apartment, she left a trail of clothes on her way to the bedroom. Only pausing long enough to pull on her nightgown, she climbed under the covers. She forced herself to stop obsessing over how quickly things had turned bad tonight.

Selene was just drifting into an uneasy sleep when a tapping jarred her awake. She sat up, looked around, and then spotted the bird perched on her window ledge. Great. One of Crow's little minions. Did everyone in the damn city know where she lived? Was the amazing Gastor sitting in a nearby tree shooting a video of her? Fury drove her as she rose from her bed, strode to the window, and flung it open. Selene glared at the bird. "Yes?"

The crow cocked its head to stare up at her from shiny black eyes. It opened its beak. "After Fin uses you, he'll toss you away like day-old trash." Then it flew into the darkness.

Selene stood at the window for minutes after the crow had disappeared. It seemed Crow had joined forces with someone. Because he might be able to control his birds, but he wasn't powerful enough to speak through them. So, who?

Not her father. She didn't think he'd gained that much power over the ages. Besides, he wasn't the type to use birds to deliver his messages when he could send in a troop of his mercenaries. Dad was into overkill.

Zero? Made sense. She'd expected him to reach out to her. Her ex-boss knew his people. Sowing doubts in her mind would work where direct threats wouldn't. The bird had reminded her that Adam and the rest of the Eleven weren't her friends. She couldn't forget that.

Determined to harden her heart and other body parts against the Siren call that was Adam Endeka, she made her way back to bed and eventually fell into a restless sleep.

———

Adam slammed the door of his apartment shut behind him. He would rather have kicked it in, but he decided that wouldn't be in keeping with the low-profile Fin demanded they observe. He was in a foul mood. Adam decided he might go back outside and kick the freaking door down just for the hell of it.

His mood didn't improve any when he saw Jude lounging in the same spot Fin had chosen when he'd shown up uninvited. His beast stirred. His raptor would just fit in this space. The vampire would find himself in a real-life *Jurassic Park* scene.

Jude looked up from the magazine he was glancing through. He grinned. His grin faded, though, when he saw Adam's expression. "Hey, you left the door unlocked."

"No. I didn't." Adam soothed his beast with promises of bloodbaths to come. "I had a rotten ending to a night that started out great. I'm looking for someone to punish for that shitty ending."

Jude nodded. "Got it." He dropped the magazine back onto the coffee table. "I have some news that won't brighten your night."

Adam exhaled wearily. "Of course, you do."

Jude stretched before standing. "Our clan wasn't happy when you told them they wouldn't be included in the kill-a-thon Zero is planning. They're afraid of you, but not enough to keep them from slithering off to meet with Zero's man. This will be a sneaky revolt; one they hope you won't notice until it's too late."

Adam breathed his favorite curses. "A revolt always has a leader. Who is it?"

"Dirk. He whipped everyone into a fury with tales of what they'd be missing."

Adam allowed himself a tight smile. "Soon he'll be Dirk the Dead. Permanently. It's almost dawn, so I can't do anything until tonight. But once the sun sets, we hunt."

Jude bared his fangs in a smile that didn't bode well for Dirk. "I can't wait." In two strides, he reached the door and was gone.

After a shower, Adam crawled into bed naked. God that felt good. Wearing clothes still didn't feel natural. His bed was one place where he could be rid of them.

Too bad he wasn't ready to sleep. Instead, he thought

about where he might find Dirk. The revolt leader would be trying to stay out of sight just in case Adam discovered what he'd done. Adam was eager for a battle but didn't relish a long search for the clan's rotten apple. He yearned for the good old days of hunting with his brothers—the stalking of their prey, the chase, and then the bloody takedown. Quick, deadly, and final. He smiled. Fin would despair of ever turning him from his savage past. But then, a lot of humans shared his violent nature. They just hid it better.

He stared at the darkened ceiling as his thoughts turned to Selene. He might not trust her, but his body didn't put trust at the top of its priority list right now.

She'd be sleeping. Did she wear anything to bed? He'd like to think not. Adam imagined her long limbs splayed out in the moonlight, the tempting shadow between her spread thighs, her full breasts soft and—

Tap, tap, tap.

What the . . . He threw himself from the bed, already in a crouch when he hit the floor, ready to spring.

Tap, tap, tap.

The window. A crow perched on the ledge, peering in at him.

Tap, tap, tap.

Adam came out of his crouch and reached the window in one stride. He flung it open.

The crow stared up at him from shiny black eyes. "She will betray you."

The bird spread its wings, ready to fly away.

"Not so fast, my little friend." With reflexes inherited from his raptor past, he grabbed the crow before it could take flight. "We have some things to discuss." He only knew one woman likely to betray him. And it wouldn't surprise him a bit if Selene did sell him out. Then why did the crow's words infuriate him?

The bird squawked, flapped its wings, and twisted

madly as it tried to peck him. Adam muttered a curse as its sharp beak stabbed his thumb.

He held the crow at eye level as he bared his fangs. "You're the perfect snack size, bird. My beast would crunch you up and then spit out your feathers. Don't tempt me."

The crow stared into his eyes. It stilled.

"Now you're being sensible." This had to be one of Crow's birds. Adam didn't doubt the jerk would love to sow all kinds of dissension among them. He'd lie like the slime he was to see Fin toss Selene out the door. *But was Crow lying?* Suspicion had a bitter taste.

Adam shoved those thoughts aside in favor of wondering how Crow had found them? Maybe Adam could return the favor. Once he set the crow free, it would probably return to its master. Adam intended to see where it went.

Problem. He didn't have as-the-crow-flies capabilities. Adam wasn't even supposed to drive a car. Selene? Without stopping to think things through, he dropped the bird into a box, put a book on the lid to keep the captive inside, and then threw on his clothes. Adam retrieved the box before charging over to Selene's place and pounding on her door.

He was thinking about waking Dave when Selene flung open her door.

"What's going on?" She stood there blinking at the box.

Adam had a moment to register disappointment at the short gown she wore. It bared a little leg and not much else. But that was enough. She looked all soft and warm from sleep. Thoughts of Crow, Dirk, and the looming end of humanity faded, replaced by images of her slipping off that gown and . . .

Adam had enough sense left to realize what might come next. Something stupid on his part. He mentally shook off the lust clinging to him with clawed hands.

Her puzzled expression turned hard as angry bird sounds came from the box. "Let me guess, you got a visit from a crow, too. What did it say?"

"Something about your boss grinding us into the dirt beneath his all-powerful heels." Adam was surprised at how easily the lie came. "Get dressed. We have to get moving." The crow cawed its outrage at the whole box thing.

"What? Now?" She didn't offer to tell him what the crow's message for her was.

Quickly, he told her his plan.

"So, you want me to create a bird that will follow this one back to wherever Crow is hiding?"

He nodded. "You can see through the eyes of your creations, can't you?"

"Sure." She frowned. "What will we do once we find Crow?"

"Nothing. I'll fill Fin in and let him make the decision." Another lie. Adam was hoping for violence and bloodshed.

"Fin won't do anything. He's convinced I'm the one who will banish Crow, and that the number six will be Crow's downfall. Personally, I'm not all in with Team Six just yet. I mean, we don't even know for sure that Crow is the right number. And six of what? One-legged trolls? Dancing virgins?"

"Whatever." No more talk. He wanted them on the road. "I'll call Dave." Their driver wouldn't be happy about Adam dragging him from bed. Adam smiled at the thought.

She nodded, not an enthusiastic nod. "I'll get dressed." Selene backed into her apartment and then closed the door in his face, leaving him alone with a pissed-off bird and a bunch of unfulfilled sexual fantasies.

Adam returned to his apartment. Leaving the box with

its noisy captive on the coffee table, he called Dave. He stored away every curse the driver flung at him for future use, even the ones in foreign languages. Fin had neglected that part of his education. Then he changed clothes. All dark to blend into the night. Now that he was vampire as well as raptor, he felt an affinity for the darkness.

It didn't take long for them to gather in the parking lot. Their driver limited his conversation to mumbled promises of a slow death to the one who had dragged him out at this godawful hour. Adam ignored him.

Adam concentrated on Selene. She'd also dressed in dark clothes—dark pants shoved into black boots along with a black jacket. He noticed she wore a red top but had zipped up her jacket to hide it. Too bad. He liked her in red.

"I guess you turn the bird loose now and then create another crow to follow the first." He glanced at Dave. The driver speared him with a death glare. "She'll tell you where the bird is flying, and you'll have to find a way to take us there. You must know the streets here pretty well or else Fin wouldn't have hired you."

Dave didn't reply. He slid into the driver's seat, slammed the door shut, and started the SUV.

Adam shrugged away their driver's mood. Too bad he was losing sleep. That's why Fin paid him the big bucks. Then he released the bird. It cawed its joy at being free before winging into the darkness.

Suddenly, an owl appeared perched on her arm. She tossed it after the crow before climbing into the back seat.

Adam joined her. He cursed quietly as their driver gunned the motor, flinging both Selene and him back against their seats. Once on the street, Adam turned to her. "Why an owl and not a crow?"

She took a moment to tell Dave which direction to take before answering him. "Crows fly during the day, owls at night. This bird was only here because Crow ordered it. Owls are predators. When the crow sees my owl, it will head straight for its master and safety."

He nodded before peering out at the darkened streets flashing by. For whatever reason, he was happy. Adam shoved aside what the crow had said along with his renewed distrust of Selene. He'd live in the moment. He sat beside a woman who heated his blood as they headed toward a confrontation that could turn violent. His raptor thought a good time might be had by all.

CHAPTER TEN

———

SELENE CLOSED HER EYES. SHE tried to block out everything as she watched the crow's flight through her owl. Silence filled the car except when she had to give Dave directions. On some level, she was aware of Adam beside her—his tension, his anticipation of violence. But that was all as she followed the crow across the night sky.

"We're headed for the bay. I didn't sign up for boat duty." Dave didn't try to hide his still-simmering outrage at being dragged from bed.

Beside her, Adam muttered a few threats. She made a shushing gesture at both of them as she worked to maintain her focus. Selene kept on telling Dave what she saw.

"Looks like you lucked out. We're taking the Coronado Bridge. And here I was looking forward to a refreshing dip in the bay." Dave let the sarcasm flow.

She opened her eyes in time to see the long, curved bridge that would take them into Coronado.

"Just shut up and drive." Adam peered into the darkness.

She closed her eyes again until finally, *finally*, the owl landed. Selene sighed her relief as she gave Dave the last direction. "The street sign says Ocean Boulevard."

She opened her eyes to see her owl perched on the roof of a mansion, a huge brick home built on a million-dollar piece of ocean-front land. A low brick wall surrounded the corner property. The front yard wasn't huge, but the side lawn was spacious and perfectly manicured with trees and bushes. The front of the mansion faced the road, and beyond the road stretched the beach and the Pacific.

Something bothered her. "You know, this doesn't seem like a great choice for Zero. It's a busy area. I bet during the day tons of beachgoers park on both sides of the street. And the homes are pretty close together. Hard to maintain lots of privacy."

"You're assuming it belongs to him. Maybe it doesn't." Adam studied the house. "You worked for him. You'd think he'd ask you over."

"No, he never invited me to visit." She pondered the why of that for a moment. "But this sure doesn't belong to Crow. Crow has more colorful tastes. Besides, this would be way above his pay scale. Crow along with the rest of us who're under Zero may have unusual gifts, but we're still just the hired guns of the universe."

"I'll drive on by and then let you out down the block. Don't want anyone noticing you. Because then I'd have to save your asses. Saving asses isn't in my contract either." Dave passed the home slowly and kept on going.

"Your loyalty touches me." Adam climbed out as soon as Dave stopped. He leaned back in to speak to their driver. "I'll let you know when you can pick us up."

Selene joined Adam in time to watch Dave drive away. Seeing those taillights disappear into the darkness made everything real. Excitement touched her. Every sense sharpened as the night's silence wrapped around her.

And then there was Selene's awareness of the man beside her. He was a walking, talking threat to whatever little peace of mind she had. But he was also the right one to stand with her if whoever was inside discovered them.

She recognized the adrenaline rush that came right before walking into danger. She poked Adam's arm. "Let's do some sneaking and peeking."

They hugged the shadows as they worked their way to the mansion. It was late, and no lights shone through any of the windows. They hunkered down in the shadow of the brick wall—staying outside it to avoid motion sensors and security cameras—searching for evidence that someone was still awake. Selene just hoped no nosy neighbors saw them.

Adam made an impatient sound. "We need to see what's inside." His harsh whisper hinted that he was battling to contain his beast.

Selene kept her response to a quiet, "Don't even think about it. This yard probably has the best security system money can buy. Besides, if Zero is home, he'll make us the moment we enter his house." Too bad she didn't know the layout of the place. But the bird had come here, which meant Crow was probably inside. She couldn't control her twinge of jealousy. Why him and not her?

Adam nodded. "Sure. I know that. It's just . . ."

"I understand." And she did. "It's tough to rein in your instincts." She paused as she studied the mansion. "I have them, too."

His unasked question hung between them. Maybe she'd answer that question, but not now. "Let's see what I can do." Selene willed a creation into being.

Adam leaned close. "What is *that*?"

She smiled as she glanced at the large insect on her palm. It looked like a flying spider, with long hairy legs and wings. "This is from a world you'll never see because it blew up centuries ago. If there's an opening anywhere in the building, he'll find it. If not, he can secrete acid that will eat through almost any substance. He makes an excellent spy." Selene released the insect and watched it begin its quest for an opening in the house. "Let's hope someone is still awake and hasn't activated the inside security system for the night."

His soft laughter warmed her. "You're something, lady. You could make a fortune selling those little guys to burglars everywhere."

She smiled into the night. "Making a fortune has never been my life's goal."

"Then what is?"

Selene barely heard his question. She didn't need to think up an answer because she realized her little spy had found an opening. "He's in."

Adam tensed beside her while she focused on cataloguing everything the insect saw. "Nothing yet, just lots of big rooms and expensive furniture. Wait, I hear voices." She guided her spy towards the sounds. "There are people in what looks like a media room."

He moved closer, his arm and thigh pressing against her as she knelt on the sidewalk. Selene edged away from his distraction. "Zero is there. So is Crow. And there's some guy I don't recognize."

"Describe him."

"Tall. Thin. Blond hair in a buzz cut. Looks like he's wearing cowboy boots and fingerless gloves. He's facing away from our spy, so I can't see his face. Oh, and he has a long black duster and shades. Why sunglasses?"

"Sounds like Dirk. The showboating traitor." Anger lived in every word.

"Dirk?" Selene stared at Adam. Where had all that rage come from?

Adam waved her question away. "I'll explain later. What are they saying?"

Selene moved her spy into the ceiling's shadows and hoped no one looked up. Then she focused on their words.

"The crow is back, so it delivered the messages." Zero sounded satisfied.

Her ex-boss lounged in a leather recliner. He held a glass in his hand. Probably whiskey. That seemed to be his liquor of choice.

Crow sat across from him. He had his own glass. "My birds do their jobs. So, when are you getting rid of Selene?"

Something in Selene snarled at Crow's question. It was one thing to know someone wanted you dead, but hearing the words spoken took her anger to a new level. She would get lots of pleasure from kicking him and his murder of crows off the planet.

Zero laughed softly. "Why would I get rid of Selene when she's being so useful?"

Useful? Selene didn't know what Zero was talking about, but she didn't like the sound of it at all. And she didn't think Adam would want to know how useful she was to Zero, so she'd delete that part when she repeated the men's conversation.

Crow gulped his drink and then slammed the glass down. "She can't do anything that I can't do better."

Zero shook his head. "Crow, Crow, there are some things that require a subtler approach. Subtle isn't your strong point." Then he turned to where Dirk stood near the door. "Are you sure you don't want to sit down?" He gestured toward a couch.

Dirk shook his head. "Just wanted to report. I've got my plans all set up to take over. I'll challenge him, kill him, and they'll be yours by next week."

Who was he going to kill? Selene ground her teeth in frustration. She was collecting more questions than answers. And she might not be able to see Dirk's face, but she knew body language. He was terrified of Zero. He was sticking close to the door so he could bolt at the first sign of danger.

"Excellent." Zero lifted his glass. "Here's to the end of humanity and the rise of all Earth's nonhumans. May the earthquake, tsunami, and the ensuing collapse of society spare this beautiful home."

"Earthquake? You never said anything about an earthquake." Crow looked uncertain.

Dirk edged closer to the door.

"Relax. It was a joke. Maybe." Zero didn't hide his amusement. "I hate minions with no sense of humor," he murmured as he stared into his glass. Then he glanced up at the ceiling. He narrowed his eyes. "Interesting. Hello, Selene." He smiled.

Selene absorbed her spy's energy as she jumped to her feet. Adam joined her. "He knows we're here. Don't bother running because—"

Zero appeared in front of them.

"Never mind." Her first thought right after *we're done* was that Zero didn't want them dead. If he had, he could've killed them from the comfort of his chair without even having to put down his glass. Selene sent Fin a frantic plea for help right before she slammed her mental shield closed. She only hoped he was listening.

Zero's smiled widened. "Selene, I'm so glad to see you again." His smile faded. "I hope you didn't just attempt to call your new employer. If you did, it's useless. He and I have been doing some mental chatting today, and I for one have one hell of a headache. I assume he has the same. He's probably asleep with an icepack on his head."

Zero looked at Adam. "And you've brought a friend. I don't have any idea why you're hiding behind the wall." He offered her a fake puzzled frown. "Next time just ring the bell."

Selene sensed Adam gathering himself.

Don't change, don't change. As far as she knew, Zero didn't realize that Rap was now Adam. It was best for everyone that he didn't make the connection. She grabbed Adam's hand and squeezed, hoping he got the message.

Just then Crow and Dirk charged from the house. They

flung open the gate on their way to join Zero on the sidewalk.

Dirk stared open-mouthed at Adam. "What're you doing here?"

Adam's smile was a mere baring of his fangs. "More to the point, what are *you* doing here?

Zero looked intrigued. "You know him, Dirk? Perhaps you could introduce us."

"This is Adam."

Selene heard all the hate he felt for Adam in those three words.

"Your clan lord? Fascinating." He focused on Adam. "You know who I am. Now, tell me how you met Selene and why you've chosen not to remain aligned with me."

Zero's voice still sounded pleasant, but Selene heard the threat behind it.

Only a slight narrowing of his eyes showed Adam recognized the danger. "How I met Selene is none of your business. I fought for your side in Oregon and got my butt handed to me for my trouble. Why would I do it again?"

Zero looked thoughtful for a moment and then nodded. "A fair observation." He glanced at Dirk. "Since we have everyone gathered here, why don't we take care of business now?"

Startled, Dirk looked from Adam to Zero. "Now? But I—"

"It's time to resolve the issue."

This was the Zero she knew—hard, implacable, while always maintaining a civilized front.

Dirk wouldn't meet Zero's gaze. "I don't think now is the best—"

"Now is the perfect time. It's simple. Kill him. Please don't disappoint me, Dirk."

Dirk looked torn between staying and fleeing. He must've realized that fleeing wouldn't keep him alive, because he swallowed hard as he met Adam's gaze. "I challenge you for leadership of all vampires in North America."

Selene hid her shock. Had Adam known about Dirk's takeover plan? She remembered his earlier anger when he mentioned Dirk. So maybe he had. But why was Zero pushing the issue now? She had the impression Dirk's coup wouldn't have involved a one-on-one battle. More likely he would've sent a gang of twenty into a dark alley to behead Adam while he stood safely in the background. He seemed that kind of guy.

Adam's smile was slow and taunting. "My pleasure." He glanced around. "Isn't this a little open, though? A vampire fight out here might draw an audience. I'm surprised you have a place this close to all these humans."

Zero waved Adam's concern away. "This is California. Strange things happen every day." He shrugged. "If any humans come to watch the show, I'll erase their memories or them." He paused before continuing. "And I find I somehow enjoy humans surrounding me. The crowds going to the beach send off waves of mindless happiness. Such a simple joy. And my neighbors are always trying to befriend me. It's warming. Perhaps I'll regret destroying these particular people, but I can't play favorites."

Selene interrupted Zero's musings with a practical suggestion. "At least let's move this off the sidewalk." She gestured to his side lawn. "The wall will hide a little."

Zero nodded, although she thought he still looked distracted by the thought of all those happy beachgoers and friendly neighbors. Well, she was a little distracted, too. She hated the idea of Adam fighting this other vampire, even though logically she knew he could become raptor in a second if he felt endangered.

But if he freed his beast, Adam's vampire cover was blown. Besides, Adam in his raptor form might be safe from Dirk, but not Zero. Her old boss could and would

kill him. It was a lose-lose situation. Selene knew she
wouldn't allow that to happen. Adam was her partner.
And maybe he could be something more. She discarded that
last thought.

They all filed through the side gate and gathered on
the lawn.

Adam turned to Dirk. "Bring it, traitor. Let's see what
you have without someone else doing the dirty work."

Crow crouched down to watch, eager for bloodshed.
Selene knew he wouldn't care who won as long as someone died.

Zero moved to her side. "Please don't interfere, Selene.
I'd have to stop you. It wouldn't end well."

She hated that he was right.

Dirk made the first move. Baring his fangs, he leaped
at Adam. Dirk hadn't bothered to take off his coat. It
would slow him down. Good. She bit her lip as Adam
avoided his charge. Dirk swept by and then turned to
meet Adam's attack.

Everything became a blur. She couldn't follow what
was happening because they moved so fast. But there was
blood. Lots of it. She clenched her hands into fists as she
strained to see who was winning. The worst part of the
battle was the silence. No screams, no sounds of blows
landing, no heavy breathing. Just nothing.

Zero spoke beside her. "I assume you've never seen a
vampire battle before. There's no punching, wrestling, no
grunts and groans. Each of them is searching for that one
moment when the other lets down his guard. Then it'll
be over."

She took her attention from the fight long enough to
look at Zero. "You enjoy this, don't you?"

"I see it as an artform." Zero didn't smile. "They're the
most lethal predators on Earth. They're solitary hunters,
and they don't give second chances." He patted her on
the shoulder. "That means you won't be able to help

Adam because he'll be dead before you even realize it."

"You seem sure Dirk will win."

He shrugged. "You roll the dice."

Selene met his gaze. She hoped he could read the determination in her eyes. Adam would *not* die. Then she turned back to the fight.

It didn't last long. Suddenly, the world seemed to freeze. Adam crouched over the other vampire. Dirk's coat and shirt were shredded. Blood covered his bare torso. And Adam held up a bloody piece of flesh.

Selene was weak with relief as Zero stated the obvious. "Dirk lost."

Crow chimed in. "He took Dirk's fricking heart." He sounded impressed.

Unable to look away, she watched as the bloody heart began to smolder. It quickly became ash in Adam's hand.

Adam rose to face Zero. Blood smeared his clothes. He didn't try to wipe it away. Selene worried. Did all that blood come from Dirk? Was Adam hurt?

"Dirk was your guy, so you can take care of the corpse. I made sure he wouldn't rise again." He held out his hand to Selene. "Let's get out of here."

"Wait." Zero stepped in front of them. "You can't leave now. I need someone to replace Dirk."

Adam met his gaze. "Too bad."

Uh-oh. Selene heard the intent in Adam's voice. If Zero pressed him, he'd free his soul and disaster would follow. Someone had to break the tension. It wouldn't be Crow. Silently, without anyone noticing, his birds had joined him. They perched on his shoulders and covered the grass around him. He was ready to kill.

She spoke up. "Why did you encourage the battle if you didn't want to lose Dirk?"

Zero glanced at her. "Because he was a coward. I sensed his fear—of me, of Adam, of a battle where he might be in personal danger. Even if he had won, I would've had to replace him almost immediately with someone stronger. He had only one purpose: to destroy Adam. He failed."

Adam shrugged. "Do I look like I care? Next time pick a winner. Hope you can't find anyone else to do the job. But happy hunting."

Selene knew Adam's casual words hid his intent. His grip on her hand tightened. She could almost feel him gathering himself, ready to become raptor in mid leap as he launched himself at Zero. He had to know it would be futile. Zero would bat him away like a mosquito.

She made her decision. Selene searched her memory for something to distract Zero. Something small that wouldn't panic the neighborhood. Something that would give them precious seconds to flee.

Zero smiled. "But that's the good part. I don't have to find someone else to kill you. You're here. I'm here. I can eliminate you myself." His smile faded. "Although I really wish I could find more competent people, because I have to make sure whatever vampire replaces you is willing to join me."

"Hey, I can take care of him," Crow offered.

Zero threw him a contemptuous glance. "No, you can't. I need you alive." He focused on Adam. "Time to die, vampire."

"Not nearly." Selene focused her energy. She chose something from her home planet, the bane of everyone's picnic. Suddenly, a swarm of what looked like winged toothpicks appeared. They circled and then dived toward Zero.

Zero's eyes widened as he swatted at the cloud of insects. But he never took his gaze from Adam. "Really, Selene? That's the best you can do? Wait, this is a distraction, isn't it?" The insects suddenly combusted and disappeared in tiny puffs of smoke.

Beside her, Adam crouched while she focused her

energy for a pull-out-all-the-stops, last-ditch effort to save Adam.

Zero's eyes gleamed with anticipation. "Both of you do your worst. I love a challenge."

He didn't raise his arms or his voice. A shimmer formed around him, and for just a moment, Selene thought she saw someone, *something* take his place.

Then the moment was gone as Adam grabbed her hand. He jerked her away from Zero, and then they ran. If she wasn't gasping from adrenaline overload, she'd explain that Zero didn't want *her* dead. After all, she was *useful* to him in some way.

She never thought she'd reach the wall. Every second, every step she took, Selene expected to see Adam disintegrate as she'd seen so many of Zero's enemies die. Gathering her essence, she prepared to fling one of the deadliest creatures she'd ever seen at Zero. It was colossal, it would probably destroy the neighborhood, but she didn't give a damn. Let humanity get a wake-up call to what lived among them.

Her ex-boss would have to put Adam on his to-kill-later list while he saved his home and all those friendly neighbors. The lengths she would go to in her effort to keep Adam alive shocked her. As she raised her hand to release her creation, someone behind her spoke.

"That won't be necessary, Selene."

She turned and looked up. Beside her, Adam skidded to a stop.

"I'll take care of this." Fin smiled at her.

CHAPTER ELEVEN

AS RELIEVED AS ADAM WAS to see Fin, he figured the apocalypse would begin any second now. It depended on how trigger happy his leader and Zero were. A shootout between the two could level all of California. Beside him, Selene's softly breathed "Uh-oh" told him she was thinking the same thing.

"Shootout?" Fin sounded amused, but he never took his attention from Zero.

Adam should have known. Fin was the ultimate multitasker. He could be in Adam's head at the same time he was planning how to take down an enemy.

"Fin. I'm impressed you've shown up to save these two. After all, they're not members of your Eleven club."

Zero looked unconcerned, but Adam felt the gathering violence in him. A rumble of thunder in the distance warned of a coming storm.

"I have a wide circle of people I care about. Selene is a useful part of my team. And Adam isn't in your pocket, so I want him to continue as vampire leader."

Adam watched Selene as Fin spoke. She winced when Fin mentioned her usefulness. What was that about?

Zero sneered. "Don't talk to me about useful. Those wolves at the zoo were useful, but you killed them. You've deprived me of many valuable tools."

"That's all his people are to him. Tools." Then Adam

remembered who stood next to him. "I'm sure you were more than that, Selene." Did he sound sincere? Nope.

Her expression said he'd flipped her switch. Anger gathered behind those amazing eyes. "They're both users." Bitterness filled her harsh whisper. "We're only pieces in some galactic chess game. They move us around, and if we get knocked off the board, so what? They'll just get someone else."

Adam figured he should've kept his mouth shut. Maybe he'd remind her that Fin had come to their rescue, so he at least wanted to keep his pieces on the board. Too late. Selene strode across the lawn to confront Zero.

Zero's smile should've coated the whole neighborhood in ice. "You have something you want to say, my sweet traitor?"

Selene's eyes widened and then narrowed. "Traitor? You fired me."

"You didn't stay unemployed long. Does the enemy treat you well?" His expression darkened. "You took Ace with you. The boy thinks you need protecting. You don't. So, send him home."

Guilt touched Selene. She hadn't thought of Ace once today. That would have to change. He was with Fin because of her, so he was her responsibility. "He's old enough to decide where his home will be."

Her thoughts shifted back to her burning question. "Why did you fire me? I refused one order because it was tactically unsound. Crow is a loose cannon, but you're okay with that. What was the real reason you fired me?"

"I thought I made it clear. You're too emotional. You wouldn't destroy that building because there were children in it. And the kittens? I put them there." He shrugged. "In simple terms, you don't have the stomach for the tough stuff."

She stilled. "It was a test?"

Zero nodded. "And you failed. Crow can be impulsive,

but I've never doubted his willingness to kill with cold-blooded efficiency. He wouldn't hesitate to bring down a building filled with babies, kittens, puppies, and a roomful of teddy bears."

"Teddy bears? Really?" Selene drew in a deep breath, outrage written in every tense line of her body.

Crow gave her a satisfied smirk that had I'm-the-chosen-one smeared all over it. She ignored him.

Adam knew she was about to let loose on her ex-boss. He opened his mouth to yell a warning at her. He never got the chance.

"But I'm a forgiving man, Selene. I believe in second chances. I want the vampire destroyed. Dirk disappointed me." Zero's glance slid to Adam. "Kill the vampire, Selene, and all will be forgiven."

Adam's beast roared. His primal soul knew how to meet danger. Attack. Kill the woman before she could decide. He tensed, ready to change. Then he glanced at Fin. His boss wore a distant expression, one that said what will happen will happen. Not a look that made Adam confident of Fin's support. This would all be on him.

Adam returned his attention to Selene. She met his gaze. There was no indecision in her eyes. She'd made her choice.

Would he have to kill her? No, he couldn't. She was an immortal. Zero or Fin were powerful enough, but he wasn't. She could destroy *him,* though. Within a heartbeat, she could create a dozen raptors to tear him apart before he could shift. Adam had to believe Fin wouldn't allow it to go that far. Then what was his boss waiting for? Adam should free his beast now, get in the first bite.

Selene took a step toward Adam. All the distrust he'd felt for her from the beginning urged him to act. She would kill him. *Attack before she can sic her creations on you.* Still, he hesitated. It all came down to trust. Not by a twitch of a facial muscle did she show what she'd chosen.

She kept walking toward him.

He couldn't wait any longer. He had to decide.

A memory intruded. That night on the mountain, her riding on his back, her laughter as he'd dumped her in the weeds. They'd had fun together. And then there was the zoo. Her raptors had fought beside him. But that could've all been a plan to win him over, to infiltrate the Eleven. What did he really believe?

What did his gut tell him? And, yes, he was honest enough to admit his attraction to her played into his feelings about this whole lousy moment.

Adam chose. He ignored his beast's screams as he watched her approach. She stopped a few feet away from him. Adam speared her with a hard gaze. "What will it be?"

She turned to look back at Zero. "Sorry, I guess I won't be working for you again. I don't kill friends."

Adam closed his eyes briefly as he released the breath he'd been holding. *Friends.* Relief was soaring hope and fist-pumping triumph. They were friends. And if they survived the next few minutes? Hopefully more than friends. That thought didn't surprise him as much as it should.

Zero didn't react. He simply returned his attention to Fin. Adam had the feeling the main attraction was about to begin.

Zero smiled. "Such loyalty, Fin. I'm jealous. But is it loyalty to *you*, I wonder? Enough about them, though. We have things to discuss."

Then Adam forgot everything except the threat of death thickening the air. Crow moved closer, his birds sweeping behind him like some feathered black cloud. Fin and Zero stared at each other. Tension hummed between them. Adam figured they were mentally cursing each other out.

Lightning skipped and flickered over the Pacific. Thunder followed it. Closer this time.

In the silence stretching between the two leaders, Adam sensed something other than the hatred he'd expected. He studied each of them. It was just out of reach, something . . .

He lost his train of thought as Fin spoke in his mind.

"Go. Take Selene with you. He won't try to stop you now that he's focused on me. Your driver is parked around the corner."

Adam considered the order for a second before dismissing it. He turned to Selene. "Fin wants us to go."

"Without him?" She must've seen the answer in his eyes because she shook her head. "He's here to help us. I won't leave him to face Zero alone."

Adam turned back to Fin. "We're staying. Someone has to keep the bird guy from causing trouble." He nodded toward where Crow paused to study them.

"We'll have to discuss the meaning of insubordination once we're done here." Fin's attention stayed on Zero.

"Deal." Adam waved at Crow. The bird man scowled. He could do his worst, because right now Adam felt invincible. And Selene's decision had nothing to do with his sudden euphoria.

Crow met his gaze. "I don't think we've been introduced. I'm Crow. Vampires don't impress me."

"Well, prepare to be impressed." Adam grinned. "Because I'm the vampire who's going to kick your feathery butt." Luckily, Crow had never seen his human form at the zoo, so he wouldn't associate Adam with the raptors. It would stay that way for now, because Adam couldn't afford to trigger an avalanche of calls to Animal Control.

Selene put her hand on his arm. "Be careful." Her expression warned that this was a no-raptor zone. "We don't want to wake the neighbors."

He patted her hand. "Don't worry. I have enough vampire mojo to take him." Adam glanced at her. "Get behind the wall while I pluck some feathers." Her outraged expression said he shouldn't have worded that as a command, but it was too late now. He only knew it was important that she stay safe. She opened her mouth to say something, but then shut it as Fin spoke to Zero.

What language was that? Not any that Adam recognized. But Selene stood rooted as Zero answered in the same language. Then he forgot about what the two were saying as lightning lit up the sky above them. A thunder clap shook the earth. No, wait, it wasn't the thunder doing the shaking. The ground rolled beneath his feet. He fought to keep his balance. An earthquake?

Didn't matter because Crow was charging across the lawn, bringing his birds with him. He hadn't taken his monster bird form, so Adam figured Zero had warned him to keep a low profile. Adam and Selene ran to meet Crow. They collided in a roiling cloud of feathers, angry caws, and the buzzing of hundreds of bees from Selene. Damn, he wanted to free his beast. But the neighbors would absolutely notice a raptor leaping and screaming outside their windows.

Meanwhile, the wind came. It roared off the Pacific, whipping the ocean waves to towering peaks. He had to do something before the anger popping and snapping between the two leaders generated a tsunami.

Adam allowed Selene to do her thing while he rooted in his pocket for the packet of salt he always carried. Fin and Zero had stopped talking out loud and were back to their death stares. Their mental conversation must've been intense because the storm grew in fury around them. Lightning strikes that sounded like cannon blasts rattled the neighborhood, and somewhere nearby a transformer exploded. The scent of ozone filled the air.

Thunder deafened him. The earth beneath him rose and sank. Cracks began to open. Sirens screamed in the distance.

Then Adam heard the first shouts as people rushed from their homes. It was California, and they'd think earthquake, the dreaded "big one."

Someone had to stop that staring match before Southern California crumbled and disappeared into the ocean. He found a sheltered spot next to the wall where the wind wasn't nearing hurricane force and then crouched to draw a summoning circle with the salt. Thank the gods the original Adam had a few useful skills. Luckily, he'd inherited all that knowledge. Now, who to summon? It had to be the most powerful being he knew who'd be susceptible to his call.

A headless crow hit his shoulder, and Crow's screams suggested the bees were working their magic on him. Selene was holding her own. But the madness was escalating, so he couldn't waste time.

Adam didn't have everything he needed for the ritual, but he couldn't worry about that now. He hoped the circle would be strong enough to contain a mistake, because the original Adam had been known to make them.

Blocking out the chaos around him, Adam called.

Selene's bees had Crow on the run. She had opted to move the attack to him rather than his birds. Luckily, he'd left his cloak inside. While the bees stung his face, hands, and any other exposed part they could find, she'd kept his crows at bay with one of the knives she always carried.

Without warning, Crow shouted his frustration, and then he changed. Selene shielded her eyes as the monstrous bird flapped its wings. For a moment, she thought Crow would attack her, but instead he took wing, his cawing army close behind him. He might be willing to murder helpless teddy bears, but hundreds of tiny stingers defeated him. Still, he should've stayed to fight her. She decided he was a bit of a coward. Zero wouldn't appreciate him fleeing the scene.

She didn't hesitate. Selene absorbed the bees and created her owl to take their place. She flung him into the sky. She wanted to know where to find the jerk when this was over.

Then she got a look at Zero's face. Crow's boss had taken a moment from his staring match with Fin to watch his minion disappear into the night sky. He looked ticked. No wonder. Turning into a giant bird didn't qualify as keeping a low profile. Flying away with your tail feathers between your legs wouldn't impress the boss either.

But she forgot about Crow's troubles, because something else was happening that made her jaw drop.

A form was taking shape inside the circle Adam had drawn. She hoped whatever he was summoning wouldn't make things worse. Who or what was inside the circle?

Fin and Zero wanted to know, too. They cut off their silent war to watch.

The man, fully formed by now, stepped out of the circle. He wore only a towel around his waist. He pointed at Adam. "You'll have to practice your circles if you want to hold something powerful in them." Then he turned to Fin and Zero. "Scaring the crap out of everyone in Southern California isn't going to solve anything."

As if to prove his point, a neighbor's SUV roared past the yard loaded with the family and pets. Selene figured people hoped to get away from the coast before the inevitable tsunami struck.

The man glanced down then back at Adam. "And next time give me time to pull on some clothes."

Adam moved to Selene's side. She glanced at him. "Who's this guy?"

"That's Seir. Fin's brother."

Shocked, she took another look at the man who by

now had reached his brother. He was not quite as tall as Fin, with long blond hair that seemed to flow with dozens of different shades. The wind whipped it back from his face revealing the same cold unearthly beauty as his brother. But instead of silver eyes, Seir's were ice-blue. And his body? Perfect, as she'd expect of anyone related to Fin. But it was Adam's body she wanted to see draped in that towel, or no towel at all. She shook the thought away. Wrong time, wrong place.

As Selene stared at the three, something occurred to her. They didn't look alike, but they all had the same *feel*. She'd have to think about that once they got away from here. *If* they got away.

Seir distracted her from that thought.

"Time to dial it back a notch, guys. You're tearing the place apart. The human population is in a panic. You don't want to bring everything down around our ears *now*." Seir glanced at Adam and Selene. He winked.

Winked? The two most powerful forces on the planet were on the brink of trashing the world and he *winked*? Seir was taking this whole thing too lightly. She looked at Adam. "We have to do something."

Adam raised one brow. "Ideas?"

Selene didn't have any. Yes, she could create a diversion. Adam could, too. But either Fin or Zero could slap them down without even looking. Then Seir reclaimed her attention.

"I say we relax, all join hands, and sing "Kumbaya" together."

It was as though he'd set off a bomb between them. Zero backed up. Fin turned on his brother.

"We will never join hands. *Never*. And don't treat everything like a damn joke, Seir. In fact, why don't you go home? This doesn't concern you."

"Oh, but it does."

Adam frowned. "Something's going to happen. I feel it."

Selene knew what he meant. The air around them thickened, making it hard to breathe, squeezing her lungs until she wanted to gasp.

Just when she thought she'd pass out from lack of air, it felt as though a bubble popped. She was able to breathe again.

And as she gulped in all that beautiful sea air, Fin and Zero disappeared.

Immediately, everything around them returned to normal. No more storm. The ground beneath them stilled. It was over. Not for the humans, though. Their panic would take a while to subside. Selene didn't doubt that Fin and Zero's temper tantrum had done lots of damage.

"Where are they?" Adam sounded uncertain.

Selene didn't blame him. The evidence pointed to Seir as the sender, but could he have that kind of power?

Suddenly, Seir became a lot more interesting. "What did you do with them?" she asked him.

Seir grinned as he walked over to join them. "Fin is in his condo. He's probably ticked off and wondering if it's worth it to come back here. But now that he has a few minutes to think things through, he'll use his common sense." Seir looked at Adam. "Frost makes Fin lose his temper, yanks him out of his cold and totally cool persona. Fin won't like to think he almost lost control. So, he'll stay home."

Adam nodded. "And Zero?"

Selene watched Adam scan the area, checking to see that Zero had really left.

"He's up in his room watching us." Seir saluted the second window from the right. "He got to engage with Fin in person, so his night was a success. The time wasn't right for a final confrontation." He gazed into the distance for a moment. "But it'll happen. Soon." Seir blinked and his attention was back on them. "Crow is having a temper tantrum, in San Diego. Frost is still too focused on Fin to notice. You might want to take care of the bird." Then Seir walked out of the yard and was gone.

Selene stood beside Adam, absorbing the silence around them compared to the pandemonium everywhere else. Emergency vehicles raced past, shouts still echoed throughout the neighborhood, and dogs howled. "Well, they created a mess, didn't they?"

Adam raked his fingers through his hair. She smiled. The wind had whipped it into a tangled mess. She liked it.

"We have to find Crow." There was an eager note in Adam's voice.

"My owl is following him. Fin said Dave was around the corner, Let's go." She started toward the gate. Adam followed her.

"Wait up." The voice was right behind them.

Selene spun to face the new threat. Beside her, Adam laughed.

Utah and Tor grinned back at him.

"Why're you here?" She might not sound too welcoming, but she didn't like people creeping up behind her.

Utah pointed at Adam. "He needed us. We know when one of us is in trouble, and we always know where to find him."

Must be nice. Selene tried not to feel jealous. She didn't have exactly the same relationship with Meg. "What now?"

"We find Crow." Adam practically glowed with excitement. He joined his brothers.

Tor nodded. "We're pack. We hunt together."

If they thought their pack was going to run off without her, they could just think again. "Since I'm the only one who knows where Crow is, I guess I'll be going along with you." She smiled at them. "I can be pack too."

CHAPTER TWELVE

———————

A DAM ENJOYED EVERY INCH OF Selene's body pressed next to him in the SUV. He absorbed her heat, her *feel*. She didn't notice all this enjoyment going on because she was concentrating on tracking the flight of her owl through the night sky.

Dave followed her directions, cursing as he made his way back across the Coronado Bridge and around closed streets, aimlessly wandering pedestrians, and emergency vehicles. "No lights. How am I supposed to drive with the damn power out?" He glanced in the rearview mirror for answers.

Adam gave him a thumbs up. "Hey, you're doing great."

Utah and Tor had left their car for their driver to take back to Fin's place, and they'd crowded into the SUV with Adam. Now, they sat silent, but he recognized his brothers' eagerness for the expected fight. It was the same excitement he felt.

He had to rein in his predator instincts, though. Too much of an adrenaline rush and he'd do something stupid. Besides, right along with the urge to hunt was that other craving, the one for the woman sitting beside him.

He battled on two fronts, and he was losing both. Still, he fought—silent, determined. But determined didn't work tonight. Rage drove him, anger born of the raptor who screamed its need to hunt free. He hoped Crow was still in his bird form, because if he was, then Adam and his brothers could let their freak flags fly without guilt. With dawn approaching, some early risers would already have seen the massive bird, so a few raptors wouldn't make much difference on this night of the bizarre.

He wasn't doing so great on the second battle front either. His emotions were sky high after the confrontation with Zero. All those feelings fed thoughts of what he wanted to do after they took care of Crow. He slid a glance at Selene.

She opened her eyes to stare at him. He saw the knowledge there. Not good. He was broadcasting. He'd thought he was learning to control feelings that bled into others. Obviously, he wasn't ready to graduate.

"Stop what you're doing." She didn't look horrified, only worried. "I need to concentrate." Then she closed her eyes again.

Adam smiled. She didn't hate his message. Good. But he didn't want it to mess with the search for Crow, so he edged a little away from her and closer to where Tor was jammed in next to him. He grunted as Tor drove his elbow into Adam's side.

"Hey, you're in my personal space. Shove over a little."

Adam didn't move. He almost wished Tor would make a big deal of it. Not that a close-quarters fight in here would satisfy either of them.

"Stop. Park here. The owl has landed." Selene opened her eyes. She pointed.

Dave pulled to the curb and then peered into the darkness. "That's Seaport Village over there. We get out and walk now."

"Seaport Village?" Utah spilled out of the vehicle as he followed their driver's gaze.

"Tourist spot. Walk along the water, buy stuff at small shops, and eat at a bunch of restaurants. Shops and restaurants are all closed now, of course. That's good. No people wandering around. You can see a couple of big hotels there." He pointed. "Lots of folks in those hotels with great views. That's bad." Dave didn't look as though he much cared. He held his sword ready. "Let's find this Crow and carve him up."

Any hope they could keep this disaster under wraps died when they reached the water. There were people standing on the balconies of the nearest hotel; staring, pointing, and trying to get pictures. Worse yet, it looked as though a bunch of them had fled the hotels when the shaking started and were standing outdoors peering up at Crow. At least the lights were still off, so maybe the black bird wouldn't show up too well. But the lightening sky as dawn approached wasn't helping their cause.

Selene made a disgusted sound. "Look at the jerk. What does he think he's doing?"

Adam thought the jerk's agenda was pretty clear. Crow was still in his giant bird form with his murder of crows flapping around him, cawing loud enough to wake any-one who might have slept through the lightning, thunder, and shaking.

Utah whistled. "Wow, he must be mad. Look at him go."

Way past just mad, Adam decided. Crow was taking out his humiliation and frustration by raining down destruc-tion here. He dived, attacking shops and restaurants. Windows shattered, and crows poured into the buildings to destroy whatever they found.

Adam glanced away from Crow long enough to scan the area. "This will make the news right along with the 'earthquake.' Look around you."

Selene moved close to him. "All those people in the hotels. I thought we were safe because it was so early. Nobody would be outside to see Crow." She swept her hand to show the full extent of the disaster.

Dave paused to listen. "I hear sirens. Cops are on their

way." He pulled a phone from his pocket and took a few selfies.

Adam speared him with his you're-dead stare. Dave shrugged and put the phone away.

Then things got really serious. Not satisfied by attacking buildings, Crow turned his anger on the gawkers. Swooping down, he plucked a middle-aged man from the crowd of watchers. Holding him in his claws, Crow rose, flapping his massive wings. He carried the screaming man over the water. The rest of the shouting crowd scattered, running in every direction. The sirens sounded closer.

"Where's our air support?" Tor looked around. "We need Q."

Selene coughed. "Good thing you have a pack member who can take his place. I'll knock Crow out of the air. You take care of him when he hits the ground."

Tor looked unconvinced she could live up to Q's reputation. "That's all great. But what about the guy hanging from his claws?"

The guy hanging from his claws yelled and windmilled his arms in a futile attempt to escape. Crow flew low over the water. His victim finally got smart. He reached into his pocket and pulled out what looked like a pocket knife. He reached up and drove the blade into Crow's foot. Crow's caw probably shattered a few more windows. Then he simply dropped the man. The guy hit the water and immediately swam for shore. Adam let go of the breath he'd been holding. "Problem solved." He nodded at Selene. "Go."

She grinned. "Showtime." Selene took a moment to wonder at the joy she felt. This was a battle. She'd been here before. But this time was different. All the other times, someone had hired her. She'd sent her creations out to do their thing, but hadn't really felt emotionally involved. Her creations fought, she collected her money, and then she left. Now, though, she was pack. She had tons of emotion involved in the outcome. And she loved the thought of winning one for her team. Okay, so some of it was showing off for Adam, too.

Gathering her energy, she created . . . Uh, what? Not some terrifying animal from another world. Not a giant manifestation of one from this world. The humans were already traumatized. What might give them a warm fuzzy feeling on a scary night? She laughed out loud as she launched her hero. And just to make everything perfect, the lights suddenly came back on.

Beside her, Adam fist-pumped his opinion of her choice.

Thor, in all his blond glory, rocketed into the sky. His red cape whipped behind him as he brandished his hammer, Mjolnir.

Selene ignored the slight weakness she always felt when losing a bit of her essence in favor of savoring the moment.

She heard gasps from behind her, the sounds of running feet as the police arrived, and the voice of a reporter doing a live feed. She could see cameras pointed at the sky. Selene knew she should be horrified, but she wasn't. Tonight, she was her father's daughter, allowing the rush of battle to take her. She didn't fear Crow. He would go down under Thor's mighty hammer.

Selene allowed the police to herd her, along with all the stupid people who had stayed to watch the battle, away from the danger area. They didn't realize that in a few weeks there would be no safe zone. The entire planet would be in play. This was just a warm-up to the main event.

She sort of felt bad for the cops. They didn't know how to deal with Crow and Thor. How could they?

She only had time to hear Adam's whispered, "You're amazing, woman," before Thor reached Crow.

Selene went with all the stuff she remembered from the movies she'd seen since hitting Earth, and maybe added a little of her own flair.

Crow flapped his enormous wings as he met Thor's attack. The wind generated by those wings rocked nearby boats at their moorings. He fought with beak and talons, attempting to overwhelm Thor. But hey, the mighty god of thunder wouldn't be taken down by an oversized bird.

Thor swung Mjolnir—Selene created an impressive lightning flash to go with the swing—and slammed his hammer into the crow's side. Selene added the expected thunder as Mjolnir connected.

Crow's pained caw was fingernails dragged across a chalkboard amplified to eardrum-shattering decibels. Then he fell. As quickly as that, her part was done. Color her disappointed. She'd just gotten started.

Selene backpedaled away from Crow's projected landing spot as she reclaimed her essence from Thor. The jolt of power she got from its return energized her.

The giant bird landed hard and lay still for a moment. Then he flapped his wings, smoothed his feathers, and looked up. Maybe all was not lost. Maybe he'd come back for more.

He didn't have a chance. The screams and shouts around Selene told her that the Brothers Grim had freed their beasts.

The raptors leaped at Crow. Chaos. A mad whirl of feathers and raptor screams. Bird bodies flew in every direction as Crow's small minions tried to help him. Selene couldn't see what was happening. The action was that fast.

She wanted to send Thor in to help, but she figured Adam wouldn't want any interference. Besides, the brothers seemed to have things under control.

Dave appeared at her side. He looked sulky.

"Didn't get one shot at the dumb bird. Way to ruin my night."

Selene started to answer him, but then she heard the police talking. One thought they should just shoot the dinos and the demon bird. That brought down the wrath of some guy in a suit. He mentioned things like extinct species. The cop countered with the safety-of-citizens-first argument. Words like tasers and tranqs were thrown around.

Selene didn't like the direction of the conversation. But she didn't have to think about it long because suddenly the fight was over. Crow returned to human form. His clothes were torn and he was bloody. Without waiting to see what would happen next, he stumbled away, bounced off of some guy wearing a hoodie, and was gone. His birds drifted after him. The raptors let him go as they swung to look at the crowd, cameras, and the police. The police had their guns out and aimed.

Uh oh. Selene prepared to supply a distraction, but she needn't have bothered.

Into the tense silence—even the gawkers had shut up—strode Fin.

Every single human turned as one to face him. All expression had been wiped from their faces. It was just plain creepy.

Fin stopped, looked at the three raptors, raised one brow, and then turned his attention to his human audience.

Once again, Selene felt the push of his enormous power. He spoke.

"You just saw a scene we're shooting for a new film. Since all the shaking had ended, we decided to go ahead with it. Time is money in this business. The movie is about dinosaurs defending humanity from immortals bent on our extinction. Look for it in June. You'll love it. This is what you'll tell everyone. This is all that you'll remember." Fin turned again to the raptors. "Go."

They didn't waste time leaving the scene. Selene went with them. Once out of sight of the crowd, the raptors returned to human form. But before they could pile into the SUV, Fin was there. He leaned against the vehicle.

"Everyone back there is talking about the scene we shot. You're lucky I showed up in time. Even the guy Crow dumped into the water thinks we hired him as an extra."

Selene decided he didn't sound ticked off. But her relief was short lived. Utah couldn't keep his mouth shut.

"Maybe if you'd shown up sooner, the whole *scene* wouldn't have taken place."

"Way to poke at the bear," Adam muttered.

Utah glared at his brother. "Well, am I right?"

No one answered.

Fin threw him a hard stare. "You know, my disagreement with Zero didn't end just because Seir sent us home. We continued the battle long distance. So, forgive me if I wasn't there earlier to bail you out." His glare said he didn't need anyone's forgiveness.

Adam looked offended. "We didn't need saving. We took care of Crow without your help." He glanced at Selene. "Too bad we don't know how Selene is supposed to toss him back into the cosmos. She could've taken care of the whole business tonight."

Selene still wasn't sure she even believed Fin's prediction, but that didn't matter right now. She had another question. "Why give those people that movie memory? Wouldn't it have been safer to wipe their memories of the event completely?"

Fin seemed to remember she was there. "First, there would've been a time lapse if I hadn't filled it with something. People notice things like that. Then there were the ones who took pictures of you in action and then left. Once they were in their cars and gone, I couldn't reach them. Those photos and videos will already be circulating. We needed a reason for what they saw that people would accept."

She nodded. Made sense.

"What would you have done if I hadn't turned up? Just curious." Fin's question included all of them.

Selene didn't buy the "just curious" part. He was testing their ability to adapt to situations. Zero did that too. Once again, she noted how alike the two leaders were in some ways. Then she let the thought go. Since the other three weren't answering, she jumped in. "I was going to launch a distraction, something that would take everyone's attention from the raptors. I thought a battle between a pod of killer whales and a bunch of great white sharks would do it. Blood in the water always attracts attention. Most humans are predators at heart." Sure, that was pretty cynical. But she'd fought on enough planets to know that whatever was at the top of the food chain was always a predator. Why would this world be any different? "And while everyone watched the fight, the guys could drop into the water and then return to human form beneath the surface. If they swam around to the side of one of the boats, they could climb from the water with no one noticing. My whales and sharks would swim away once it was safe."

Fin smiled. "Good."

She returned his smile. "Thanks." His praise made her happier than it should. She had to remind herself not to allow this world to change who she was.

Tor made a rude sound. "Wouldn't have worked. No one would pay attention to whales or sharks while raptors were in the house."

Adam rode to her rescue. "At least she had a plan. I know I didn't. How about you?"

Tor looked away.

Fin didn't comment. He seemed to forget them for a

moment. His expression turned thoughtful. "Look, I'll meet with everyone tomorrow. We have things to discuss." He turned away to join the people still wandering around aimlessly. The darkness swallowed him.

No one spoke as they piled into the SUV. Selene thought the vehicle would explode from all the compressed energy inside. Once again, she was pressed against Adam. She may as well have cozied up to a live wire for all the sparks arcing between them. Neither of them had come down from their battle high.

All three of the brothers were broadcasting loud enough to deafen her. Utah and Tor's beasts were still screaming for more blood, for more rending and tearing, for *death*. She was able to ignore their needs.

Not Adam's, though. His need had morphed into something different, something powerful aimed right at her. And she responded to the raw sensuality of it. Tonight wasn't a thinking night. It was darkness and passion and feelings that tore at you until you screamed. She held onto her control by a thin shrieking thread.

Dave dropped Utah and Tor off first, and by the time he parked the vehicle outside their apartment building, Selene's anticipation had the bit between its teeth and was galloping off into all kinds of erotic fantasies. She didn't think she'd make it past the first shadowed alcove.

Their driver didn't linger. Dave was still busy being angry at not getting into the fight. He slammed the door behind him.

Selene didn't make it as far as the door. By the time Adam reached her, she'd already chosen her group of dark shadows with a convenient hedge to hide the action.

He didn't hesitate. She didn't have second thoughts. Adam wrapped his arms around her and claimed her mouth in a long, drugging kiss. He tasted of *yes* after untold *absolutely-nots* through all those long years, on all those long-forgotten planets.

Adam kissed a path along her jaw, down to the hollow of her neck. She buried her fingers in his hair to pull him closer while she whispered a litany of sensual promises in his ear.

As he tugged her top low enough for his lips to trace a searing path across the swell of her breasts, she slid her hands under his shirt front. The sensation of smooth warm skin beneath her fingers almost made her forget what he was doing with those incredible lips. Okay, that was a lie.

He shoved her top up to unclasp her bra. Definitely impatient. And if his fingers trembled just a little, that too was a turn-on for Selene. She waited, waited, waited for his mouth to touch her breasts. Right *there*. She could almost feel his tongue sliding across her nipples, pausing to tease and torment each one.

Her heart pounded, and heaviness built low in her stomach as she imagined the path of those lips moving lower and lower. She clenched as anticipation urged her to pull him down behind that hedge and . . .

And then he stopped. He freaking *stopped*.

Outraged, she looked up.

His eyes glowed, and his lips were slightly parted. She could see the tips of his fangs. In that moment, he looked totally vampire. And Selene realized she was so far gone that even a bite from him sounded sexy.

Then she remembered that he'd *stopped*. "Why?" The question was torn from thousands of years of deprivation. Her heart still pounded, and her breaths came in hard gasps. He couldn't do this to her.

Adam released her and took a step back onto the walkway. Away from her and what they'd almost had. "Almost" was the operative word.

"You're responding because of my broadcasting. This is the way it works. I can't control my emotions, and they bleed over into you. You believe the feelings are your own, but they're not. They're mine. I don't want us to start out with a lie."

Selene was so furious she was speechless. A first for her. She would *not* waste her words trying to convince him she wasn't that weak, that her passion was her own. She straightened her clothing with angry jerks. "Fine." If he were any judge of women, he'd recognize that everything wasn't fine. But of course, he didn't know squat about women. Otherwise, he wouldn't have stopped.

She marched ahead of him into the building. He trailed behind her until they reached her door. He hesitated.

What would he say. That he was sorry? That he wanted to come in so they could continue what they'd started? That he'd never again leave her hanging in midair between earth and fulfillment? Selene imagined all the crushing put-downs she'd deliver.

She opened her door and stood waiting for his groveling to begin.

"I've been thinking."

Fine, so that was a start. She tapped her foot. *Come on, say it.*

"I don't think Crow is Six."

Selene slammed the door in his face.

CHAPTER THIRTEEN

———

A S ADAM PULLED ON HIS boots, he wondered if he'd broken any world records last night. Not only had he put his foot in his mouth, he'd managed to cram both of them in there. Too bad Guinness hadn't been around to record the moment.

He glanced out the window. Late afternoon. It would be nice just once to get up early enough to spend a whole day in the sun. Adam thought about his vampire limitations. Okay, maybe not a whole day.

He straightened, took a deep breath, and headed for the door. Dave was already waiting in the parking lot to drive them to Fin's condo where they, along with his brothers, would have the discussion Fin wanted. The boss would probably already have a Power Point presentation ready to show all the ways they'd messed up.

But that didn't bother him as much as having to walk over and bang on Selene's door. And, no, he still didn't like to ring the bell. It had a weak sound compared to the solid thump of a fist on wood.

He managed it all, though. The walk, the knock, and then the waiting.

Selene opened her door. She threw him a frigid stare. He could feel icicles hanging from his cock. She was already dressed in jeans, boots, sexy top, and leather jacket. She didn't waste words on him as she closed the door before striding ahead of him all the way down to the SUV.

Adam thought about calling shotgun beside Dave, but that was the coward's way out. He climbed in behind the driver and next to the ice queen. Utah in his raptor form could've fit between them. Dave ignored them as he pulled into early-evening traffic and then ramped up the radio volume. Adam tuned out the news and traffic report in favor of hacking away at the icy wall surrounding Selene.

"I noticed you reacted when Fin called you useful last night. Want to talk about it?" *Apologize, idiot.* No, he wouldn't do the I'm-sorry thing. That was a weakness. And any kind of weakness was deadly for raptors and vampires.

"No."

At least she'd spoken to him. "Have you thought over what I said about Crow?" *Apologize.* Why? He didn't say anything wrong last night. She should be glad he had enough strength to stop when he did. He'd done the right thing.

"No."

A woman of few words. *Apologize.* Nope. "Look, if we had kept going last night, you'd regret it today. My emotions got to you before I could put a cap on them. They do that to everyone. You would've felt used." There. That was logical.

"Don't tell me how I would've felt." She paused to think. "They do that to *everyone*? Do you mean you've thrown those lust-filled bombs at lots of women, so you know exactly how we feel?"

Her glance seared him with the heat of a thousand suns. At least now his cock could defrost.

Dave offered a disgusted grunt as he turned off the radio. "Jeez, for crying out loud, apologize to the woman. This whole conversation is painful. It brings me down, and I do violent things when I'm down."

Now Adam was mad. "Damn it, I tried to do the right thing, and all I'm getting is crap for it." He glared at Selene. "Do you think my beast wanted to stop? You don't have a clue how tough it is sometimes to remember that I'm a freaking human. I didn't stop for me. I stopped for you." The truth.

Silence cloaked the vehicle in storm clouds. Adam figured she'd let loose on him now. Maybe that was a good thing. She could get all the anger out of her system, and they could go from there.

He was wrong. Selene didn't answer, but she didn't sneer either. Instead, she stared out the window. He'd live with that. But he was through trying to explain himself.

Dave switched the radio back on. "Pissed-off silence works for me." He began to whistle.

The uncomfortable wall between them lasted for the rest of the way to Fin's condo. Shen ushered them into the dining room instead of the boss's office. Utah and Tor sat at the long table. But so did the rest of the Eleven. Why? Coffee along with breakfast stuff was laid out. This better not be a public humiliation followed by a late breakfast. As Adam and Selene joined his brothers, he was already ramping up his mad when Fin entered the room.

A stranger wearing a hoodie followed him in. Adam narrowed his eyes. No one in the room seemed to be looking at the new man except Adam. The guy turned to meet his gaze. Adam had only a moment to register essentials—tall, dark hair falling around his face, cold eyes, *not human*—before it hit him. It was like one of those lust bombs Selene accused him of tossing around had flattened him. Adam's beast roared to life. He almost couldn't contain it, didn't *want* to contain it. Every color in existence disappeared except for the flaming red of sexual starvation. It broke off into shards that stabbed him. He bled desire. He wanted Selene right on this table, taking him inside her while they rocked the coffee cups and trays of eggs and bacon.

Beside him, Selene flung her hand across Adam's eyes. "Look away. Now."

No, he didn't want to look away. Adam wanted to drown in his need for her. But thanks to her interfering hand, he couldn't see the man anymore. Slowly, the sexual compulsion faded and he could breathe air again instead of fire. He gripped the table edge to ground himself. "I'm okay."

Selene removed her hand.

Tor spoke from his other side. "Sorry. I forgot your soul was sleeping in Arizona when we worked with Kione in Portland. I should've warned you."

"Who *is* he?" Adam glanced at Selene to see her reaction to his loss of control.

She kept her gaze averted from the stranger as she answered. "That's Kione. Zero warned me about him. He's one of the High Fae. An unseelie prince. Very powerful. You just experienced one of his talents. Meet his gaze and get hit with uncontrollable lust for whoever is closest to you. Even your worst enemy would set you afire."

He must've made a threatening sound, because she hurried on to explain. "Don't blame him. It's just part of who he is. He can't turn it off. I bet he wishes he could."

Adam didn't comment. He was still busy calming his beast.

Fin sat at the head of the table. Kione sat to his right. Fin chose to ignore what almost happened. "I called everyone together to discuss Crow. Just in case anyone is unaware of what happened last night, here's the video." He clicked the TV on. Cable news was busy running film of the fight.

No one spoke as they watched, but Adam heard a few

mutters of envy. Everyone loved to mix it up with the enemy.

When the video was over, Fin turned off the TV. "I won't make you suffer through the panel of experts talking it to death. I'm taking steps to make sure our cover story of a movie shoot holds up to investigation. The man Crow carried away will of course be paid for his work as an 'extra.'" He threw the brothers a cranky glare.

Here it comes. Adam waited for it. Fin would explain in excruciating detail how they almost blew the Eleven's cover. How they never should engage the enemy in front of humans, especially when none of them could erase memories. Oh, and definitely not when those humans all had phones to immortalize the whole fiasco.

But Fin did none of those things. Instead, he asked Adam a question. "What was your impression of Crow?"

Adam didn't see any reason to lie. "I don't think he's Six."

He ignored the surprised murmurs from the others in the room. "Look, Zero's people are super powerful." Adam nodded at Selene as a prime example. "Sure, Crow can do lots of damage, but I don't think he's in the same league as Zero's other numbers. And I got the feeling we could've killed him tonight if he hadn't run away." He shrugged. "Maybe I'm wrong, but that's my take on Crow."

The muttering died down as everyone waited for Fin's reaction.

Fin pointed at Selene. "You would know Crow best. What do you think?"

"I agree with Adam." Selene met Fin's gaze. "I'm not friends with Crow, but from what I've seen of him, he's pretty one dimensional. He turns into a giant crow and his murder backs him up." She frowned. "I don't know enough about him to say whether he's immortal or not."

Ty spoke up. "Why don't you know more? You were part of Zero's pack."

He didn't sound friendly, and Adam bristled at Ty's attitude. "Hey, give her a break. She's one of us now. She did her part to defeat Crow."

Ty grumbled, but chose not to argue.

Selene refused to back down. She stood to face the rest of the Eleven. She met each of their gazes. Some of the guys looked as suspicious as Ty, but Adam's brothers gave her a thumbs up. Lio, Al, and Q smiled their support.

She stared down all of them. Except for Kione. She wouldn't go there. "Here's what I know about Frost's 'pack.' He made sure we never did anything more than meet each other in passing. We never hung out, we never did anything social together. Each of us was our own little island. Frost told us what to do and we did it. Ace and Meg were my only friends." Selene blinked. "By the way, where is Ace?"

Fin looked distracted for a moment before answering. "He's still sleeping. I didn't think he needed to be part of this meeting."

Selene was just getting started. How dare these men judge her? They knew nothing of her life, of how much she'd sacrificed to become what she was today. "Oh, and where are Kelly, Lia, and Jenna? Aren't the women *useful* enough to be here?" Now where had that come from? Adam's question about her usefulness must still be rattling around in her subconscious.

Fin ignored her question. "Getting back to the original discussion. I agree that Crow isn't Six. I also agree that he isn't powerful enough to be one of Zero's immortals. That's not saying he isn't dangerous." His expression turned thoughtful. "I wonder how loyal he'll be to Zero after his boss gets through pointing out how stupid he was?"

Selene sat down, but not before envisioning a dramatic

exit from the room. She'd look back just before leaving to yell, "I quit" at Fin. Then she'd slam the door behind her as she left. And she'd never speak to any of them again. Satisfying, but then Zero would destroy humanity and she wouldn't be there to stop him. So what? Who cared? *She cared.* The truth was an anchor tethered to her heart, holding her here with these people.

Unaware of her budding desire to mutiny, Fin kept talking. "I think we should explore the possibility that our feathered friend might be lured from the dark side."

"You're kidding, right?" Adam sounded amazed that anyone would ever think that.

Fin's glance suggested that Adam had no imagination. "Everyone has his or her price." He must've noticed the outraged glares from the others because he amended his comment. "Except for all of you. I have complete faith in your loyalty."

Selene didn't believe him. Fin was a cold creature. He probably wouldn't even trust his mother. Then she thought of her own family, and decided he wasn't alone in his distrust of parents.

Fin stood. He paced as he spoke. "Adam and Selene, find Crow's nest. See if you can convince him to speak with me." He didn't look at either one of them as he gave his orders. "We need as much help as we can get—no matter how unreliable—in these final weeks."

No matter how unreliable. Selene wondered if that's how he thought of her. *Was* she to be trusted? Not at the beginning, not when she'd planned to act as a mole in order to win her way back into Zero's elite group of killers. But now? Yes, she was committed to the Eleven, and to Adam.

Fin wasn't finished. "Oh, and Adam, check in with your vampires. They need to see their leader. Make sure they understand their role in the coming battle."

Adam raised one brow. "And that would be?"

Selene thought he was treading a little close to Fin's line of patience.

Fin ignored Adam's tone. "Vampires are the ultimate night stalkers. I'll give you a list of humans they'll need to protect if the nation is to remain intact. Have Jude pass down the information to every vampire clan in the country." He turned his attention to the others at the table.

Selene stopped listening. She was still focused on Crow. There were a few holes in Fin's logic. "Wait. Let's go back to Crow for a moment. How're we supposed to turn him? We don't even know where he lives." Personally, she didn't think they stood a chance of winning him over. In fact, Crow would be so ticked off about getting beat up by the raptors that he would probably try to kill them before they even opened their mouths.

Fin actually smiled. "I bet Crow is true to his nature. He probably loves shiny stuff. Bribe him. Use your creativity. I'd suggest a trip to Old Town Market."

Then Fin put his hand on Kione's shoulder. "Our friend here has another interesting power besides the obvious. He can find any person he's ever come in contact with. And if you didn't notice, Kione bumped into our feathered friend as he escaped you last night." His smile widened. "He'll go with you tonight."

Sadist. Fin was enjoying this. She didn't miss the look of horror on Adam's face. It would be funny if she wasn't going to be shut up in the car with both of them. Selene had never experienced what the dark fairy could do, but she'd heard the tales.

She blocked out Fin's instructions to the rest of the Eleven as she thought about the direction of her life in general. Something had to change. Soon. The scrape of chair legs pulled her back to the present in time to see Fin rise.

Without waiting for any more questions, Fin turned

his back to the table and then left the room. Adam rose to follow him while the rest of the Eleven continued their interrupted meal.

Selene wasn't about to allow him to corner Fin without her. She followed him to Fin's office and slipped in just behind Adam.

Fin was already sitting at his desk, his gaze fixed on a paper in front of him. Adam stood on the other side of the desk, his back a rigid line of rebellion. Selene moved to Adam's side.

Finally, Fin looked up. He sighed as he pushed the paper aside. "Ask."

"Do we have a chance of stopping Zero before December 21? I want an honest answer."

Silence gathered as Fin leaned back in his chair to study the ceiling. When he lowered his gaze, all his frustration, his anger, shone in his eyes. His pupils were solid purple.

"No. The best we can hope for is to find and eliminate Six from the fight. We're running out of time." He swiveled his chair so he was looking out over Petco Park. "I thought maybe Zero would recall the rest of his immortals so they could stand with him in his battle against us. We would've had a chance if they were all in one spot. We can only hope he still does it."

"He never discussed his plans with me." Selene tried to remember if Zero had ever mentioned anything about the final battle. "All he ever spoke about was making sure the word got out to his nonhuman horde to rise as one on that day."

Fin nodded as though that made sense to him. "He hit Earth running before I got here. He's had more time to organize. I have people all over the world, but they won't be enough to stop what will happen."

Adam clenched his fists, his lips thinned into a tight line of determination. "He won't win."

Fin spun his chair back to face them. His smile was the scariest thing Selene had ever seen.

"He's underestimated me before." Fin's gaze grew distant. "Many times."

"Tell us you have a backup plan." Selene had to hang onto that belief or lose hope.

Fin leaned forward; his stare intense. "I'll deal with Zero. That's all you need to know."

Adam looked frustrated. "That's all, huh?"

Fin rubbed his hand across his face as he slumped back in his chair again. He closed his eyes. "That's all. Now leave so I can think. Your dark fairy and Dave are waiting in the car." He opened his eyes. "No, wait." He reached into a desk drawer, drew out a credit card, and shoved it across the desk at Selene. "Here. This is yours. You'll need it if you're going shopping. All of the Eleven have one."

She scooped it up and dropped it into her jacket pocket. "Limit?"

He shrugged. "None."

Selene fantasized about buying expensive shiny things as they left the office.

Neither of them spoke until they were in the elevator going down to the parking garage. Then Selene couldn't contain herself for another minute. "You know, Fin and Zero are a lot alike. Zero is a control freak, and Fin plays in the minds of you guys whenever he feels like it."

That triggered her earlier feeling that there was something similar about them. Maybe they came from the same world. A possibility. Fin had given a hint when he'd said Zero had underestimated him many times. She sensed a history between them that went beyond what everyone knew. How could she find out more? Her father? He had certainly been around the universe for a lot longer than she had. Selene hated the thought of searching him out, but she'd have to if she wanted to know more. Then she realized Adam hadn't replied. A side glance showed him wearing a bemused expression.

"Fin worried me. He's our all-powerful leader. He's cold, calm, and always has the answers. Back there, he wasn't wearing his cape. He sounded worn out, and I didn't hear any encouraging words. How do we deal with that?"

"Are you going to tell the others?" She didn't think it would help morale for them to know.

Adam shook his head. "What good would it do?" He looked at her. "I wonder why he didn't erase our memories before we left? I don't think he'd want us spreading the news that we can't stop Zero."

Selene thought about it. "Maybe he's tired of erasing memories." It was as good an answer as any.

They'd almost reached the SUV when Adam put his hand on Selene's arm to stop her. Luckily, she hadn't taken her jacket off during their brief visit to Fin's condo, so there was no skin-on-skin contact. Good thing, because even through the leather separating them, his touch made her want to self-combust. He was just that hot. She couldn't stop the mental picture that brought up. Selene smiled.

He looked puzzled at her smile before dismissing it. "You didn't ask about Meg. Why didn't you include her in your list of women who should've been at the meeting?"

Selene thought about her answer. *Be careful.* "Meg wouldn't have any interest in our battle plans. Besides, we stay in touch. I keep her in the loop."

Adam nodded. Relieved, she hoped he wouldn't ask any more questions about Meg.

"Looks like you're talking to me again. Does that mean you're over your mad?" His glance was wary.

Selene shrugged. "We only have two weeks until the

twenty-first. I won't waste it on anger." Left unsaid was
that there might not be a twenty-second.

He looked way too happy at her answer. Selene
wouldn't ruin his moment by adding that she'd make
sure their next skin-on-skin meeting ended more satis-
factorily. No need to warn him.

"Good. Believe me, it won't happen again."

An ambivalent answer. Did he mean he'd never try to
make love with her again? If so, he had a surprise coming. Or did he mean that the next time he wouldn't end
the moment on a down note? She chose to believe the
second choice.

"Sure." They'd reached the SUV. She peered in through
the darkened windows. Kione sat next to Dave. Excellent. Selene chose to sit behind their driver, and Adam
sat beside her. This time Adam made himself comfortable
much closer to her. She immersed herself in his scent of
all things wild and unexplored. If she had her way, he
wouldn't stay unexplored for much longer.

Selene leaned back, prepared to enjoy the ride. "Okay,
Kione, let's find our giant feathery friend."

CHAPTER FOURTEEN

A DAM RELAXED ON THE WAY to Old Town. The tension with Selene was gone, and he had hopes of . . . Well, he just had hopes. Thankfully, Dave and Kione talked to each other and left him alone. All was pretty much great in his world until Selene's voice pulled him out of his cloud of contentment.

"Tell me who you are, Adam. Really." She kept her voice low so the ears in the front seats wouldn't share their conversation.

He met her gaze. "Why do you want to know?"

She shrugged before glancing away. "You asked me to share a bit of myself, so I'd like a bit of you in return. Hey, it's only fair."

"What makes you think I'm not exactly what you see?" *Just an ordinary guy who loves to kill monsters and hates saying no to his soul.* Now wasn't the right time to share emotional reveals. Adam would rather save those kinds of things for when he was basking in the afterglow of great sex. Or maybe never.

Selene made a contemptuous sound. "Give me a break. You're a closed door. Too bad for you that I can see a light underneath it, so I know someone's home."

Adam thought about just not answering, except he did want to know more about her. He opened the door a crack. "I hate to disappoint you, but I don't have a clue who I am. It's like parts of me are scattered all across freaking time. I don't even remember the name of where my soul first existed, or of anyone who was important to me then. What did I do each day? What did I look forward to in the future? Then there was the raptor's time. Not much to know about that. I killed, ate, slept and mated. Not a lot of memories to worry about. Next came the human Rap with a predator's soul. The human and raptor were still fighting it out when the vampires killed me. Fin yanked my soul from my body and then dumped it into Adam's recently vacated one. Now I'm Adam, an all-around great guy and soulless bloodsucker." Good luck with her figuring out who the real Rap-slash-Adam was from that.

She nodded. "I get it. Dealing with an identity crisis is tough."

"No kidding." Adam hated the sympathy he heard in her voice. That's not what he'd intended. He'd said too much. "Look, I didn't mean to unload on you. I'll take my multiple personalities into the corner and shut up." He was trying to treat his outburst lightly, but the emotions churning inside startled him. An identity crisis? Was that the fancy name for the panic he felt, the worry that at any moment he could become someone else, someone he'd have to add to the mob duking it out for control of him?

Selene watched him, a strange expression on her face. He didn't want to know what it meant. Time to redirect the conversation. "Your turn."

"Right." She took a deep breath. "I've—"

"We're here." Dave pulled into a parking space, shut down the SUV, and climbed out.

Everyone piled out after him. Adam stretched and hoped his expression didn't show his disappointment at their interrupted chat. He met Selene's gaze. "We'll continue this later."

She nodded but didn't look happy about it. Tough. The baring of souls went both ways.

He chanced a glance at Kione. The prince had pulled up his hood so Adam couldn't see his face. Good thing. He shifted his attention to their driver. "Maybe you and Kione have some shopping you want to do." Hint.

Dave shook his head. "Nope. The boss wants us to keep you guys in sight. Wouldn't want anything to happen to the little lady."

Damn. Adam wanted to be alone with her, or as alone as he could be with crowds of people wandering around the brightly lit shops. "Look, I can protect—"

Selene interrupted. She turned the full wattage of her fury on Dave. "Call me little lady again and die."

"Sure." Dave didn't seem bothered by her death threat. "Anyway, we'll just tag along and maybe pick up a few things."

Then they walked. Shop after shop after shop. Hand-crafted stuff from Mexico and South America, clothes, jewelry—Selene bought a necklace—art, candy, and dolls. Adam smiled. Maybe he'd get a Day of the Dead doll for Crow. Bands played and people danced. They lost Dave to a candy store. He hoped choosing took lots of time. Kione didn't seemed tempted to linger anywhere.

Adam leaned close as Selene scoped out a display outside a clothing store. He allowed himself to bathe in her scent. He wasn't sure what it was, but it was hardwired to his sexual hunger. *Not here.* He moved out of the danger zone, or as far away as he could without being obvious. "Do you have something in mind, or are you just doing a random search?"

"I have a few ideas, but whatever I choose, it has to be amazing and sparkly enough to blind you if you make direct eye contact."

He grinned. "Sort of like our dark prince."

She returned his smile. "Exactly like our dark prince."

"I'm right here. Why not turn around to speak with me?"

Kione's voice sounded way too close for Adam's comfort. "I'll pass on turning around." But he thought about it. He'd turn around, stare into the prince's eyes, and since this was *his* fantasy, she'd do the same. Then he'd lay an invisibility shield over the two of them and they'd make love right here in front of the shoppers, the band, and the dancing people. It would be awesome. And he could blame it all on Kione. The only thing missing? Invisibility shields weren't in old Adam's skill set.

A soft chuckle behind him assured Adam that Kione knew exactly what he was thinking.

Selene seemed too busy studying the clothes to notice anything. "I'm going in here. Want to come?" She turned to Adam.

He glanced at the place. Small. And unlike most of the others they'd passed, this one had a shadowy interior. Adam shook his head. "Small, dark spaces bother me. I'll wait out here." Vampire Adam thought the shop felt sort of homey. His raptor soul hated enclosed areas. He decided to humor his beast this time.

She nodded before disappearing inside. Adam watched the hypnotic swing and sway of her hips until she was gone. Then he scanned the area. No Dave. Good. Kione moved up beside him.

"You can look at me now."

Adam turned and then relaxed when he saw that the prince had pulled his hoodie so far forward that no one could see his features. "It must be tough always having to hide your face."

Kione shrugged. "It is what it is. At least I never feel unwanted."

Adam heard the bitter undertone. He'd bet the fairy would love to walk down the street without being noticed. "Some would say that was a gift from the gods."

Kione's silence said it all.

"Okay, I get it."

"No, you don't. I can never know who my true friends are because the compulsion touches everyone. If I walk into a room, every person falls into lust with their partner. Or, if I'm unlucky, with me."

"Tough." And Adam meant it. "Was there ever anyone who—"

"I loved?" Kione watched Dave making his way back to them loaded down with candy bags. "Yes. Once. She died." He looked back at Adam. "Vampires captured both of us."

Adam winced. "How did she die?"

"She took her own life so I'd be free to escape."

Adam knew there was more to the story, but he wasn't about to ask for details. He didn't know what to say. His beast stirred at the thought of something like that happening to Selene. "I hope you got revenge." He would've torn every one of the vampires into bite-sized bits and then rolled in their blood.

"I returned. Only blood and the memory of their screams remained after I left." His voice was cold with satisfaction.

"You still hate them even though they're dead." It was a statement. Any idiot could feel Kione's loathing.

"Always."

"Do you hate all vampires?" Adam sort of cared. This guy had suffered and survived. And then he'd taken his revenge. Adam respected that.

"I only hated the members of that clan." The prince was quiet for a moment. "Although I discovered later that five of them weren't there when the clan captured us. I met them later. We worked things out. Take my suggestion and appreciate what you have while you have it. Tomorrow isn't guaranteed."

Adam didn't have time to process that thought before Dave reached them.

"Lots of people here." He reached into a bag, retrieved a chocolate, and stuffed it into his mouth.

The people, the noise, the bright colors all made Adam want to close his eyes for a moment. He still wasn't used to it all. His beast snarled, reminding him of what would happen if he ever freed it in a place like this. This wasn't his world. He still didn't feel as though he belonged.

Adam found a bench and settled to wait for Selene. Kione joined him. Dave wandered over to where a band was playing and a few people were dancing. Eventually, he too sat on the bench to wait.

When Selene finally left the shop, she saw Dave eating candy, Kione gazing at the ground, and Adam staring at her. For just a moment, she swore his eyes lit with happiness. And then he stood, his expression smoothing out.

"See you bought something." He closed the space between them.

The others trailed behind him.

"I found the perfect temptation." She surprised even herself with how happy her purchase made her. Who knew she loved to shop? Selene held up the garment bag.

Dave licked his fingers and then tossed his empty bag into a nearby bin. "Well, let's see it."

She should probably wait until they got back to the SUV, but she was too excited to show off her find. "I couldn't believe when I saw it hanging in the back of the place. It's Crow. He'll love it." She hoped. Maybe it was a bit overdramatic, but he was a *crow*. She pulled off the plastic covering. "What do you think?"

Silence greeted her. They all stared. Fine, so she couldn't tell if Kione was staring, but she assumed he was. As the quiet dragged on, she grew defensive. "Yes, it's a bit much, but can't you see Crow wearing it?"

Kione spoke. "It's brilliant. I'd wear it everywhere."

"It's a long cloak made from crow feathers." Adam's voice was noncommittal. "Each feather is tipped in gold." He shook his head. "I was okay until I got to the gold tips. That's a little too over the top for me." He glanced at Kione. "And you'd wear it everywhere?" He shook his head. "To each his own."

Dave laughed. "It takes a certain kind of stupid to wear something like that."

Kione stepped closer. He reached for his hood. "Look me in the eyes and say that."

Dave suddenly found something fascinating to stare at on the ground. "I guess it would take lots of courage too. It says you're not afraid to be an individual. I salute you."

Kione dropped his hand. He turned his attention back to Selene. "I saw something in one of the places we passed that would be perfect with that." He strode off.

Selene watched him go before looking at Dave. "You need to work on your people skills."

Their driver shrugged. "It isn't my style. What can I say? I'm honest." He frowned. "I don't like backing down like that, but it's all about survival, you know. I'm good at sensing power in people. That fairy is more than just a killer face. He's scary, and I don't say that often."

Adam changed the subject. "You said it was the perfect temptation for Crow. What would *your* perfect temptation be?"

His question made her forget all about Dave's survival instincts and Kione's killer face.

Suddenly, she was staring at a blank wall. No one had ever asked her that. Selene didn't like being caught off guard, so she gave an automatic answer chiseled from all those cold years of just-not-giving-a-damn when she had convinced herself she was happy that way. "Nothing. I can't think of one thing that would tempt me to do something I didn't want to do." She believed it was true.

Adam just smiled.

She didn't like that smile. It was filled with an arrogant male "knowing." Ha. He knew nothing. And she believed that too. Sort of. Thank heaven, Kione's return distracted her from Adam's smile.

Selene still couldn't see Kione's face, but she heard amusement in his voice.

"This will go with the cloak. Crow can wear it when he's trying to intimidate all those humans." He held up a full-face mask.

A Mexican wrestling mask. "Wow. It almost makes me want to buy one." Selene reached for it, and Kione handed it over. It was all shiny black except for the wings that swept up from the sides to almost touch above the head of the wearer. The tips of the wings were painted metallic gold. The mask's nose jutted out above the wearer's nose to form a short beak. "You're right. It's perfect."

Adam glanced at his watch. "Time to find Crow and see if he's open to bribery." He nodded at Kione. "Ready?"

"Sure." Kione retrieved the mask before leading them back to the SUV.

Selene had a few minutes to think while the prince guided Dave through a poorer and darker section of San Diego. She chanced a side glance at Adam. He seemed lost in thought. Did she know any more about him than when she'd asked her question? Yes. He was dealing with lots of inner conflict, and he wanted to know what her greatest temptation was. She allowed herself a sly smile. It could be him. Maybe. Or not. Selene would have to take him for a test drive first.

Dave parked on a street of sad and neglected houses. Overgrown yards, fences that leaned like drunks marching to war, and homes with peeling paint. She couldn't see much more detail in the dim glow of the few streetlights still working. Kione pointed at a corner house that had zero curb appeal. Drab and colorless came to mind. Not what she'd expect from Crow.

Selene turned to the others. "The direct approach will be best. We don't have a chance of sneaking up on him if he's home." She glanced at the house's roof where beady black eyes shone in the darkness. His murder was on watch.

"I'll knock on his door." Dave sounded eager. "He doesn't know me, but he'll sense I'm only human. No threat. I'll explain the situation to him."

"If he lets you live that long," Adam murmured.

"Why so anxious to die?" Kione sounded sincerely interested.

Dave met Kione's gaze, or as close as he could get with the dark fairy's hood pulled over his face. Selene recognized their driver's expression. Dave was reclaiming the self-respect he'd lost to Kione when he'd backed down from the prince. Kione nodded his understanding. She did a mental eyeroll. Men and their egos.

Dave didn't wait for everyone's okay. He strode to Crow's gate—the one hanging by a hinge—and flung it open. He boldly climbed the porch steps—avoiding the one with a hole in it—and then banged on the door. She didn't see a doorbell. Then they waited.

And while they waited, Selene slipped the covering off the cloak. Kione handed her the mask. She held them up where anyone opening the door could see them. Adam did his part by using the small flashlight he'd taken from the SUV to spotlight the awesomeness of the gift they were offering Crow.

At the third knock, Crow opened the door. This time he wasn't depending only on his crows to help him win any battles. He wore jeans, boots, and a red shirt. She leaned in for a better look. Okay, a silk shirt. And he carried an assault rifle. Who said you couldn't teach an old crow new tricks?

Adam whistled softly. "Will you look at that gun. He's out for big game."

Selene studied Crow. He was still tall and cadaverous, but he looked somehow diminished standing in the darkened doorway. Maybe it was in his slight stoop or the way his head-feathers stood straight up as though he'd run his fingers through them a lot.

Crow's gaze snagged on the cloak. His eyes widened. He didn't blink or look away from the feathered offering. Good.

She couldn't hear what Dave said, but she saw the moment Crow realized what was happening. He shoved Dave out of the way and stepped onto the porch. His stoop was gone and he radiated fury. He pointed a clawed finger at them and mouthed, "You!"

Showtime. Selene moved forward slowly. Didn't want to scare the birdie. She tried to look harmless as she waved the cloak in front of her. Olé! Behind her, Adam sighed.

"Isn't working, sweetheart. You just look dangerously sneaky and cunning now." He moved up beside her.

Everything stilled—the night sounds, their breathing— as Crow studied them. This whole plan hung on Fin's belief that Zero would kick Crow to the curb for his failure. If the cloak and mask didn't at least get them into Crow's house to talk, they'd probably have to kill him. Selene didn't flinch away from spilling blood, but she hated having to admit failure to Fin.

"Relax." Adam spoke quietly. "He knows he can't destroy us all, even with the gun, so he probably won't try. Especially with the memory of what happened last night."

Even in the dim light, Selene could see bruises on Crow's face.

Kione nodded. "He's probably considering a run for it. I'll—"

Crow beckoned to them.

Kione backed into the shadows. "I'll stay out here to

cover any escape routes and to keep an eye on his murder."

Selene could hear the rustle of hundreds of wings as Crow's birds shifted restlessly on the roof.

"Good idea." Adam started forward. "That's an old house. Probably has small rooms. It might be tough for me to free my raptor if he tries anything." He pointed at Selene. "At least she can create a colony of killer fire ants."

Selene ignored his comment. "Time to get serious. Fin wants this guy on our side. We have to stay firm but play nice in there."

Adam made a rude sound. "Play nice? After he tried to kill us? I don't think so."

She threw him an impatient glare. "At least try."

He widened his eyes. "For you? Okay, I'll smile while I'm removing his head. I might even apologize afterward."

Forget christening him as her greatest temptation. He was unpredictable and undisciplined. Selene took a deep breath before marching toward the porch. She held the cloak in front of her like a feathered shield. This was something she understood—negotiate or destroy. She only hoped they wouldn't have to kill the jerk.

CHAPTER FIFTEEN

DAVE ENTERED THE HOUSE FIRST. Adam noticed his sword had appeared from out of nowhere. But Crow didn't seem worried about Dave's weapon. His gaze never left the cloak and mask. He'd dropped the rifle to his side. Adam would have to point out to him that focusing on objects of lust left him open to sudden death from his enemies. He glanced at Selene. A lesson for him too.

As Selene passed Crow on her way inside, he reached out to slide his fingers down the cloak's arm. He actually shivered from the contact. Adam shook his head. Was this the guy Zero had sent out to take them down? Show him something shiny, and all of the Eleven could troop past and Crow wouldn't give a damn.

But then Crow shifted his attention to Adam. His eyes narrowed, and Adam saw the killer in them. Maybe not so clueless.

"You're the vampire lord."

Adam nodded. He waited to see if Crow would put it all together.

"But your driver said one of the Eleven was here to negotiate a deal for Fin."

Adam didn't say anything. But he saw the lightbulb blink on in Crow's head.

"So, you must moonlight as one of the Eleven."

Adam gathered himself, ready to act if Crow attacked.

"I'm not going to ask how the hell you can be both, but I guess you are. Which dino are you?"

Here it comes. "The one who almost ripped out your tailfeathers last night at Seaport Village."

Crow surprised him. He chuckled.

"Frost doesn't know you're both?"

"Not unless you tell him." Adam tensed, ready to react if he gave the wrong reply.

"Why would I do that? Secrets have power."

Great. The bird was probably already planning to blackmail him.

Crow entered the house last and closed the door behind him. The hallway was narrow and dark. It smelled of age and dust. Adam didn't notice much more about the hall because he was too focused on the man behind him. The one with the big gun. Crow walked quietly, but Adam could still hear his soft footfalls, his quickened breathing, and any sound that hinted he was raising his weapon. Heightened senses, a gift from Adam's primal past.

Just before they entered a small room on the right, Crow closed the gap behind Adam. He spoke softly. "I assume since I've guessed your little secret, you'll try to kill me if I don't buy what you're selling. Don't underestimate me, raptor. The three of you beat up on me last night, but here in my nest I'm king. Just because I admire your offering doesn't mean I've forgotten what you are." Then he reached out to switch on the lights.

Adam blinked. He resisted the urge to cover his eyes.

Dave said it for all of them. "Insane! How do you live here?"

Selene laughed. "Mirrors on the ceiling, Crow? Glitter on the walls? Velvet on the floor? And a sequined couch?"

Crow sniffed. "I'm a crow. I like color, shine, and texture. My home, my choices." He sent her a defiant stare.

Adam recovered. "Everyone has a right to their own

taste. I sort of like that cat statue." About a foot tall. Purple metallic paint with diamond eyes. Hey, what wasn't to like?

Crow smiled, and the killer in his eyes receded. "Yeah, I liked it, too. Cats are predatory. I relate to that. I was cruising past a high-rise condo when I saw it on a table. No one was home. I opened the window—people don't lock their windows when they're ten stories up—and nabbed it."

"Cool." *See, Fin, I'm trying to be diplomatic.* Adam hoped the boss was tuned in.

Everyone found a place to sit. Adam ended up on the sequined couch with Selene. He shifted, searching for a comfortable position. There was none. Sequins were great until you had to kick back at night to watch a game. The little suckers poked the hell out of him. He wondered where you'd put a drink if you did want to relax. Every table surface was filled with shiny objects—statues, jewelry, and even colored rocks.

Crow sat on a chair covered in what looked like peacock feathers. He set the gun on the floor beside him and then leaned forward, his gaze intense. "What's your deal?"

Selene had her laughter under control. "We thought you might be interested in working for someone else, someone who appreciates your skills."

Crow looked suspicious. "What if I already have an employer?"

Adam asked the all-important question. "Do you?"

Crow dropped his head. He stared at the floor. "No. Frost didn't like the way I handled last night. He said I was too impulsive, that I never should've lost control and gone on a rampage. He said he wouldn't be able to depend on me when it counted." Crow raised his head. Rage and humiliation lived in his eyes.

Selene offered sympathy. "I know how you feel. He kicked me out with no second chance too."

Dave chimed in. "Tough. Not the way to treat a loyal employee."

"No kidding." Crow sat up straighter. He looked at Adam. "I would've destroyed you last night if I hadn't been outnumbered."

"Sure." Adam spoke through clenched teeth. He wanted to abandon diplomacy and punch Crow in his big fat beak. He swore he heard Fin's laughter in his mind.

Selene cast Adam a warning glance before smiling at Crow. "Well, tonight is your lucky night. Fin appreciates someone with your talent. He'd like to offer you a position with us."

Crow didn't seem convinced. "Why would he do that? I tried to kill all of you."

"Yes, you did, didn't you?" Adam smiled with his fangs on full display. "But we're all warriors. That's what we do. Once the battle is over, everything is forgotten." *Not.* "That's how professionals act."

Dave's expression said he'd never heard that much bull in his life.

Selene ignored them both. "What do you say? I'm sure Fin will be generous with you. He gave me a credit card with no limit."

Crow's shiny black eyes lit up. "No limit?"

Gotcha. Adam gave Dave a cautious thumbs-up while Crow probably contemplated buying out every jewelry store in San Diego.

Crow's attention switched to the cloak Selene had draped over the back of the couch. She held the mask in her lap.

"I get the cloak and mask?" He didn't try to hide his glee.

"Of course." She kept the smile pasted on her face.

"I want your necklace too."

Selene narrowed her eyes. Adam figured Crow was treading on dangerous ground.

Finally, she sighed and lifted the necklace she'd just bought from around her neck. The colored glass beads glittered as she handed it to Crow. He slipped it over his head and then looked up to admire himself in his mirrored ceiling.

"We have a deal." Crow studied each of them. "But try to double-cross me, and I'll tear you up."

Adam just stopped his instinctive eyeroll.

"Good. Now that we have that settled, I have a few questions for you." Fin stepped into the room. Ace followed him.

Startled, everyone leapt to their feet. Adam exhaled as he wrestled his beast back into its cage. He wished Fin wouldn't do that. Why couldn't he just knock on the door like everyone else?

Dave and Selene returned to their seats. Crow remained standing. He'd grabbed his gun. Adam didn't miss the uneasiness in the bird's eyes. Above him, he could hear the distant caws of crows on the roof. Something from his far distant past—the one he didn't remember—intruded. *Always confront the enemy from a position of power.* He glanced at Crow, and then his gaze shifted to Fin. For only a moment, he wondered which to confront. *Where had that come from?* He looked down. When he finally raised his gaze, Fin watched him, expressionless.

Adam chose to stand.

Fin moved into the room. He took the seat Adam had vacated. Ace perched on the arm of the couch beside Selene. She reached over to pat him on the knee. Ace grinned down at her, the perfect image of a carefree teen. Was that picture a little too perfect? Adam shook his head. He had to get rid of the paranoia. It could distract him from focusing on proven enemies like Zero. But when he glanced up at the mirrored ceiling and caught Fin's reflection, something hazy seemed to superimpose itself over his leader. Adam blinked it away. No more chasing shadows.

"Does your ex-boss have more of his immortals coming to town?" Fin flicked a sequin off his leather pants as he scanned the room.

"I don't think so." Crow shrugged. "Frost said everyone he needs is already here. I guess he feels he can handle San Diego alone. Besides, you guys took care of three of his main weapons, so he's a little shorthanded. Frost wants what's left of his posse handling things elsewhere." He paused to think. "By the way, what's with Fin and Frost? I mean, couldn't you have picked a name that started with a different letter?"

Fin actually laughed. Selene marveled at the moment. She wished she'd had her phone out to record it.

"I like the name Fin. Just because he got here first doesn't mean he has the F words locked down." His laughter faded. "I bet he's using plenty of them every time he thinks of me. He's always wanted to be unique, the alpha wolf in every pack. He doesn't like sharing." Fin smiled. "Annoying him makes me happy, always has."

Always has. Those words bothered Selene, just as something about Fin had tugged at her from the beginning. They hinted at a familiarity between the two that went beyond what she knew of them. She pushed the thought away. She'd take it out to examine some other time.

Crow wasn't finished with his name questions. "Why do you call him Zero?"

Fin didn't try to hide his impatience. "Forget about names. We have other things to worry about." He turned to Adam. "You need to mobilize your vampires. Get the word out that I want these people watched and protected." Fin pulled a small notebook from his jacket pocket and handed it to Adam. "When Zero launches his attack, he'll try to kill important world figures first to throw nations into chaos. That list only covers people of power in the United States. I've sent other lists to our reps around the world. I want it done tonight. We only have a few weeks left before the Winter Solstice."

Selene hoped Adam's frustrated expression had at least a little to do with Fin's postponement of what she hoped would happen once they were free for the night. "I don't know how either you or Zero can be ready for Armageddon. There're too many variables involved. Humanity will fight back. The world's nonhumans might not react the way you think they will. Can you even depend on the allies you believe are on your side?" Her list was endless, but she didn't think Fin would want to hear it. She waited for him to wiggle his way out of answering her. After all, he wouldn't want to show weakness in front of his new recruit.

Fin met her gaze. "I don't know about Zero, but I have a few secret weapons." He turned back to Crow as though that's all he needed to say. Not even close. She opened her mouth to ask about those "secret weapons." But Adam distracted her.

"I want to be done with this before dawn, so if you don't have anything else for me to do, I'm leaving."

"Go." Fin waved him away as he focused on Crow.

Adam glanced at Selene. "Coming with me?"

She nodded and then followed him from the room. Dave trailed them as they left the house and headed for the SUV where Kione already waited. Her last thought about Fin was to wonder if he knew that Zero had a few secret weapons, too. Her father would count as one.

Adam paused long enough to send a text. When he saw her watching, he explained, "I've asked Jude to meet us at an open-all-night restaurant on El Cajon Boulevard. Great food."

"You're delegating? Don't you think your vampires need to hear this straight from their leader?"

"Don't try laying a guilt trip on me." He looked away

as he started walking again. "Jude is more their leader than I am. Sure I wear Adam's face, but I don't think I'm fooling the clan. On some level, they know he's gone." He opened the SUV's door for her. "Accept it, I live in an in-between world. Not quite here, but not quite there."

She didn't miss the frustration in his voice.

"Hey, wait for me. I want to hang with you guys for a while." Ace caught up with her just as she was about to climb into the car. "Fin doesn't need me for anything else, so I'm free."

Kione—with his hood still hiding his face—rode shotgun after introducing himself to Ace. Selene ended up in the middle between Adam and Ace. She marveled at the teen's lack of questions about the dark fairy as well as his general silence once he'd climbed into the back with Adam and her. All that was good, though, because then she could concentrate on Adam.

The sexual hum between them was so loud she was surprised Dave wasn't singing to it. She rested her hand on Adam's thigh and smiled as he clenched his muscles. But he got his own back when he leaned close to whisper in her ear.

"Tonight. Naked. In my bed. You'll scream."

"Well, you certainly have a high opinion of yourself." She laughed, but it was a little shaky because the warmth of his breath teasing the sensitive skin behind her ear made her shiver.

His laughter was husky and filled with dark promises. "Okay, so maybe I'll do some shouting, too."

Selene was reaching out to touch his jaw when Ace kicked her. Hard. She jerked her hand away and then turned on the teen.

"What was that about?" She tried to keep her voice down, but she wasn't sure it did any good. Kione half turned to look back at them.

Ace met her glare. He wasn't smiling. "I'm reminding you of who you are."

"What?" Who had stolen the real Ace and put this troll in his place? "This from the guy who is all for fun, exploring life, and believing people should mind their own business?"

Ace didn't look away. There was something in his gaze that bothered her. It was too mature, too not the kid she knew.

"Just want you to think before you test the waters." He shrugged and then started to turn away.

Adam joined the conversation. "Don't you think Selene is old enough to make her own decisions?"

He didn't sound angry, only curious.

Ace leaned toward Adam. "Hey, it's my job to keep her safe. That means when I see her getting too involved with someone she's only known a short time, I say something about it."

Adam thought that over for a moment. "I'm glad someone is watching out for her, but you can relax. She's safe with me."

Selene realized Adam was trying to allow Ace to escape with his pride, but his words sort of irritated her. What if she didn't want to be safe with him? She loved a challenge. The thought of a dangerous Adam was sexy. Besides, Ace's insinuation that she was so weak she needed a seventeen-year-old to ride herd on her was insulting.

She wasn't sure where the talk would've gone because Dave interrupted.

"That was great, folks. I was so entertained I didn't even turn on the radio. Afraid you'll have to bring down the curtain, though. We're here." He parked and they all piled out.

Dave stretched and yawned. "I think you'll be safe inside. I'll stay here to guard our ride." Translation: he could listen to the radio, maybe relax with some music.

Jude was waiting for them inside. Once again, Selene marveled at the star-power of the vampire. He was all dark flowing hair, warm sensuous eyes, and a hot mouth. Still, she preferred Adam with his tousled hair, golden eyes that burned when they touched her, and tempting mouth that said, "Kiss me hard."

She was glad to see only a few couples scattered throughout the restaurant. Between Kione's deadly everything, and the vampires' overwhelming sexual pull, lots of relationships would've ended tonight if the place was crowded.

Nothing was said until everyone had ordered. Except for Jude. Blood wasn't on the menu, so he abstained. He finally lost patience. "What's this about, Adam?"

Before Adam could answer, Kione stood. "Our driver is calling. He needs one of us. I'll be back."

Selene, along with everyone else, watched him leave. Strange, no one else acted as though they'd heard a shout or even a mental call. And none of them seemed motivated to follow Kione. But then the dark fairy was more than capable of handling any emergencies. She shrugged and settled in to enjoy the burger and fries the waiter placed in front of her.

"Again, why am I here?"

Jude sounded frustrated. She didn't blame him.

Selene focused on her meal as her mind wandered while Adam explained Fin's directions to Jude. The words shifted and faded as she thought about other things—tonight with Adam, her father's anger if he discovered her involvement, Adam naked, how her budding feelings for him would impact her in-control self-image, and finally, Adam moving inside her, touching . . . She blinked. Wow. Luckily for her, Adam had stopped talking. A few more minutes, and her thoughts of him would've incinerated the place.

Jude was speaking. "Got it." He took the notebook

Adam offered. "I'll get right on this." Without even a goodbye, he rose and left the restaurant.

Selene frowned. That didn't sound like a Jude goodbye to her. But he was probably focused on passing the info to his clan. She looked at Ace. "My mind wandered a little. Did I miss anything?"

Ace seemed startled. He pulled earbuds from his ears. "What? Are you guys through talking? I was just sinking into my music."

Before she could answer, Kione returned. "Nothing important. Some thugs thought the SUV would be easy pickings with just Dave in it." He smiled, all teeth but no eye contact. "They thought wrong. While they were busy trying to have sex with each other, Dave knocked them out with his sword. They're lucky he didn't use the pointed end." He stopped smiling. "I would've."

Adam remained quiet as he paid the bill and they left the restaurant. He avoided the bodies without commenting. While they stood by the SUV, Selene prepared to talk about what would happen when they got home. But Adam seemed distracted. "Is there anything you want to tell me?" *Please don't say you've changed your mind about us.*

He shook his head. "Something weird happened back there."

Other than thug bodies scattered around the vehicle? "I don't think so. At least I don't remember anything." Fine, so she was so lost in her thoughts of him that a pack of werewolves could've invaded, eaten everyone in the place, and then left, and she wouldn't have noticed.

"No, something definitely happened to me in that place."

His intensity bothered her. "Explain."

He massaged a spot between his eyes. "I don't remember a word of what I said to Jude."

CHAPTER SIXTEEN

ADAM'S THOUGHTS RACED. WHO HAD messed with his mind? Because someone definitely had. Memory loss wasn't one of his weaknesses. Fin? Not likely. What would be his motive? This whole meeting with Jude was Fin's idea, so why would he interfere? Dave or Ace? Fin protected the Eleven from mental attacks. Dave seemed completely human, or near enough not to make a difference. Adam still didn't sense any power in Ace. Kione? Who knew what the dark prince could really do? Sure, he had the power, but where was his motive?

That left Selene. Again, not likely. Her power was something else entirely. But there was always the chance she had concealed a talent for mind manipulating. He pushed the thought away. No, he wouldn't go there. Then *who*?

"You think someone made you forget." Selene didn't sound disbelieving.

"I think someone got to all of us." He speared each of them with a hard stare.

Selene looked thoughtful. "I don't usually lose focus during an important meeting."

Ace shrugged. "I don't think anyone did anything to me. I always go for my music when I'm bored." He paused. "But I wasn't bored, so . . ." He didn't finish.

"And I didn't call for help." Dave seemed offended by

the idea. "I could've taken care of that bunch by myself."

"I heard you calling." Kione narrowed his eyes. "Or thought I did. Another point: what made those men think they could rob Dave in a lighted area right here in front of the place where someone could come out of the restaurant or pull into the lot and see them? They could've found easier prey somewhere else."

"A distraction?" It made sense to Adam. "It got you out of the place while I was speaking with Jude." Maybe whoever was controlling their thoughts didn't feel confident fooling around with Kione's mind for long. Adam certainly wouldn't have.

As though on cue, one of the fallen men groaned.

Adam crouched beside him. He was young, tough-looking, and unlucky tonight. The man opened his eyes and looked around. What he saw mustn't have comforted him because he immediately started babbling. "It wasn't my idea. Hammer said we had to rob him, that something told him the guy had more cash than we'd ever seen before. None of us say no to Hammer, not if we want to live." He stared up at Adam, panic in his eyes. "Did someone call the cops?"

"I did." Dave grinned at him.

"I'd run if I were you." Adam straightened. He didn't wait to see what the man would do before climbing into the SUV next to where Selene was already seated. Dave, Kione, and Ace followed suit. They pulled out of the lot just as the first police car arrived.

"Where to?" Dave glanced in the rearview mirror.

"Just drive for a moment. I have to think." *About the press of her body warm against his side.* Adam forced his mind onto a different path. Connecting with Jude came first.

"What happens next?" Ace leaned past Selene to look at Adam.

"I talk to Fin." He closed his eyes and reached for the

mental link to his boss. Nobody answered. Strange. Fin could usually sense when something wasn't right with any of them. He opened his eyes. Selene watched him, her hand resting on his thigh. *Don't think about her hand.* He was only partially successful. Funny how an adrenaline rush heightened all his senses. "He must be busy. I'll try the old-fashioned way." He pulled out his phone. It rang for long enough to worry Adam. Finally, Fin answered.

"Now isn't a good time."

Adam frowned. Fin sounded exhausted. "Sorry, but this can't wait." When Fin didn't comment, Adam told him everything.

Adam could almost feel Fin gathering his strength. What was going on with their leader?

"I'm in the middle of a mental conference call with Zero and Seir. We're discussing the coming apocalypse. We can't agree on the details yet, but we all know it'll be amazing." His bitterness seeped through the phone, belying his sarcastic tone. "Find Jude. I'll get back to you as soon as I finish here." And then he was gone.

Adam met the curious stares of everyone except for Kione. "Fin is handling something else." He could understand a mental battle with Zero, but what was Seir doing in the middle of it? Sure, he was Fin's brother, but definitely not a favorite one. "We have to find Jude. Kione, do you know where he is?"

Kione shook his head. "I've done a scan. Nothing. He's either dead or hidden in a way I can't detect him." His tone said that didn't happen often.

"Just freaking great." Adam found Jude's contact info and sent a text telling the vampire to meet them at the condo or at least let them know where he was. Then he shoved the phone into his pocket. "If we're lucky— and we haven't been so far—he'll get back to us right away. If he doesn't . . ." Adam didn't want to think about that. "While we're waiting to hear from him, let's head to Adam's place. I need something from there." The *old* Adam, the one who's skin he wore, but never comfortably. He might have to answer to the vampire lord's name and rule over his nation of bloodsuckers, but he refused to live where the stench of death leaked from the walls and the screams from his victims still echoed in dark corners. A place of slaughter. New Adam was a predator, but the blood he'd spilled was honest, won in a hunt for food or to protect himself and others, not in a massacre merely for the pleasure of watching people die.

He'd never think that way. Okay, so *maybe* never. Adam considered the joy he'd get from watching vampires die. Oh, yes, vengeance still burned in his heart.

Selene leaned close. Adam breathed in the scent of warm female and desire. She drove away thoughts of the condo, its previous owner, and vengeance. He wanted her. *Not now. Later.* That was a promise.

She spoke quietly. "I have a bad feeling about this. Other than Zero—who was busy with Fin—I don't know who would have the power to manipulate so many thoughts at once."

Dave had good hearing. "Maybe this Six you're looking for is that strong." He didn't elaborate.

No one answered him. Adam figured none of them wanted to imagine that kind of mental muscle tramping around in their brains. On a personal level, who or what would be strong enough to override Fin's protection of the Eleven?

They remained silent for the rest of the ride to the condo. The quiet continued in the fancy elevator that took them up to the penthouse. Adam studied his face in the mirrored wall. That face didn't feel like home, maybe it never would. But which one of his many faces would he choose if he could? He didn't have to think about it long. Rap's face, the one that branded him as belonging with his brothers, the one that made him feel most human.

Selene finally spoke as they entered Adam's home.

"Jude didn't get in touch with you." She stated the obvious.

"Nothing." Adam wandered to the wall of windows that looked out across San Diego. Not much of a view now in the darkness with mist rolling in from the Pacific. He shivered. Unlikely that someone was walking across his grave, but you never knew. He shook himself out of his mood and then strode toward the office. He noted that Ace was heading into the kitchen while Kione stood alert by the door. Dave threw himself onto the couch and grabbed the remote.

Selene followed Adam. "Why are we here?"

Adam sat at the massive, elaborately carved desk the vampire lord had felt suited his greatness. He pulled out the top drawer. There. He took out the large book containing names and contact information for every vampire in North America. He opened it. "We need to find out if Jude passed on my message to anyone. I have to start calling clan members in the area until I reach someone who knows something. And one of them will."

Selene leaned over his shoulder; her cheek brushed his. He sucked in his breath. *Ignore it.*

"Why isn't all that information in a computer file?" She sounded horrified. "In this day and age, he actually kept that stuff in a book?"

Adam shrugged. "The old bloodsucker didn't trust technology. Jude probably has everything on his computer, but I don't know where Jude lives. He hasn't shared his address with Fin. I don't blame him. It doesn't pay to trust anyone completely." She tensed beside him. He didn't rush to assure her that he no longer suspected her. Because on some level he still had a few doubts. But he chose to bury them beneath his joy in her company and his desire.

She didn't ask why the new and improved Adam kept the book in this desk instead of at his place where he could get to it fast, or why *he* didn't have the info on a thumb drive. He was glad she didn't. Because he would then have to explain how he didn't want to drag around one more anchor tethering him to the vampire world. He had too many already. Adam left the book open while he spent a few moments rooting through the drawers.

"What're you looking for?"

"Pieces of myself." The truth. If he was doomed to live forever as Adam the vampire lord, then he wanted to know as much about himself as possible. Lots of clues were often buried at the bottom of desk drawers.

He found nothing but a tourist guide to San Diego. Couldn't hurt to take a look. Fin still didn't have a clue where the big confrontation with Six would happen other than knowing there was a catchy tune involved. "Hold onto this." Adam handed it to Selene before going back to the book of names.

Kione chose that moment to join them. "I can't find Jude, but if you merely want a vampire, I sense two coming up in the elevator."

They all ran from the office. Friends or enemies? After tonight's weirdness, Adam wouldn't take any chances. He scanned the room. The condo was open concept, lots of room and super high ceilings. Large enough for his beast to maneuver. Unfortunately, two vampires didn't warrant the appearance of his raptor. He couldn't deny his disappointment.

Selene looked relaxed, but Adam knew she was ready to create any number of horrors capable of destroying a horde of vampires.

Ace came from the kitchen, still clutching a bag of chips. "What's going on?"

"Vampires coming." Selene didn't take her attention from the door.

Ace's eyes widened, but he didn't retreat to safety.

Dave interrupted his TV-watching long enough to stand and draw a wicked-looking knife.

Kione waited in the middle of the room facing the door, ready to meet the vampires eye to eye.

Someone rang the bell. Adam decided that wasn't the way hostiles usually asked to enter.

Adam shouted, "Name?"

"Miguel. I have Xavier with me. Jude sent us."

Kione concentrated on the door for a moment before turning to nod at Adam. "They're who they say they are."

Adam made a note to question the fae prince about the strength of his mental powers, because he sure hadn't seemed to strain himself IDing the two vampires. But he still didn't see a motive for Kione messing with all of them. Adam strode to the door and flung it open before quickly stepping aside.

The vampires walked in and then froze when they saw the others.

The smaller of the two vampires spoke first. "Hey, looks like you're ready for trouble." His gaze skittered around the room, cataloging the various threats. He stopped when he reached Adam. "Yo, we're friendly, boss. I'm Miguel. Don't think we ever met personally, but I've seen you in action before. This here's Xavier." He nodded at the big vampire behind him.

Xavier was made to live in shadow—dark jacket, dark face, dark eyes, dark smile. "Jude told us to hurry over because you wouldn't be here long." His gaze slid to Dave's knife.

Adam nodded. "Let's hear his message."

Miguel looked a little nervous. "Why's everyone so tense? You're making me jumpy."

Xavier didn't comment, but his eyes gleamed with

anticipation. "Do you have a reason to distrust us?"

"Not yet." Adam forced himself to relax a little. On the couch, Dave returned to watching an old movie. Selene smiled, and Kione looked away. But if Miguel and Xavier were smart, they wouldn't be fooled into thinking everyone was now ripe for an attack.

Xavier stepped in front of Miguel. "I'm Jude's second in command while he's here in San Diego. He wants you to know that our people have already grabbed some of the ones on your list." He reached into his jacket pocket to pull out a paper and then handed it to Adam.

Grabbed them? Adam glanced at the list. They were screwed. The vampires had nabbed the mayor of San Diego along with a bunch of city officials. They even had a military officer. "How did you move so fast?"

Miguel looked as proud as a vampire could look. "We're just that good, boss."

Selene moved to Adam's side so she could look at the list. "What did you do with the people you grabbed?"

Miguel blinked. "Just what the boss asked us to do. We took them to Jude."

Ace asked the obvious question. "What did Jude do with them?"

Xavier answered for Miguel. He stared at Adam. "Why all the questions when you're the one who gave the orders?"

Adam met the vampire's gaze. "Humor us." He could feel his fury building. Since the moment Fin returned his soul to Adam's body, he'd held it together, shoved the rage deep inside. But this was all too much. He hated vampires. They'd killed him, ripped his head from his body. Fin had taken his soul from the ruined body and shoved it into a vampire. Sure, he was glad to be alive, but not in a vampire's body. Now, he was supposed to rule them, make like he was one of them. He, Wanted. To. Kill. All. Of. Them. He sucked in air. *Breathe, breathe.*

Xavier shrugged. "Jude took all of them to . . ." The pause dragged on until the vampire's expression turned puzzled. "I can't remember." For the first time, he seemed upset. He turned to Miguel. "Where did he take them?"

Miguel's expression was blank. "I don't know. Why don't I know?" His voice rose in panic.

Adam's anger was bubbling and building, but he kept his voice calm. "Do you remember where you met with Jude?"

"No." Xavier's voice was sharp with controlled rage. "Why can't we remember?"

Selene answered. "Someone has made you forget. The same someone has manipulated all of our memories." She glanced at Adam, her expression troubled.

Adam could almost see waves of darkness enfolding Xavier. The vampire's anger was a living thing.

"Who?" Xavier curled his upper lip back exposing fangs that gave new meaning to deadly.

Adam understood Xavier's fury. But at least the vampire's anger was controlled. Adam's wasn't. It was wild and irrational. There was no reason for his impending explosion. *Yes, there is. It's been coming for a long time.* Tonight's events had simply lit the fuse.

Still on the couch, Dave snorted his opinion of the question. "If we knew that, we wouldn't be jawing with you. We'd be out killing his ass."

Kill, kill, kill. Adam liked the rhythm of the words repeating over and over in his head. He tried to disconnect from what was happening in his mind. He had to concentrate on what was happening now.

Adam was about to speak when Fin stopped him. *"I've been listening in. We all need to talk. That means the two vampires as well. Crow too. He's on his way. I want all of you to meet me at our restaurant. I won't chance everyone coming to my condo. And where you are now is too exposed. A lot of people know about it. Whoever is responsible for tonight doesn't* seem to want the people on my list dead right now. We might be able to free them if we can find Jude." Fin paused. "Are you okay?" His voice was sharp.

No, he couldn't allow Fin to realize what was happening. Fin had a safe room in every condo he bought where any of the Eleven who lost control were kept until they pulled themselves together. He *wouldn't* be locked up. "Sure, I'm fine." He held his breath as he waited to see if Fin would buy it.

"Good. I'll see you soon." And then Fin was gone.

When he looked up, everyone was staring at him. "Fin was talking. He wants all of us to meet with him. Now." Adam was holding everything together with duct tape and a will that was a long way from iron. He met Xavier's gaze. "That means you and Miguel as well." He transferred his attention to Dave. "Drive everyone to Fin's restaurant."

Selene's gaze sharpened. "You sound as though you're not coming with us."

He held back a curse. She saw too much. He forced himself to look relaxed, to smile. "I'll be along as soon as I can. I have something I want to do here before I leave."

She returned his smile. "Then I'll keep you company."

No! "That won't be necessary." Had he put the right amount of coldness into his voice to convince her to leave. He'd rather hurt her feelings than let her see what happened when his personal volcano erupted.

"Oh, but I want to." Her smile might be sweet, but her eyes were ice chips.

"I think I'll stay with you and Selene." Kione's tone said that Adam may as well accept his presence because he wasn't changing his mind.

Adam didn't argue. He just had to get the rest of them out of here right now. "Great. Dave, get moving with everyone else. Tell Fin I'll be there as soon as I can." As soon as he'd exhausted his supply of rage. And if Selene and Kione tried to stop him? No, he wouldn't hurt Selene. He didn't know if he even had the power to injure Kione.

Miguel shuffled his feet. "I don't think I want to talk to this Fin. Jude is the only one who meets with him." He looked at Xavier for support.

But Xavier was all too eager. "We're going. I've wanted to see this person that scares everyone." He turned to Adam. "Since Jude's out of the picture right now, I guess I report to you. Here's my info if you need to get in touch with me." He pulled a card from his pocket.

Bemused, Adam watched all of them leave. Vampires carried business cards? Then he was alone with Selene and Kione.

Selene returned from closing the door behind Dave and the others. She gazed up at Adam. "What's the real reason you wanted to stay behind."

Kione said nothing. He waited.

Adam knew his smile was merely a baring of his teeth. "This is what's been building since I woke up in a vampire's body."

Selene said nothing.

Adam tried to make it clearer. "I'm angry. I've stored it for way too long. I have to get rid of it before I see Fin. He'd know as soon as he looked at me that I was ready to explode."

"Anger management wouldn't help?"

Adam could hear the amusement in Kione's voice. He wondered how long the fae prince would be laughing

"The Eleven have their own version of anger management." Adam watched Selene's expression.

She didn't look scared or horrified. She simply nodded. "Then let's do it, raptor."

CHAPTER SEVENTEEN

———

SELENE POUNDED DOWN THE STAIRS behind Adam. He'd refused to step into the elevator because, "The walls will close in on me, and I'll have to kick them down." She didn't think kicking down elevator walls would be a winning strategy. So, they ran down and down and down.

She glanced behind her. Kione had disappeared. Not a surprise. Selene couldn't imagine him running down all of these steps when he had another option. No doubt he had many options.

They reached the bottom of the stairs—her huffing and puffing, him casting deadly glares around the condo lobby. Luckily, the area was deserted.

"Now what?" Maybe she should've clarified what he had in mind before agreeing to accompany him. *You know you'd stay with him no matter what. If he needs help, you'll supply it.*

The smile he turned on her was his beast's smile. There was nothing of the Adam she knew in it. A weaker— or smarter—person would've bailed on him right about then.

"Now, I run until I fall down. Exhaustion is a great cure for crazy rage." He noticed her expression. "You'll just have to keep up." His tone said she'd probably drop out of the chase quickly.

"No destination in mind?" She'd address the keeping-up problem in a moment.

"Crow's house. If he's in the meeting with Fin, he should be gone for a while. I'll hunker down there until he comes home and then find another place to hide until Fin's temper cools." He shrugged. "Not that I care what he thinks. But I don't want to end up in the safe room."

"You're just going to race across San Diego in raptor form?"

"Yes."

"And you don't see a problem with that?"

"It's late, dark, and I run fast. I see no problem. There won't be many people around." He strode to the door, yanked it open, and stepped into the darkened street.

She followed him. "You won't lose control and kill someone?" That was her greatest fear. If it seemed like it might happen, she'd have to stop him.

He turned his gaze that already had lost its human warmth on her. "I won't kill anyone." But his expression said he'd be fighting the temptation. "Unless it's a vampire. Then all bets are off."

Or if her father showed up. Selene was certain Adam hadn't forgotten who besides the vampires had killed him

He glanced around. "At least we've lost the prince. Good."

Then he changed. The biggest raptor to ever walk the earth—over two thousand pounds of concentrated rage—stared down at her. She gulped. *Don't hesitate. Don't even think. Just do it.*

"Crouch down. I'm buying into this nightmare." Selene thought he might just race off without her, but then he lowered himself so she could scramble onto his back. She planted herself right behind his shoulders. When she'd ridden him the first time, he'd flattened out and the ride had been almost comfortable. Then she held her breath.

They flew, or at least it felt like that. She could feel his powerful muscles moving beneath her as she leaned forward to lessen wind resistance. She wanted to bottle this feeling of glorious freedom as he ran through the darkened streets. Selene didn't miss the surreal quality of the whole thing. She longed to shout for everyone to come out of their houses to see one of Earth's ancient predators with an alien on his back right there in the middle of their very modern city.

Gradually, she felt the tension ease in his body, knew exactly when the rage was replaced with the joy of his beast's freedom. Selene drew in a deep breath of crisp air and then released all of her doubts, her worries about Zero, her father, and Six. Everything. And just gave herself over to the night, the darkness, and the thrill of the moment.

Suddenly, a dog raced from a side street. It was a big fierce dog, probably one that thought of itself as a top dog, and rightly so. It was loud and threatening. It barked and growled loud enough to alert the entire block that enemies were loose in the night. Not good.

Adam's beast was having none of that. It stopped and rose up on its back legs. Uh-oh. Selene hung on to keep from sliding off the raptor's back end. No, they didn't need a battle for supremacy in the middle of one of San Diego's peaceful streets. The raptor screamed its challenge.

Selene didn't know quite how to describe that cry. It was sort of like a ticked-off eagle magnified to angry-elephant volume. Guaranteed to wake the neighborhood.

Luckily, the dog had great survival skills. It took one look at the raptor's mouthful of teeth and forgot all about being top dog. It disappeared into the darkness. Unluckily, some people had heard the raptor's challenge.

A man stumbled out of his townhome wearing only his pjs and holding a phone.

"Get us out of here!" She pounded on the raptor's neck.

"Now! Fin will kill both of us if that man gets a picture."

Adam's beast paused only long enough to scream at the man before taking off. Selene breathed a huge sigh of relief as the man dropped his phone, leaped back into his home, and slammed the door shut. The raptor turned the corner at the end of the block just as other people leaned out of windows to see what was going on.

The rest of the journey passed in a blur. When the raptor stopped in front of Crow's house, Selene slid from its back. Her legs were jelly as she stumbled to the curb and collapsed. She put her head in her hands. "That was a rush, but let's not do it again soon."

When she glanced up, Adam was standing watching her. Kione stood beside him.

Adam grinned. "I thought it was fun. Did you see the look on that guy's face when I screamed at him? Priceless."

Selene just stared at him.

Adam's grin faded. "At least it took the edge off my need to kill a bunch of my fanged subjects." He looked at Kione. "Where were you?"

Kione pointed up. "On the roofs. I could see if any danger was coming better from there."

Selene shifted her attention to the prince. "Didn't see the dog, though, did you?"

Kione shrugged. "I don't count dogs as threats. Besides, that dog wasn't too smart. He barked before he looked." Then he changed the subject. "Let's get off the street. Crow's not home, so I opened his door."

She didn't ask whether he'd picked the lock, kicked it in, or used magic. She didn't care. Once inside, Kione flipped the hall light on and then turned to study them.

"What?" Adam kept his gaze fixed on the prince's chest. No eye contact.

"You'll be safe from Fin here. I assume that's who you don't want to face."

Adam's expression hardened. "I was losing control. Now I'm fine. I'm staying here until Fin has a chance to realize I'm not running across San Diego slaughtering half the population, that he doesn't have to lock me in his safe room. This is strategic planning on my part, not cowardice."

"I didn't think it was. I apologize if you had that impression." Kione walked to the door. "I'm heading out to take care of a few personal chores."

"You're not going to Fin's meeting? She didn't particularly care where he went. All she wanted was to have Adam to herself.

Kione waved the question away. "Why would I? He'll be trying to find out who manipulated our memories. That means rooting around in our minds. No one gets into my brain." His expression promised that when he found the one responsible for tonight's invasion, the person would not die happy. "Keep an ear open for Crow. Make sure he doesn't catch you searching his place, because I know that's what you intend. It's what I would do."

Adam's smile was slow and sensual. "You have no idea what I intend."

Selene felt that smile as a slide of heat across her breasts, spreading until it curled low in her stomach. Wow, some smile.

Kione grinned. "Have fun." He left, closing the door quietly behind him.

Adam interrupted her thoughts. "I figured all that exercise would make me hungry. I was wrong." He swung her to face him. His eyes burned with how much he starved for something a lot different than a ham sandwich.

Desire pushed everything from her mind. Forget about searching the place. "I can't wait any longer." Selene reached up to slide her fingers along the side of his face.

His skin was smooth beneath her touch, and she could feel his jaw tighten as she touched him.

"We have to find somewhere secure in case Crow gets home early." He grabbed her hand and pulled her down the hall.

They passed the living-room that still starred in Selene's nightmares. Adam opened each door as they came to it. She caught sight of a bedroom with a comforter on the bed that could have doubled as a Picasso painting. But, hey, it was a bed with a soft mattress. Adam closed the door and moved on.

She tugged on his hand, stopping him. "What was wrong with that room?"

"Not safe enough." He was almost grinding his teeth with impatience.

She thought for a moment. "I want the master bed-room."

They didn't find any more bedrooms on the ground floor, so they climbed the steps. They hit pay dirt when Adam opened the door to the room at the head of the stairs. Selene squeezed past him to enter first. She ignored the inviting bed with its glittery comforter and instead looked for the closet. One door led to a bathroom—yes, with multicolored towels, shiny gold floor tiles, and a glass shower with embedded gold crystals. When she turned on the lights above the sink, they blazed like a rainbow in need of a tranq. She controlled the instinct to shield her eyes against the glare.

"What're you searching for?" Adam stood by the window staring down.

She might've just thought he was scoping out escape possibilities but for the way his hands gripped the window sill with white-knuckled intensity. Any minute now they'd both lose it.

"The closet." Only one door remained, so she yanked it open. If this wasn't the closet, she was ready to pull

Adam over to that bed, tear his clothes from his body, and mount him. Crow? Let him come home. He could wait in the hallway until they finished.

"Why not one of the closets in the other rooms?" He raised the window and leaned out.

"Because the master bedroom closet is the one most likely to be a walk-in." She flipped the light switch beside the closet and then took a good look. "Holy—" There was absolutely no word she could pair with "Holy" that would do justice to Crow's wardrobe. It was the color apocalypse—brilliant, shiny, sparkly, and every over-the-top adjective she could recall. It was all hanging in this closet.

"Is that what you were looking for?"

"Yep." She heard Adam close the window. Quickly, she yanked a bunch of coats from their hangers and dropped them onto the floor. Then she turned off the light. No need to blind him when he entered. Then she sat on them. Luckily, the closet was large enough to make for comfortable love-making. She waited.

"Don't turn on the light," she warned as he entered.

He didn't argue. As he closed the door, the darkness wrapped around him. The sliver of light shining under the door cast him as a black silhouette, dangerous in a way that chilled her body but heated her blood. Her want was a physical pain, a yearning that tightened her chest and turned her breathing into a harsh rasp.

Then he dropped to his knees in front of her. Now she could see all of him—his powerful body, the tangled glory of dark hair that fell forward as he leaned toward her, the shine of his eyes where the violence of his raptor still lingered, and his full, sensual mouth that made decadent promises. She believed those promises, oh how she believed. She breathed in the scent of him, not the city odor, but the remembrance of forest, desert, and shadowed places.

He stripped off his shirt, baring hard muscles rippling beneath warm, smooth skin. She reached out to run her fingertips across his chest. Yes. Warm. And too tempting to resist. He sucked in his breath at her touch even as he fumbled in his pocket.

Selene placed her hand over his. "Don't. Females of my race are fertile only once a year. This isn't it." She sensed his relief.

"This won't be the way I imagined, Selene. I wanted it slow, building and building until everything exploded." He shook his head. "Not a great description." He got rid of his jeans.

Selene laughed. "The only thing you got right was the explosion." She pulled off her jacket and yanked her top over her head. "Maybe the other stuff will come later, but right now I want it fast, hard, and absolutely delicious. The explosion is the whipped cream on top. No time for the cherry."

His soft laughter was an invitation to play. He reached behind her to unclip her bra, and when it slid off, he cupped her breasts in his large palms. "Do you need help with the rest of your clothes?"

"Nope." Four letters were about all she could manage right now. She had no memory of slipping out of her boots, and everything else below her waist. Then they were wrapped in each other's arms.

Selene ran her hands over his back, a back strong enough to bear every one of her many weaknesses and worries. No, she'd never use him that way. She leaned into all that heat and naked male flesh.

And when he claimed her lips, she was ready. The rest of him might be excitingly hard, but his mouth? It was soft, pliant, and tasted of everything that made her happy right now. She'd learned long ago to grab all the "happy" you could in life because there wasn't a lot of it floating around.

With a gasp, he broke the kiss, and then pulled her down to the coats. She lay on her back staring up at him. He was all dark predator doubled—raptor and vampire. And she loved it. The danger. The incredible sensual realness of him.

She spread her legs and he knelt between them. Then he leaned over her, his hands on both sides of her head to brace himself. Selene skimmed her fingers over the hard muscles in his arms. And while his hands were occupied, she continued her exploration. When she gently pinched his nipple, he shuddered before kneeling up and grasping her roving hand.

"Be careful how you tempt me, witch. I'm holding onto my control by a worn thread."

She laughed at him. "Oh, a challenge." Selene pulled her hand free and continued her journey south. She splayed her palm over his ridged stomach, memorizing the velvet over steel feel of his skin.

"Two can play that game." And if his voice shook a little, his hands didn't.

He bent over her again, his hair a silken slide across her skin as he touched his tongue to the sensitive skin behind her ear. Then he whispered, "I have to touch you. Now."

True to his word, he kissed the base of her jaw, her collarbone, and finally her breast. Selene arched her back to gain maximum contact. She moaned as he slid his tongue over her nipple before closing his lips around it. And when he gently nipped it as she had done to him, she shoved her fist against her mouth to keep from crying out.

Men had done this before, but it hadn't felt like this, hadn't moved something inside her that had lain dormant forever.

It had to stop. When he touched her, she wanted to let go—of her control, of her thoughts with their warning lights flashing. All she wanted to do was *feel*.

If he was as close to the edge as she was, Selene knew one way to shove him over. She slipped her hand between his thighs and cupped his balls. He shuddered and leaned back on his heels.

"Too fast," he ground out.

"Not fast enough," she countered.

She drew the tips of her nails across them before closing her fingers around his cock. The heat pooling low in her stomach promised *soon.* Closing her eyes, she pumped her hand up and down, up and down his shaft, not thinking, simply glorying in the heat, the texture, the *readiness* of him.

With a muttered curse, he pulled away from her. She opened her eyes as he slid his hands under her bottom then lifted her to meet his lips. Selene had no time to prepare, to brace herself, before he kissed the inside of her thigh as he worked his way up to *there.* There where the center of all sensation hid—waiting, hopeful.

Adam put his mouth on her. He glided his tongue back and forth, back and forth across that one tiny piece of flesh.

She screamed. "Now!"

This time he listened to her.

He lowered her, just enough. And when she felt the nudge of his cock pressing there, she rose to meet him.

After that, who the hell knew. She turned liquid to become all sensation—the push and then stretching as he entered her, the friction, the clenching of her muscles that longed to hold him inside her forever, the unspeakable feeling of total fulness and completion.

Then he moved, and she realized completion hadn't quite arrived yet. He pressed into her and withdrew almost, *almost* all the way out. Repeat torture over and over again until she knew something earth changing was within reach. The pressure built and built until she was about to shatter into a million shards of something amazing.

Seemingly from a distance, she heard herself crying out instructions that were totally not in her usual voice. "Harder, deeper, faster, faster! Yes, yes, yesss!"

And with her last "yesss," *it* came. All thought disappeared in a searing flash of pain/pleasure. Too intense to bear. As every nerve in her body sang the song of its people, she clenched around the moment and tried to hold it within her. But it was too powerful to be contained. It escaped her in a long moan. Yes, this time it *was* completion.

She lay, breathing hard, listening to the mad pounding of her heart, and wondered when they could do it again. Adam collapsed beside her, and she realized—selfish witch that she was—that she hadn't given a thought to whether he'd enjoyed—weak word—the moment as much as she had.

Finally, when her body was once again almost calm and her heartbeat had slowed, she turned her head to gaze at him. "That was absolutely amazing." *Was it good for you, too?* Now she was thinking in clichés.

He didn't turn his head to look at her. "Remember when you promised you'd explain why the word 'useful' bothered you?"

Selene tensed, her euphoria leaking away. Why was he bringing this up now when everything had been . . . No, not perfect, because she'd learned the hard way never to be too positive, too hopeful. Maybe their lovemaking had just been "useful" to him, a way to finish off an invigorating run with a little sex. She sat up and then pulled on the closest piece of clothing, his shirt—it was chilly in this dumb closet—and started to scramble to her feet.

Adam grabbed her arm to pull her back down. "Listen to me." He rolled partially on top of her to hold her in place.

Her traitorous body responded to the pressure. Even suspecting that this had all been false on his part, she still wanted him. She tried for cold and calm. "So, this was a useful moment for you, a way to keep from getting bored in a closet? No problem. It was pretty good sex. Now it's over."

His muttered curse said what he thought of that. "What I want to say is that I would never call you useful. The right word is . . ." He took a deep breath. "Essential. I think you're becoming essential to me."

Selene hoped her expression wasn't as dopey as it felt. She tried to stop grinning. After all, "essential" wasn't the most romantic word. Lots of things were essential—air, food, shelter. But the gleam in his eyes and the way his heart pounded as he pressed against her said he meant *really* essential. And face it, "essential" was a big step up from "useful."

Selene knew that later when she had her head together and had detached it from her naïve emotions, she'd find ways to reject what she felt now. That's the way she lived her life. Never hope for too much because too much never panned out. If her expectations were low, her disappointments were low, too.

She opened her mouth to say something appropriate just as someone yanked the closet door open.

CHAPTER EIGHTEEN

$$\longleftarrow\!\!\!\blacktriangleright$$

ADAM LEAPED UP TO FACE the danger. He expected Crow. An embarrassing situation, but not deadly now that the bird worked for Fin. And just in case Crow got aggressive, Adam could disable him long enough for them to make their escape.

Instead, he met the hard gaze of someone else, a man he knew. No, not *knew*, had seen through Fin's memory— tall, short blond hair, cold blue eyes, and what looked like a perpetual sneer. This was the man who had killed him in that first life, who had led the forces that destroyed everything and everyone he'd cared about. Violence coiled hot and eager in him, flame with a superheated blue center. Its name was Revenge, and it burned away all sane thoughts.

The man peered around Adam at Selene. "Please tell me I don't have to challenge him to avenge your honor. It would all be so tiresome." His voice oozed sarcasm. The gaze he turned on Adam was filled with contempt. "Maybe you should get dressed before we talk." He held a sword pointed at Adam's gut.

The bastard didn't recognize him. Of course, he wouldn't. Adam didn't look like the person he'd slaughtered millennia ago. Not that he'd even remember all his victims. "I don't need clothes to tear you apart."

The man's eyes widened in alarm for a moment and

then they narrowed. "I've killed bigger monsters than you on a thousand planets in this galaxy. And all I need is this to get rid of you, vampire. Or is it raptor?" He raised the sword point a few inches until it was exactly where it needed to be to pierce Adam's heart with one thrust.

Adam watched his eyes and saw the tiny flicker right before the killer tried to skewer him. The guy was fast, but he'd underestimated Adam's speed. Adam jumped aside even as he tried to judge the size of the room. Too small. His raptor might be able to cram itself inside, but he wouldn't be able to maneuver. He tried to push past his killing rage long enough to *think*.

Adam didn't get the chance to figure out his next move before Selene charged from the closet wearing only his shirt. It reached mid-thigh and did great things for her long, long legs. Her only accessory was the gun she held pointed at her father.

Her father. In his fury, Adam had forgotten that fact. What would she have done if he'd ripped the head off her loving dad? Neither of them looked loving right now, though. Her father's eyes blazed with fury, and Selene's smile was a frigid twist of her lips. Nothing remained of the warm sensual woman of a few minutes ago.

"Get out of the way, Selenetaya. And for heaven's sake, don't you have anything else to wear besides *his* shirt?"

"Concerned about my style choices, Father? How comforting." She didn't try to hide her scorn. "Put away the sword and leave."

Her father's laughter mocked Selene. "You won't shoot me. Not over him." His expression said Adam was expendable, just another monster among a thousand others.

Selene widened her eyes. "Of course, I'll shoot you. Oh, and isn't it time to diversify your weapons? Swords are so last century."

"This sword has served me well." His sneer said it was

the only real weapon in the room. "And I taught you, so I'd bet your sword is in that closet along with your clothes."

"I brought a knife tonight. Less obvious." She shrugged. "But guns are more efficient. Now, go away."

Adam wanted to stop the conversation by pushing Selene aside so he could end her father forever. That's what he *should* do, what the spirits of all those murdered by this animal demanded. *Kill him, kill him.* The words pounded at Adam until he wanted to scream and let the madness take him. She couldn't blame a crazy man if he punched through the murderer's chest, yanked out his heart, and then tossed it in the trash can. Maybe Adam wouldn't find a heart in that body. It wouldn't surprise him.

Adam couldn't fool himself, though. He wasn't insane. And the man—jeez, Adam didn't even know his name—*was* her father. The choice was clear—kill him and serve justice or allow him to live for his daughter's sake. *Kill!* His beast was definite on this point. Adam's vampire doubled down on the idea. His inner bloodsucker yearned to tear out the bastard's throat and bathe in his blood. Could he do it in front of Selene? At that moment, he knew he was lost, because the answer was no. The man would live. He imagined the condemnation in the eyes of a million dead people.

Unaware of Adam's inner battle, Selene and her father still talked.

She held the gun steady. "Why're you even here?"

Her father's expression showed frustration as he clenched and unclenched his hand around his sword. "Now that Crow isn't working for Frost anymore, the boss wanted me to take a look around to see if the bird had anything that didn't belong to him. The thief would steal the rings off your fingers if he had the chance."

For the first time, Selene's lips tipped up in a real smile.

"Good luck with finding anything in this place."

Her father's expression softened a little. "I could still use you, Selenetaya. Frost would be willing to take you back. Your talents are wasted on *this*." He glared at Adam. "Come with me and be on the winning side."

Adam couldn't allow that to pass unanswered. "The only reason you're leaving this room alive is because of your daughter. Go now while you have the chance."

"I can fight my own battles, raptor." Selene sent a ferocious stare his way. "Keep out of this."

Adam blinked. What? No one spoke to him that way. Then he smiled. She had the heart of a raptor. He love . . . admired her for that. His breath deserted him as he firmly denied what he'd almost thought. It was a mental blip brought on by stress. He sucked in a deep breath. There. He was fine again.

"He's right, though, Father. Leave. I'm not coming back to you no matter how 'useful' I'd be."

Adam could see the guy thinking about his chances of getting past Selene for another shot at his enemy. The dumbass was arrogant enough to think just because he had a sword that he had the advantage. *Bring it.* Selene couldn't blame Adam if he killed her father while defending himself. *No, but she'd always remember.* There was no way to win.

Then Adam realized the fool was really going to attempt it. He readied himself as he saw the man tense. Then . . .

Selene shot her father. Coldly. Calmly. "Get. Out."

Wow. The woman didn't mess around. Adam hoped the sound of the gun didn't bring unwanted visitors.

Her father paled as he stared down at his bleeding hand. His sword lay on the floor. Clumsily, he reached for it with his uninjured hand while pressing the bleeding one against his chest. "This isn't over, daughter." His expression was filled with rage mixed with grudging respect.

He sent Adam one more hate-filled glance before backing out of the room.

Adam waited until he heard the slam of the front door before relaxing. He looked at Selene. "Are you okay?"

"Sure." But she was trembling.

He raced through his possible reactions. Act cool because she wouldn't want him to make a big deal of it. Get her mind off her father by mentioning that they should clean up and leave before Crow got home. But in the end, he went with his heart.

Stepping in front of her, he gently removed the gun from her hand, tossed it onto the bed, and then wrapped his arms around her. He pressed her head against his chest. "Thanks for saving my butt."

He felt her shaky laughter. "It's such a great butt."

Speaking of butts, Adam suddenly remembered how almost-bare hers was. He slid his hands down her warm body and then reached beneath his shirt she wore to cup her amazing bottom—firm, round, and perfect.

She tipped back her head and reached up to grab his hair so she could pull his head down to her level. Then she covered his lips with hers for a long, drugging kiss.

He was ready to drag her back to that closet, but when she broke the kiss, all she had to offer was a common-sense suggestion. Major buzz kill.

"We need to get dressed and go. If we revisit the closet scene,"—her gaze was hot with how much she'd enjoy that scene—"Crow could surprise us like my father did."

He merely nodded. She was right, but that didn't stop him from wanting to break a few pieces of furniture to express his disappointment.

They dressed in silence. Adam would love to have known what she was thinking, but he wasn't certain her mind was a safe place to be right now." He helped her hang up all of Crow's coats before heading downstairs.

Adam stopped at the bottom of the steps. "We don't have a ride home."

Selene shrugged. "Can't you run us home?" She wandered over to the living room doorway and then stepped in to turn on the nearest lamp. "I want to take one more look at this. Maybe the first time was just a stress-induced hallucination." She looked around. "Nope. And it doesn't get any better the second time you see it." She paused to simply stare.

He joined her to see what had caught her interest. "Has Crow added something new and horrific?"

She pointed. "I didn't get a good look at it last time."

"The Christmas tree?" Adam somehow couldn't connect Crow-the-killer with this small tree resting on a corner table. But he supposed even bad guys had sentimental moments. The tree was in shadow, and he'd been focused on other things during his first visit, so he hadn't paid much attention to it. He watched her walk over to take a closer look.

Selene turned to smile at him. "He's decorated it with jewelry. I wonder if some of this belonged to Zero?" She reached out to touch a sparkling bracelet.

Adam noted the wistful quality of her smile. "Do you want a tree?"

"No." She seemed pretty definite about that. But she didn't look at him when she said it.

"Why not?" He wondered if Fin would buy a tree. Probably not. The boss was too focused on his ongoing battle with Zero. Besides, how could anyone get excited about Christmas when humanity might not even exist by the twenty-fifth? A depressing thought.

Selene didn't answer for a moment. She just continued to touch the decorations. Finally, she sighed and turned from the tree. "I ignore holidays—all those special celebrations on the hundreds of worlds I've visited." She headed for the couch and then sat gingerly on it. "Holidays bind you to a place, make you feel emotions for it, maybe enough to start you thinking about staying." She met his gaze. "And I never stay." She patted the couch beside her.

Adam ignored her invite in favor of taking a closer look at the tree. He took a moment to plug in the lights and then went over to turn off the lamp. Selene's exclamation of pleasure made it worthwhile.

"So pretty. Come over here and sit for a few minutes. Enjoy the tree. We'll hear Crow coming before he gets inside. His birds are noisy creatures." She returned to an earlier topic. "So, can you run us home?"

"I've already taken a chance by allowing my raptor to run through the city once tonight. What if the police had spotted me, or someone with a camera had gotten lucky? Fin was able to cover up our fight with Crow, but people might not be so ready to believe him the next time. No, I won't do that again. How about if you create a gigantic bird to fly both of us there? Birds are harder to spot at night."

She shook her head. "Too worn out. Making love in a closet is exhausting. But in an amazing way. That means no giant birds to fly us home."

Her smile was just plain sexy. It made him want to strip and take her on . . . He glanced around, his gaze returning to the couch. He grimaced. Okay, he'd even make love to her on that sparkly couch. Yeah, he'd be picking sequins out of his butt for a week, but she was worth it.

Since they wouldn't be making love, though, he'd pass on the torture couch. The rest of the chairs weren't any better, so he sat on the floor. At least the velvet was soft. He patted the carpet beside him, and she joined him. He pulled her against his side, and then they watched the tree with its soothing lights. He felt his stress, rage, and general urge to rain death on his enemies fade away. Beside him, Selene relaxed into his side.

"A tree is a good thing." Adam decided he'd remember that.

She sighed. "I could sit here all night watching it, but we have to leave."

He nodded. "Right. Crow." Adam pulled his phone from his jacket pocket. "I'll text Utah and Tor. See if the meeting is over and if one of them can pick us up."

As he was texting, she rose to pull out the cord. Once on that side of the room, she stopped in front of a CD player with a bunch of CDs piled on top of it. Selene looked through them, and then chose a few to take with her. While she was on her way back to him, Tor returned his text.

Adam stood. "The meeting is just getting out now. Tor is on his way. He'll meet us at the corner. If Crow flies, he'll be here before my brother, so I'd suggest we get out now."

Selene followed him down the hallway and out the door. They walked to the end of the block where they stood in the shadows of some tall hedges. She didn't say anything.

The silence bothered him. It spoke of second thoughts and maybe-I-shouldn't-haves. Adam was tempted to start a conversation, but he wasn't sure he wanted to know her thoughts right now, especially if she had regrets. He certainly didn't.

Together they watched Crow come in for a landing on his lawn and then go inside while his murder settled onto a large Ficus tree. Just as Crow closed his door, Tor drove up in the black sedan he favored for stealth missions. Meg sat beside him. Adam wondered if Fin knew Tor had ditched his human driver.

Adam and Selene piled into the back seat, and Tor peeled away from the curb. He glanced in the rearview mirror and grinned at them.

"Fin is ticked off, brother. What were you thinking?" Tor seemed to be enjoying himself.

Adam glared. "Thanks for the sympathy, *brother*. I was feeling twitchy tonight. And you know how Fin likes to toss us into his cooling-off room at the first hint we might go all prehistoric on the local population." Not that Adam could really fault the boss.

Meg turned to stare at Selene, her eyes dark with worry. "Are you okay?"

Evidently the thought of her sister spending time with a twitchy raptor concerned her. Adam could assure her that Selene had no problem handling his twitchiness. He squashed his need to smile at thoughts of that closet.

Selene waved Meg's worry away. "I'm fine. Adam just thought we should stay off Fin's radar for a little while until his raptor calmed down. Since Crow was in the meeting, we figured his house would do for a brief lay-over." She grinned at the last word and cast Adam a sly glance. "It was fun. Crow has some great closets."

Meg looked confused, but recovered quickly. "I wish you wouldn't put yourself in danger so much."

Tor reached over to pat her knee. "Don't preach, cup-cake. It won't do any good." He laughed. "I know. Rap—" He met his brother's eyes in the mirror. "Sorry, bro, but you'll always be Rap to me. I can't stomach this Adam crap." He didn't wait for Adam's reaction. "Anyway, Rap was always hardheaded. And I get the feeling so is your sister."

"Glad you've come to terms with that." Adam studied the back of Meg's head. Same blonde hair, but Meg's was long and wavy while Selene's was short and choppy. He had a perfect memory of Selene's eyes. They were a clear, winter-sky blue—beautiful but with a cool sharpness to them. He hadn't noticed Meg's eyes, but he thought they were soft. He shook his head. Just soft. Tor evidently liked their softness.

Then there was Selene's scar. That scar should bother him, but it didn't. It went with the woman. She was strong without any vanity. Someone to stand beside a man and . . . *Stop that*. He didn't need anyone standing beside him other than his brothers.

Selene didn't react to Tor's assessment. She seemed caught up in her own thoughts. No one had much to say for the rest of the ride.

When Tor pulled up in the apartment's parking lot, he turned to look at Adam. "Will you guys be okay?"

Selene didn't waste any time opening her door. "I'm not the one who has to worry." She glanced at Adam. "Will Fin hunt you down here?"

Adam opened his own door. "No, I think I'm safe for the night. I closed my mental connection so he can't read my thoughts, but he can still sense my emotions. He'll know I've stepped back off the ledge for now."

Tor nodded. "Great." Then he grinned. "Try to stay off that ledge at least until tomorrow. Utah will want to have a heart-to-heart with you about flying under Fin's radar."

Adam did a mental eye-roll. Utah had hatched a few minutes before Tor and him, so he figured he had the right to big-brother status. He climbed from the car, closed the door, and then watched until Tor drove away.

He followed Selene and found her standing in front of her door waiting for him. She seemed a little nervous, unusual for her.

"Would you like to come in for a few minutes?"

"Sure." Adam answered quickly. He didn't want to give her a chance to rethink her invite.

He followed her inside and then settled on her couch, which was *not* covered in sequins. He loved her couch.

"Could I get you something to drink?" She didn't meet his gaze as she took off her jacket and tossed it over a chair in the small dining area.

"I'm fine." Adam watched her set the CDs she'd taken

from Crow's place on the table. "Won't Crow miss those?"

She shrugged as she turned toward him. "I think we could carry off half of everything he has in that house, and he wouldn't notice. I'll return them after I've made copies."

Adam laughed as he took off his own jacket. He patted the seat beside him. "Let's talk for a while." What came after for-a-while hung between them.

She sighed as she settled in close to him. He put his arm across her shoulders and pulled her close.

He decided to defuse the sexual tension thrumming between them, at least for a few minutes. She needed breathing room. "Will you teach me how to fight with a sword? You were right about diversifying your weapons. I've depended solely on my raptor for too long. Your father could've gotten lucky tonight, and I would've been dead." Adam felt her relax a little.

"Sure." She turned to offer him a grin brimming with sexy wickedness. "But you have to do something first before you pick up a sword."

He waited for it.

"A wise Earth man named Confucius said, 'Never give a sword to a man who can't dance.' Can you dance, raptor?" Her expression said she'd bet he couldn't.

"Hey, not fair. Raptors don't dance." He wore his most outraged expression. "Besides, if dancing is supposed to teach me agility and speed, I already have those. I don't need to dance." Adam tried to push aside his feeling of inadequacy. This was just one more human skill he lacked. No way did he want to make a fool of himself in front of her.

She leaned closer. He tried not to get sidetracked by her scent, a mixture of cinnamon and vanilla. "You smell like a cookie."

"What?" Selene look startled for a moment. Then she just looked irritated. "So maybe I ate a few cookies today." She swept her hand down her body, brushing off imaginary crumbs. "Stop changing the subject."

He could've told her it was the sexiest thing he'd smelled since he awoke into this world. But he wouldn't, because she was still lecturing him.

"All living things dance in their own way, Adam. And dancing isn't just to gain agility and speed." Her lips tipped up, hinting at those other things dancing taught. "Did raptors have a mating dance? Hmm?" Selene's expression said she knew exactly what she was doing by throwing those words into the mix.

Adam didn't feel strong enough to answer without dragging her into her bedroom to demonstrate his own version of a mating dance. He merely nodded.

"Great. I picked up a few dance music CDs from Crow's place." Selene rose, dragging him with her. She led him into her bedroom, into her bed.

"Tomorrow we dance, raptor. But tonight . . ." She turned off the light.

CHAPTER NINETEEN

—◆—

THE TEXT-MESSAGE PING WOKE HER. Selene rolled over onto the spot where Adam had lain. He was gone, but his memory wasn't. She longed to curl around those mental images like a contented cat and just immerse herself in yesterday—the closet and last night in this bed. She opened one eye.

Late afternoon sun shone weakly through the blinds. Sighing, she opened the other eye. The not-so-amazing recollections wouldn't be denied—her father, mind invasions, and kidnappings by vampires.

The text. Selene reached for her phone on the nightstand. The message was from Adam. Lucky for him, his vampire shared the house with a raptor and human, so he could be out and about during the day. Unlucky for him, he was in Fin's office. The boss wanted her there, too. Fin was angry.

Just great. Way to begin the day. Selene crawled out of bed and stumbled to the bathroom for a quick shower. After doing a minimum of makeup and hair stuff so she wouldn't horrify any humans she met, she pulled on jeans, a top, and her boots. Before throwing on her jacket, she called Dave.

Then she listened to him gripe all the way to Fin's condo about how he'd had to make *separate* trips to the same place with each of them. Selene was so worried about what Fin would say she didn't even bother to apologize. She left Dave still grumbling to himself as she got out of the car and headed up to face Fin's quietly terrifying fury, one of his most effective weapons.

Shen answered the door. Fin's assistant didn't smile. "He's in a bad mood today. Zero gave him another migraine this morning, and he's ready to bite someone."

Selene wondered if Shen meant that literally. "I'll keep it in mind." She followed him back to Fin's office.

Shen knocked quietly and then opened the door for her. She stepped inside.

Fin sat behind his massive desk with the huge windows behind him. Night falling over San Diego made an ominous backdrop to the Eleven's leader. He hadn't switched on any lights. She got it. Migraine.

Adam already sat in one of the chairs facing Fin's desk. He turned as Selene entered. She didn't need the warning in his eyes to remind her to tread carefully. She took the seat beside him, but she didn't even pretend to relax. Fin was a predator, a *silent* predator, the worst kind. She didn't fear the Crows of the world, the ones that attacked with noise and bluster. It was the killer who lurked in shadow, watching with cold eyes until the exact right moment to pounce. *Fin.*

Fin's silver eyes gleamed in the fading light. He smiled. Selene didn't believe that smile.

He focused on Adam. "You ran from me last night. Did you think you could escape?"

Adam met Fin's gaze. He didn't show weakness in the face of his boss's unspoken threat. "I wasn't running from you. I was trying to wear myself out enough to control my rage. It worked. My beast is calm."

Selene doubted his beast was ever calm, but at least he'd shoved it back into its cage. Fin couldn't ask for much more from any of his men considering that, as far as they knew, a few months ago they'd been dinosaurs. Even thinking that felt weird.

Fin's smile didn't change. "Don't ever run from me again."

His warning hung heavy, coating the room with all the horrors he could unleash on Adam's disobedient head.

Adam didn't flinch, his gaze didn't waver. Selene was proud of him. She didn't know if she could do the same faced with Fin's immense power.

"I'll make sure I inform you next time I have to subdue my beast." Adam's tone bordered on sarcastic.

She waited, breathless, to see if Fin would rip Adam's soul from his body and then deposit it in a more submissive one.

The moment dragged out as Fin decided his fate. "I'll let it go this time because I have more important things to deal with than you." His smile faded. "If I'd wanted your presence badly enough, though, I would've come for you. You wouldn't have enjoyed that."

"No, I wouldn't." Adam drew in a deep breath as he placed his hand on Selene's knee.

Selene shared his relief, but she still wasn't ready to relax. "What did you learn from the meeting?"

Fin rubbed a spot between his eyes before replying. "Nothing. I reached into their minds, but whoever was there before me buried the memories too deeply." He focused on Adam. "Of course, I only had five at the meeting. But I don't think I'd have any different outcome from you." He looked at Selene. "How about you?"

"No." She raised every one of her mental defenses, listened as they clanged into place. "Don't mess with my mind." Selene knew Fin could rip her walls down, but she was counting on his not wanting to antagonize her. After all, she was his weapon against Six.

Fin seemed to think about it before nodding. "My headache is ramping up again, and I don't need to help it along by putting any effort into searching through your thoughts."

She barely had time to celebrate before he continued. "Tell me what happened after Adam ran his rage into the ground."

Selene thought about lying, but then abandoned the idea. "The truth?" She didn't glance at Adam to see if he agreed. "We stopped at Crow's house." She told Fin about almost everything. Except for the closet. The closet was none of Fin's business." When she'd finished, Selene waited for Fin's reaction.

He leaned back in his chair and closed his eyes. "Keep in touch with your father. We'll find a use for him."

Selene couldn't help it. She smiled. At some point down the road, she'd have to tell her father that he'd been "useful." He'd hate it, and she'd love it. Maybe that made her small and mean, but after a lifetime of usefulness, it would feel glorious to pin the tag on someone as worthy as her father.

"Kione didn't show up either. What happened to him?" Fin stared at Adam from beneath lowered lids.

Adam shrugged. "Don't know. He said he had some things to take care of."

Selene wondered about those things and whether they had anything to do with Six or Zero.

Fin leaned forward, suddenly alert. "I'd like to know what he was doing." He pointed at Adam. "Find out."

"Sure. No problem." Adam didn't try to hide his sarcasm this time.

Fin chose not to notice. "Here's what else I need both of you to do. Find Jude and the others the vampires kidnapped. If we're lucky, they'll still be alive. Take Xavier with you. He's a good man." He paused for a moment. "We still need to track down that music along with the place I saw in my vision." Fin shook his head. "I have some of the others searching, but it's tough when you don't have any idea where to look."

Selene bit her lip to keep from making a snarky comment about the list of miracles Fin was expecting from them.

Fin leaned back again and closed his eyes. "Now go. Tell Shen to get me some pills. I can't think with this headache."

They rose and hurried toward the door before Fin could come up with something else for them to do. But Selene couldn't resist one more question. "Doesn't Zero ever give you a break?"

Fin shook his head. "He's relentless. Always has been."

As she closed the office door behind them, Selene was struck again by the way Fin spoke of Frost. There was a familiarity there she wanted to explore. Then she dismissed it. They had enough to worry about.

Adam left the building without texting Dave to pick them up. "I'm hungry. There's a little place around the corner. We can walk there. I don't want Dave tagging along with us."

"I agree."

She didn't say anything else until they were tucked into a booth in the restaurant. After getting her burger and fries, she broached the subject she'd been thinking about on the short walk from the condo. "You have precognition, right?" She held up her hand. "Don't ask. I know because Zero does a thorough investigation of all his nonhuman allies. He passes on helpful info he finds to his people."

Adam's expression said he had a real need to lay a raptor sized hurting on Zero. "The vampire me does, occasionally. It's unpredictable. I don't depend on it."

Selene frowned. "Power is power. You either have it or you don't. You practice, don't you?"

Adam paused with his own burger—four rare beef

patties with bacon and cheese—halfway to his mouth. "Practice? How would I do that?"

"You mentally block all outer distractions and then open your mind to the future." She couldn't believe he hadn't tried to enhance his gift.

Adam finished off half his burger before answering. "I never thought about trying to improve." He shrugged. "Didn't know I could." He glanced away from her.

She knew what he was thinking. "You don't have to like the vampires to take advantage of their powers."

He said nothing, just kept eating.

Selene forced herself not to comment on the food he was inhaling. It must be his raptor's metabolism. In some ways, he had the best of all worlds. He could enjoy a glass of warm blood after doing serious damage to a fast-food meal. "You should at least try. I'll help you. If we expect to find Jude and the place Fin saw in his vision, we'll need all the help we can get."

By the time she'd eaten half her meal, he'd devoured all of his burger and fries. Now he was almost done with the milkshake he'd ordered. She made him wait as she ate the rest of her burger and drank her ice tea. As soon as she finished, he rose to lead her outside.

"Where do we go now?" He raised his face to the night sky and took a deep breath. "I love the night."

"We go back to your apartment."

"What?" He forgot about the night. "Why?"

"To practice your gift. We need you to *see* where Jude is." She glanced up and down the street before scanning the rooftops and sky.

Adam recognized her caution and applauded it. Her plan to free his precognition? Not so much. First, what she wanted would take more than one session. Not that he believed it would work. Besides, they didn't have time. Six might decide to kill Jude and the other captives at any moment. If they weren't already dead. Second, the only thing he'd be able to concentrate on in his apartment was her. His beast and he agreed on that.

"By the time I've practiced enough to see Jude, he might be dead." The hard truth.

"I can't believe you won't give this a chance." Her expression said he was a hardheaded jerk.

"I'm just being practical."

She narrowed her eyes and studied him through the slits—assessing, looking for weaknesses. "I bet I can help you to control your power in one hour."

Adam perked up. "What do I win if you can't?" He knew what he wanted.

"Nothing."

He frowned. Not the right answer. "And if you win?"

"If I win? I get your body tonight to use as I see fit." Her gaze turned smoky and sensual.

Adam didn't know whether to be angry or aroused. "Why play games?"

She pulled out her phone to text Dave. "Because this way I know we'll be working for the same outcome." Selene cast him a piercing glance. "At least I hope we will."

He brooded over that until Dave showed up. She was right. He'd bust his butt to see that she won. And because he didn't like being tricked, he remained silent on the drive home.

Unfortunately, Dave didn't seem to notice.

"Been listening to the news. Lots of bad stuff happening all over the world. The prime minister of Canada just went missing. Riots in some places. Unexplained explosions. Strange-creature sightings."

"Looks as though Zero is starting the party early," Selene murmured.

Dave didn't hear her. "You need to talk to that Ace boy."

Selene frowned. "Why?"

Their driver shrugged. "I watched him at that meeting last night. He was pale and sweating up a storm. Looked as though he was about to keel over. You might want to see if he's sick."

Selene nodded as she reached for her phone. Adam only half listened as she spoke with Ace.

After a short conversation, she put her phone away. "He says he's okay. But there's something not quite right." She stared out at the night. "I can't put my finger on it, but he doesn't sound normal."

Adam didn't comment, and she didn't offer any other explanation. He shoved Ace to the end of his worry list while he tried to figure out where in San Diego Six—he assumed Six was the culprit—had stashed his victims.

By the time they reached his apartment, Adam's thoughts were focused on something very different.

He followed her into his living room and silently cheered when she only stopped long enough to peel off her jacket and then fling it onto his couch. He did the same before following her into the bedroom. *Yes.* His hopes soared. But his elation faded when she only sank onto his one chair and crossed those long, long legs.

She gestured toward the bed. "Lay down."

He raised one brow even as he obeyed her. "Alone?"

Selene gazed at him from lowered lids. She slowly slid her tongue across her full lower lip, leaving it shining and so tempting he hurt just thinking about . . . No. He gathered what remained of his fleeing brain cells and waited.

She smiled, a lifting of her lips that tempted and promised at the same time. "Do you want me to win, Adam?"

"Absolutely." He watched her glide her fingers over the arm of her chair and imagined those fingers caressing every inch of his body.

"Then I suppose you need to put lots of effort into making it happen."

She drew out the word 'lots' until it became a sexual

tease, an emotional stroke of her warm tongue the length of his cock.

Adam had only two choices. Allow her to drive him insane until he was willing to do anything for her or . . . get mad. He chose anger. "I don't like cheap games, Selene."

Her gaze went from sexy siren to hard-eyed warrior. "There's nothing cheap about it. We're playing for high stakes—the lives of a bunch of people. And I'll do what needs to be done. Are you ready for your lesson?"

It didn't take her long to switch roles. The idea bothered Adam. Was her whole desire for him only an act? He thought about last night. No, that had been real. "Sure. What do you want me to do?" If he sounded grouchy, too bad.

"Great." She transferred from the chair to the side of his bed.

Adam scooted over so none of him was touching any of her. No contact meant no distraction. He'd made a deal, so he'd give this whole dumb lesson his best effort. When he failed, she wouldn't have any complaints. *And you'll sleep alone tonight.* "What now?"

"Close your eyes."

All he saw behind his closed lids was her smooth, bare body. He forced himself to think of kale. He hated kale.

"Focus inward. Go to the place where you keep your vampire power locked up. Visualize it."

Adam could do this. Blocking out all sound, along with all of his other senses, he pictured a cage right next to the one that held his beast. This cage trapped old Adam's power behind bars forged by his will. Gleaming eyes stared out at him.

"Now, I want you to release your vampire power." Her quiet voice was his only tether to his life outside.

He met the thing's hungry gaze as he stood in front of the cage door. Hesitantly, he reached for the lock. Then he stopped. Did he really want this? Did he want to free this part of bloodsucker Adam, a part he might not be able to control? *You hate everything vampire. Don't accept anything more from the creature Adam was.* He shoved the thought aside. If Selene was prepared to do what needed doing, then so was he.

A collar and leash. He visualized them and they appeared hanging on a hook by the door. He took them down and then again reached for the door.

He opened it.

Adam just managed to fling the collar around the thing's neck before it exploded from the cage, a creature of fire and fury. It dragged him in its wake as he tried to gain control. But he couldn't, because suddenly he *"saw."* The body he wore had been witness to the original owner's savagery and cruelty. Flashes of scenes piled one on top of another that went on, and on, and on. Too many, too powerful. They ripped at his soul leaving agony behind. He gripped his head between his hands and screamed. "Stop them!"

Then he heard her voice. Felt her touch. An anchor in his sea of chaos.

"This is a part of you. It will listen to your commands. Put it back. Now." She stroked his cheek as she spoke.

Her touch, her warmth, gave him courage. His eyes still squeezed shut, Adam grabbed the leash and yanked. His vampire power turned its massive head to stare at him. For a moment they stood frozen while Adam fought with every ounce of his will, and his power fought back. *"You'll return to your cage, but before you do, show me where Jude is."*

The picture flashed for a millisecond and then was gone. Adam watched his power disappear into its cage. He mentally locked it. Then he opened his eyes.

"I know where Jude is."

CHAPTER TWENTY

A DAM SAT UP. "MAYBE NOT exactly *know.*" He rubbed the back of his neck. "But I have a clue." He met Selene's gaze. "Why don't these dumb visions ever just give you the freaking answer? They have to tease—a tune, part of a fence, a name."

Selene could barely contain her impatience. "*What* name?"

"Yankee Jim Robinson." Adam swung his feet to the floor and strode into the living room with Selene right behind him. He sat on the couch as he pulled his phone from his jacket pocket and did a search for Yankee Jim Robinson.

She hung over his shoulder. Selene whooped when she saw the results. "He was hanged on the spot where the Whaley House was built. What's the Whaley House?"

Adam took a minute to read before answering. "It was the Whaley family home. Two-stories. The first brick building in California. Original structure built in 1857. Lots of paranormal activity. It's supposed to be the most haunted house in America. Tourists love it."

"We're about to add to the legend." She took the phone from him to check on the house's location. "Looks as though we'll be going back to Old Town."

"See what else you can find out about the house while

I contact Fin." He leaned back against the couch and closed his eyes. "I hope his mind is free."

"Why not just call him?" She found another site with the history of the house.

"This is too important. He might ignore a call if he's messing with Zero. But me pounding on his mental door will get his attention."

Selene dropped onto the couch beside him to read. Silence settled over the room. It lasted a while, so she assumed he'd connected with Fin. Finally, he opened his eyes and then stood.

She returned his phone. "What's the plan?"

"We wait here until the rest of our team arrives. And while we're waiting, *we* come up with a plan." He paced, stopping for a moment to gaze out the window.

"Is Fin part of our team?"

"No. He didn't give me any names, but I didn't get the feeling he'd be joining us."

Now that just irritated Selene. "It seems to me the boss is doing a lot of delegating. If Six is involved, shouldn't Fin be front and center in the rescue mission?"

"I guess he trusts us to be able to handle this." He met her gaze. "I'm proud he thinks we're capable of freeing those people."

Selene figured he had a lot more confidence in his glorious leader's decisions than she did. She'd experienced enough stupid moves by supposedly smart bosses to give her a healthy skepticism when it came to those in power. She decided to keep that thought to herself. "This is what I know about the house. It's a California historical landmark, so try not to destroy it. The house has an interesting history, but I'll let you read about that on your own. Here are the important details. It has a bunch of rooms tourists tramp through each day, so we won't find our kidnap victims there. As far as I can see, there's no basement. So maybe we're simply supposed to pick up a clue somewhere in the house. Or maybe our people are in one of the outbuildings." She watched him pace.

"I don't know. I doubt they'd be in any nearby buildings. I think the vision wants us to focus on the house." He raked fingers through his hair. "What kind of vision only gives someone one name? Would it hurt to add a small picture, maybe an arrow pointing in the right direction?"

She had no answer for that, so she continued. "Supposedly, lots of spirits call the place home. Yankee Jim Robinson and a daughter, Violet, seem to be mentioned the most, but according to witnesses there're a lot more family members who still hang around."

"Great. Maybe we can find a chatty one who'll know where Jude is stashed." Adam's sarcasm was laced with real anger. "I'll text Dave so he'll be ready as soon as the others get here."

She considered her next move while Adam texted. There was no reason she couldn't enjoy this brief time alone with him. She waited for him to finish. "We're wasting time. We need a plan." Selene patted the spot beside her. *Close* beside her.

He smiled. "I enjoy an intimate working relationship with my partner." He sat next to her and then wrapped his arm around her waist to pull her close. "Let's collaborate."

Selene's thoughts scattered in the sensual gale generated by his touch. Maybe she should've patted a spot a little farther away. Foolishly, she'd thought she was strong enough to control her emotions near him while still enjoying his closeness. He leaned in to nip her earlobe and then kiss the sensitive spot right behind her ear. Fine, so maybe control was overrated. She tried to formulate a plan for Jude's rescue, but it kept morphing into one for their next lovemaking event. She smiled. And with him, it would definitely be an *event*.

Whoa! Just in time, her common sense asserted itself. You'd think after so many years she would've remembered how often sex between team members—not her, never her—had led to disaster. She'd always been too smart for this. Obviously, her brain cells had scattered along with her thoughts.

She pulled away from his grip, rose, and then stalked over to a chair. Selene felt his surprise, but she refused to meet his gaze. If she saw his face, she might weaken. "Plans. First, we go in after the last night tour at about 10:30. If there're any stragglers, I think a hair-raising haunting by Yankee Jim Robinson looking for vengeance over his totally unfair hanging might empty the place." Selene didn't give him a chance to comment. "I saw a photo of him on one of the sites. I can create him. Then—"

"Be quiet, Selene."

Surprised, she looked at him.

His lips turned up in the beginning of a rueful smile. "I understand. As much as I enjoy knowing I distract you, it works both ways. I can't concentrate near you. So, no togetherness." His smile widened. "For now."

She refused to comment on that. "I don't think there's much more planning we can do until we get to the scene. Let's just wait until the others arrive."

"It's a good plan. I like the haunting." Silence filled the empty space between them. Selene mourned the time spent in useless quiet when they could instead be . . . She caught herself. *Focus.* Someone had to say something.

"It didn't take you long to master your power. How did that happen?"

Adam didn't answer as he rose to walk into the small kitchen. He opened the fridge. "Want something to drink?" He grabbed a Coke.

"No thanks." She watched him return to the couch and wondered if he intended to answer at all.

After taking a swig from the bottle, he met her gaze. "I

have a vampire's body, a vampire's instincts, and a vampire's talents. I hate all of them. Not that I consciously rejected Adam's precog gift." He shrugged. "I just never thought about it, never considered using it at all. Subconsciously, I guess I was saying, 'Absolutely not,' to everything I got from Adam. When I purposely reached for the power, it was there waiting—eager and ready to give me dumb clues."

Now that she had a conversation going, she didn't want to let it go. Selene knew so little about him. "Do you have any plans for when this apocalypse thing is over?" She tossed him a casual look that said the tension between them meant nothing to her. She lied well.

Adam practically lit up. "I want to be a paleontologist."

She blinked. "What?"

"A scientist who studies fossil records. Who could know more about dinos than me?" He leaned forward. "I have it all planned. Fin said he'd pay my college fees."

Selene blurted the first thing that came into her mind. "Do you really think there'll be much civilization left after December 21? Maybe 2012 will be the end."

"I don't know. But that doesn't stop me from thinking about what I want to do with the rest of my life. Everyone needs something to give them hope. What about you?"

He studied her, and she straightened as she put on a mock warrior's face. "In my world, each citizen hones their gift to a sharpened point and uses it to commit mighty deeds." Selene thought of her father. "Mostly evil." She winced. Her sarcasm had come off a little too close to the truth. "I only have one skill. How much demand do you think there'll be for me?"

His expression softened, and she drew in her breath at what she imagined she saw in his eyes. She couldn't be weak, though. Selene had always tried to face the truth as she saw it. "Besides, why should I plan for a future on

Earth when Zero has made it clear as soon as the Winter Solstice passes, we'll have to leave the planet until the next time period ends."

He frowned. "I'd forgotten you were one of his." Then his expression cleared. "But you're not one anymore. The rules might not apply to you."

He was venturing into areas she didn't want to think about now—the end of everything, leaving him. But she couldn't stop her mouth. "Will you hold my hand when the clock strikes eleven-eleven? A tug of war between you and whatever power is trying to banish me would lack dignity, but still . . ."

His eyes turned feral as he bared his fangs. "I would win."

She never got a chance to respond because suddenly three people appeared in the middle of the room. Selene leaped to her feet.

"Seir! What the hell?" Adam stood.

Seir grinned. "This was faster than driving. Is Dave ready?" He held the hands of two others.

"Good to see you, Xavier." Adam nodded at Jude's second.

Xavier batted Seir's hand aside as he returned Adam's nod. "I'm in the mood to rip out some throats." Jude's second glared at Seir. "Next time I'll walk."

Fin's brother showed no regret. "Some enjoy the trip, some don't."

Shen also dropped Seir's hand. "Fin said we're headed for the Whaley House to rescue Jude and the others."

Selene pulled on her jacket. "Adam saw the name of a man who was hanged where the Whaley House stands today." She paused to study Shen. "Why did Fin send you? No offense, but I didn't picture you in this sort of role."

He smiled. "You tagged me as the mild-mannered assistant type?" Shen held up his hand. "I understand why you'd think that. No offense taken. But I have my talents."

Shen's smile turned sly and ruthless. It warned that she might have misjudged him. Too late she realized Fin wouldn't keep anyone around who wasn't dangerous. "What are you?"

Seir laughed. "Stop being coy, Shen." He turned to Selene. "Our mild-mannered assistant here shifts into one of the most venomous snakes in existence. One bite and it's all over."

Shen tried to look humble. "You're lucky to have friends in low places. I can slither into spots where you couldn't go. And if you need an advance spy, I'm your man. No one will see me if I choose not to be seen."

Selene decided not to ruin Shen's moment of triumph by mentioning that she could create any number of creatures that might be able to slither just as well as he could. She admitted, though, that her creations would never have the knowledge and experience he brought to the job.

Adam slapped Shen on the back. "You're perfect for what we need." He shrugged into his jacket. "Let's go. Dave will be waiting."

Once on the road, Adam tried to focus on what they might meet at the Whaley House. But his thoughts kept returning to the woman beside him. Of course, her hand resting on his thigh didn't help matters. By the time they reached the Whaley House, her palm would've seared a permanent image into his flesh. When tonight was finally over, he hoped they'd have some serious conversations along with lots of sexy interludes.

Too soon, though, she removed her hand to root for her phone. She attempted a call.

"Hmm, I can't reach Ace." Selene shifted uneasily as she put her phone back into her pocket. "I promised myself that I'd keep a closer eye on him, but he's never available. We'll have to talk about that."

Adam refocused. "He's a boy. He's probably hitting all the night spots in San Diego."

She still looked troubled. "Zero wants him back. Ace needs to be careful or else someone will snatch him off the street and deliver him to Zero. He doesn't have any power to defend himself."

Shen commented, "What makes you think he doesn't have power?"

"Zero told me, and even Ace admitted it. His lack of power always bothered him." She turned to gaze past Adam at the dark streets. "I've wondered why Zero kept him around. My ex-boss isn't known for being soft-hearted when it comes to his recruits."

Shen thought about it for a moment. "Strange." He shrugged. "Fin doesn't seem to mind having him around. Maybe he just feels bad for the boy."

Adam doubted Fin had a sympathetic bone in his body. Then he remembered his brothers telling him how Fin had mourned *his* death. Maybe the boss *could* actually feel sorry for someone. The idea boggled the mind. Adam forgot about Fin, though, as Dave parked on a side street.

"Give a shout if you need me to get you out fast." He patted the dash. "Me and Betty Sue here will come flying."

Xavier cast him a disbelieving stare. "Betty Sue?"

Dave didn't flinch from the vampire's contempt. "Had a girlfriend once by that name. Great performance with low maintenance. Just like this baby."

Xavier didn't comment as they climbed out. He turned to Adam and Selene. "Now what?"

"We check to see if anyone's still in the house." Adam nodded at Selene. "The place should be empty, but if it's not, Selene will convince them to leave."

Seir looked bored. "Why don't I just pick up the house, turn it upside down, and shake it until they all fall out? I call it my saltshaker move."

Selene didn't honor the suggestion with an answer. She checked her watch. "Okay, let's do some sneaking and peeking." She ghosted around the corner and the others followed her.

They all stopped in the deep shadows where they had a clear view of the house. Adam moved closer to her. "I can see a faint light. Not a lamp. And I saw someone move past a window."

She frowned. "I wonder why?"

Shen spoke up. "Why don't I go in so I can find the breaker box. I'll throw all the switches so no one can turn on the lights when you do your Yankee Jim imperson-ation. Nothing like darkness and a ghost to scare the crap out of people."

Seir added his thought on the house. "Anyone taking a tour of a haunted house this late is hoping to see a spirit. And ghosts don't dance in bright lights. Ergo the only light in there will be a small one, maybe a candle the guide is carrying."

She nodded. "Great. While you're getting situated, I'll send in a small spy to see what I can see."

"The rest of us will hunt for any lookouts Six posted. Because there's no way he'd just stash his loot and then abandon it." Xavier faded into the night.

Seir glanced at Adam. "I'll let you take down any look-outs that Xavier misses. I'm going to look at those nearby buildings to make sure none of our people are in them." He disappeared before anyone could comment.

Adam remained next to Selene. "I'll stay here while you conjure your flying spy." He'd seen her do it before, but the way she formed her creations from her very essence still made him marvel.

She shooed him away. "Don't try to keep me safe. I've kept my heart beating for longer than you've lived, rap-tor."

He tried to think of an excuse not to leave her side,

but couldn't think of any she'd accept, certainly not the truth, that he wanted to protect her from harm with a fierceness that almost embarrassed him. Tor would laugh. Utah would understand.

"I'll leave you to it then." Adam slipped into the darkness, hugging the shadows while keeping an eye out for anything unusual. If by chance Jude and the others were really being held here, he had to be prepared for a possible confrontation with Six. Not something Adam relished considering how easily Six manipulated minds.

He crept around the corner of the Whaley house, looking not only for sentries but also random strangers walking along the street. The place was too open, too easy for ordinary people to see anything strange taking place. That made him think this whole thing was a waste of time. Six wouldn't be able to hide a bunch of people here without being noticed.

As he got his first view of the back of the house, he caught a glimpse of a snake slithering around the far corner. Shen looking for an opening. He couldn't see Selene at all. As for Xavier, Adam didn't expect to see him. The vampire would be in the wind. And forget about Seir. Fin's brother would handle things in his own way. "His own way" was what worried Adam, though. Seir wasn't a lowkey guy.

Time seemed to drag while Adam crept through the darkness searching for lookouts. He watched a few cars pass and one or two pedestrians walking the street. Luckily, the shops had closed for the night and the area was emptying.

He was just thinking about heading back to Selene when something dropped onto him from the house's roof.

Instinct took over as he hit the ground and rolled, taking the assailant with him. He saw a flash of fangs and gleaming black eyes. *Vampire.* Adam flung the lighter vampire from him as he leaped to his feet and lunged. His attacker rose quickly to meet his charge. The dance of death began. His beast cheered him on from the sidelines.

Kill. The need to bury his fangs in his enemy's throat, to taste the blood as it slid down his throat hot and rich threatened to overwhelm him. Some part of him, still sane and aware, recognized that old Adam was in control now. This wasn't like his beast that killed to protect and nourish itself, to survive. Okay, so his beast did enjoy taking down its prey. But this was a selfish need to inflict pain, to watch death dim the other's eyes, to revel in slaughter for its own sake. Anticipation of a kill reached fever pitch as he pinned the smaller vampire to the ground.

In his last moment before blood lust took him completely, Adam realized this was probably one of his own people. Under Six's power? Most likely. The truth hit with a cold blast of reason. "I'm Adam, lord of all vampires in this country." Wow, he sounded like an arrogant jerk. "Tell me the name of the one who dares challenge me." Adam breathed hard as he denied himself the kill.

The other vampire stopped struggling. "Lord Adam? I didn't recognize you." Fear quivered in his voice.

Adam figured he had the right to end him just for that stupid answer. "How could you not recognize me?" Almost every vampire—other than Jude and his people—lived in fear of old Adam.

"I'm Martin." A hesitation. "And I don't know why I didn't recognize you."

Of course, he didn't. Six had been busy tinkering with lots of minds. Adam allowed Martin to rise. "What are your orders?"

Close up, Martin looked young and pretty clueless right now. He cast Adam a puzzled look. "Jude said you wanted us to guard this place. We weren't to allow anyone in except for the tourists who came for the tours."

"Did Jude share why you were to do this?" How much

time had passed? He had to get back to Selene. But first he needed a few more answers from Martin.

The other vampire's eyes widened and the first sign of panic appeared in them. "No. I mean . . ." He clasped his head between his hands as though if he let go it would bounce away over the lawn. "I don't know why I'm doing any of this. I can't remember anything—not what happened yesterday, not why I'm here." He looked up at Adam. "Why?"

Adam had a very real fear the young vampire would come apart right in front of him. "It's okay, Martin. I'm changing your orders."

"But, I don't know, I can't—"

Adam grabbed him by his hair and pulled him close. "I am your lord. You answer to no one but me." He didn't expect to break Six's compulsion, but at least he could sidetrack this one vampire. "Go home. Sleep. You'll understand everything when you rise again." Martin wouldn't understand a thing, but at least he could hang onto Adam's promise long enough to get him home.

The other vampire nodded before staggering away. Adam watched him until he was well on his way down the street. He didn't want Xavier to pop out of the shadows and ruin all Adam's hard work with Martin. Then Adam headed back to Selene.

He found her standing in the same spot. Seir and Xavier were with her.

Seir yawned. "Nothing in the outbuildings."

Xavier smiled. "I dined in style on that idiot Bennet. He acted like he didn't recognize me. I always knew he was stupid. I took enough blood so he'll stay groggy for the time we'll need."

Adam quickly told them about Martin. "Six has made them into focused weapons. We need to find a way to break his or her control."

No one offered any ideas.

Selene finally spoke. "Shen is in and has found the breaker box. I watched through the eyes of my flying spy. Three people are inside—a couple who've evidently paid for a private tour, and the tour guide." She took a deep breath. "We need to go in now. We don't have any idea when or if Six is going to decide to kill his captives." She sighed. "Maybe they're already dead."

She bit her lower lip as she thought. No matter how grim the moment, Adam almost groaned at the damp fullness of that lip. *Focus.*

"You can stay here, Selene. You don't need to be inside to control your Yankee Jim spirit." Adam horrified himself. He'd never wanted to be one of those men who gave into his primitive urge to protect the weaker woman. His "weak" woman could blink and generate an army of angry Yankee Jims who'd stomp his sexist butt into the dirt.

She smiled, a wicked baring of her teeth. "Absolutely not. I want to be inside with the rest of you." Her eyes gleamed at the possibility of a showdown with Six.

What a woman. He really—*careful*—really admired her. Adam turned to Xavier. "Maybe you should stay outside to warn us if anyone else shows up."

"Will do. Shout if you need me. I'll hear you." The vampire blended into the shadows and was gone.

Seir finally joined the discussion. "Hold my hand and I can take both of you inside with me."

Adam was curious. "How do you know you won't land in someone's lap?"

Seir waved the possibility away. "I know exactly where to go."

"How do you know if you've never been inside?" Selene took his hand.

Seir gave her a sly smile. "I've already scoped it out." He held up his hand. "I know, I said I was just going to check out the other buildings." He shrugged. "I lied. It's a weakness."

Adam snorted his opinion as he reluctantly grabbed Seir's other hand. He hated conceding power to Fin's brother. He wanted to be all things to Selene. Yep, Alpha Man was alive and well.

There was an instant of terrifying nothingness and then they were in a small bedroom.

A man stood on the other side of the bed. Tall, thin, angry. The room was too small for Adam's beast, so his vampire might get another chance to prove itself. "Who are you?" He kept his voice to a harsh whisper. No use in notifying everyone else in the house about their arrival.

Beside him, Selene answered. "Yankee Jim." She sounded breathless.

Adam glanced at her. Right, she'd seen his picture online. "You amaze me. How did you create him so fast?"

She stared blankly back. "I didn't create him."

CHAPTER TWENTY-ONE

———

"A TRUE SPIRIT." SEIR WALKED AROUND the foot of the bed to the ghost's side. He reached out to touch it. His hand met resistance. "Interesting. Semi-corporeal."

Yankee Jim didn't move, but his eyes blazed with fury. The room's shadows seemed to coalesce around him even as the faint light from a streetlamp shining through the window gave him an otherworldly glow. She'd remember to recreate that look with her version.

Seir cocked his head to the side as he studied Jim. "It must grow tedious haunting the same building year after deadly year. Do you get out once in a while, perhaps visit the neighborhood cemetery? I hear it has an active night life." He winked at Jim.

She wanted to punch Seir. "Forget the ghost. We have some business downstairs to take care of." She drew in a calming breath. Maybe she should show a little compassion. "Look, Jim, I'm sorry about how you died, but it's time to move on, to escape those memories." She returned her attention to Fin's brother. "Can we go now?" She kept her voice low, tough to do when she wanted to scream at him.

Seir didn't bother answering. Instead, he spoke softly to the ghost. "What gives you the strength to maintain some of your physical body in this realm?"

Adam ignored Seir, instead aiming his comment at her. "Maybe he can't 'move on' because he's trapped here. Besides, give the guy a break, Selene. How often does he get a chance to unload his grievances? Some of us need time to get over the bad stuff that's happened in our lives."

Adam stepped quietly to the bedroom door. Selene opened her mouth to point out that he wasn't the only one dealing with stuff, but Yankee Jim didn't give her the chance.

The ghost glowered at Seir. "Hatred lends me power. Loathing for the men who hanged me, for the ones who built this place, for all those who walk these halls each day ignorant of what I suffered, and for the intruders who now desecrate the spot where I died." His voice faded to nothing and then he disappeared.

Adam returned to Selene's side. "Hate is a powerful motivator. That last part about intruders and desecrating the spot where he died gave me an idea, though."

She nodded. "Hold on to it. While Jim is brooding over all the wrongs done to him, I'll scare off the three downstairs. Luckily, they've been talking, so they didn't hear us." She crept to the door.

Seir stepped past her. "I'll check with Xavier, make sure he's eliminated all the lookouts. Send me a thought when your creation is ready to make its entrance. I can be close if things go wrong."

She paused to study him. "You'll be in my head?"

He looked surprised. "Of course. I'm Fin's brother. It's a shared talent. We use it often."

She couldn't contain her anger. "That's mental breaking and entering. Doesn't that bother you?"

He met her gaze. "Never. I don't have much of a conscience. It comes in handy. Now, when your Jim appears to them, make sure he ramps up the menace—maybe works up a growl, bares his teeth, utters lots of death threats." Seir slipped into the hallway and was gone.

"Don't try to tell me my business." Wasted anger. He couldn't hear her. She waited while Adam joined her. "Doesn't he have any personal limits?"

Adam shrugged. "Not that I know of."

She said nothing more as they crept to the top of the stairs and then paused to listen. Below them, Selene could hear the murmur of voices. Beside her, she could feel Adam tense in readiness.

"Now." His whisper brushed warmly over her, making her feel less alone. Strange that she'd never minded being alone before. She pushed the thought aside as she sent her mental message to Seir.

Then she created her Yankee Jim, capturing his bitterness and hatred, twisting his lips into an angry sneer, and filling his eyes with dark menace. Finally, she gave him a suggested course of action. He was ready to perform. Selene guided him down the dark staircase and from there she sent him gliding around the corner toward the voices of the guide and her charges.

She felt Adam slip past her. "Where're you going?"

"I'll be there in case Jim isn't enough." He didn't wait for her reaction.

She hung onto the railing as she padded silently down the stairs. A tumble would ruin the whole haunted-horror affect. Selene almost tripped when she heard the heavy tread of footsteps behind her. She paused to allow her heart to slow. A quick glance behind showed an empty staircase. Yankee Jim. Of course, he'd want to watch the show.

Startled shouts told her the exact moment her victims saw her creation. She reached the bottom of the stairs and then hurried to catch up with the faux Jim. Even though he could act independently, and she'd told him what to do, she'd still feel more secure with him in sight.

Once close to her victims, she crouched behind a chair

to watch. Good. He'd stopped close enough to a window to capture a little of the glow. And he was snarling as he started to edge nearer to the three women frozen in place.

"I am Yankee Jim, and this is my home. I died where this house stands, and I don't want you here. Leave or suffer my curse."

Suffer my curse? Not exactly how she'd express Jim's feelings. That was the danger with her creations. She made them from her essence and explained what she wanted from them, only once they left her, they could interpret things in their own way. Jim punctuated his demand by baring his teeth and growling. At least he got that right. Seir would be happy.

Two of the women, both older, backed toward the front door. Perfect. They were afraid to turn their backs on the apparition. Just as long as they continued backing out the door.

The guide, a younger woman with long blonde hair and dressed in period costume tried to stop them. "A ghost can't hurt you. If you leave, you'll miss an amazing event." She set the lantern she'd been carrying on the floor and then fumbled in her pocket for her phone. "This is what you paid for." The guide took a photo.

Selene turned her head from the flash. When she looked again, the two older women were at the door. One of them reached back, yanked the door open, and then both fled into the night. They hadn't uttered a word. Selene was thankful for that. The bar across the street was still going strong. They didn't need screams bringing customers pouring into the street.

Now for the guide. She was busy taking more photos and trying to talk to Jim.

"Hi, I'm Bonnie. Thank you so much for materializing. This is amazing. Do you want me to pass on any messages? Any words of wisdom from all your years of existence?" She took a step forward. "This is my first night as a guide. The regulars will be incredibly jealous. Could I take a selfie with you?"

Was the woman for real? She ground her teeth. Fin didn't want the fool injured, just scared, but not so much that she'd call 911. While Selene was thinking over her options, Adam stepped from the shadows.

Bonnie gave a small cry of alarm. "Who're you?" She glanced at the door.

Adam didn't answer her. He stared at Selene's Jim. "Go. Your time here is done."

For just a moment, Selene wondered if he could handle this. That was her warrior-woman, go-it-alone attitude speaking. Then she faced reality. He was a vampire and could shift into a raptor. Adam could take care of this woman. Selene just hoped Bonnie didn't say anything to tick him off. His raptor could just about squeeze into the room. She almost smiled. Let the guide try to explain that to the police.

Selene absorbed the part of her essence that was fake Jim, and he disappeared. The guide stared at the spot where he'd stood before turning back to Adam. She wore a dazed expression, but she didn't run. Selene couldn't decide whether she was extremely brave or just stupid.

Adam became the sensual creature that modern books and movies portrayed.

"You are worthy of knowing the truth, child. I am vampire." He bared his fangs, but in a sexy way. "Because of your bravery in the face of the angry spirit, I'll allow you to leave unharmed."

The woman's eyes widened. "Really?"

"Really." And he smiled.

Selene thought that smile would be too much for a mere mortal to withstand.

"Leave? But I want to know more about you." She breathed the words out on a sigh.

Brave or stupid? Definitely stupid.

"I'm Adam. I have no time to speak with you tonight, Bonnie. Go home. Sleep. Return tomorrow night and we'll converse." His heavy-lidded gaze suggested the many other things they'd do.

Selene's eye-roll was wasted in the darkness.

Bonnie smiled. "Wow. I've always believed vampires existed. But I thought only ghosts lived here." She frowned. "I can't tell anyone, can I?"

Adam offered her an understanding smile laced with a message that said, "This will be our secret alone." "If you tell someone, they'll want to see me, too." He shrugged. "I'd be forced to leave. You'd never see me again."

She nodded her agreement while staring at him from wide eyes. "Oh, I won't say a word to anyone." Bonnie looked around. "I'll have to lock up before I go. Will that be a problem?"

He waved the idea aside. "Locks mean nothing to me. Now, go."

The guide spent long minutes closing down—setting alarms and securing doors. Finally, she was ready to leave. Bonnie stood at the door as she took one last look at her very first vampire. "This has been the most exciting night of my life."

You have no idea. Adam waved her out the door before turning to where he knew Selene stood. "Now we start searching. I want us out of here as quickly as possible just in case Bonnie decides to come back for a final peek."

Selene walked to his side. "Or worse yet, notifies some-one not quite so infatuated that there's a vampire in the house." She frowned at him. "I can't believe how easy she was to manipulate."

Adam shook his head. "Selene, Selene, don't act so superior. Old Adam had centuries to perfect the art of seduction." He shrugged. "I know what he knew."

She snorted her opinion of his vampire talents. "Right.

Well, that wouldn't have worked on me."

Adam raised one brow. "Are you sure?"

"Of course." Well, maybe.

He grinned. "I see the lie in your eyes, Selene."

He'd never know what her retort would've been because Fin's brother joined them.

"That was amusing." Seir didn't look amused. "I would've taken a more direct approach. Bonnie would've slept until morning and woken refreshed although quite confused. But I suppose you got the job done."

Adam decided they'd messed around long enough. Outside, Xavier would be wondering what happened to them. "I think I have an idea where we should search first." He led them into the parlor and pointed to the arch leading to the next room. "When I was reading about the house online, the site mentioned that Yankee Jim supposedly was hanged on the spot where that arch is. Of course, back then the house didn't exist."

Selene joined in. "Now I get it. Jim said he hated the intruders who were desecrating the spot where he died." She grinned at Adam. "Brilliant."

Her smile lit up her face and Adam truly believed that no vampire, even one as old as the original Adam, could've outshone her. But that was just his opinion, and he admitted to some bias.

Adam crouched down to study the floor under the arch. "The problem is, the house doesn't have a basement, as far as I know. So maybe we're back to simply finding a clue beneath the floorboards." He stood. "But how do we search without leaving behind evidence that we were here?"

Selene knelt beside him. "We still need a look under the house." She stared as though her eyes could become lasers by her will alone. "I'll create a snake to—"

"I'm done with this crap."

That was all the warning Seir gave them before the

floor exploded. Adam grabbed her as they were both flung across the room. His head bounced off the wall and for a moment he saw nothing.

"Are you okay?"

Her voice. The explosion hadn't knocked her out. Relief turned to rage. Adam glanced at her to make sure she was really unhurt, and then he turned his anger on Seir. "What the hell do you think you're doing?" He rolled to his feet and glared at Fin's brother across the crater that now occupied almost two rooms in the treasured historical house. Worse than the damage was the ominous creaking of the rest of the house. "You idiot! You took out walls, *load-bearing walls*. The building is too old for this stress. The whole thing could come down on our heads."

"Luckily for you, I'm in a good mood, so I'll overlook the insults." Seir wore a manic grin. "Fin is the patient one, the careful one. I'm the impulsive one, and I don't do patient. He should've remembered that when he sent me in his place. This was taking too long, so I fixed it."

Adam could hear the house's alarms going off as he cudgeled his beast back into its cage. Not enough room for him to maneuver in. Besides, as much as he wanted to wipe that grin off Seir's face, he knew they didn't have much time before the police came calling.

"I don't believe it!"

Selene's voice. She was peering into the chasm where the floor had been. Adam walked to the edge. Seir joined him. They stared down.

"How is there a room down there?" Adam reached for the still-lit lantern Bonnie had left sitting on the floor. He aimed it into the opening.

Jude stared up, along with a crowd of terrified humans. He waved at Adam. "Hey, I could do without the exploding floor, but it's great to see you. Is it safe for us to come out?"

Safe? Adam wondered what Jude was talking about. They didn't have time for questions right now, though. He could hear sirens in the distance, and the ceiling was making serious creaking sounds.

"Yeah, it's safe. Let's get you out of there." Adam was ready to leap down to help the humans up when Xavier joined them.

"What happened?" The other vampire took in the scene at a glance. "Whatever it was has attracted a bunch of gawkers from the place across the street. Those alarms aren't quiet."

Selene put her hand on Adam's arm. "We may have neutralized Six's lookouts, but I'd bet he's powerful enough to sense that his hidey-hole has been breached."

The sirens drew closer as Adam's thoughts raced. Too many people to save and too little time. He stared at Seir. "This is your fault. Can you get the humans away from here?"

"Of course." Fin's brother dropped down to join Jude. "The vampire goes with you. I can take the others."

Adam's tension eased just a little. "Take them to Fin's restaurant." No way would Fin want his brother or the humans in his condo. He glanced at the panicked faces of the humans. Would they be a problem? He'd soon see.

Seir spoke to the humans. "I'm teleporting all of you to another location where you'll be safe. But each of you has to be touching me when I do it."

A woman—tall and slim with a hard stare—spoke up. "*Teleporting?* How?"

Selene answered before Adam had a chance to speak.

"Military. Top secret." Selene looked away from the woman to throw Adam a frantic glance that said they were out of time.

The woman nodded her acceptance of Selene's explanation. She turned to the others. "Do what the man said. Now."

Adam wasn't surprised when they all rushed to touch Seir. He for one wouldn't disobey that voice. Adam looked closer. She wore a uniform. Army? Thank the gods for military discipline.

As soon as everyone had contact with Fin's brother, they disappeared. One problem solved.

Jude escaped the sunken room in one fluid leap. A vampire perk—enhanced strength.

Together they all rushed to the back door and out into the night. Adam heard the police pulling up to the front of the Whaley House.

The two vampires were mere streaks in the darkness as they raced away. Adam could've done the same, but Selene didn't have a vampire's speed. He couldn't leave her to face the police.

His decision made; Adam freed his beast. Selene didn't hesitate. She scrambled onto his raptor's back, then he took off.

Too late he saw the police car pull to the curb on the side street next to the house. He'd have to pass close to it. There was no time to change course, no other direction that would lead to freedom.

The cop threw open his door, leaped out, and pointed his gun over the roof of his car.

Adam was now close enough to see the man's eyes widen in shock, his mouth open to shout. Too bad his gun hand didn't even tremble a little.

He knew the man was shouting at him, but Adam was too focused on gaining enough speed to pass the car before the cop could react to listen.

The gunshot got Adam's full attention, though. The fool had actually shot at a Utahraptor. *Him.* But he swallowed his outrage as he increased his stride and blew past the officer.

He turned into the first dark driveway that was out of sight of the Whaley House before stopping to give Selene a chance to slide off. Then he returned to his Adam form.

"I can't believe he had the guts to shoot at me." Adam turned to share his disbelief with her. "At least he missed."

"Not quite."

He was just in time to catch her before she crumpled to the ground.

CHAPTER TWENTY-TWO

N O! FEAR STABBED HIM. NOT Selene. Adam lowered her gently to the ground and then dropped to his knees beside her. He glanced around. No lights in surrounding houses. Bedtime for most humans, so no traffic. Good.

"Don't move. I've got you." He didn't waste time denying his panic. He acknowledged it and kept going. "Let's get your jacket off."

She nodded. "Side. Don't think it hit anything major."

Adam forced his hands not to shake as he lifted her just enough to slip off her jacket. She didn't cry out, but he heard her suck in her breath. He cursed silently.

Once free of the jacket, Adam saw the blood soaking her top. It looked black in the darkness and seemed way too much to not be serious. He thought of all the blood he'd seen in his life, so much that it didn't bother him anymore. Her blood did. He must've made a noise, because she laughed weakly.

"Don't pass out on me, raptor."

"I wouldn't dare. Because while I was out, you'd probably dig the bullet out of your side, bandage yourself, and then carry me to the SUV."

"You know it."

Her voice grew fainter. Time to get busy. Adam shrugged off his jacket and then pulled off his T-shirt.

"Fin made us all learn basic first-aid, so you're in good hands." Adam hoped he sounded more confident than he felt. "I'll stop this bleeding before getting you to the hospital."

"No!" She tried to sit up but fell back with a gasp of pain. "No doctor. They have to report gunshot wounds. Besides, I don't have human blood. They'd notice." Her voice faded. She closed her eyes.

Adam muttered a few curses. He hadn't thought about her nonhuman blood.

Grimly, he got to work. He peeled her blood-soaked top away from the wound. Adam winced at the blood oozing from the bullet hole. Was the piece of lead still in her? Carefully, he slid his hand beneath her, feeling for an exit wound. None. No time to clean away the blood and do a thorough exam, though. Fear tore at his gut. What if he couldn't stop the bleeding? He pushed his rising panic aside.

He tore a long strip from his shirt before folding the rest into a pad that he pressed against the wound. Then he tied the strip tightly around her to hold the pad in place and pulled her top back down.

Now to get her to someone who could fix that wound. He leaned back on his heels. "I'm calling Fin. He can be here in a few seconds. He'll teleport you back to the condo. He'll heal you." Adam never doubted the boss's power to do anything. If he could take the soul from a man, he could heal a mere bullet wound.

"I don't—"

"Shh, Save your strength." He reached down to stroke her hair. Then he jerked his hand away. She wasn't a freaking puppy. And what did he know about comforting her anyway? Raptors weren't the touchy-feely types. The petting was just a substitute for what he really wanted to do—pick her up, hold her tight, and then heal her himself. But that wasn't part of his skill-set. Killing yes, healing not so much. So, Adam closed his eyes, ready to reach for the boss.

"I'm here, I'm here. I'll help."

Adam opened his eyes. Ace was already kneeling on the other side of Selene. "Where did *you* come from?"

The kid glanced up. For a moment his expression was blank. Then it filled with emotion. "Dave. He called Fin. Said that Jude and Xavier had gotten back to him, but that you guys were still missing."

Adam didn't have a chance to ask another question.

Ace wrapped his arms round her. "I'll take her to Fin." He stared down at Selene. "You'll be okay. I've got this."

The gaze he turned up to Adam was filled with panic and fear. *You and me both, kid.*

Then Ace looked down at her again. "I promise."

She reached up to touch the boy's cheek. "It's okay. I'm fine. Calm down."

Adam frowned. How would Ace take her to Fin? Something didn't feel right. He'd learned to listen to his instincts. He made a grab for Ace just as Selene and the boy disappeared.

Adam leaped to his feet. He spun, knowing even as he did so they were gone. Was he the only one in the world who couldn't teleport? He wanted to free his beast and tear the whole city apart.

Scooping her jacket from the ground, he took a deep breath and tried to think past the fact that Selene was gone. Then he closed his eyes and reached for Fin. Adam would only relax when the boss said he had her and she was safe.

"Where are you? Dave just called. He said you and Selene were missing."

Adam's heart plummeted. His adrenaline spiked. Fin wouldn't claim they were missing if Ace had reached him. Adam asked anyway. "Isn't Ace with you?"

There was silence for a moment. *"Should he be?"*

Adam gave him a brief rundown of events as his mind screamed, *"Find her!"*

"The boy shouldn't have been able to teleport."

Fin's voice wasn't in his head this time. Adam turned to face his boss. "You might want to warn me when you're going to do that."

"I don't have time for warnings. We have to find them. I'm sure Selene will be safe with Ace. She's a big sister to him. But there's more to that boy than I thought. I want to know what's going on."

That made sense, but Adam couldn't think past Selene long enough to worry about Ace. "Any idea where to search?"

"We'll look at the Whaley House first. I need to get a sense of what happened there." Fin wore his someone's-going-to-die expression. "Seir mentioned there was some collateral damage during the extraction."

"You could say that." Adam sat on his impatience. Right now, Selene was at the top of his to-do list. The Whaley House couldn't compete. "Look, you go see the house, but first tell me where you think Ace took her and I can start the search."

"You'll start the search after *we* see the house." Fin pointed. "This way?"

Adam nodded while trying to keep his anger from showing. He wanted to fling his defiance in Fin's face, but an argument right now wouldn't help Selene. Besides, he didn't have a clue where Ace had taken her.

Fin must've sensed how mad he was because he ratch-etted down the arrogance a little.

"I know you care for Selene." Fin held up his hand to stop Adam's response. "And, no, I didn't need to be in your head to sense that." He exhaled wearily. "Human emotions make things a lot tougher."

Adam couldn't keep quiet. "You wouldn't know about those kinds of emotions, would you?" Harsh but true.

Fin's expression hardened. "You'd be surprised. But I don't allow them to interfere with my common sense."

"This conversation isn't going anywhere." They were almost at the corner where they'd be able to see the house. Adam paused. "After the house, what?"

"I've called Kione. He's been around Selene, so he should be able to find her. He'll meet us here at the house."

Adam mentally banged his head against a wall. Why hadn't he thought of the fae prince? *Because you're not thinking straight right now.* Maybe Fin had a point about his emotions. He nodded. "Great."

They turned the corner.

Fin cursed softly when they came within sight of what had once been a historical treasure.

Adam shook his head. "Wow! I didn't know it was this bad." As he and Fin joined the crowd gathered behind the police line, Adam realized how lucky everyone had been to get out when they did. The house had collapsed in on itself. He glanced at his boss.

Fin was livid, showing a lot more emotion than Adam was used to seeing from someone who claimed to have so little.

"It was the perfect storm." Fin worked his way to the front of the crowd with Adam beside him. "Six had already injected a large empty space beneath the house, and then Seir took out a huge chunk of the floor and foundation along with some walls of the already compromised structure. The integrity of the building was shot."

"Injected?" Adam scanned the gawkers, searching for Kione. He hoped the prince got there fast. "Not dug?"

Fin shrugged. "Magic, Rap. Magic. Powerful beings who can manipulate reality don't 'dig.'"

Hearing his true name jolted Adam. He had to make

sure not to lose it or forget he *was* that person. "You think Six did this, not Zero?"

Fin started to answer just as a thin balding man shoved between Adam and the boss so he could have an unobstructed view. Not a wise move when Adam was in a dangerous mood.

He reached out and grabbed the man by the back of his shirt. Then Adam lifted the guy until he could do the eye-to-eye thing.

The man cursed as he turned his head to meet Adam's gaze. "What the hell! Put me down before I—"

Adam smiled, revealing the tips of his fangs. "Yes?" He allowed his beast to stare out of his eyes.

The guy gulped, his eyes wide, his mouth trembling. "Nothing."

"And you'll never do that again?" He drew his tongue across the point of one fang, drawing it out, loving it.

Beyond words, the man just shook his head. He frantically scanned the crowd, probably searching for help. But everyone around them conveniently looked the other way. Adam didn't fault them for that. Smart people.

"Good." Adam dropped him and then watched as he scuttled back the way he had come. That had been too easy. He'd wanted the man to put up a fight. He needed to work off some aggression.

"You have an enhanced reaction time and intuitive intimidation skills. I've always admired that about you." Fin listed Adam's high points with detached interest. "Now, if you're finished, I'll answer your question."

Adam dragged his attention back to Fin. "Reaction time and intimidation skills? Really? Is that what you have in my file?"

"Of course." This was Fin at his most analytical and least emotional. "It helps me assign the right people to each job. The files will also help if someone has to take my place."

Adam hadn't known Fin kept a file. And he couldn't conceive of *anyone* taking the boss's place. The whole file thing bothered him, though. "That's cold, Fin. We're more than reaction times and intimidation skills." He thought about his growing feelings for Selene. Had Fin ever warmed up enough to love someone?

"You wanted to know if Zero did this. The answer is no. I also have a file with a log showing exact times when he and I were . . . interacting. During the probable time frame when the basement was created, he wouldn't have had time to form it. Besides, our mental battles are grueling. Even with his immense power, he wouldn't come away with enough strength to do the job."

While Fin was going on about mental battles and time frames, Adam's thoughts went back to Selene. How much blood had she lost? Did Ace have enough sense to call in a doctor?

The big-picture question: who was this kid with enough power to teleport, and how had he kept Fin from finding out?

"A messy demolition. Who's responsible?"

Kione spoke from beside him. Adam had never been so glad to hear his voice.

"Seir. He owes San Diego a completely restored Whaley House. I'll make sure he makes restitution."

From Fin's tone, Adam figured Seir should run while he had the chance.

Kione studied the destruction. "I assume you want me to find someone. Who?"

Adam didn't wait for Fin to answer. "Selene." He gave Kione the important details.

When he finished, Fin took up the narrative. "Once we find where Ace has her, we don't just charge in."

Speak for yourself. Adam thought charging in sounded like a good plan. "Do you know something we don't,

Fin? Is there a reason why a raptor, a fae prince, and someone with your power need to show caution?"

Fin didn't respond.

For the first time, Kione showed real interest. "If Ace only took Selene because he wanted to get help for her, then I don't see why there would be a problem. Just knock on his door and ask to see her. Am I wrong?"

Fin remained silent as he led them away from the crowd. He stopped in the shadow of a closed café. Finally, he turned to face them. "We'll discuss this when we find them. Until then, I have things to think about." He nodded at Kione. "Whenever you're ready. Dave is still parked where Adam left him. Jude and Xavier decided to make their own way home. It'll just be the three of us."

Adam took one last glance at where the Whaley House had stood, just in time to catch Yankee Jim doing a victory jig in front of the ruins. *"Fly free, Jim."* Adam wished he could share the ghost's joy.

No one spoke as they walked the short distance to where Dave waited. Their driver shut down his phone and unlocked the doors. They all piled in. Fin sat next to Dave.

Dave studied Fin before turning to look at the two behind him. "From the police cars, ambulances, and firetrucks along with the sound of a collapsing building, I assume a good time was had by all. I checked out the local news online. They're throwing out wild guesses right now—gas explosion, terrorists, electrical glitch." He paused for a moment. "Although it seems to me a terrorist would look for a more high-profile target."

Fin didn't choose to explain other than to say they had to find Selene. Dave didn't take being shut out quietly. As Kione gave their driver directions, Dave complained about their lack of trust in him, Fin's willingness to put his life in danger, the ingratitude of bosses in general and on and on. Adam ignored him and thought instead about Ace and Selene.

Ace. How had he even known Selene needed help? Everyone said Ace didn't have power. Even Selene, who'd known him the longest, agreed on that. But he'd teleported himself and her out of there. *Not* powerless. How had he cloaked all that from Fin? And why?

Selene. Was she really safe with Ace? Would he get her help or try to heal her himself? Could he heal her? Who knew what the kid could do? And would she be safe if they arrived and Ace felt threatened? Adam allowed himself a brief smile. She'd hate his questioning her ability to protect herself.

Finally, his thoughts returned to Ace.

Had power to spare.

Hid that power from everyone.

Had ingratiated himself into Fin's condo and into his trust.

Why?

Adam closed his eyes against a growing suspicion.

Six?

CHAPTER TWENTY-THREE

———

SELENE LAY WITH HER EYES closed. Remembering. The flight from Whaley House. The bullet's impact. Pain. Adam close, holding her, stopping the bleeding. Then Ace was there, arguing with Adam. Ace picked her up. Adam tried to stop him. Then? Nothing. She must've passed out.

She didn't sense anyone nearby, so she opened her eyes. Instant impression—expensive hotel room, large, contemporary, neutral with a wall of windows that looked out over the Pacific. She lay on one of two queen beds. The sun and the balcony called to her.

A glance at a brochure on the bedside table confirmed her assessment. How had Ace afforded this room?

Gingerly, she poked at her side. No pain. Swinging her legs to the floor, she sat on the side of the bed and took stock of herself. She still wore her own clothes except for her top. She recognized the shirt as one of Ace's. She lifted the shirt away from her side. Smooth skin with not a trace of a bullet wound. Good as new.

She looked around for her phone before realizing it was still in her jacket pocket, and her jacket was back with Adam. Had Ace called Fin to let everyone know she was okay?

She heard the door open and started speaking before

the person entered. "Did you heal me, or did you call in someone else, Ace?" An important question.

"What if it hadn't been me at the door?" Ace neatly avoided her question as he walked past her to deposit a bag on the desk.

Selene shrugged, hoping it looked more casual than she felt. "Who else would it be? The last thing I remember is you taking me away." *And Adam trying to stop you.*

He nodded, evidently satisfied. "I brought food. No fancy hotel stuff for us. Donuts and coffee, the breakfast of champions."

Her grin was automatic. No matter what the problem, he'd always been able to make her smile. Suspicion clouded it this time, though. "Great. I'm starving. Let's eat on the balcony."

Once settled in the sun with coffee and a huge box of donuts on the small table between them, Selene got down to business. Too bad the gorgeous ocean scenery would be spoiled by the tough questions she had to ask.

"You didn't answer my question. Did you heal me?" She watched his expression, reading the exact moment he chose to go with the truth instead of a lie. Ace couldn't hide his emotions, and even though he'd count that as a weakness, Selene mentally put a check mark in the plus column for him.

He glanced away. "Yeah, I took care of it for you. The blood made it look worse than it was."

"How did you do it, Ace? Did you have to dig the bullet out? Did you have medical instruments? An amazing job, because there's not even a tiny scar."

His was angry as he finally met her gaze. "Stop the sarcasm. You know how I did it." His expression turned defiant. "I willed it healed, and it was."

Selene softened her tone. "That took a lot of power for someone everyone thinks is powerless."

The corners of Ace's lips tipped up. "Well, there are lots of clueless everyones out there."

She couldn't stop now. "You teleport."

He took another donut, stuffed it in his mouth, and didn't answer.

"What else can you do, Ace?" Her voice dropped to almost a whisper. Yes, she was afraid of his answer to this one. Mentally, she pictured Jude and those people trapped beneath the Whaley House.

When he glanced at her, he was as close to shifty-eyed as she'd ever seen him.

"Lots of stuff."

Time to stop dancing around things. "So, you've been hiding behind a shadow person?"

He shrugged. "We all hide behind shadows, Selene."

"Not me." That came out way too aggressive. She dialed it back. "What you see is what you get." Selene offered him a quick smile.

He didn't smile back. "Really? I don't think so. I've been talking to Meg."

His words froze her. "And?" One word was all she could manage.

"Tor is getting serious about her. She feels the same. I see a problem in your future."

He knew. She closed her eyes, feeling the empty spot inside her. Then she took a deep breath and opened her eyes. "Meg talks too much. What are you going to do about it?"

"Nothing. Not my business. The question is: what are *you* going to do—about Meg, about *me*?"

This time she was the one who grabbed a donut to stuff in her mouth while she thought. Stress called for stuffing, not nibbling. Finally, the donut was gone along with her hesitancy. She had to ask the big questions. "That depends. Did you mess with everyone's minds? Did you create that room under the Whaley House? Did you imprison those people?" Selene took a deep breath. "Are you Six?"

He changed. Oh, not his physical appearance. Ace still had the body and face of a teen. But the person looking out of his eyes was a man—hard, bitter.

"Yes to everything." He paused. "Even though I think that number crap is stupid."

Selene reverted to the person she'd been for so many years before joining Zero, the cold mercenary. Instinct took over as she readied a defense to counter this dangerous stranger.

Ace laughed as he raised his hands above his head. "Please, not the plague of a thousand fruit flies. Hey, we're friends. Let's talk this out."

Against her better judgment, Selene relaxed a little. She'd liked Ace, had felt protective of him—what a joke—and it was tough to suddenly think of him as the enemy. After all, she'd joined Fin with the intention of spying for Zero. *So, what happened?* She'd consider that question later.

"Fine. Talk." His smile bothered her. It was the sunny mask hiding killer clouds behind it. She'd never seen that darkness in him. Why not?

Ace's smile faded; his gaze grew distant. "Your rescuers are coming. Kione's good. I was able to throw him off my trail a few times, but he's a freaking bulldog." His attention returned to her. "I guess I better talk fast."

Rescuers? Was Adam with them? Would he be mad? Sure, he would. Ace had grabbed her and evidently not contacted anyone. "Tell me everything and then leave before they get here. You don't want a confrontation."

"Maybe I do."

Selene recognized that stubborn expression. She'd seen it enough times. It made her sad to realize the boy she thought she knew was gone forever. "No, you don't. If you go, I can settle everyone down and explain your side of what happened." The trouble was, she wasn't sure his side would calm Fin or any of his merry men.

He dropped his gaze to his clasped hands. "You can't fix this, Selene. They know I lied to them." Ace looked up and tried for another smile. It didn't work.

He took a deep breath before speaking. "Okay, here's the important stuff." Ace reached for another donut, but instead pushed the bag away. "Those people I put underneath the Whaley House? I saved their lives. Zero was ordered to kill them." He shrugged. "I don't murder people."

Wait. Things didn't make sense. "Who ordered Zero? And didn't he get angry when you disobeyed him?"

"I don't know who gave the orders. Zero never talks about things like that."

Selene watched his gaze grow distant again. He looked uneasy.

"They're almost here. I need to wrap this up. Anyway, he didn't get mad because he didn't know the people weren't dead." He sent her an accusing glare. "He will now. Everyone will be blabbing about it."

"What have you gotten yourself into?" She couldn't maintain her anger. "Let me help you." She'd done a lousy job of keeping him out of trouble so far.

Ace shook his head. "Can't. I have to get away from both sides now, go into hiding."

"Zero will get over it. He—"

"Zero didn't know I had power. He sent me on this job because he figured I wouldn't need power to kill a bunch of humans if they thought I was harmless. I cloaked it from everyone. He'll know now." Ace stood and then moved to the railing. "He'll want me to do more things for him. Things I don't want to do."

"Maybe Fin will—"

Ace's laugh was harsh. "Fin? I lied to him. He'll never trust me again." He rubbed his hand across his face. "I really like Fin, but I'm the enemy now. The infamous Six."

"Yes, well . . ." Lost for words. She could create anything, but not the words to give him hope.

He held up his hand to stop whatever mumbled nonsense she would've spouted.

"They're here." He glanced over the railing. "I'll be in touch."

Then they heard Dave's voice clearly through the door.

"I don't know what you guys are worried about. He's a runner. A coward. I can read people. I bet he's gone already." Short pause. "What do you mean, shut up?"

Uh-oh. Selene saw the outrage in Ace's eyes. Dave had challenged his manhood. She wasn't surprised when his stubborn expression made a reappearance.

"On second thought, I'll stay long enough to show Dave how much trouble a big mouth can cause." He strode back into the room and stopped in the middle of it.

Selene wasn't about to allow this to turn into an immortal shootout that would level the city. She followed him inside, walked around him, and then planted herself right in front of the door.

"Get out of the way, Selene."

"No." She didn't turn to look at Ace. No matter if he was Six or Sixty, he was still the boy she'd promised to keep safe. For the moment, she refused to remember Fin's vision.

She raised her voice so everyone on the other side could hear her. "Hey, guys. Selene, here. I'm fine. Everything's under control. If I let you in, will you play nice?" She prepared Ace's plague of fruit flies just in case she needed a distraction while cooler heads prevailed.

She held her breath until Adam answered.

"We just want to talk."

Right. Famous last words uttered before millions of

barroom brawls. But she supposed she wouldn't get more of a guarantee than that. She opened the door.

Adam couldn't enter because Selene was in the way. He took in what he could see of the room. Just the two of them in there. She was blocking Adam's path to Ace, or Six, or whatever he was.

Adam wanted to wrap his arms around her and then carry her from the room, from the hotel, from the coming insanity, to somewhere safe where Zero and his people couldn't touch her.

She'd tear him apart, though, if he went all protective on her. He loved her independence, but it drove him crazy. She'd reject his protection, but that's about all he had to offer her. He didn't think occasional rides on his raptor was a basis for a deeper relationship. A *deeper* relationship? What was he thinking?

Her eyes narrowed as she looked past him to Kione and Dave. "No violence."

Adam simmered. He wanted to say, "No, please, don't thank me for running around all night searching for you, worrying if you were okay, hating Ace for . . ." *taking care of you when it was my job.* He shoved the thought aside and instead said, "Unless you want to talk in the hallway, we'll have to come in."

She threw him a last warning glance and then stepped aside.

Before entering, Adam turned to Dave. "Wait out here and guard the door." Better to keep their driver and his sword away from Ace. He wouldn't put it past Dave to attack the kid. Adam didn't think it would end well for Dave.

He strode into the room with Kione behind him. The prince closed the door on Dave's string of complaints.

Adam faced Selene as Kione slipped past him. The prince sat on the end of the nearest bed instead of choosing one of the two chairs.

"You led me quite a chase, child. None of my prey have ever eluded me for so long." Kione slow-clapped his contempt for Ace's effort.

"I'm not a child." Ace sounded outraged.

Kione ignored Ace's tone. "When you've lived as long as I have, everyone's a child."

"You have no idea how old *I* am, boy." Ace seemed to have forgotten everyone except Kione for the moment.

Which was good, because Adam needed to focus on Selene. "You say you're fine, but are you? If Ace is who I think, he could make you believe you're healed." A little farfetched, but not beyond Six's ability.

With a hiss of irritation, she pulled up her top so he could see the smooth skin beneath. Not even a pale scar.

Adam couldn't help himself. He slid his fingers over the spot where the bullet had entered. Warm, vital, *alive*. Finally, he released his fear.

Her voice was soft as she leaned close. "Thank you for coming to my rescue. I should've said that first, but Ace had me worried."

"Sure." Before he could give into the temptation to keep his hand on her, to draw her into his arms, he stepped around Selene to confront Ace.

The boy bristled with hostility.

Even faced with evidence that Ace wasn't the power-less, likeable kid he'd thought, Adam didn't want to place him on the enemy's side. Best to get right to the point. "Are you Six?" Adam wished he'd get more chances to ask questions like that outside where he had room for his beast to maneuver. He loved his beast. The sun didn't bother his raptor. Another reason to reject his vampire side.

"I'd like to know the answer to that, too."

Startled, Adam looked past Ace to where Fin stood in the balcony doorway. Even though he'd known the boss intended to sneak in behind the kid, Adam still wasn't prepared for how Fin could just appear like that.

Ace's reaction was instantaneous. He spun to face Fin at the same time a cage of living vines bearing trumpet-shaped black flowers erupted from the floor and reached the ceiling within a breath.

The shocked silence lasted for maybe ten seconds. While Ace focused on Fin, Adam crept closer to study the blooms. He whistled softly. "Would you look at this." He had to hand it to the kid. As protections went, this was an original. "Each flower has a mouthful of pointed teeth." He leaned in to get a good look. The flowers snapped at him. He stepped back. "Plants as a weapon. I'm impressed."

Behind him, Kione chuckled. "So, this is your true power, Ace? I bet you have your own savage garden back home."

"This isn't funny!" Selene's voice shook with rage.

Ace punctuated her comment by destroying his living cage in a spray of snapping flowers and writhing vines. "Don't laugh at me. Don't the fuck *ever* laugh at me!"

Before anyone could do more than duck, the room began to shake. Pictures fell from the wall, lamps crashed to the floor, and outside, black clouds churned as wind whistled around the hotel. Jagged streaks of lightning lit the clouds followed by booming thunder.

Fin didn't move. The gale pulled at his shirt and his silver hair whipped around his face.

Why was everyone just staring? Adam turned towards Selene as a crackling sound filled the room followed almost immediately by a tingling sensation. He looked down. The hairs on his arm were standing straight up. Realization gut-punched him. "Run!" He leaped toward Selene.

Too late. A brilliant dagger of lightning struck the balcony with the sound of a gunshot. The explosive boom of thunder masked the disintegrating of the whole thing along with the table and chairs. At the same time, the windows imploded.

Adam flung his arm up to protect his eyes from flying debris as he stumbled toward Selene. Had to get them out of this crazy room before the ceiling came down on top of them. The kid was out of control.

Instead of joining him, Selene waved madly toward Kione. Adam followed her gaze.

The dark prince glowed, his arms stretched out in front of him, his palms facing Ace. He'd pulled down his hood, exposing his deadliest weapon.

Selene struggled toward the boy. "Kione's going to hurt him."

Personally, Adam sort of thought Ace needed to have a hurting put on him for all the trouble he'd caused. But more likely, the kid would have enough power to counter whatever Kione would try. There'd be more destruction and . . . What was Fin doing?

Fin hadn't moved. He still stood in what remained of the balcony doorway. "Kione, no. Pull up your hood." He sent the prince a hard stare. "Calm down, Ace. I guarantee no one is laughing at you."

Ace remained as he was in the middle of the room. He was breathing hard, his only sign of any inner turmoil as broken glass, bits of cement, and flowers settled around him.

Silence enveloped the room until Dave flung open the door, his sword in one hand and knife in the other.

"I knew you'd need me. I'll fix everything." He charged Ace.

"Stop." Fin didn't raise his voice.

Dave froze as he met Fin's gaze.

"Leave. We're fine."

Adam could tell Dave wanted to argue, but one look at Fin's expression and he simply left, shutting the door behind him.

Selene turned toward the door to follow Dave. "We need to get out of here. Hotel staff will be all over this. You can't hide what that lightning strike did."

"Yes, I can." Fin moved into the room, closing what remained of the door. "Take a seat." He glanced around the room. "Everyone."

Reluctantly, Selene sat on the bed closest to the door. Adam joined her. Kione dropped onto the other one. Ace seemed to hover between either sitting or continuing his assault on the world. Everyone except for Fin tensed as the kid made his decision. Finally, he slumped onto the chair next to the desk where he looked like nothing more than a sulky teen.

Adam felt everyone exhale in relief. He pointed out the obvious. "The room shook. That means rooms around it shook."

"A few minor tremors, that's all. California is used to them." Fin sat on the remaining chair nearest to where the hapless balcony used to be. He crossed a leg over his knee before brushing some concrete dust off his shirt."

Irritated now, Adam continued, "At the least, someone from the hotel will knock on that door. Look around you. I don't think they'll buy the partying-hard excuse." He heard sirens in the distance. Just great.

Fin nodded. "You're right."

Amazing. Fin admitted he was right. Adam would note that on his calendar with a star beside it. He closed his mouth on the rest of his argument.

"Look at me." Fin spoke to Ace. His tone didn't leave any doubt he expected to be obeyed.

"What?" Ace still sounded defiant, but he did meet Fin's gaze.

"Put everything back the way it was, *exactly* the way it was. Now."

CHAPTER TWENTY-FOUR

———

A DAM WATCHED ACE'S EYES WIDEN in shock and then narrow. He felt the kid's rage along with his intention to bolt. Sure, Fin could force Ace to stay, but no one wanted a battle of the Goliaths with all the sound and fury that went with it. Time to derail the boy's plan.

"If you leave now, Ace, Dave will drive us all crazy bragging that he had you pegged as a runner from the start. Stay long enough to hear what Fin has to say. Then you can tell us your side of the story. Maybe even make us understand everything." Adam wondered if leaving would even be an option by the end of this talk.

Would Fin allow the kid to walk away? Why not? After all, according to his boss's vision, Selene would banish Six as some stupid tune played while she waved a stick around. That wouldn't happen here. And trying to contain Ace might take more energy than Fin wanted to expend right now as he fought his daily mental battles with Zero. Adam hoped so, because even with all his suspicions, he still liked the kid.

Silence fell, and in the distance those sirens drew closer.

Finally, Ace nodded. "Sure. I'll fix the place, but not because you ordered me to. Then maybe I'll talk. If I feel like it." His shrug said it was no big deal.

The boy didn't move, didn't gesture, didn't even blink, but suddenly everything in Adam's world seemed to shimmer and rearrange itself. He closed his eyes against the feeling of vertigo. He opened them again when he heard a gasp beside him.

"Impossible." Selene's eyes shone with pride. "Look what Ace did?"

Like everyone else, Adam scanned the area. "Whoa!" Who was this boy with enough mega power to recreate the room and balcony? It was as though nothing had ever happened here. Except for one thing.

"You really like flowers, don't you?" Kione's words were light, but his expression said Ace had impressed him.

Selene rose and walked to the desk where a vase filled with a dozen long-stemmed pink roses sat. She touched a petal. "These are beautiful."

The boy shrugged and tried to looked cool. "I thought you'd like them." Then he blushed.

Good grief. This was Six, the deadly immortal who would help destroy humanity? Adam shook his head. He just couldn't picture it. He glanced at Fin to see how the boss was reacting to all this power. Fin looked surprised with a side order of worried. Not an expression Adam associated with the boss.

That thought didn't go any further as someone pounded on the door. Adam was the closest, so he stood and went to answer it.

Dave called from the other side. "The cops are here."

"Let them in." Fin didn't take his gaze from Ace as he spoke.

Adam pulled the door open, and then smiled at the two policemen on the other side. "Can I help you, officers?"

They didn't smile. "Several people reported a lightning strike destroyed your balcony and shattered the windows."

"Destroyed the balcony?" He hoped he sounded puzzled.

"There were also reports the building shook." The

officer speaking looked apologetic. "Everything seemed normal as we pulled up, but we'd like to inspect the inside."

Adam motioned them in and waited as they took a look around the room and balcony. Then they returned to the door. "Sorry about disturbing you. Must've been crank calls."

Adam nodded. "No problem. Kids these days." He shot Ace an accusing glance.

The officers agreed and then left.

The door had barely closed before Selene blurted her question. "How did you do that, Ace?"

Fin answered for the boy. "He manipulated time. We'll save the how of it for later."

Ace glared at Fin for stepping all over his big moment but didn't bother arguing.

"Betraying me was Zero's idea, wasn't it?" Fin wasn't about to allow Ace time to gather his thoughts.

Adam didn't even pretend to know what Fin was feeling most of the time. The guy was Mr. Inscrutable. But for a moment, he swore he saw hurt in the boss's eyes. Then it was gone, and Fin was back to being cold and unreadable. Adam decided he'd been wrong, because Fin wasn't one to waste the few warm fuzzies he had on a kid he'd only known for a short time.

Selene interrupted. "Maybe if you back off and let him tell his story, we might learn something."

Fin's gaze would've frozen a strong man's blood in his veins, but Selene simply returned his glare. "Well, it's true."

Adam reached for her hand, hoping she understood that he supported her. She sent him a grateful glance.

"That's okay, Selene. I'll answer him." Ace smiled at her.

Adam gave the kid props for that smile. There was genuine affection in it.

Ace turned his attention back to Fin. "Yes, it was Zero's idea."

Fin didn't look happy that he was right.

"I owe Zero *everything*." Ace shifted in his seat, his gaze skittering around the room before settling on a wall print of a ship tossing on a stormy sea.

Adam figured Ace could relate with the sailors on it.

Ace focused on Fin. "You've heard my story. Never knew my mother. Raised by an old woman. When she died, men took me away and tossed me into stasis. I was twelve. I would've rotted there forever unless they needed me to fight and die for the planet. Zero rescued me from that living death."

Adam glanced at Selene. She was trying to keep her expression neutral, but sympathy for Ace shone in her eyes.

He wasn't sure how he felt about the kid. The human part of him was sorry for Ace and wanted to believe his story. But the vampire Adam had lived for centuries and knew all the ways people could lie. Vampire Adam was a cynical bastard.

Ace paused. His gaze grew distant. "They took my clothes and sprayed me before forcing me into the stasis chamber. I was nothing but another decontaminated piece of trash to keep stored so I wouldn't bother any of the good citizens of their planet again. I didn't know anything more until Zero woke me. He gave me clothes, fed me, and then loaded my mind with info about this world and its language. But his greatest gift was hope for a future." Ace stared into each of their eyes defiantly. "In return, he only asked that I supply him with information. I would do much more than that for him." He glanced away. "Except kill people."

"How heartwarming. Loyalty is so rare these days." Pause. "But I wonder why you hid all your amazing power?"

The new voice whipped Adam's attention to the balcony. The door was open, and Zero stood leaning against the doorjamb. He waved at them. "Please, don't get up for me."

Everyone except for Fin ignored Zero's invitation to remain seated. Adam leaped to his feet along with the rest of them. Unlike the others, he acted instantly. After all, a raptor who stood around gawking when the enemy appeared was a dead raptor.

Initial evaluation: his raptor wouldn't help him here. Instead, he called on his vampire. His hatred for the original Adam meant he'd closed the door to exploring a lot of the powers the old bloodsucker had wielded. Adam flung open that door now. No time to get fussy about where he got the help he needed.

Beside him, he heard Selene shouting something at him, felt her hand on his arm pulling at him. He ignored her.

His vampire's preternatural speed and strength carried him across the room in one leap. Adam took only a moment to enjoy the startled expression on his enemy's face before he lunged for Zero's throat, fangs fully extended.

Zero sprang back, avoiding having his throat ripped out by inches.

Adam had survived all those millennia ago with a combination of speed, savagery, and an instinct for the kill. Now, his gut told him he had only a few breaths before Zero retaliated. He didn't weigh his chances of living, he didn't hesitate, he reached into his vampire's memory and pulled out five words in a language he didn't know, didn't have a clue what they'd do. They were old Adam's words. He hoped they equaled the viciousness of their originator.

Adam shouted the words into the room. Then all hell broke loose. Literally.

He heard the cries around him at the same moment part of the floor collapsed underneath Zero. A huge hole gaped open spewing smoke and flames. Adam stopped breathing as clawed hands reached up through the hole followed by grotesque heads with mouths open to display teeth that would make him cry jealous tears if he wasn't frozen in place. Adam did manage to fling his hand in front of his face to protect it from the heat. He coughed as smoke billowed into the room.

"What the . . ."

Adam didn't blame Zero for not being able to come up with an awesome curse. He couldn't think of one either. Adam watched his enemy rise above the groping demons. Then, horrified, he saw the abominations trying to hoist themselves from the hole. This wasn't turning out exactly as he'd hoped. Frantically, Adam searched his vampire memories for something to stop them.

Selene spoke from beside him. "I have this." He glanced her way. She was surrounded by a mob of demons she'd created especially for this occasion. Of course, she had. A glance in the other direction assured him that Fin had finally stood. He didn't notice what Ace or Kione were doing, but he was certain they were also getting ready to jump in to save his butt.

No! At a moment when he should simply back away and allow the others to do their things, pride raised its stupid head. He'd started this, and he'd finish it. He glared back at her. "Relax. *I* have this."

Somehow. Adam delved deeper into his murky old Adam memories. There. Words that had a similar feel to the ones he'd just said. Before he could lose his nerve, and without allowing himself to think of the consequences if they were the wrong ones, he shouted them.

The hole began to shrink. The last thing Adam heard was the angry bellow of a demon whose claws got trapped in the closing portal. The smell of smoke lingered.

Then, silence. Two long claws lay on the undisturbed floor. Zero drifted down from his perch near the ceiling. Fin just sighed.

Zero ignored Adam as he reached back to drag one of the balcony chairs inside. He sat then met Fin's gaze across the room. "That was a shock. Not something I experience often. I had no idea one of your Eleven could reach beyond his dino roots." He glanced at Adam. "If you ever feel the need to earn a promotion from someone who will treasure your gifts, text me."

"Do you have a card?" Adam figured if Zero wanted to play it casual, he'd do the same. It was a lot better than the guy turning him into a pile of ash. Not that Adam believed Fin would allow that. Although, if Fin was furious enough at Adam, who knew.

Adam couldn't hide his surprise when Zero reached for his wallet and produced a card. He took the card but didn't look at it before shoving it into his pocket. Total coolness demanded he seem unimpressed with Zero's offer.

Zero switched his attention to the others in the room. "Relax. Sit. I'm not here for any of you."

Fin returned to his chair. He sat and then stared at Zero with an expression that said he was barely interested in whatever his enemy might have to say. Adam decided if his boss could toss around an I-don't-give-a-damn expression then he should do the same. He reclaimed his place on the bed. Kione and Ace also sat, although the kid looked as though he was teetering on the brink of another explosion. Adam hoped not.

Selene controlled her need to scream at Adam for his suicide mission long enough to recall her demons. She took a deep breath. There. She felt complete again. Or almost. She sat beside Adam. But before she could tell him exactly what she thought, Kione spoke.

"Interesting. I was there when the original Adam tried

to summon a demon in Portland. He would've succeeded if I hadn't intercepted the demon and taken its place." He smiled at the memory.

Selene saw the smile, but the unseelie prince's eyes were still hidden within his hood. Good thing. Even without being able to look into his eyes, she could feel the dark fairy's erotic pull. She glanced at Adam. Or maybe that was just her now normal reaction to being in the same room as her raptor. *Her* raptor? She backed away from the word.

Kione wasn't finished. "The important part of this story is that the original Adam had to rely on a summoning circle to call forth his demon." He paused for effect. "Our Adam didn't. I'd say the mixture of raptor and vampire has increased his vampire power. That's a good thing for our side." He glanced at Zero. "And a bad thing for yours."

Zero shrugged his lack of concern. "I'll deal when the time comes." He directed his stare at Adam. "Remember, no matter what you do or how powerful you are, you can't destroy me."

Adam's smile was evil. "But tearing you apart would give me so much satisfaction."

Selene ignored all of them as she pondered why she was so angry at Adam. She relived her emotions as she watched him leap at Zero. When she realized what he intended, her first instinct was to stop him. Fear for his life took her breath away. Then came the thought that everyone else in the room had more of a chance of stopping Zero than Adam did. *She* was more powerful.

Not from what she'd just witnessed. Shame made her look away from Adam. She had admired his pure physicality, his predatory savagery, but didn't believe it measured up to what she could do. Looking at it from his perspective, she was an arrogant jerk. Sure, she was angry because he'd acted impulsively. But if she looked deeper,

Selene realized she'd enjoyed feeling a little superior. Not something she liked recognizing in herself.

When she glanced back, Adam was watching her. He smiled and then turned away. But not before she saw the heat in his gaze. Her own hunger rose to meet his. Kione? No, this was pure desire for Adam, no outside interference needed. They'd celebrate their escape from death later.

Fin spoke to Zero. "Why are you here?"

Selene admired that Fin never stepped out of character. His voice was as cold as his gaze.

Zero stared at Ace. "I came to collect what is mine." He smiled at the teen. "I followed the call of your power. Come, Ace. Together we'll do wonderful things."

Selene tried to distance herself from Zero's charm. He was beautiful, and when he'd turned the full power of that smile on her in the past, she'd felt like the most important person in the universe. She recognized that same emotion in Ace's eyes. He belonged to Zero.

Fin didn't ask Ace to make a choice. Instead, he asked Zero, "How much of all this did you plan?" He glanced at Selene as he spoke.

Zero's smile said, "All of it." He lifted his hands in a self-deprecating gesture. "I fired Selene because I knew she'd be angry enough to search out you and your men on her own." He shot Selene an I-know-what-you'll-do-before-you-do-it glance. "I told Ace to go with her, to protect her from the evil men with dino souls and their wicked leader."

What? Selene interrupted. "But I thought—"

Ace spoke over her. "Hey, you told me—"

"I know, I know." Zero waved their outrage away. "I lied. I knew if Ace followed you, Selene, you'd do everything you could to protect the powerless boy. And of course, Ace, you thought I wanted you to protect her as well as doing a little spying. My plan was simple. Since

I didn't know you could protect yourself, I made sure she would be there to keep you safe while you gathered information. It worked, as do most of my plans."

Selene wanted to wipe that self-satisfied smirk off his face. She settled for a few well-chosen words. "You manipulative, arrogant piece of crap."

"Why thank-you, Selene. It's gratifying to know I've lived up to expectations." He didn't give her a chance to reply as he turned to Ace. "Are you ready to go home with me?" Zero stood.

Ace remained seated. He cast desperate glances at Fin, at her. "I'm sorry. I didn't want this." His words faded, replaced by a shrug that said it all—regret, sorrow, resignation. He got up to stand beside Zero.

Fin ignored the boy as he spoke to Zero. "Do you value anything other than yourself?" He stared at his enemy; his silver eyes flooded to purple.

Selene thought it ironic that he could control every one of his body's tells except for those eyes. There was a lot of some emotion going on inside Fin. Now that she stopped to think, he hadn't had much to say since Zero arrived. Strange. He wasn't one to cede the stage to his enemy. And what a strange question to ask Zero.

Zero paused in the act of leading Ace to the balcony door. He turned to stare at Fin. He didn't even try to hood his eyes. They were a kaleidoscope of whirling colors. "Once, a long time ago, I thought I valued family." He turned away but paused at the door. "I can't even remember why anymore." Then he and Ace disappeared.

The silence was a blanket of lead, its weight bearing her down, taking away her breath, while her thoughts wove together the things she'd just heard and seen. The emerging tapestry disturbed her.

Adam broke the silence. "You just allowed him to walk in and then walk out with the kid." He didn't try to hide the accusation in his voice.

Fin didn't even look at him. "There was nothing to be done. This wasn't the time or place."

"Really? You couldn't have talked Ace into staying? When your favorite numbers finally roll around, we'll be facing that kid on the enemy's side. You didn't even try to fight for him."

Selene couldn't remain quiet. "Who do you think Ace is, Fin?" She thought she'd figured out that much, but she wanted to hear it from Fin's lips.

Fin met her gaze. He rose from his chair, and for the first time, Selene thought she saw his millions of years of existence in his eyes. Fin looked tired.

Kione had remained silent until now. "Perhaps we don't need to look deeply into another's life. Some pain is best not shared."

He cast Selene a meaningful glance, reminding her of the horrific details of his own life she'd heard from some of the others.

What? Then she remembered that Kione could sneak into minds. Maybe Fin had left himself unprotected for a moment. She looked at Adam. He shrugged.

"It's okay, Kione." Fin stared at the balcony door, and it closed with a quiet click. "I don't care if all of you know." He walked to the hall door but didn't open it. He waited.

Kione shrugged. "You think Zero, or Frost, or whatever you call him just left with his son."

Fin didn't reply. He opened the door, strode into the hallway past a surprised Dave, and was gone.

CHAPTER TWENTY-FIVE

"WAIT. WHAT?" FIN COULDN'T JUST walk away after dropping that bombshell. Adam grabbed Selene's hand and followed his boss into the hallway where he joined a puzzled Dave. Kione stopped beside them. Then they all stared at the spot where Fin had been and now wasn't.

"I hate when he does that." Adam gloried in his raptor's strength and ferocity, but there were times when his beast wasn't enough. Maybe he needed to get over himself and work on his vampire powers. He probably would never teleport, but he sure could summon demons or whatever those things coming out of the floor were. Of course, before summoning anything else he'd have to work on his control.

Kione started to leave. "I'll find my own way home." He glanced back at them. "You've banished three of Zero's team so far, but I think the toughest will be Six." His attention fixed on Selene.

"Why?" She lifted her chin but remembered not to meet his gaze.

"Because your heart is in play. Emotional involvement always makes things harder." He drew in a deep breath. "I know." Then Kione walked away.

She turned to Adam. "I'll do what needs doing when the time comes."

But he saw the shadows in her eyes, the sadness she couldn't hide. "I know you will." He hoped she wouldn't have to, though. Past takedowns hadn't gone exactly as seen in Fin's visions. If Adam could lift this burden from her, he would.

Dave spoke for the first time. "Let's head out. And unless you have somewhere else to go," His expression said they wouldn't dare. "I'll try for some shuteye once I drop you off."

Adam remained quiet on the drive back to Fin's condo. Selene stared out the window at the sunny San Diego streets, at the ordinary people doing all those ordinary things. Ordinary was something he'd never experienced. He fished in his pocket for his shades. Even though the SUV protected him from direct sunlight, the glare made his eyes hurt. Did he mention the long-sleeved shirt and jeans? No tanned anything for him ever again. But at least he was in a body, not a lone soul stuck underground somewhere.

He studied Selene. She was there beside him, so all was not dark in his world. *Enjoy her while you can, because she'll run screaming if you try to make her your mate.* When had he made the leap from lover to mate? His heart wasn't waiting for his mind to catch up. Anyway, now wasn't the time to plan that far ahead. December 21 was almost on them. Surviving till December 22 should be at the top of his to do list.

But at the moment, all he wanted to think about was sliding his fingers along the smooth curve of her neck and then leaning close to whisper the many ways he'd make her thrum with pleasure. *Nope, get rid of that thought. Bad timing.* His body disagreed.

Since he was only torturing himself, Adam forced himself to think instead about discussing Fin's big reveal. He glanced at Selene. Her eyes were closed, her lips drawn into a tight line. No, not now. She was hurting. Ace had a lot to answer for.

Once back in Fin's condo, Adam knew they couldn't postpone their talk with the boss. He didn't get to suggest that, though, because Selene spoke first.

"We have to find Fin and get some answers before we plan how to go forward." She headed for Fin's office.

Adam wasn't surprised when the boss didn't answer to knocks on his office or suite doors.

She took out her frustration when door-pounding didn't work by shouting at Fin. "I know you're in there. Come out and talk to us like a . . ." She paused. "Okay, not a man. But we deserve an explanation if we're putting our lives on the line for you."

Adam exhaled wearily. "You're not putting your life on the line. You're immortal." He shrugged. "For the most part. And why would Fin come back to the condo when he knew we'd be bugging him for an explanation? He's not stupid."

She turned to glare at him. "Where would he go?"

He gave that some consideration. Damned if he knew. "I don't have a clue. I've never thought about it before. He's never mentioned going out to relax or have fun." If he had thought about it, Adam would've assumed "fun" was an alien concept to the boss. Why? Because he'd never seen Fin doing anything other than working to foil Zero's plans for the coming apocalypse.

"Didn't you ever think about inviting him out with the guys for a night's entertainment? Maybe take in a game and then have a few drinks? Everyone needs to unwind once in a while."

Put like that, Adam felt like a selfish jerk. He rarely thought of the boss as someone with normal emotions and needs. Maybe he was due for an attitude adjustment. "No, I didn't. None of us did. But part of that's Fin's fault. He never tried to be a one-of-the-guys type boss. He's always kept a degree of separation from us." If Adam had ever reached out . . .

Then he remembered how Fin had wiped their memories. Maybe Fin had some penance to work out before he deserved to be taken out for drinks and a game.

"Well, if Fin isn't here to lead a discussion, we need to gather everyone in the media room and have one ourselves." Selene raised one brow as she waited for his response.

He nodded. "I think it's time. Check to see if Greer is up for some sandwiches and coffee. I'll hunt down Shen."

Adam didn't wait for her approval before looking for Fin's assistant. He found Shen in the media room slouched in a recliner watching a video. "What's that?"

Shen got up and stretched. "We've set up cameras in spots our spies have said are likely places to find Zero's fighters. Not the numbered ones, but the troops that'll do the grunt work, the slaughterers of innocents still alive after the nonhumans have finished." He nodded at the screen. "That man going into the warehouse is Horatio, Selene's father. He's the backbone of Zero's forces, the planner. Take him out and there's no one at the top to give orders to the ordinary troops." Shen looked away. "From what Fin's told me, he was the one guiding the destruction of your original civilization."

The one who killed me. Hate burned through Adam, searing every nerve ending until he wanted to leap through that screen and rip the man apart. He wanted to see the spray of blood, feel the tearing of flesh, smell the stench of death. He wanted all of those things. *Now.*

He is Selene's father. Adam shook with his need to kill. *He's Selene's father.* Slowly, he brought his raging beast under control, stuffed it back into its dark space, and fought to slow his breathing, to ease the drumbeat of his heart.

He recognized two truths. First, he could not allow

Selene to be forced into killing her own father no matter how vile he was. Second, if Adam destroyed her father, she would never forget even if she realized the necessity. She might say she forgave him, but the man's death would always lay between them. And knowing how fate worked, the opportunity to kill Horatio would fall to Selene or him. Fate was a bitch that way.

He closed his eyes, searching for a way out but finding none.

Shen spoke. "Did you want something?"

Adam opened his eyes. "Fin isn't here, but the rest of us will be meeting in the dining room. Would you text everyone telling them to come as soon as they can?" He could do it himself, but he wanted a few minutes to collect his thoughts, to figure out exactly what he wanted to say.

"Sure." Shen turned off the video. "Something Fin might not have had time to tell you, but he's called back the rest of the Eleven. They should be arriving by tomorrow morning. He's gotten word that Zero is doing the same with his people."

Adam figured Shen should know about Ace. "We found Selene with Ace." He took a moment to acknowledge his regret. "Ace is Six."

Shen shook his head. "Too bad. Fin liked the kid."

After Adam left Shen, he found Selene in the dining room. Greer was already loading the table down with food and drinks. The man was a wizard. Adam sat beside her. "It won't be long now." Should he tell her about seeing her father on the video? No. He could at least spare her that small hurt. "We'll get everyone up to speed on Ace."

Selene nodded. "We still have to come up with a plan to ID the stupid tune. We're running out of time."

She rested her hand on his thigh, and even that small gesture made him believe he could topple mountains.

He didn't know what she was thinking, but he chose to believe touching him gave her confidence, that she trusted him that much. Or, as his body pointed out, maybe she just wanted to touch him because he was so awesomely hot. He smiled at the thought.

"What's so funny?"

He shrugged. "Nothing."

Her stare said she didn't believe him. But she didn't get a chance to grill him because Ty and Kelly arrived.

Saved by the T. rex. Adam met Ty and his wife at the door and guided them to their seats. And if his greeting was a little more enthusiastic than usual, hey, let them wonder.

Before long, the others arrived. Utah and Lia, Al and Jenna, along with the single guys—Q and Lio. The last arrivals surprised him—Tor and Meg. His brother must be serious about Selene's sister if he brought her to a meeting like this. Adam put off the questions he wanted to ask Tor for a later time.

Once seated, he waved them toward the food and drink. "You can eat and listen at the same time." From the way the guys fell on the sandwiches, he knew he'd won their goodwill for the rest of the meeting. That was important, because without Fin here to soothe the savage beasts, things could get out of hand fast.

"Why the meeting?" As usual, Lio didn't waste time on small talk.

Adam had leaned toward Tor, listening to something his brother was saying, so Selene answered Lio. "First, let's get you caught up with the latest." She ran through everything that had happened at the Whaley House up until now except for Fin's last revelation about Zero's son. If she mentioned it, they'd never get to the rest of the agenda. She'd save that announcement for last.

"Ace is Six?" Al looked confused. "I never sensed any power from him."

Join the group. Selene sighed. "Nobody did. Which is scary, because that means Ace is so strong he can shield himself from everyone." She tried not to feel betrayed. Selene had been closer to him than anyone, but he hadn't trusted her enough to share his secret.

Al still didn't look convinced. "Why're you so sure he's Six? We only tossed three of Zero's people off the planet so far. Zero still has a bunch of them left."

Adam chimed in. "Here's what I understand. Fin's visions always show the woman who will do the job, and he automatically knows where to find the number he's hunting. Up until now, every number has been the only one of Zero's people in that city. So, we can assume this will be the same. Zero's other people are scattered around the world organizing their forces the same way ours are. That leaves Ace as our obvious target."

Kelly frowned. "He seemed like such a nice kid."

"Yeah, that's why he's so dangerous." Q snagged another sandwich. "It's easy to kill a butt-ugly old troll who's spouting hate at you. But things get complicated when your enemy is your friend. You meet him on the battlefield, think about the good times you had together, hesitate for just a moment, and bam, you're dead."

Selene didn't miss the quick side glances the others cast at her and Meg. "My father sent me to war when I was twelve. I understand where my loyalties lie. I *won't* hesitate." She caught Adam's frown. Was he thinking about her, not Ace? Did he still wonder if she belonged to Zero? She thought they'd gotten past that. Thankfully, Lia changed the subject.

"Next up, how're we going to find out what that stupid tune is that Fin heard in his vision? We're close to the big day, and if we don't find a way to eliminate Six, he'll be using all that power to destroy us."

Selene's thought exactly. She tried to ignore the small inner voice still screaming, "No!"

Adam finally spoke up. "We've tried to ID it. Lio did his thing on Google and came up empty. It's tough when all you have is the tune itself. Evidently, it was never a big hit."

Tor made a disgusted sound. "Maybe we all need to stand on corners and hum it until someone says, 'Hey, I know that tune.'"

Everyone laughed. Adam didn't. Selene sensed the lightbulb going on over his head. Uh-oh. She had a bad feeling about this.

"That's it!" Someone groaned, but Adam kept talking. "The tune must have some special connection to San Diego, not the rest of the world. That's why online searches haven't worked. We need to get people who play instruments or sing to stand on corners until someone recognizes the tune. We can offer a prize for the first one who names it." He threw her a triumphant glance.

No one spoke for a minute. Selene could see some of them opening their mouths to say it was a dumb idea, and then closing their mouths again. It *was* a dumb idea, but until someone else came up with a better one, it was the only idea they had.

"None of the Eleven play an instrument, and I have a voice like one of Crow's murder. I don't know about anyone else, but it won't be me." Ty grinned at Kelly. "Luckily, I have a talented wife who plays a mean flute."

Kelly offered them a mock bow. "I'll be happy to entertain the masses, but are buskers even allowed in the city?"

Not surprisingly, Lio spoke up. "I've checked out the city's laws. They're allowed as long as they don't block pedestrian traffic."

"Lio, our resident lawyer." Utah laughed.

"If we survive past the twenty-first, I'm going for it." Lio hit him with a defiant stare. "With the idiot things you guys do, the Eleven will always need legal help."

Selene pulled everyone back on task. "Okay, where do we find more musicians?"

"I hear the High Fae have musical talent." Adam glanced at Selene. "We need to contact Kione."

Al stood then stretched. "Anything else we need to know? Jenna and I want to get in a little more sleep so we'll be ready for our nightly hunt. Even an Allosaurus needs some down time."

Selene opened her mouth to speak, but someone beat her to it.

"There are two more items to discuss. I can fill you in on the details." Fin rose from a chair in a corner filled with unnatural shadows.

Startled, everyone turned to stare. Selene admired Fin's talent for dramatic entrances along with his cloaking power. But it would be nice if he sometimes chose to just knock on the door.

Adam slid his arm around her waist and pulled her close. He whispered in her ear. "Al has the right idea. How does a nap sound to you?" He flicked her earlobe with the tip of his tongue.

Selene turned her head to give him a stern gaze. "Business first." Then she smiled. "Play after."

"Where've you been?" Jenna's question sounded casual, but her eyes shone bright with curiosity.

Selene figured all of this was going in Jenna's computer file for her future bestselling book. Al's wife might not work for a tabloid anymore, but you couldn't take the journalist out of her.

Fin dropped into the seat at the head of the table. He poured himself a cup of coffee before answering. Then he faced his people. "I visited the King and Queen of the Seelie Court. I asked if they'd support our fight. They said their court would not involve itself in human battles."

Adam huffed his disgust. "Their fairies certainly stick

their noses into humanity's business everywhere else." He leaned forward. "Are we that desperate for fighters?"

Fin reached for a sandwich. He took off the top slice of bread and scraped off the pickles. Finished, he answered Adam. "We need help. Sad to say, the nonhumans around the world are more likely to fight for Zero than for us. They don't love how humans have treated them and the planet. We need a few more large bodies of nonhumans to join us or things look grim for our side."

Now that was scary. Selene felt the first twinges of fear. For Fin, with his seemingly limitless power, to admit they might lose wasn't exactly a morale booster.

Adam continued, "You have the vampires and the Houston wolves. What about Seir? Doesn't he control a bunch of demons?"

Fin laughed, not a pleasant sound. "Most demons can't wait to destroy humanity. And my brother doesn't have kind feelings for me. He'd love to see me humbled."

Selene wasn't sure of that. Adam had told her that Seir had helped the Eleven on a few occasions. She couldn't believe he hated Fin.

Q offered his suggestion. "What about the Unseelie Court? Have you asked Kione?"

Fin nodded. "I asked him some time ago. He wasn't encouraging. Besides, I don't know how wise it would be to turn such malevolent forces loose on humanity."

Adam offered, "We're desperate. Malevolent forces that are on our side work for me."

Quiet settled over everyone until Fin spoke. "Two other announcements and then you can leave. I can feel your aggression already reacting to my presence."

Selene held her breath. She knew at least one of them would shock the Eleven.

"First, I've called the rest of the Eleven home. As it stands now, I'm convinced the only way we'll win is if I can defeat Zero here in San Diego. I've never mentioned it, but both Zero and I will be feeding a portion of our powers around the planet during the battle, giving strength to those who fight for us. If we stop Zero here, his followers will weaken and lose the will to continue without his help. That's why all of you must be here to support me. Extending my reach to blanket the world will weaken me in this city. You'll have to pick up the slack. Second, I believe Ace is Zero's son."

Fin held his hand up to silence the clamor of voices. "I'm not taking time to explain my reasons for saying that. They're not important in the big picture. Now, go home and get some sleep. Things will grow more intense the closer we come to the twenty-first." Fin ignored the grumbling as everyone stood except for him. Then he pointed at Adam and Selene. "Stay for a few minutes. We need to talk about your plans for exiling Six from Earth."

Selene couldn't stay quiet. "How do you know it will even happen? What if we can't find the place?"

Fin's expression said he was shocked she'd doubt him. "Because I *saw* it."

"Right." Selene started to turn toward Adam, when another voice rose above the sound of people standing up. A voice they hadn't heard from yet.

"Wait!" Meg knocked over her chair in her rush to stop them from leaving.

Surprised, everyone paused. Selene was probably the most shocked of all. Meg never injected herself into important discussions. She rarely spoke up even among the people she knew. This was a new Meg, one who could cause problems depending on what she said.

Meg tossed a rebellious glance her way before speaking.

"It's time you talked to the humans. After all, they have the most to lose."

CHAPTER TWENTY-SIX

———

"LET'S HEAR YOUR THOUGHTS, MEG." Fin waved the others out of the room. "Meg and Tor, please stay behind with Adam and Selene for a few minutes. The rest of you keep going." When the room was finally empty, he focused on Meg again. "I'm waiting." He didn't ask them to sit.

Adam watched Selene and not her sister. He'd noticed something strange when Meg first spoke up. Instead of looking interested in what Meg might have to say, Selene had first looked shocked and then worried. Now, she even seemed a little afraid.

Selene turned and caught him staring at her. "What?" Her expression smoothed out the worry and fear.

He shrugged. "Nothing."

She accepted his excuse with a suspicious glance before turning back to listen to her sister.

"You've said the Eleven have some nonhuman supporters in high places. Maybe it's time to use them. If any of them are in the military, they can at least give humans under them a heads-up that something big is about to happen. Our allies don't have to say anything too specific. Maybe they can hint at a terrorist attack." She shrugged and blushed as she leaned into Tor. He wrapped his arm around her shoulders and hugged her. Meg seemed to take strength from his support. She straightened and met

Fin's gaze. "You have a whole planet filled with people who could fight Zero if they only knew their world was in danger. I think you underestimate what humans are capable of. Now is the time to find out."

Selene jumped in. "Hey, remember that woman who took control of the people under Whaley House? She was military." She looked at Fin. "Did you get her name? Where is she?"

Fin leaned back; his sandwich forgotten. "I gave all of them a fabricated story that didn't involve nonhuman activity. Then I sent them home."

Adam decided it must've been some story to make people believe the unbelievable. But then Fin was doing the telling, so, yeah, it was possible. Adam thought about his own lost memories and how Fin had filled the empty spaces with lies. He forced himself not to get mad all over again.

Tor had Meg's back. "I think she's right. We should at least warn officials and the military that something big is about to go down."

Meg smiled at him, and even Adam, who was pretty sure he lacked a sensitivity gene, could see the adoration in her eyes. Surprisingly, Tor returned the look. Well, what do you know?

Selene didn't smile. In fact, if Adam had to name her expression, it would be alarm. What was that all about?

Fin finished off his coffee before commenting. "I agree. I should've realized that sooner. At first, I didn't want to involve humans in my plans. They're physically weak, unpredictable, and I couldn't depend on them. Besides, if word leaked to the press too soon—and it would, because people can't keep a secret—we'd have billions of panicked humans in the streets before Zero's attack even started. But I can't be choosy anymore. We need their help if we can get it." He rubbed a spot between his eyes.

"It's no excuse, but this constant mental battle with Zero has fried my brain."

Adam waited for the lightning to flash and the thunder to roll, because the mighty Fin had admitted he'd made a mistake. That had happened twice lately. If Fin didn't watch out, admitting mistakes could become a habit.

Fin continued, "Tor and Meg, you're in charge of doing what you can before the twenty-first. Talk to Shen. He has the list of our nonhuman allies who could influence the humans around them. Oh, and make sure to contact the woman from the Whaley House." He paused to think. "All humans must understand this will be guerilla warfare. Their enemy will attack at night from the shadows and after killing everyone fade back into the darkness. They'll be facing nightmare beings with abilities never seen by humans and with weapons superior to their own." He raked his fingers through his hair. "Zero's people will be slaughtering them anyway, so we may as well give them a chance to defend themselves."

Adam watched as Tor and Meg left the table and headed for Shen's office.

Then Fin turned to Adam and Selene. "You two will have to arrange the street corner performances. Do you have any ideas?"

"We'll contact Kione. Maybe he has a few Fae friends who'll agree to play the tune or hum it for us. Humans don't ignore fairies." Adam would prefer to use a few of his vampires, but, well, daylight.

Fin frowned. "Keep it under the radar. I don't want the Unseelie queen involved. We don't need an angry fairy on top of everything else."

As they were leaving, Adam glanced back at Fin seated at the long table by himself. The boss looked tired, and if it wasn't Fin, Adam would say defeated. But he could never imagine tagging Fin with that word. Amazingly, he felt a fierce protectiveness for this leader he didn't understand and sometimes didn't even like. Fin belonged to the Eleven, and they protected what was theirs.

Once down in the condo lobby, Adam texted Dave. As they waited for their grumpy driver, Tor and Meg joined them.

"Do you think your driver will mind dropping us off at my place?" Tor yawned. "We need to sleep."

Selene's eyes widened. "Meg, you're staying with Tor now?"

Meg met her gaze. "Yes."

Adam smiled. Meg didn't believe in multi-word answers. He switched his attention to Tor. "Dave will complain the whole trip, but he'll take you home."

Selene was still focused on her sister. "Did you get anything planned with Shen?"

Tor answered. "Wow, did she! Meg took right over. Shen is sending her files with contact info on all the influential nonhumans around the world who are on our side. She's building a planet-wide chain that will connect—"

Meg interrupted. "They don't want to hear all the details, Tor." She glanced at Selene. "I promise all of you, I have this."

Adam turned thoughtful. Was that a challenge Meg was tossing at her sister? Interesting.

Selene started to comment, but Meg stopped her.

"Oh, look. Here's Dave. He doesn't look happy." Dave's unhappiness didn't seem to bother Meg as she climbed into the SUV first.

Not much talking went on during the drive because Dave never shut up. "Do you know how long I've gone without sleep? I didn't sign up for this bullshit. Accidents happen from sleep deprivation. Google the stats. I hope you guys aren't hitting the streets at sunset because . . ."

Adam blocked out the rest of his rant while he sent Kione a text. He also sent the prince a file of Fin humming the tune. As soon as Kione answered, Adam leaned close to Selene. "Kione will have a few of his people at my place within an hour." He could almost see her wilt.

"I'm tired. Ace healed me, but I guess I'm still feeling the effects of the blood loss." She yawned. "Please, tell me once they leave we can sleep."

Sleep? His beast was banging on its bars and demanding sex that would light up the sky like the Macy's fireworks display. Adam ground his teeth as he blocked out the noise. "Our songsters won't be going out until tomorrow morning, so we'll get a night's sleep." Well, she might, but he'd be sitting under a cold shower spray for a few hours. Way to end a perfect night.

Dave dropped Adam and Selene off at their apartment building before taking Tor and Meg to theirs. His last words before he peeled out of the parking lot were, "This job sucks. No job security and shitty work hours."

They dragged themselves up to Adam's apartment. Once inside, Adam got them both drinks before settling onto the couch beside her. With a sigh of contentment, she tucked her feet onto the couch and rested her head in his lap.

Adam didn't even try to keep his hands to himself. At least he was controlling his baser nature. But it was tough. His beast had gone from beating on its bars to slamming two pot lids together while it howled, "Take it all the way."

He stroked her hair. She closed her eyes and purred. "I noticed you were a little uneasy when Meg spoke up."

Adam felt her stiffen. The purring stopped. When would he learn to keep his mouth shut? "Never mind. It doesn't matter."

She burrowed into his lap before answering. "Meg is my twin, but I've always thought of her more as a younger sister. She's the perfect one, the one I always have to protect. Besides, she doesn't have any powers, so I wanted to keep her out of what's coming."

Adam took a moment to catch his breath. Her lap burrowing was having the expected reaction. "I don't know where you get the idea that she's the perfect one. And she didn't sound as though she needed any protecting tonight. Besides, I don't think there's any way she won't be involved in this. In case you didn't notice, she's with Tor."

"Yes, Tor. I'll have to talk to her about that." Selene slipped her hand under his shirt to slide her fingers over his stomach. "And of course, she's perfect. No scars and great hair." She smiled to lighten what she was saying. "I'll never stop protecting her. That's the way it's always been. Whenever my father would haul me off to some battle . . ." She hesitated. "Meg stayed home. Safe." She'd stopped smiling.

He would like to have questioned her further, because he might not have much sensitivity to emotions, but he was very good at reading people's words. That end part hadn't been the truth. Why would she lie?

While he was mulling that over, he stroked the side of her neck. Her skin was smooth, warm, and so welcoming he wanted to lock the door, scoop her up, and take her to his bed. Let Kione bang on the door all day if he wanted.

Thoughts became reality, because someone knocked on the door. Damn! He gently lifted her head from his lap and got up to answer it.

Selene sighed, opened her eyes, and reluctantly sat up. Did she want to talk to Kione and whoever he'd brought with him? Nope. Could she avoid it? Nope. She ran her fingers through her hair and tried to look alert.

Adam flung the door open and stepped aside for Kione and another fairy to enter. Just one? Selene frowned. That didn't look promising.

Kione dropped onto the recliner. He pointed at the

other fairy who stood in the middle of the room giving everyone the stink eye. Selene could tell him the glare wasn't working. He was too beautiful—tall, slender, with features carved from night shadows and moonlight, and eyes too blue to be real. His full pouty lips wouldn't scare anyone. Even dressed in jeans and a T-shirt, Selene was afraid he might not fool people into believing he was human. At least his long, blond hair hid his ears. She glanced down. Bare feet. Well, shoes weren't essential as long as he got the tune right.

"This is Birch. He was the only one I could convince to come, and he only agreed because he owed me a favor." Kione cast Selene and Adam an apologetic glance. "We don't like to perform in front of human audiences. And we definitely don't like to do our thing in daylight."

Adam looked at Selene. "Fine, so we make do with what we have." He spoke to Birch. "Can you show us how you'll play, sing, whatever?"

Birch's stare turned murderous as he whipped a wooden flute-like instrument from the back pocket of his jeans. He put it too his lips and played.

Selene widened her eyes and forgot to breathe. Yes, the tune coming from the pipe was the same one Fin had hummed, but the melody skipped, spun, and leaped, filling the room with golden notes that were sweet enough to taste, dripping with cool drops of springtime rain and sparks from warm winter fires. It was magic. It made her want to dance and dance and dance. She stood.

"Sit down." Adam put his hand on her shoulder, gently easing her back onto the couch. "Don't dance to fairy music. It'll trap you within the song and you won't be able to stop until the piper stops." He glanced at Birch, who shrugged before putting away his pipe. "If the piper doesn't stop, you'll dance until you die."

"Wow. Tomorrow should be fun." She narrowed her gaze on Birch. "Tomorrow, you'll stop for a few minutes between performances. No dancing until anyone drops."

Birch looked disappointed. "Sure."

Adam rejoined her on the couch. "Is there anything special you noticed about the melody, Birch?" His expression said he didn't expect anything useful to come from the question.

Birch shifted from foot to foot, not hiding his eagerness to leave. He stopped his foot-shifting just long enough to consider the question. "It's a palindrome. It has the same notes played backward or forward." He searched for an example. "Like the word 'madam'."

Selene frowned. "That's important, but I'm not sure why. It'll come to me. Eventually. When I'm not so tired."

"What time do you want him and where?" Kione stood.

Adam looked at Selene. "Would nine be good?"

She nodded. "We'll find a corner downtown." Selene spoke to Birch. "If you could be here in the morning at nine, we'll go together."

Birch deigned to nod his agreement and then was gone. Kione followed him out.

Relieved, she returned to the totally comfortable position with her head on Adam's lap. "If we're lucky, we'll have our answer by tomorrow night."

Adam leaned his head back on the couch and closed his eyes. He returned to stroking her hair. "You know, I'd be just as happy if we never found out. I can't wrap my mind around the idea of Ace as a cold-blooded killer. That's not what the kid is."

Selene agreed, but she was too tired, too content with Adam's stroking to answer. "Hmm." That's about all she was up for. Sleep pulled at her. But before she drifted off, she heard Adam mumbling to himself. "What did you say?"

"My beast is having a sexual-deprivation attack. It's screaming, 'This isn't enough.'"

She smiled. "So, what did you tell it?"

"I told it to shut up."

Selene was still smiling as she fell asleep.

———◆———

She awoke feeling disoriented, like she wasn't where she should be. Selene opened her eyes to her own bedroom. Adam must've carried her here. Too bad. She'd enjoyed the feel of her head in his lap, his fingers stroking her hair, her . . .

Wait. She was still in her top and jeans, but he'd slipped off her boots before pulling covers over her. How tired had she been not to wake up while he did all that? A glance out her window assured her night had fallen. She turned her attention to her bedside clock. Midnight.

A note lay beside her clock. She read it. *Couldn't get to sleep with all the noise my beast was making. Cold shower didn't help. Only way I could get it to shut up was by removing the temptation. Sorry. Good night.*

Selene was still smiling when the pebbles hit her window. She froze. That's the sound that had woken her. Sitting up, she swung her feet to the floor and then padded over to the window. She stared out to meet the gaze of her father staring in at her.

When he saw her watching him, he made a gesture for her to join him. She balanced the danger of connecting with him again against the possibility that he might have some information she could use. In the end, she pulled on her boots and met him in front of the building.

"Why didn't you just come inside and bang on my door?" She knew he could get past any code needed to get into the building.

Her father shrugged. "Fin has the place warded. It would've taken too long to get past it."

She cast him a knowing smirk. "In other words, it was too strong for you."

He scowled. "I'm not here to discuss Fin. Have you reconsidered my offer?"

"Why would I do that?" She gave him her wide-eyed puzzled look.

"Maybe because the solstice is just days away. When it's over, you and the Eleven along with most of the humans will be dead. And don't give me that immortal garbage. If Frost takes your soul, you're done." His eyes didn't soften or show any sorrow at the thought of her dying.

Selene went cold inside. How could she have any of him in her? No matter how many times she'd looked for caring, kindness, *love* in him, she'd found none. The closest she had ever come were the times when her power helped win a battle for him. Then he'd shown her his approval. And, God help her, she'd lived for those moments when she was young, when she'd cared what he thought.

She considered her options. Walking away from him now would gain her nothing. Maybe if she showed even a faint interest in joining him, he'd give her info she could pass on to Fin.

"I don't know." Did she look torn by indecision? "Living is important. But Fin is powerful, and his allies will be tough to beat. I think he'll win. Then where will you be? No pay if your side loses." Her taunting smile was meant to enrage him. His pride wouldn't allow him to even consider failure. When he got mad, he grew careless. She was counting on his anger pushing him into revealing something useful.

He grabbed her hand. She forced herself not to jerk it away.

"You think Fin has any chance of beating us? Come. Take a look at what we have." Without waiting for her to agree, he pulled something small from his jacket pocket and pointed it to a spot in front of him. A space opened, showing someplace very different from where they stood.

Selene couldn't stop her gasp. A portal. "When did you learn this trick?"

"Frost gave us the technology as a gift for staying with him. Pillaging became so much easier with this." His smile was triumphant. "Now we don't have to land our ships." He stepped through the opening, drawing her with him. "You're on my command ship. Frost has cloaked my entire fleet. Earth's military has no way of detecting us. Amazing, right?"

Selene's heart sank. How could the Eleven beat this? They had no allies charging from portals to save the day. She took a deep breath. No matter what, she had to learn as much as she could from her loving dad. "How about a tour?"

"Of course."

By the time he'd finished the tour, her father's ego probably looked like one of Earth's puffer fish. His pride knew no bounds. "So, what do you think?"

"The ship is amazing." But the number of fighters it held was horrifying. She had seen what had to be thousands of fighters, most humanoid, but not all. She could picture those thousands pouring through the portal to descend on and destroy some unsuspecting town. The slaughter would be total. And that was only one ship. There were hundreds of ships like it in his fleet.

Her father stopped in front of the spot where the portal would open. "Have you decided?"

He didn't say it, but Selene knew how badly he wanted the use of her power. She was nothing more than a weapon to him. "I'm not sure."

He sneered. "I can't believe you're still considering staying with the Eleven. Winners fight with winners."

She shrugged. "I'll have to be sure I choose the winning side then. Please open the portal."

"I could keep you here."

"I could release a plague of insects that would destroy

everyone on this ship." She narrowed her eyes, her expression promising that she, too, had learned a few tricks over the centuries since they'd fought together.

Gazes locked, they warred. She was determined to win this one.

Finally, he nodded and turned to the portal. As it opened, he said, "Oh, I forgot to tell you. Your mother is dead, Selenetaya."

Dead. The word drove every breath from her lungs.

Her father watched her. Cold. Expressionless.

Selene dragged in a breath. "How? When?" Barely a whisper.

"She died with her lover in a flash flood." He shrugged. "I can't recall the name of the world where she met her end. The authorities notified me on the day after you ran off swearing never to fight another battle for me." His gaze grew distant. "You kept your word."

So long ago? Rage rose on a wave churning with all the hundreds of times he'd shown how little he cared. For her. For her mother.

Selene's heart shrieked and tore. "You didn't tell me! *Why*, Father?" In her memory, the years spiraled back to her childhood when she'd longed for his love, but even then, knew she'd never have it. How many millennia since she'd wanted to believe?

No longer distant, he met her anger with his own. "You didn't leave a forwarding address, Selenetaya."

No, he wouldn't make her the villain. "You talked to me only weeks ago. You. Didn't. Tell. Me."

"My enemies were nearby. I couldn't afford a scene like this one."

Misery was a sour coating on her tongue. "Do you hate me that much?"

For a moment, she thought she saw surprise in his eyes, but then it was gone.

"I'm a warrior. Emotions like love and hate are distractions that will get you killed. So, I avoid them." His scowl said he was definitely distracted now. "You rejected me, after all I did for you. I made you the strong and ruthless fighter you became. It was all me." He thumped his chest while his expression twisted, grew feral with his fury at her perceived betrayal. "A true daughter would've shown gratitude. You're just like *her*. She never appreciated me either."

Selene stepped back from the force of his rage. But she couldn't allow him to bully her into retreating. "My mother loved me." Even as she said the words, she silently added, "sort of." Her mother had never said, "I love you," although she'd taken care of Selene and kept her safe.

His sneer destroyed any truth in her words. "Your mother carried out what she felt was her responsibility. Nothing more, nothing less. Love never entered into it. On her home world, women are expected to birth and raise one child until it can survive on its own. It was duty, Selenetaya, and only duty. Once you were old enough, she left . . ." He drew in a deep breath, and turned away, "both of us."

She loved me. She loved me. Tears filled her eyes, because lords-of-the-universe help her, she knew he told the truth. And it savaged her soul as she allowed the hope she'd clung to for all those years slip away.

Before he could see her sorrow—tears were a weakness—she raced through the portal, panting as she stood once again in front of her building.

Her trip had taken longer than she'd realized. Dawn was breaking, a new day. Great symbolism. This was a new day in her life's story as well. She'd turned the page. Selene was now motherless. No tears, no grief, no regrets. She'd save all of those for another day, another page.

When she reached her apartment, Selene hesitated. What to do? Go inside and call Fin with her information? Or . . . She glanced at Adam's door. She didn't want to be alone right now. It would be too easy to throw herself onto her bed, pull the covers over her head, and cry buckets of tears for her mother, for all Selene's lost hopes of reuniting with the one person she'd thought loved her a little. Option? Knock on Adam's door. Tell him what happened. They could contact Fin together, and she could forego the tears and sorrowful memories until she'd taken out some of her anger at fate on the enemy.

She knocked on Adam's door.

CHAPTER TWENTY-SEVEN

—————

A DAM WOKE TO THE POUNDING on his door. He glanced at the clock. Who the hell ...? He stumbled from his bed, not taking time to throw on his robe, and padded into the living room. He'd worked up a good mad by the time he reached the door. He flung it open, ready to rip off a few heads.

Selene stared at him; her fist raised to knock again. She lowered her arm. "I have news. We should talk."

It must be important for her to wake him at the break of dawn. Then he saw her eyes. They were haunted. Whatever this news was, it was personal. All thoughts of sleep fled. He stepped aside and watched her walk into the middle of the room. She looked lost. He couldn't imagine this strong woman ever being lost. Had something happened to her sister?

"Sit down." He closed the door before walking to where she still stood staring vacantly at the couch.

"Oh, sure." She started toward the couch and then hesitated. "Look, maybe I should come back later, let you get back to sleep." She started to turn toward the door.

"Nope. Isn't going to happen. Sit and tell me about it." He guided her to the couch and pulled her down beside him. For a moment, he thought about leaving her long enough to pull on jeans over his briefs. Then he took another look at her expression and decided the jeans could wait. "Talk to me."

She leaned her head back against the couch and closed her eyes. "My father dropped in after you left. Okay, not exactly dropped in. Fin has the building warded, so he stood outside and threw pebbles at my window. I went out to see what he wanted."

"He's dangerous. You should've woken me."

She smiled, a bitter twist of her lips, and Adam knew if she opened her eyes the same bitterness would be reflected in them.

"I was perfectly safe. He'd never kill me as long as there was a chance I might be *useful* to him." She packed all her sadness and disillusionment into that one word.

Something hot and vicious coiled inside him. Something that licked its lips and craved blood. Not his raptor. His vampire. "Go on."

"He sang the same old song. I should join the winning side. I should help him destroy the human race." Still with her eyes closed, she shook her head. "And I gave him the same old answer. *Never.*"

"Did he try to change your mind?" Of course, he would. From the little Adam knew of the man, he'd formed a picture of an arrogant ass who was used to getting what he wanted.

She nodded. "He opened a portal right there and led me through into his command ship. I got a guided tour of thousands of fighters—some humanoid, some not. And that was in just one ship. He made sure I understood he didn't have to land any of his ships. He could open a portal anywhere, and those thousands would pour out to spread carnage." Her smile wasn't really a smile at all. "I still said no."

His gut twisted. Portals? How could you protect against that? Did Fin know? Probably. The boss pretty much knew everything. Adam ached to free his beast, spread death in a river of blood, and then open the door to his deadliest vampire skills. *Dial it down.* He didn't show the violence churning inside him by even the narrowing of his eyes or the baring of his fangs. This was about Selene.

She wasn't finished. Something worse was coming. He sensed it in the clenching of her fists, her quickened breathing, and the drumroll of her heartbeat. Adam placed his hand over her fist and felt her relax. He hoped she sensed how much he cared, but not how much he wanted to murder her father. Adam waited.

"He was furious, so he hit me with the one thing he knew would hurt the most." Selene drew in a deep breath, and then opened her eyes. They were swimming with tears. "He told me my mother was dead." She turned her head and tried to blink them away.

Adam cursed, low and savagely. He didn't wait for her to elaborate. All he cared about was her pain, the agony she wasn't able to hide. Without thinking, he gathered her into his arms and held her tightly against him, trying to shield her from a wound that was already bleeding.

Selene didn't pull away, didn't protest that she was fine, that she didn't need comforting. For Adam, this was proof of how deeply her hurt ran.

Finally, she wrapped her arms around him and sobbed. If Adam could've reached her father at that moment, he would've torn him into bloody bits. At least he knew when to shut his mouth. Now wasn't a time for questions, it was a time for giving comfort.

Her face was pressed against his chest, so he barely heard her whisper.

"Through all those centuries, I told myself she was the only one who'd ever loved me." Selene gasped as she fought to control her tears. "I was lying to myself. She left us when I was twelve. No last loving note explaining. Nothing. And still I tried to believe. Neighbors said she'd left with a man. I told myself he'd forced her to go. My

father said she and her lover had died together. That I'd
been nothing more than a duty to her." She gulped, took
a deep breath, and pushed away from him.

He let her go. She met his gaze. Her eyes were still red,
but the tears were gone.

"She didn't love me any more than my father did. The
day after she disappeared, he took me to war with him.
I had become a useful tool." She tried on a weak smile.
"Guess I'm just not the loveable type. But that's okay. It
all happened a long time ago. I don't know why I got all
emotional over it." Her expression said she'd deny everything if he ever told a soul how she'd reacted.

Adam couldn't allow that to pass unchallenged. "You
are loved. Never doubt it." *By me.* The truth of those
two words upended all the neatly stacked beliefs he held
for his future and then kicked them all to hell. Now, he
couldn't die fighting Zero. He had to live so he could
protect Selene. Adam had to make sure she had a future,
even if it didn't include him. Sure, she was immortal, but
he was certain Zero could get around that little problem
if he really tried. Hadn't Fin removed his soul from his
dead body? What if Fin had stomped on his soul instead
of placing it in a safe spot? Adam didn't believe even an
immortal could survive that.

While Adam had been busy working through his shock,
Selene was recovering. She rubbed her eyes before turning her head away. "Sorry you had to listen to all that. It
won't happen again."

Adam huffed his impatience. "Stop apologizing. You
just found out your mother was dead. You're flesh, blood,
and heart, not stone. Crying is allowed, even encouraged."

Selene stood. She was leaving. But before he could
come up with a credible reason for her to stay, she started
walking toward his bedroom.

She beckoned. "I need something amazing to fill the
empty space in that heart you claim I have."

Adam rose and followed her. "Hey, I'm a great distraction. The best you'll ever find." He smiled, but it was a fake. She wanted *something*, not someone. This wasn't playing out the way he'd hoped. A distraction was a cold thing, a few moments to occupy the mind and body, but not the emotions. He wanted to be . . . He exhaled and let it go. Time to start thinking in terms of the long game.

Selene paused to glance back at him. She must've read his expression because her eyes widened. He dropped the phony smile.

"Oh, no. You're not a distraction. You're much more than that." She reached him in two strides.

Before he realized her intention, she reached up, grabbed his hair, and pulled his head down so she could cover his lips with hers. Her mouth was soft, and sexy, and tempting, and . . . He groaned as he deepened the kiss. Long before he was ready, she stepped away from him.

Her eyes shone as she stared up at him. "That empty space?" She tapped her chest. "You fill it. You don't make me forget the past. You give me hope for the future." She made a frustrated sound. "I'm not explaining this right. Adam, when we make love there's no past or future, only the present and *you*. It's a good feeling. One I want to hang onto. Forever."

He didn't give her a chance to say any more. Scooping her up, he carried her to his bed and laid her down there. Then he stripped off his briefs.

Even through her anger and sorrow, Selene could still pay homage to the pure beauty of his body. But looking wouldn't fill her need now.

Adam knelt between her legs, and she closed her eyes as he slipped her clothes off. In the brief moments before she was naked, Selene remembered his words, "You are loved." Did he mean she was loved by Meg? Of course, he did. She was afraid to even consider he might be talking about himself, because Selene had learned young never to get her hopes up that good things would happen to her.

"Tell me what you want." His words were soft, his breath against her skin a promise.

"I want a storm—black clouds, booming thunder, jagged streaks of lightning, wild winds, and lashing rain. I want to *feel*. All of my senses aflame." She paused to think. "I guess fire doesn't go with the whole storm image, but you get the idea. Oh, and no talking. Just every part of my body alive." Alive, the opposite of dead. She couldn't change her mother's fate, but she could absolutely celebrate her own existence.

Then he touched her.

He nipped her earlobe before whispering in her ear. "This is all for you. Keep your eyes closed and allow me to do my thing."

She smiled. "I'm looking forward to your 'thing.'" *Keep me looking forward, because back hurts too much.*

She reached up, and he kissed her palm before guiding her hands to his shoulders. She ran her fingers over their broad expanse and down the curve of his biceps—hard muscle sheathed in warm, smooth skin.

Oh, yes, she wanted this, to slide her fingers over every inch of his bared body. To breathe in the scent of him—male with a memory of the forest on a clear, cold night. To hear his voice—deep, rough—whispering sensual words only for her. "I changed my mind about talking. You can talk. A little."

He chuckled. "Only necessary words."

What she *didn't* want was to see him. To look into his eyes and recognize merely sexual hunger there. To know for sure he'd been talking about Meg, not himself. At least if she couldn't see his expression, she could continue believing there was still hope.

He shifted, kissing a path down the side of her neck,

over her breastbone, and ending when he reached her nipple. A nipple already puckered and ready for whatever wonders might come. She shivered as his breath touched her, and she hummed her joy in the moment.

He touched the tip of her nipple with his finger and she gasped. Only a precursor, she promised herself. There would be more, so much more. To prove her right, he proceeded to roll the nipple between his thumb and index finger.

She gasped her approval as she fought to keep from making any sounds that might signal a loss of control. She vaguely realized she was kneading his arms like a contented cat.

He transferred his attention to her other nipple, closing his mouth around it while he flicked it with his tongue. She bit her lip as she countered by abandoning his arms in favor of sliding her hands down his sides before trying to drive inland a little. She couldn't quite reach her destination, so she slithered down a few inches. There. Now she could massage his inner thigh and then, and *then*, she cupped him.

Now he was the one fighting for control. She could feel it in the tensing of his muscles as she smoothed her fingers the length of his cock. It had a size and strength worthy of the mighty predators he harbored.

He lifted his head, his breaths sounded labored. Good.

"How's the storm coming?" His voice was ragged.

"Black clouds rolling in. Wind picking up. Thor's chariot just pulled into the parking lot. He's waving his hammer. Lots of lightning bolts."

"To hell with Thor. I'm your lightning maker."

Before she had a chance to come up with a clever rejoinder—after all, her brain was grinding in slow motion right now—he wrapped his arms around her and then rolled so she was now on top.

Selene sat up, straddling his hips. She opened her eyes.

Now, this was a different perspective. Every luscious inch—she glanced down at the hard length of him—okay, inches, were open and waiting for whatever she might want to do to him. So many choices. She smiled. "Get ready to light up my night, lightning maker."

She knew she wouldn't remember the details, only the overload of sensations. The way he sucked in his breath as she kissed a path over his taut stomach. The warmth of his body between her legs. The way he ran his fingers through her hair before drawing her down to him for a long, drugging kiss.

And then, she wasn't thinking at all, only reaching for more and more of him. She nudged his legs apart and then knelt between his spread thighs. She wrapped her fingers around his cock and squeezed gently. He moaned.

Yes, that's what she wanted to hear. Her heart pounded with anticipation as she leaned down to touch him with her mouth.

He jerked when she slid her tongue around the head of his cock and then closed her lips over him. He cursed softly as she took more of him, her lips gliding up and down his shaft, allowing the rhythm of sex to take her. She wouldn't last much longer. Already she was clenching around the image of what was to come.

Adam didn't lay back and enjoy the moment long. Breathing hard, he gently pushed her head away from him. "Now you've done it. Don't know if we'll ever get to make slow love. But it won't be this time." His words came out raspy and tortured.

Selene gloried for a mini-moment in her power over him. Her glory was short-lived.

Without even straining, he gripped her hips and then pulled her up his body until she knelt right over his cock. Her heart pounded, and her breaths came hard and fast. Selene wasn't about to hold that position when what she wanted, no needed, was right below her.

But Adam didn't let go, didn't give her what she wanted. He'd pay for that.

Instead, he held her steady with one hand while he reached between her thighs with the other, and touched her. *There.* The spot was so tender, and she was so ready that she couldn't stifle her scream. So much for not losing control. He slid his finger back and forth, back and forth until she knew she couldn't take another second.

"Stop." She pushed his hand away. "No more coming attractions." She gave him her do-it-now-or-die glare. But the order lost some of its punch when her voice came out all weak and breathy.

Adam grinned up at her, his eyes dark with passion. He slid his tongue over his full lower lip. She stared at the sheen of it, tempting, taunting, promising what he could do with that mouth.

"Now you're just being mean, trying to make me forget about *now*." And she lowered her body until she could just feel the head of his erection pushing against her. Selene returned his torture by pausing there, wallowing in the pressure, preparing for the big climax. And it would be a nuclear event, she was certain of that.

Slowly, drawing out the exquisite sensation, Selene drove down on him. She'd wanted to make it last—the sensation of him filling her, the heaviness building low in her stomach promising, promising . . .

But her plans went to hell as he rose beneath her, thrusting into her until every thought leaked from her useless brain.

Abandoning everything to the joy of the moment, she rose and then fell again, and again, and again. She clenched around him as he touched something she'd thought out of reach.

Selene rose for the last time. She knew it was the last because every cell in her body screamed its readiness. Her breathing stopped, and it felt as though her heart did too. She tightened, tightened, tightened . . . And froze. *Hold it, hold it.* Then the storm broke.

Wind toppled her world, lightning struck, and booming thunder echoed her ragged cry and his shout of triumph.

Then she stilled, held hostage in that eye-of-the-storm moment when old worlds died and new ones were born. And even during this ultimate moment of touching the untouchable, Selene knew nothing would ever be the same for her.

Suddenly, it was over. Selene could move again, breathe again, and her heart pumped blood again. She collapsed on top of Adam, falling to earth once more. But at least she had a soft-landing.

Beneath her, she could feel his pounding heart, and hear his labored breathing. His chest was sheened with sweat. She rolled off him and lay still, allowing the after-shocks to bring her back to the real world.

Selene could take one thing away from her lovemaking with Adam. He was definitely magic.

He rolled onto his side to face her. "That was . . ."

Amazing? Incredible? Earth-shattering? Breathlessly, she waited for his judgment. Because anything less than those superlatives would crush her.

When he didn't continue, she glanced at him. His eyes were half-closed, an expression of peace on his face. Peace? Not the reaction she'd hoped for. And was he actually going to fall asleep without finishing his comment? He needed a nudge. "That was what?"

His lids drooped further. "That was *you*. The only you in the universe."

Well, that was cryptic, and not at all satisfying.

He blinked, trying to stay awake. "Would you consider walking into the heart of my beast?" Sleepiness slurred his words.

Her reply was all impulse. "I'd walk anywhere for you."

"Good." He smiled, and then he shut his eyes.

She listened as his breathing evened out. Asleep. What did he mean about walking into the heart of his beast? Probably nothing. He was half asleep when he said it.

Selene lay awake staring at the ceiling, thinking about all the things she wanted to say to him, all the things she hoped to hear from him. Maybe he'd have nothing to say when he woke, but at least now, in the dawn of a new day, she could hope.

Eventually, her thoughts returned to her mother. A woman she hadn't seen since she was twelve. A woman who'd abandoned her. A woman who hadn't truly loved her. Someone she'd never really known. And her hurt slowly faded into the distant past where it belonged. She gazed at Adam. *Thank you.*

She was still awake when someone banged on the door.

CHAPTER TWENTY-EIGHT

HELL'S LITTLE CORNER. SAN DIEGO'S special spot where patience went to die. Adam glanced around. They'd been out here for hours watching the crowds of shoppers. No luck yet. Selene shouldn't have answered that knock this morning. At this very moment, they could be tucked up in his bed . . . He shoved the thought aside. *Concentrate.* He was supposed to be guarding everyone against a sneak attack by Zero's minions.

Adam was working on a ticked-off mood, unhappy with most of his teammates. Utahraptors didn't humiliate themselves. A Quetzalcoatlus? No pride at all. Because Q, also known as the flying idiot, was out there by the curb dressed as Santa, ho-hoing it up while Birch, their sulky fairy, played Fin's tune on his pipe. Tor and Meg were useless as security. They were too occupied casting lust-filled glances at each other to watch for enemy infiltrators.

At least Birch had enough sense to wear a cap. Although, hiding his pointy ears hadn't stopped the human girls from flocking to him. One good thing, female adulation had brightened Birch's mood.

Adam glanced at Selene. A little female adulation might brighten his mood, too. But she was busy questioning people who paused to listen to Birch and promising them a prize for the person who could ID the fairy's tune. And there were lots of listeners. Birch was good.

Adam drew his hood over his head as he leaned against the wall of the busy cafe. The day was cold and cloudy, with mist adding damp to his discomfort. Not your usual San Diego weather. At least the sun wasn't a worry today.

As much as he wanted to continue his Grinch impersonation, the holiday spirit was starting to infect him. Happy shoppers, strings of colored lights and decorations, along with the faint sound of Christmas carols were making it tough to stay grouchy. He could almost forget that if the Eleven didn't stop Zero, these people wouldn't live to open any presents. Ever.

Adam scanned the area, watchful. The Winter Solstice was drawing closer, and Fin expected Zero to begin his campaign of human annihilation any minute now. After all, he had to have everything wrapped up by December 21 because that's when the universe would kick him and the rest of his dirtbags off the planet. They wouldn't have another shot at the world for as long as this next time period lasted. Fin might understand the whole higher powers thing that set the rules, but Adam didn't have a clue.

He allowed his attention to wander back to Selene. She laughed and clapped as a small boy danced to Birch's tune. Her smile warmed him, made him remember another smile from last night, different but just as much a celebration of the moment, of happiness.

Adam recalled every second of those minutes, and the heat from the memory reaffirmed life and . . . love. He smiled.

When he finally turned away from Selene, his gaze met the fixed stare of someone standing in the shadows between two buildings across the street. He knew that stare. He'd dropped his guard for a moment and the enemy had crept in.

Trying not to call attention to himself, he pushed away from the wall and walked across the street, pausing to glance in store windows but always keeping his target in sight. Finally, he slipped into the narrow alley and stopped facing his prey.

"Enjoying the music, Ace?" Adam offered a fake smile showing lots of teeth. "How's the spying going?"

Ace cast him a wary glance. "It's not spying when I'm standing where you can see me. Besides, everyone knows where you are. It's no secret."

Adam narrowed his eyes. "Then why're you here?"

Ace nodded toward Selene. "I like her." He met Adam's threatening gaze. "I'm liking you less and less, though."

Adam shrugged. "See me cry bitter tears." He leaned closer. "And that wasn't a very good answer. Try again."

"I like Fin, too. I don't want anything to happen to either one of them." Ace glanced away. "Or even you."

"Thanks." Adam tried to sound sarcastic, but against all reason, he was touched. The kid oozed sincerity. It was tough to think of him as the evil Six. "I assume you have a reason for being here other than your admiration for us."

Ace nodded. "Tell Fin that Zero has all of his people back, and the attacks will begin tonight all around the world."

Adam found it funny that the kid was still calling his boss Zero. Guess it was a habit. And then what he'd said registered. *Tonight.* He forced himself not to react even as his heart raced into battle mode. *Stay calm.*

Ace started to turn away, but Adam put a hand on his shoulder. "Wait. If you care so much, why not come back to us?"

The kid shrugged his hand off. "You don't get it. I *owe* him." He walked away.

Yeah, and maybe he's your dad. Adam waited until Ace

had disappeared before crossing back to the sidewalk circus they were putting on.

He joined Tor and Meg, who were standing against the wall behind Birch and Q's act. His brother and Meg were supposed to be doing the same thing Adam was—making sure nothing happened to Birch and his pipe.

Adam slapped Tor on the back. "Hey. You're supposed to be watching for anything suspicious. That's not going to happen if you can't keep your eyes off of Meg." He smiled at Meg to lessen the bite.

"There's no danger here. I'd sense it if there were." Tor flushed and wouldn't meet his brother's gaze.

"Maybe you're right, but I just finished talking with Six. He was standing across the street watching everything." Adam smiled his best fake grin, the one that said Tor was being an idiot.

"What the hell, Rap?" Tor scanned the street before turning to stare at his brother. "Why didn't you yell? You should've taken me with you. We could've dragged his butt back to Fin. High-value hostages are money in the bank."

Adam started at the sound of his human name. It almost sounded unfamiliar now. He hardened his determination not to lose that part of him. "Right. Like he'd come peacefully. We don't need a battle in the middle of San Diego that might involve human shoppers when we're trying to find Fin's freaking tune."

Tor hesitated and then nodded. "Guess you're right. What did the kid want?"

Adam started to answer, but a high-pitched squeal scattered his thoughts. He spun to face the new threat, and then relaxed.

A girl with long dark hair jumped up and down as she shouted, "I know that tune. It's the 'Crab Carillon.'"

Adam along with Tor started to push through the crowd that suddenly seemed a lot bigger. The people clapped and craned their necks to see the girl while not moving aside to let them through. What was that about?

Selene called to the winner as she tried to reach her. The crowd wasn't cooperating. "Congratulations! You win the prize. How did you know that tune?"

Selene was smiling, but Adam recognized her underlying tension. Out of all of Fin's people, this girl's revelation would impact Selene the most.

"It's the melody the 25th Street Bridge plays when you drag a rod or something along its railing. I used to walk over the bridge a lot when I was little. Mom would let me run a piece of metal along the rails whenever we crossed. It was a big deal for me."

Meg backed away. She pulled out her phone. Adam figured she'd be researching the bridge as they finished up here.

"What do I win?" The girl's expression said she was hoping to walk off with Birch in her shopping bag.

"You've won . . ." Q, still impersonating a slightly predatory Santa, reached into his sack.

Birch spoke up. "Come over here, sweet thing, and see the real prize." The fairy's voice was a dribble of caramel—sticky and sweet.

The girl didn't hesitate. She rushed over to Birch without a glance at what Q was offering. Adam cursed as he forgot human courtesy and began shoving people aside. But it seemed for every idiot he pushed away, three took his place. Adam was pretty sure the crowd response wasn't normal. He'd kill the fairy along with his fae magic.

Birch bowed before the girl, his long blond hair falling around his face, probably hiding his sly expression from his victim. Adam renewed his attempt to reach the girl before she did something stupid.

"What is your name, lady of my heart?" Birch smiled, all fae beauty and wicked intent.

Adam rolled his eyes as he fought harder to get through

the crowd that was now packed tight. He'd wipe that smile off Birch's face. But first he had to reach the fairy. For just a moment, he considered how much fun it would be to free his soul. Then he'd see how fast the crowd scattered before an enraged raptor.

"No! Don't tell him your name." Selene's shout was lost as the crowd upped its noise level.

Adam gave Selene props for trying to warn the girl.

"I'm Cindy." Her voice quavered with excitement.

Almost there, but way too late. Birch knew her name now. Adam could see Tor and Q yelling, with the same result. Who gave the go-ahead for a fairy to do this job? Oh, yeah. Fin.

"Well, Cindy, you've won this." The fairy held out a bracelet glittering with what looked like diamonds. He slipped it on her wrist. "Wear this and remember me always."

Cindy's eyes widened as she stared at the prize. She opened her mouth.

"Don't say it!" Adam was almost close enough to clamp his hand across the girl's mouth and the consequences be damned. But he was seconds too late.

"Thank you." Cindy spoke the words in hushed wonder. She stared up at Birch from eyes shining with adoration.

Stupid human. Adam stopped trying to reach the cursed fairy. It was too late. The girl left with a mob of giggling friends. He wanted to break Birch's pipe over his conniving head. The crowd was dispersing, and Selene had finally gotten to Birch.

She glowered up at him. "Typical fairy. Manipulative, cunning—"

Birch looked puzzled. "Your point?"

Selene threw up her hands. "Never mind. But if you hurt that girl—"

The fairy interrupted. "She is safe for some years yet.

Cindy is too young." He frowned. "I don't understand your anger. She will take pleasure from anything I ask of her."

Selene wasn't a screamer, but she was willing to make an exception here. "Cindy didn't know the rules of your game. She didn't know the danger of giving a fairy her name, because names have power. Cindy didn't know she should never accept a gift from a fairy, and absolutely never thank the sneaky . . ." Selene took a deep breath. *Stay calm.* She was sure flames must be shooting from her eyes. "The girl didn't understand that the moment she thanked you, she admitted owing you a favor."

Birch's smile was slow, sweet, and deadly. "Yes. A favor. I'll treasure the moment always."

Selene sensed Adam joining her, but she didn't take her gaze from Birch. "If you're going to work with us—"

The fairy's eyes iced over. "I'm *not* working with you. You offered no pay for my effort. I owed Kione a favor. It is now paid." His smile was cold. "But Cindy now owes me a favor, so I've gained my reward for today's music."

Before she could launch another verbal attack, he turned away, walked into the mist, and disappeared.

"Damn fairy." Frustrated, she turned to Adam. "If they're all like Birch, I can see why they won't fight with us. They have rocks for hearts. They're selfish and . . ." She searched for more words to describe them.

Adam shrugged. "Kione's not like that. So, don't judge. Besides, it's just the Seelie Court that turned Fin down. The boss won't ask the Unseelie Court for help. He knows the dark fairies would be as dangerous to humans as Zero's people. Let Birch go. He's young. If he hangs around Kione long enough, he might change." He shook his head. "And why am I defending the snake? Forget what I just said. Birch is a jerk."

Selene wanted to keep ranting, but she closed her mouth on any further insults as Tor and Meg walked up. Q was missing. She glanced around, and found him talking to a pretty woman obviously interviewing for the job of Santa's helper. Q had removed his hat and beard as he bent close to the woman.

Adam followed her gaze. "Even the apocalypse doesn't slow Q down."

Selene didn't miss the admiration in his voice. She harrumphed her opinion of Santa Q and his search for the perfect helper. "What now?"

"I think we should report to Fin before we do anything else." Meg spoke quietly, but her words carried weight.

Tor nodded. "She's right."

Q frowned. "Quiet. Getting a message from the big man right now. Fin agrees with Meg. He wants us to get over to his condo now." Q shook his head, trying to dislodge the pesky mosquito that was his boss. "I hate being his messenger boy."

Selene turned to Adam, but his attention was on Meg. Worry tugged at her.

"You give good advice, Meg, but you don't join the conversation much." Adam smiled. "I'm not criticizing, just saying that we'd like to hear your voice more."

Treading on dangerous ground, raptor. Selene hoped her sister chose her next words carefully.

"I hear her voice plenty," Tor reminded his brother.

Adam waved his comment away. "You don't count."

Meg glanced at Selene. "My job is to watch, listen, and offer logical conclusions." Her smile held a bitterness only Selene would understand. "I don't do small talk."

Adam was impatient. "Want to explain that?"

Be careful, Meg. Selene drew in a deep breath, ready to jump in and deescalate the situation if her sister said too much.

Meg seemed to relax. She grinned and shook her head. "Nope. Explaining would ruin the fun."

That should've satisfied Adam, but Selene saw he wasn't

about to let it rest. She wanted to grab her sister's hand and run away with her.

"*Your job?* That's a strange way to put it. You know, you can have more than one 'job' in your life." Adam's narrowed gaze said he scented something strange.

Selene readied a verbal attack to be launched at the next careless word her sister spoke. Selene would drown them all in her meaningless chatter. She reached out to clasp Adam's hand. Every little distraction would help.

Meg's eyes widened. She looked at her sister before giving Adam her whole attention. "I didn't mean it that way. I meant that observing is more my strength than talking." She tried on a smile that didn't quite work. "Selene is the extrovert, I'm more comfortable being alone." She brightened. "And reading. I enjoy books." Meg threw Tor a playful look. "Oh, and now I have something I love more than curling up with a great read."

Adam subsided. He didn't ask any more questions, and Selene hoped he'd forget Meg quickly.

Selene began talking to focus everyone's attention on her. "The rest of you should report to Fin. Adam and I will do something else."

Adam raised one brow. "Like?" His heated gaze suggested the "something else" would take them back to his apartment.

Too dangerous on lots of levels.

She reached for the logical next step in the investigation.

"We'll take a look at the 25th Street Bridge." See, Meg wasn't the only one with a flair for logic in the family.

CHAPTER TWENTY-NINE

———

WHILE SELENE GOT DIRECTIONS TO the bridge from Meg and then passed them on to Dave, Adam waited. The silence in his head was ominous. Fin was at his deadliest when he went quiet.

To blunt their leader's anger, he called Fin. As he'd hoped, Adam's call went straight to voicemail. Fin wasn't in a call-answering mood. He passed on Ace's message along with a mumbled excuse for not showing up at the condo with the others. He hoped that would pacify Fin a little.

Once on their way, he glanced at Selene. She sat close beside him in the seat behind Dave. Luckily, their driver was focused on the news, not on them. *Bad* news. A surge in murders all over the world meant some of Zero's killers were starting their party early.

She sighed as she turned her head to stare at him. "You don't think going to the bridge is a good idea."

Adam shrugged. "If all you want is a look, we can find plenty of pictures online. So, no, I don't think it's necessary to go there today," *and tick Fin off*. "But something important will happen at that bridge, and it revolves around you." Adam had a gut feeling it wouldn't all be about banishing Six. "I guess you have a right to check it out ahead of time."

She rested her hand on his thigh. He covered it with his own.

"Thank you." She looked away but didn't remove her hand.

Didn't she know he'd lay his vampire empire at her feet and then meet the sun for her? He'd rip his predator's soul from his body and die a human death for her if that's what she wanted. Didn't she understand that? Of course not. She couldn't read his mind. Besides, all that emotion over one woman was pretty extreme for him, wasn't it? *No, not even close, not for* this *woman.*

"No need to thank me. We'll have fun with music while the others are turning to stone under Fin's thousand-yard stare. He won't be happy that everyone stood around as Birch made the winner pay the price of doing business with a fairy." He tried to smile. Luckily, she wasn't watching so couldn't call him on an obvious fake.

Dave parked close to the bridge. He started to get out.

Adam put his hand on their driver's shoulder. "Don't bother. Wait here. We won't be long."

Dave turned to stare at him. "But Fin said I had to—"

"Fin isn't here, is he? He's tied up with his meeting. Selene and I will be fine. Besides, you can see the bridge from here. Anything happens, you come running."

Dave yawned. "Fine. Just don't get killed. Fin would blame me."

Selene climbed from the car. Adam started to follow her but then paused. "Hey, do you have something that won't break if she has to do a little whacking with it?"

Their driver reached beneath his seat. He pulled out a length of thin pipe and handed it back to Adam. "It pays to have a weapon to fit every occasion."

"Right. Thanks." He closed the car door and then followed Selene into the thickening mist. Darkness was already starting to fall. Short winter days put his vampire in its happy place. But with the night came Zero's minions looking for an easy kill. He smiled. *Bring it.*

She waited until he pulled even with her. "Why didn't you want him along?"

Adam shrugged. "He's worn out. I felt guilty. We've kept him on the run without much down time. Besides, I'm tired of having a constant shadow when we're out. We'll only be here for about ten minutes. We'll be okay."

She nodded absently as she pulled her collar up. "I'm suspicious. This mist is growing thicker by the minute. And it's getting dark a little early, isn't it?"

Now that he thought about it . . . "We'll take a quick look at the bridge and then head home." He had a bad feeling about this. Not that he'd mind a fight. He was in the mood. But now wasn't the time, and the bridge wasn't the place. *How do you know? This might be exactly the right time and place to fulfill Fin's vision.* But the boss's vision had included Meg. Adam relaxed a little, very little.

Their footsteps echoed in the mist. He didn't see anyone else walking nearby, although in the almost-fog, he probably wouldn't. Still, he sensed something out there, something just out of sight. He kept alert.

Finally, they reached their goal. There was nothing special about it after all of Fin's buildup—an ordinary bridge crossing over a busy highway. The railing separating the walkway from traffic did look a little like a giant xylophone, though. The mist now qualified as fog, and the cars passing beneath the bridge were nothing more than shadows with headlights dimmed. He hoped Dave would move the SUV a little closer so he could keep them in sight.

Selene stopped before stepping onto the bridge. She took the pipe from him. "Meg said to walk quickly as I hit each rail. So here it goes."

She began walking. As she struck each rail, the note

echoed in the fog. He counted the notes. She paused when she reached the sixth rail.

"Hit it."

The familiar voice sounded way too close. Adam spun, searching the fog. His predator's vision spotted Ace behind them right before the kid stepped forward.

"No!" Selene waved him away. "Go away, Ace. This isn't the time or place."

Ace moved closer. Adam sensed no threat from him, so he held his raptor at bay while he waited to hear what the boy had to say. And where was their driver? Dave was supposed to be making sure surprises like this didn't pop up.

"Why not?" Ace's voice was flat, emotionless. "You're here. The bridge is here. I'm here. We can get this done now. Fin can check Six off his list."

Selene reached him in two strides. "Stop that." She spoke through clenched teeth. "Stop acting as though your existence doesn't matter."

The boy shrugged. "If I don't care, why should you? Besides, this won't be the end of me. I'll just keep busy somewhere else in the universe until the next end-of-time rolls around."

"No." Her voice was made of steel and grim determination. "I won't do it. I care about you, Ace."

The kid blinked, and Adam looked away. The tears in the boy's eyes touched a part of him that his raptor and vampire didn't understand. The human, Rap, sort of understood, though.

"If you care, Selene, you'll do this for me. I'm tired of being pulled in different directions. I don't want to be forced to choose one or the other in this battle. I just want it all to go away." He shoved his hands into his jacket pockets to still their shaking.

Adam pushed aside his sympathy. "Running never solves anything. You'll be out of it, but what happens when you get the word that Zero killed Selene, or maybe even Fin?" He didn't think it would happen, but he was fine with laying guilt on the kid. It was for his own good.

Ace glared at Adam. "Shut your mouth. You don't get a say in this."

"Don't I?" Adam narrowed his eyes as he advanced on the boy. "This is my world, too. I'm human." Surprised, he realized it was true. His vampire and predator might still be a part of him, but it was the human Rap he identified with now. "I won't stand around while Zero wipes out humanity. If you're too much of a coward to stay and make the tough decisions, then I guess you'd better leave."

"Adam." Selene touched his arm.

Yeah, maybe he'd come on too strong, but the kid had to understand that everyone had choices to make. And if he made the wrong one now, he'd regret it later in his life.

Ace set his mouth in a mulish expression. "Do it now, Selene."

Her eyes shone with unshed tears as she walked back to the sixth rail. Without another word, she struck it with her pipe.

The note echoed in the swirling fog. Time seemed to stop. Adam held his breath, waiting for the inevitable unraveling of Ace's body before he was flung from this world. Selene didn't turn around to look. She stood, frozen, staring at the sixth rail.

Nothing. Happened.

Adam muttered a few low curses to express his relief.

Selene turned to see what had caused his reaction.

"I'm still here." Ace glanced down, making sure all of his parts were accounted for. "*Why* am I still here?" He turned an outraged stare on Selene. "You did something wrong."

Selene closed her eyes, her relief obvious. "I didn't do anything wrong. But we were one person short."

Ace slumped. "Explain. I had to work myself up to do this. Don't think I can do it again."

"Good." Adam nodded. "We don't need any more of that drama." He might sound unsympathetic, but Adam was angry at how much the kid was hurting the woman he loved.

Selene opened her eyes. She turned away from Ace as she scrubbed the moisture from them. Then she put her back to the railing and slid down it until she was seated. She tilted her head to stare up at a sky she couldn't see. "Fin's vision included Meg. I think I've figured it out. Birch said the tune was a palindrome. That means both sixth notes have to be played at the same time." She gestured toward the other end of the bridge. "Meg isn't here to hit the other rail." Finally, she smiled. "That means I can't help you disappear from Earth without her. And Meg is with Fin right now."

Ace didn't smile. "So, what do I do when the killing starts?"

Adam tried to ignore the lost look in the kid's eyes. To take his mind from Ace, he thought about Fin's vision instead. Why did it have to be Selene and Meg? Okay, he could understand Selene. She had power. But what was so special about Meg that she had to also hit the rail?

"Come stay with me, Ace." Selene stood. She covered the space between them in two strides. She wrapped the kid in her arms. "You'll always be safe with me."

Ace just nodded. She dropped her arms and then stepped away from him. "Promise you'll think about it."

"Sure." He turned away.

"Wait." Adam had a question for the kid. "Did you have anything to do with this fog and early nightfall?"

"Yeah." He started to walk away. "I didn't want any witnesses to what I thought would happen. Wasted effort." With that last bitter comment, he disappeared.

Adam shook his head as he turned back to Selene.

"You might regret not tossing his butt off the planet. We have no idea how powerful he really is. I'd bet even he doesn't know."

"He'll make the right decision. I have faith in him." Selene hoped she sounded more confident than she felt. She'd allowed emotion to interfere with her common sense.

He took her hand as they walked back to the SUV. "Changing the subject. I've been thinking about this sixth-rail thing. I don't know why it has to be you and Meg. In the vision Fin had of the Philly bell, he saw Jenna ringing it. But in the end, Utah rang the bell. Same result. Number Eight was gone."

She shrugged. "But Meg and I make sense. We're twins, almost the same person."

When he didn't reply, she changed the subject. "We'd better head back to Fin's condo. He won't be happy with us, but the news that Ace isn't an enthusiastic participant in the apocalypse should put him in a better mood."

Adam nodded. He opened his mouth to answer her. Then he froze. She recognized the distant expression on his face. Fin was in his head. Finally, he turned to her. "Fin has word that something is happening at Crow's place. His birds are going crazy. The boss wants us to check it out before someone calls the cops."

They raced back to the SUV. Adam peered inside. "I don't believe it. He's asleep. Now we know why he didn't ride to our rescue when Ace showed up."

Selene banged on the window.

Dave's eyes popped open. Faster than she could follow, a gun appeared in one hand and a knife in the other. He shoved his door open and leaped out. "Where's that little worm? I'll carve him up like a Thanksgiving turkey."

Adam held up his hands. "Whoa. Calm down. It's over. You slept through all the drama."

"Slept?" Their driver's voice quivered with outrage. "I

never sleep on the job. I . . ." He blinked. "I remember seeing that young punk walk past me. He waved and smiled. Then . . ." Dave shook his head. "I don't remember anything else until now."

"See, it wasn't your fault," Selene soothed. "Ace obviously sent you to sleep because he knew you'd cause him trouble if you followed him onto the bridge. He feared you." Was she laying it on too thick? Probably.

"You think so?" Dave brightened. "I'll make him pay the next time we meet."

"We don't have time for ego-stroking." Adam yanked open the back door and waited while Selene scrambled inside. Then he joined her. "Fin sounded worried. He said to get to Crow's and take care of the situation." He slammed the door closed, not trying to hide his irritation. "Too bad he couldn't tell us what the 'situation' was."

Dave had returned to the driver's seat. He gunned the motor and they took off.

For what seemed hours but was probably only minutes, Selene listened to their driver muttering threats aimed at Ace featuring death preceded by unending pain. Until she'd heard enough from him. She was trying to focus on what they might meet at Crow's, and she didn't need Dave's rants.

She leaned forward until their driver could see her narrowed eyes and totally ticked off expression. "Please shut up, Dave. I'm trying to concentrate on battle strategies."

Dave met her glare for glare. He must've sensed something, though, because he nodded and stopped grumbling. Ah, blessed silence.

Adam smiled and winked. Then he pulled her up against him. He whispered in her ear, "You sure know how to handle your men, woman."

She smiled. That would probably be her last smile for a while.

As they drew closer to Crow's house, Selene noticed

the fog was thinning and the darkness had lifted a little. Figured. Ace didn't need to hide anymore.

Dave rolled down his window. "Do you hear those birds? Something has them plenty riled up."

For the last few blocks, all they had to do was follow the cries of the crows. Selene rubbed the goosebumps that had suddenly popped up on her arms. Weird. Suddenly, she wanted to tell Dave to turn around and get them the heck away from there. Afraid? Why? She couldn't spot any danger.

Finally, Crow's house came into view. The dark shapes of Crow's murder circled the building. Their angry and confused caws echoed along the strangely empty street.

Dave pulled to the curb halfway down the block. "No use advertising we're here if something bad is going down inside. Besides, I don't like the feel of this place. We have to be ready for a quick escape."

Selene was fine with that. "Stay here. We'll text if we need you." Not that she foresaw anything powerful enough to challenge the two of them.

She piled out of the SUV with Adam close behind her. Then they crept down the street, using trees and bushes to hide their presence. Finally, they crouched in front of Crow's house.

Adam leaned close to whisper in her ear. "No people outside. No traffic. And it's not fully dark yet. I don't think we even needed to do any sneaking. The whole area feels deserted."

She stepped onto the walk leading up to Crow's house. Adam whistled softly and added a "damn" at the same time she got a look at the front door. Or what was left of it.

Something huge had gone through the door leaving pieces of it scattered over the porch. Not only had the massive thing taken out the door, but also the frame and the walls on either side.

"I'd bet it's still in there." Adam sounded hopeful.

They didn't have long to wait for confirmation.

An immense body filled the doorway. And as it moved into the light, Selene whispered a horrified, "Oh, no." Adam's sharply indrawn breath expressed his feelings better than any words.

The creature scuttled out of the house. Once in the open, Selene could get the full effect.

The thing looked like a giant octopus. It was at least seven feet tall with a huge, bulbous body and tentacles that stretched from the doorway to the porch steps. No, Selene corrected herself. Not exactly tentacles. Because at the end of each one was a hand sporting impressive claws.

The similarity to an octopus ended quickly. It had ten tentacles rather than eight along with five eyes as opposed to the octopus's two. And all five of those eyes gleamed with feral intelligence.

Selene didn't take her attention from the creature. "It looks as though Zero's main weapons are really back in town. I never met any of them, but I have their descriptions. This guy is mainly aquatic, but he can function on land."

It spoke, its mouth moving in a creepy parody of human lips. "Don't forget to mention I'm rabidly carnivorous. Oh, and smart. I would love to go for my law degree, but I'm afraid I would upset the dynamics of a human classroom." His—definitely a male voice—mouth parted in a grin that exposed deadly fangs. "Professors tend to get upset when you eat your fellow students."

Selene felt Adam tense beside her. She placed her hand on his arm. "Don't. This isn't a good place for a battle."

The creature focused its attention on Adam. "Don't even think about attacking me, raptor. It would take all of your feeble Eleven to even make me sweat." Pause. "Oh, wait. I can't sweat. But before you call in your buddies to try to prove me wrong, remember I'm immortal. Nothing you can do will stop me." Its mouth spread in a self-satisfied smirk. "My name is Bernius. Remember it."

Relieved, Selene felt Adam relax a little.

Adam returned Bernius's smile. "A thought. If I dug that huge brain out of your overlarge head, could you regenerate it and retain the same thoughts and knowledge that you have now, or would you have to start over? It would make a great science experiment."

Surprisingly, Bernius seemed to be considering Adam's question. "Interesting conjecture. Immortality does have some gray areas. Perhaps we shouldn't explore it." Bernius turned his attention to Selene. "And, yes, I get it. We carnivores are hard-wired to fight and kill. But this time we should practice self-control. The final battle will be in a few days." Again, that smile. "It'll be like a cosmic Showdown at the OK Corral. I can hardly wait."

Selene was over the small talk. "Where's Crow?"

Bernius gestured behind him with one of his arms. "Inside. Dead. I came to peacefully request that he return something he stole from our boss. It had sentimental value. He attacked me, so I killed him." He shrugged, dismissing the death.

Adam didn't seem surprised. "What did you do with all the humans in the neighborhood?"

Bernius waved his arms in the air. "I used my Tentacles of Terror to cast a blanket of doom over several blocks. My blanket throws fear into those it touches. It encourages them to stay inside in a safe area away from windows and doors. Drivers are reluctant to drive down those streets. You obviously were less affected. I would expect no less. When I leave, I'll release them. They'll be puzzled, but not alarmed."

Adam snorted. "Tentacles of Terror? Blanket of doom? You're kidding, right?"

Bernius looked insulted. "I've watched movies and TV.

Humans crave drama. So, I've given my powers colorful names. Now, if you have nothing else to discuss, I'll be going."

As he started to scuttle away, the crows attacked.

For a few minutes, the area around Bernius was a whirling maelstrom of waving tentacles, distressed and angry caws, and a cloud of black feathers. It was over almost as soon as it began. When everything cleared, dead birds lay scattered over the lawn. Bernius dusted himself off and disappeared.

"Poor crows. They died protecting a dead master." Selene turned to Adam. "I wonder what Bernius's other powers are? I suppose we'll find out soon enough."

"I can't wait to pop the bubble of superiority Octopus Guy is living in." Adam's lips were drawn into a thin line, his eyes narrowed. "But that can wait. We need to take care of Crow. He was a jerk, but Fin made him one of ours."

Selene nodded as she followed him up the steps to the trashed door. Just before entering, she heard a low caw from a nearby tree. Turning, she saw one lone crow perched on a branch. "He's gone, buddy. You're on your own now." Then she went inside.

CHAPTER THIRTY

A DAM STRODE DOWN THE DARK hallway. The coppery scent of blood led him to the living room where they'd met with Crow for the first time. He ignored his vampire's cravings.

Bernius had destroyed the door and wall next to it in order to squeeze into the room. One lamp lit the scene of carnage. The remembered kaleidoscope of shine and sparkle now had a bright overlay of Crow's life blood. Adam grimaced when he located Crow's body sprawled next to the couch. He heard Selene's soft gasp behind him. "Crow didn't have a chance. Even if he'd managed to shift, his giant bird form wouldn't have helped him in this small room."

As Adam carefully approached the body, avoiding stepping in any fresh blood, he studied Crow's ripped and shredded flesh. Octopus Guy's claws were lethal. Adam didn't like Crow, but he wouldn't wish this death on him.

Selene moved up beside Adam. She watched silently as he crouched and placed his fingers against Crow's torn throat. Shocked, Adam felt a faint pulse. "He's still alive. We have to get him to—"

"Don't bother. I'm done." Crow's voice was whispery, barely there, as he slowly turned his head.

Selene knelt on Crow's other side. She didn't offer false hope as she gripped the dying man's hand.

Crow clung to it, a last lifeline. "Just listen." He paused to gasp for breath. "Only have a few minutes left."

Adam could smell death. It was close. He rested his hand on Crow's shoulder. "What happened?"

"Stole something from Zero. Bernius came to collect. I said no. Then tried to shoot him. He ripped me up." A faint smile touched Crow's lips. "The bastard didn't get it. A crow never gives away his stash."

Adam scanned the area. There. The gun lay partially under the couch.

"He's almost gone," Selene whispered.

Adam nodded. "Anything else, Crow?"

Crow gave a faint nod. "Two things I want you to do." He lifted his hand weakly toward Adam. "Promise."

Adam never made promises when he didn't know the terms. He opened his mouth to say "no" when he caught Selene's gaze. She nodded; her eyes messaged "yes".

His vampire and beast figured he didn't owe Crow anything. Adam should just let him die. No big loss. But his human . . .? His human thought Crow wouldn't be asking for something big, and how would it hurt to grant a dying person his last wish? Adam's vampire and beast both thought his human was an idiot. He nodded. "I promise."

"Take my crows as your own. Treat them with respect, and they will be loyal."

Adam pictured the one crow left perched in the tree outside. No need to tell Crow his murder was gone except for that lone bird. It wouldn't be a problem. He started to nod, but Crow wasn't finished.

"In my pocket." Crow glanced down.

Adam reached in and pulled out a small, translucent green stone.

"It's aventurine." Crow coughed up blood. He took a shallow rasping breath and continued. "The stone controls the murder. When you no longer need them, crush

the stone and free them. My crows have served me well."
And in a barely audible voice, he whispered. "They are
the only living things I ever loved."

Adam felt death closing in—a cold that spoke of damp
earth and endless darkness. Lesson learned. At the end
of his existence, Adam would have loved many things
and many people. But most of all, he would have loved
Selene. He was sure of that now.

"One more thing." Crow was gasping between each
word, his voice barely audible. Adam glanced at Selene.
"Tell Fin to send me home in the robe you gave me. It
was the only gift I ever got."

He closed his eyes forever.

And Selene cried. Tears rolled down her cheeks as she
tried to swipe them away. "Look at me. He was a killer. I
didn't even like him."

Adam said the first words that came to him. "You cry
for someone who was so alone he'd never received a gift,
whose only friends were his birds, who wasted his life by
making all the wrong decisions."

One of the many things Adam loved about Selene. All
the violence she'd seen, along with having a bastard for a
father, hadn't hardened her.

She nodded and remained kneeling by the body as
Adam rose. He opened his mind to Fin and then told
him what had happened. Fin didn't reply immediately,
and Adam wondered what he was thinking.

Finally, Fin gave instructions. *I'll send people to retrieve
the body. Make sure you put the robe Crow wanted next to
him. Then come to the condo. Crush the stone to free the bird. If
you decide to keep the crow, make sure it craps on someone else's
building.* Without waiting for a reply, he disconnected.

Leave it to Fin to leach all emotion from Crow's death.
Adam pulled himself back to what had to be done. When
he relayed Fin's instructions, she didn't comment, only

rose and walked toward the stairs. But she paused in front of him before leaving.

"I didn't have a chance to tell Crow we had something in common. I've only received one gift since my mother disappeared from my life a long time ago. My father gave it to me—the head of an enemy. I like Crow's robe better." She went to retrieve said robe.

When they finally left the house, he took lots of thoughts with him. Of Crow. Would that be his fate if someone ended his existence? Nothing remaining but the memories of an endless string of deaths? No. He glanced at Selene who walked beside him. He'd make a better life, if he lived past the next few days. And he'd bring Selene presents. Lots of them.

Selene returned his gaze and smiled. "I refuse to remember the bad things about that house. I'll remember Crow's closet. That was a good closet."

He nodded. "I agree. A great closet." If he could only take that closet with him, he would.

Adam's thoughts shattered as a soft caw reminded him of his promise. He stared at the last remaining crow. The bird studied him from bright, intelligent eyes. Then it flew from the tree branch to land on his shoulder before he could brush it away. It cocked its head with a let's-get-on-with-it attitude. The bird deserved freedom. Adam pulled the stone from his pocket, dropped it on the cement, and crushed it with his heel.

Then he watched the bird fly away.

———◆———

"We'll discuss your disregard for orders later." Fin tapped one finger on the table, the only sign—along with a cold stare—that he was mad. "We have important things to talk about first. We'll begin in a few minutes." Distracted, his gaze flickered between the door and the wall of windows.

Selene relaxed a little. Distracted was good. Less time for Fin to think about his anger with them. Utah beckoned them over to the seats he'd saved. Selene followed Adam, and quietly took her place at the long dining room table. She glanced around. She assumed they were the last to arrive.

The room was packed. All of the Eleven along with their wives sat at the table. There weren't enough seats, so some had dragged chairs from other rooms. She spotted Jude and Xavier along with Kione and Birch sitting against the wall. Surprisingly, she saw a human female seated near Fin. Stern, with an air of command, and somehow familiar, she wore the uniform of one of this country's armed forces. Selene didn't know the names of the different branches, so she couldn't ID her. She turned to Utah. "A human? Who?"

"Lieutenant General Stapleton. Army. Remember that woman who helped get everyone out from under the Whaley House? Turns out she's a high-ranking officer. Fin showed her some things. Now she's a believer."

Selene nodded and then turned her attention to the food. Greer had performed his usual magic. Drinks, sandwiches, and pastries filled the huge table.

Selene knew she should be hungry. She wasn't. Crow's death was still too fresh. Her father would say she was getting soft. Maybe she was, but right now it didn't feel like a bad thing. So, no food.

And she sure didn't want to stare at Fin with his hard eyes and accusing glare. Instead, she thought about how serious this must be for Fin to gather everyone. Wait, where was Meg? She leaned forward to see past Utah and Lia. Nope. No Meg. She kept her voice low as she spoke to Tor. "Where's my sister?"

"Upstairs. Last room on the right. She isn't feeling well." Tor cast a longing glance at the dining room door. "I wonder if I have time to go check on her."

Selene stood. "Don't bother. I'll check now. It'll only take a minute." She turned to Fin before he had a chance to order her to sit down. "My sister is sick. I'll pop in for a quick look and be right back. Promise." She didn't wait for his reply. She was already in trouble for going to the bridge. What was one more act of disobedience?

She ran up the wide staircase and hurried down the long hall. Stopping in front of Meg's door, Selene knocked softly.

"Go away."

Meg's voice had the weepy sound Selene recognized from all the years spent together. "Let me in."

"Why?"

Selene's patience snapped. She was too tired to put up with Meg's attitude. "Just open the damn door."

After a few moments of silence, Meg yanked the door open. "I'm not in the mood for visitors."

She slipped past Meg into the room and then watched as Meg shoved the door closed. "Visitor? I'm a little more than a 'visitor.'" She walked to the small sitting area and chose a chair. "What's wrong?"

Meg shrugged. She sat in the chair opposite Selene and then stared at her across the coffee table. "Can't I just feel weepy?"

Selene tried to maintain her annoyance. After all, while she had been out kneeling in blood as she held a dying man's hand, Meg had been sitting in her room feeling sorry for herself. She took a deep breath and released her anger. "No, you can't. Tell me what's wrong."

Meg looked down, studying her clasped hands. "Tor asked me to be his mate. I said I'd have to think about it." She drew in a deep breath. "I'm going to say yes."

Each sentence was a whiplash, opening old wounds she'd hoped were healed forever. But deep inside, she always knew this time would come. Why hadn't she planned for it, lined up her arguments in a logical row to throw at Meg? *Because denying was easier and hurt less.*

While Selene was pulling herself together, Meg spoke. "Are you going to stop me?"

Shocked and hurt, Selene stared at Meg. "When did I ever give you the impression I would keep you from what you wanted?" *But you want to, you really do.*

"Will you give me my own life?"

The question. The one she'd hoped she would never have to answer. Selene allowed the silence to build between them while she faced the truth she'd always known but refused to acknowledge. Finally, she nodded. "I want you to be happy, so your life is your own."

At last, Meg met her gaze. Tears slid down her face. "It will weaken you."

Selene squared her shoulders while she attempted a smile. "I've been living with that weakness for a lot of years. Having you by my side has made every moment of that time worth it."

Meg was in full faucet mode now. She swiped at her tears as she jumped from her seat to hurry around the table to Selene. Meg enveloped Selene in a crushing hug before sinking to the floor at her feet. Her eyes shone through her tears. "Thank you."

Selene was uncomfortable with Meg's thanks. She said the words that had always held them together. "You're my sister. You'll always be my sister."

Meg dropped her gaze. "I'll have to tell Tor the truth."

Selene leaned forward to lay her hand on Meg's shoulder. "He loves you. He'll understand." She thought about Adam. Would *he* understand—why she'd indulged herself, why she'd held Meg by her side for so long? And she'd have to tell him, because if she ever wanted a future with him, she'd have to start their journey together with the truth.

Meg nodded. Her tears had dried and she was smiling. "I want to tell Tor right now. I'll go back down with you."

She started to rise, but sank down again as she seemed to really see Selene for the first time. "You have blood on you. What happened?"

"Crow is dead. This is his blood. Bernius, one of Zero's immortals, killed him." Selene gave Meg a shortened version of the event, leaving out Crow's last moments.

"That's sad." But Meg's words didn't have any real depth.

Selene understood, though. Meg didn't know anything about Crow other than what she'd seen at the zoo. She hadn't interacted with him. Crow was a symbol of their whole existence together. While Selene had thrown herself into danger, she'd made sure Meg was safely tucked away, never exposed to the agony and cruelty of life. Selene had treated her like a treasured art glass sculpture, something to be set on a display shelf, dusted occasionally, shown off to others, but never, ever placed close enough to the edge where she'd be in danger of falling and shattering on the stone floor of life.

Selene changed the subject. "Do you think Tor will stay near his brothers when this is all over?" If they all survived, she didn't want to think of Meg moving far away. *Stop creating problems that don't even exist yet.*

Wait, would Selene even be allowed to stay on Earth? After all, Zero had brought her here, and Fin had made it clear that as soon as eleven-eleven struck on December 21, all of Zero's people would be banished from Earth. No! Even the possibility made her weak. Adam couldn't be torn from her when they'd just found each other.

"What's the matter?" Meg frowned. "You just turned white."

And as she'd done for centuries, Selene protected her from the unpleasant possibilities of real life. "Nothing. I haven't eaten for a while, and I'm feeling a little queasy."

"Then move your bottom. We're going down to get some food. I'm sure Greer has set out tons of goodies. It's what he does." Meg was happy again. She stood.

"You head down. I'll catch up. I want to wash off some of this blood."

Meg seemed satisfied with her answer. "Sure. Don't take too long. Fin doesn't like to be kept waiting."

Don't I know it. Selene rose, ready to head for the shower.

She tried not to show her surprise when Meg leaned over and hugged her. "What's that for?"

Meg laughed and kissed her on the cheek. "That's for being an amazing sister." She released Selene as she pulled open the door. But then she paused to look back.

"Thank you for creating me, Sis. And thank you for freeing me." Then she was gone.

CHAPTER THIRTY-ONE

———◆———

THEY WERE BOTH SEARCHING FOR something. Fin's gaze shifted between the wall of windows— where true night had fallen, not Ace's creation—and the door to the dining room. Adam was watching that door, too. Selene had been upstairs with her sister for a while now. What was going on with Meg?

He tried to distract himself by turning to Utah. "Who does the boss expect to walk through that door? He has all kinds of wards on the building, and Shen has the alarm set, so no one can come up in the elevator without us knowing. And why is he staring out the windows?"

Adam's brother shrugged. "Only Fin knows. Alarms don't always keep the bad guys out. The windows? Maybe he expects to see Zero staring back at him. Wouldn't be surprised."

Adam lost interest as Meg entered the room. She surprised him by stopping beside his chair instead of Tor's. Leaning down, she spoke softly. "Please make Selene happy. She sacrificed a lot for me."

What exactly did that mean? He knew Selene had taken care of Meg—protecting her, shielding her from life's ugly side. But he had the feeling Meg meant something more than that. He'd ask Selene when he saw her. Meg started to turn away. "Where's your sister?"

She paused to glance back. "Selene wanted to clean up a little before coming down."

He watched her join Tor. She looked as though she'd won the lottery. Meg sat before bending close to whisper something to his brother. Whatever she'd said made Tor happy, too. He was grinning like an idiot as he turned to his brothers. "Meg said yes. She'll be my mate."

"Hey, congrats. When's the ceremony happening?" Adam was thrilled for Tor. Of course, he was. He listened as Utah and Lia added their congratulations. Then Adam admitted the truth. He was also jealous. Would Selene make him a happy man? And, yes, he was asking that as a human, not a vampire or raptor. No matter how pointy his fangs were, no matter how much the scent of blood drew him, no matter how the need to hunt, to kill, called to him . . . He. Was. Human. Selene had ended his identity crisis. His beast roared its outrage. Adam ignored it.

"We want to make the mating official before the big battle." Tor didn't add the obvious. There might not be much left of the world afterward.

Adam subsided into his own thoughts. Only Fin knew how many of Earth's humans—he glanced at the lieutenant general—and nonhumans would fight with them. How many fighters did Zero have? He had an unfair advantage. He had Selene's father along with all those mercenaries packed into the cloaked ships hovering above the planet just waiting for the word to descend and start the bloodbath. Then there were the rest of Zero's immortal minions, the ones the Eleven hadn't met yet except for the tentacled terror, Octopus Guy.

Adam wouldn't wait for the battle's outcome either. He would ask Selene to be his mate, no, wife. Humans had wives not mates. He'd ask right after this meeting. Maybe it wasn't fair to rush her, but their time together might be short. Yeah, he was nervous at the thought of what she might say. Sure, Selene had said she'd walk into the heart of his beast, but what if when everything was on the line she changed her mind? He could battle nonhuman hordes and get an adrenaline rush from the whole thing, but the fear that Selene might say no froze his insides.

"You haven't been keeping in touch, so I thought this might be a good time to get you caught up."

Startled, Adam turned. Jude stood behind his chair with Xavier hovering like a death cloud beside him. "Hey, I'm sorry about that. I've had things going on." Yeah, and that didn't sound weak. Guilt nudged him, reminding him that along with the original Adam's body he'd inherited obligations. Ones he'd chosen to ignore.

"We've all had things 'going on.'" Jude crouched next to Adam. "The vamps in the USA are ready whenever you give the word. Oh, and I want a raise. Do you know how tough it was to organize their asses?"

A rhetorical question. Adam didn't need to answer. "I appreciate everything you've done. Think of it as practice for when you take over." Had he just said that? Jude's startled expression said he absolutely had.

"What? I don't—"

Adam didn't give him a chance to voice his confusion, especially when his own thoughts were so scrambled. Adam changed the subject. "The word on the street is that all the werewolves in town lined up behind Zero."

Xavier snorted his contempt for the wolves. "All claws and teeth with nothing between their ears. You can't depend on them. It's always like, 'I have these badass aliens to hunt down and ... Oh, look, a squirrel.'"

Adam didn't believe that, but he kept his opinion to himself. "The wolves don't have one strong national leader to organize them." He nodded at Jude. "Like you." Adam raised his hand to ward off Jude's denial. "I haven't done a thing for the vampires. It's been all you. We both know it."

Jude sighed as he stood. "We can argue about this later."

He turned to Xavier. "The werewolves in Houston are with us. I've checked." Then he left still discussing the merits of the wolves.

Perfect timing, because Selene had just returned. He narrowed his eyes, studying her. She looked the same, but not exactly. There was something diminished about her. Diminished? A strange word to pop into his head, certainly not one he'd ever use to describe the woman he loved.

Adam followed her with his gaze as she circled the table and then dropped onto the chair beside him. She was tired. He could see it in the shadows beneath her eyes, in the whole way her body seemed to droop. His first instinct was to demand she tell him what Meg had done to her, because she hadn't looked this way when she'd left the room. *Don't go all protective on her.* He made the wiser choice of waiting for her to tell him what was bothering her.

"Did I miss anything?" She glanced around. "What's holding up the meeting?"

Adam shrugged. "Don't have a clue. Fin's been eyeing the door and the windows since you left." He tried to relax the ball of tension lodged in his stomach. Coiled and ready to spring was a good look for his raptor, but not here, not now. "I want to talk to you. Once this meeting is over, we——"

He didn't get a chance to finish. The dining room door crashed open to reveal Seir. He was dressed to impress in black leather with a red cape flung over one shoulder. His long blond hair was a tangle of curls around his face. Guess he wanted everyone to think he'd just flown up from Hell for the meeting. Two massive demons flanked him, all bared fangs and killer talons. They were so huge they had to bend over to enter the room. Everyone leaped to their feet.

Seir smiled and waved to his brother. "I'm here. We can start now."

Adam chanced a quick glance at Fin. He couldn't mistake the look of relief on his boss's face.

"You've decided to join us?" Fin took a step towards his brother.

Seir widened his eyes. He pointed at himself, at his two demons, and then at the windows. "Obviously."

Everyone turned to look at the windows. Adam cursed quietly. Selene sucked in a startled breath.

Beyond the windows stretched a legion of demons. They hung high above the ground, their black wings creating clouds of darkness around them. They peered in at those in the dining room from glowing eyes. The night hid their numbers, but there had to be thousands. "Won't someone notice your army?" Adam was officially impressed.

Seir waved away his comment. "The world sees what I want them to see."

"Are you sure you can control them?" Ty's expression said he didn't trust Fin's brother.

"Oh, please." Seir's eyeroll dismissed Ty's question. "Now, let's talk war." He strode to the head of the table where an empty chair waited for Fin. He reached up and pulled an identical chair from the air. He sat.

Slowly, everyone returned to their seats. But no one took their gaze from Seir and the two demons who stood to either side of his chair.

Fin sat beside his brother. Then he smiled. Selene muffled her gasp. Fin wasn't a smiler, but when he *did* break out a grin, the world stopped turning. A quick glance at Adam's scowl showed he'd noticed her reaction and didn't like it. She turned her head to hide her own grin. She was woman enough to enjoy his jealousy.

Fin's smile disappeared as he stood to begin the meeting. "Humanity's final hours or the beginning of a new era for them will be decided in the next three days. Specifically, by December 21 at 11:11PM when the old time period ends and the new one begins. At that moment, Zero and his remaining numbers will return to the cosmos, leaving what's left of this world to fend for itself. The Eleven have been gaining strength the closer we draw to that moment. Eleven is my power number." He leaned forward, his gaze raking each of them. "*Your* power number if you stand with me. Those of you in this room and the ones who fight with you will decide if the world as we know it survives."

Selene pressed her back against her chair as Fin speared each of them with a hard stare. She noticed others in the room had the same reaction. Fin's force bore down on all of them.

"Why three days?" Stapleton's voice broke the silence.

"Because numbers rule the universe. And my life. Three represents the triad. Think of a triangle—beginning, middle, end. All connected. And when you reach the end, you naturally begin again. And so, Zero will attack tonight. The next night will see the bloodiest part of the battle, with one side emerging as the stronger. The last night will see . . ." He shrugged. "Well, you know what will happen if we don't triumph. Either this planet will begin its new time period with humans safe from extinction, or it will not."

Zero would attack *tonight*? Of course, he would. With everything that had been happening, she'd forgotten Ace's message. Selene stomped on her burgeoning panic. They had to get out of here, go home, grab their things, and— *Stop.* She shoved up a white wall in her mind to block the chaos there and returned her attention to Fin.

Leave it to Mr. Detached to face what was to come with a cold, analytical prophesy. Selene glanced around. Now that Fin had finished his explanation, she noted how the Eleven were growing more restless. She knew they couldn't spend much time together around their leader without going nuclear. Selene wondered about that, but Fin didn't give her time to think for long.

He focused on Kione. "The Unseelie Court still won't help?"

"Mab says no." The prince rarely showed emotion, but his clenched fists and said what his words didn't. He nodded at Birch beside him. "He'll be with us."

Fin switched his attention to Birch. "Why?"

Birch yawned. "I'm bored. It's something to do." He shrugged his disinterest in humanity's fate.

Selene wanted to slap the sulky expression from his face.

Kione added, "His mother doesn't want him involved."

"So what? I do what I want to do." Birch's resentment that anyone would dare tell him no lived in every word.

"You treat your mother like that?" Selene couldn't stop her comment. She would've killed to have a mother who wanted to keep her safe.

Birch didn't bother to answer her.

Adam seemed to sense her feelings because he leaned close and whispered, "He's a jerk. I'd listen to my mother." He paused for effect. "If I didn't, she'd eat me. Mama raptors were intense."

She smiled. "Thanks." *Thanks for caring about my emotions and trying to lighten them.*

Fin glanced next at the lieutenant general. "Are the humans ready?"

Lieutenant General Stapleton stood. She met Fin's stare. "First, might I say you have a hell of a nerve waiting until the last minute to inform humanity of a threat that could wipe us from the planet." Her gaze challenged not only Fin but every nonhuman in the room. "And what kind of cowards skulk around in the shadows while preying on my people?" She took a deep breath. "But even on such short notice, and being forced to partner with a bunch of predators, humans will rise to the challenge as they have so many times in the past. We. Will. Survive." She emphasized each word by pounding on the table.

"Whoa. Balls of titanium." Utah grinned as he waited for the expected explosion that would annihilate the human.

"Brave but stupid." Adam glanced at Selene. "Ready?"

Selene nodded. "We stop anyone who makes a move on her."

Fin raised his hand, and the rumble of anger from the "bunch of predators" in the room simply stopped. "The lieutenant general has a right to her opinion." His cold glare said he wasn't a fan of Stapleton's opinion. "She is our ally and will be treated as such."

Selene had the feeling that once the war ended, Lieutenant General Stapleton might want to make herself scarce. But right now, Fin's word was law.

Finally, Fin turned his attention to the Eleven. "I would suggest you not return to your apartments. Their locations could be compromised. And when the fight begins, remember that these immortals destroyed your first life along with all your loved ones. Those who died so long ago cry out for vengeance. Payback is now."

The Eleven roared their desire to rend and tear their enemies. The walls shook with the pounding of their feet. Their predators were close to the surface. That made Selene nervous.

She looked around her. Not only the Eleven were primed for killing. She saw nonhumans she couldn't ID, and their hungry gazes said they weren't plant-eaters. Fin was releasing them just in time.

Selene watched Meg stand and start to leave with Tor. Then Meg paused to meet her gaze. She mouthed "Thanks," just before hurrying out of the room with all the others.

Through the mob heading for the door, Selene noticed that Fin remained. Seir stayed beside him.

Adam touched her arm. "Are you coming?"

"Wait up. This is my chance to ask Fin a couple of questions without everyone listening in. It'll only take a moment."

Adam followed her as she made her way to the head of the table. Then he sat and helped himself to two more sandwiches. Selene didn't fool herself, though. He might be chowing down, but she knew he'd pay attention to every word.

Selene remained standing. "Do you mind answering a few questions?"

Fin studied her. "Go ahead."

She hid her relief. "You've never been clear about how you'll organize this worldwide battle. Are we just supposed to go out and kill anyone who looks like an enemy? Where're the plans?" Selene had fought in many wars, but not in one with no structure, no chain of command. Only one leader—Fin. That's wasn't a winning formula. "What happens if you die?" Okay, so maybe he couldn't die, but she wanted to be ready for any eventuality.

His smile never reached his eyes. "Then you all die. Oh, and you'll know our enemies when you see them. Trust me." His smile became real. "The name of this game is unpredictability. Zero will find it tough to defend against an army that doesn't subscribe to conventional methods."

Well, that answered part of her question. He hadn't filled her with confidence, though.

Seir interrupted. "My brother-of-few-words hasn't told you the whole tale. Maybe this will help. Both leaders are masters of planet-wide battles. Fin will expand his mental imagery to encompass every place on Earth. Then he will telepathically communicate his orders to the local leaders of the fight. If there's an important area in danger of falling to the enemy, he'll send you to help." Seir smiled at her as though that solved all problems.

"What? No!"

"Yes." Fin's voice was velvet over steel. "You have the power to create whatever is needed to defeat any enemy. And if the troops need my presence to raise their morale, you can create me to do it. I have no one else with your skills. You *will* go where you're needed."

Adam spoke before Selene could respond. "Where she goes, I go. And since I'm part of a pack, Utah and Tor go with me."

Surprised, Selene shut her mouth to listen.

Fin paused to think this over. Then he nodded. "Agreed. And when I see the moment Six arrives at the bridge to meet his destiny, Selene, I'll send you there."

Selene couldn't allow that to stand. "No. I won't banish Ace from this world. I can't believe you still want me to do it."

Fin didn't even blink. "I foresaw it, and so it shall be."

"Give up, Selene. When he starts talking in his ancient-seer voice, it's all over." Adam stood and moved to her side.

Her father would probably recognize her expression now. This was her stubborn-as-hell face. "He won't fight for either side. He cares for you, Fin. Doesn't that mean anything at all?"

Fin's face was carved from a million years of rigidly controlled emotions. "Personal feelings mean nothing during a war. We can't afford to appear weak to Zero. Besides, if my vision showed you banishing him, it means he's still a danger to us in some way. My visions don't lie."

She wanted to punch him in his hard head. "But you didn't see *Ace*. Six could be anyone." She fought to control her temper.

Fin offered her his iciest stare. "He is the most likely."

"Heartless jerk," Selene muttered before turning away.

"Now I have a question for you, Selene. If you meet your father in battle, will you be able to kill him? Will you even try?"

Selene froze. She hated Fin for asking that question. Slowly, she turned back to him. "Maybe I will, but then, maybe I won't. After all, I don't have any almighty visions to make my decisions for me." Besides, her father was immortal. He'd be a tough kill. So, maybe she'd just wave goodbye as he left the planet in defeat. She started walking away. She didn't want to be in Fin's presence anymore.

Adam grabbed her arm to stop her. She waited.

"Since everyone is asking questions, I have one, Fin. Who are you? Really."

Selene felt the air around her freeze. She expected ice to form on the windows. She thought she was brave, but she avoided Fin's gaze.

"Stupid question," Seir muttered. "You're just making him mad. Run away, children."

Selene was proud of Adam for standing his ground in the face of Fin's anger. She held her breath as she waited to see what Adam's boss would do—answer or squash them.

Finally, Fin spoke. "You don't need to know who I am. It's enough to know I rescued you from the destruction of your original home and now I'm trying to do the same for this one." Then he got up and left.

Seir remained seated. He grinned. His demons didn't react at all. Evil gargoyles. Selene took that back. Who was she to judge?

"Go home and make love, or not, because Zero's goons might be waiting. And then fight for the glory of Fin-the-Numbers-Guy." Sarcasm oozed from Seir's every word.

"I'm done." Selene left Fin's brother still sitting at the table. Laughing.

Silently, Adam led the way back to the SUV.

She stopped him before they climbed in. "I know I shouldn't go back to the apartment, but . . ." Selene couldn't finish. She wasn't having much luck walking away from her distant past. She took a deep breath. "There's something I can't leave behind."

Adam laid his finger against her lips. "It's okay. You don't have to explain. We'll stop there."

She simply nodded. That's why she loved him.

Neither spoke as Dave drove them home. She should tell Adam about Meg now, before their world came crashing down. But not in front of Dave. Not when they might be facing Zero's fighters at the apartment. Selene stared at the passing streets. Evidently, not when she could think of one more excuse not to tell him.

CHAPTER THIRTY-TWO

———◆———

SELENE FLUNG HERSELF FROM THE car even before Dave had stopped. She pounded toward the front door of the apartment building. *Faster. Faster.* Beyond the mad drumbeat of her heart, she could hear footsteps behind her. Adam. *No, go away, stay safe in the car.* But he didn't hear her frantic thoughts, wouldn't have obeyed them if he had. Stubborn man. He followed her to her unit and waited impatiently behind her as she fumbled for her key. She dropped the key, scrambled after it as it skittered over a heating vent, and watched it disappear. No!

Before Selene had a chance to scream her frustration, he picked her up and moved her to the side.

"The hell with a key. We don't have time for this."

Then he changed. His raptor filled the hallway. Selene stumbled away as Adam's beast leapt for the door. His powerful back feet with their deadly talons hit the door with a force that shook the building. The door shattered, pieces of it flying into her living room.

Her next-door neighbor threw open his door and stepped into the hall. His eyes widened as he took in the raptor crouched a few feet away. He dropped the bottle of booze he held as he stumbled back inside. "Ain't gonna drink no more of that cheap shit." Then he slammed his door shut.

Adam returned to human form just in time as more doors opened and half-asleep people peered out at them. Selene offered a weak smile and a wave. "Adam was helping me with a new fridge. We lost control, and it smashed through the door. Sorry." Weak. No way would they believe that. But at least they took their disbelief back into their apartments with them.

Her mother's lucky rock. The only thing left of the woman who gave her life. A person Selene thought had loved her. But still she clung to the memories and the rock. Go figure. She turned to Adam. "My mother's lucky rock. She left it behind." Selene looked away. "She died. Should've kept it with her."

Thankfully, Adam simply nodded. Selene didn't turn on any lights as she hurried past what was left of the door. She raced into her bedroom with Adam right behind her. He waited quietly by the door as she rooted in her closet for the small fireproof box tucked into the corner behind a pile of shoes. She was backing out of the closet with the rock clutched in her hand when she glanced at Adam.

He stood frozen; his focus turned inward. Oh, no. She'd seen that look before. When he finally blinked and turned to her, she dared to speak. "Fin?"

"Yeah. He's not happy. We need to get out of here. Zero's goons are hitting the Eleven's apartments right now. He found a way past Fin's wards." Adam shook his head. "Scary power."

He reached her in one step. She shoved the rock into her pocket even as he grabbed her hand. Her first instinct was to pull free. Selene didn't need any hand-holding to make her feel brave. And yet the strength of his fingers intertwined with hers triggered a surge of adrenaline, a *knowing* that together they were unstoppable. She grinned, the thrill of a thousand past battles revving her up. They ran for the door. But just as they reached it, his phone pinged. Cursing, Adam yanked it out. He skimmed the text. Then he quickly sent a return message.

"Dave. He said Zero's people have the building surrounded. He got out of the parking lot before they noticed him. He'll meet us two blocks down at the corner with the Italian restaurant. He says he'll stay in the car, but if we need him, he'll break out his big guns."

"Knowing Dave, he'd probably wipe out the whole neighborhood." People would die soon enough. She didn't want the killing to start here if they could help it.

Adam peered into the hallway. "Everything seems quiet. They're probably not even sure if we're home. Someone will come to check. Then, they'll want to draw us out into the open where they'll have the numbers advantage. I'd expect a visitor any minute now."

"We need a diversion fast."

He nodded. "Got it." Adam punched in 911 on the phone he still held. Then he shouted his message in imitation of a terrified human voice. "Fire! Some crazy dude is shooting up the place. He's set the building on fire." He gave the address and then shoved the phone into his pocket.

"We can't go out the front door." She slipped into the hallway. With cops and firetrucks on the way, they'd be ground zero for bad stuff happening in a few minutes.

Her gaze snagged on the fire alarm at the end of the hall. She pointed. He reached the alarm in two strides, broke the glass, and yanked down the handle. The shrill scream shattered the silence.

"Let's go." Selene dashed for the staircase with Adam beside her. They ran up the stairs, and at the top emerged on the roof. If she hadn't been sweating from the climb, she'd be shivering. The temperature had dropped. A lot. Low clouds discouraged any hint of a coming sunny day. In the distance she heard explosions. Fire lit the sky to the east. No time to worry about that now, though.

Below them, chaos erupted. People poured from the building, most in their night clothes. At the same time, three squad cars pulled into the parking lot. A firetruck was close behind.

That's when Zero's people made their move. Wolves slunk out of the shadows. Huge, slavering beasts as big as ponies. With them came opaque, amorphous things. Massive, elephant-sized, and gray—to match the morning. They flowed from between the buildings, engulfing everything they met. Amoebas on steroids.

Shocked, Selene watched one slide over a squad car. When the blob moved on, the car was gone along with the officer inside it. *No!* "What are they?" Nowhere, in any solar system she'd visited, had she seen these horrors.

Adam didn't answer. He was watching with shock to match her own as another blob digested the firetruck. *Digested.* Selene decided that was the only word to describe what the blobs were doing.

"There's no blood, no screams, no bodies." Adam's comment held the bewilderment of his raptor soul that couldn't conceive of death without all of those things.

Selene had opened her mouth to answer when the wolves struck. Screaming people scattered in all directions. Blood spattered against the buildings and pooled in the street. Bodies sprawled in that loose-limbed way the dead did. All this between one breath and the next. She watched, trying for the cold distance she'd often put between herself and death before. It wouldn't come this time. Those people were dying because of *them*. Zero's monsters hoped that if they just slaughtered everyone in the area, they were bound to catch Adam and her in their net.

Adam turned to search for an escape—the roof next door. The space between buildings was narrow enough for both to leap. From there Selene saw more roofs they could use as their path to freedom.

She met his gaze. "We have to help them first. Our battle to save humanity starts one person at a time."

He nodded. "I thought I'd killed all those wolf a-holes back at the zoo. I need to finish the job."

Selene measured the distance to the ground. "You wouldn't survive that jump without broken bones."

Before he could challenge her statement, she reached deep for a creation that might have the power to stop the giant slime things. Determination overrode any fear she was feeling. Beside her, Adam bared his teeth, and she almost felt sorry for the wolves. Almost.

There. She'd found the perfect weapon. Selene brought forth her champion. The sinking, shrinking sensation she always got when losing a bit of her essence was balanced by the shock on Adam's face. His sharply indrawn breath told her without words what he thought of her creation. It took up the entire roof and then some. "Climb on. I'll stay here to navigate."

"You're amazing, woman." Then he scrambled onto her dragon.

She was ready to take on all of Zero's army singlehanded because of his words. As her dragon spread massive wings and took flight, Selene narrowed her eyes on the scene below and prepared to kick some blobby butt.

Her dragon landed in the middle of the street at the same time Adam leaped from its back. He became raptor in mid leap and descended in the middle of a shocked werewolf pack. From the corner of her eyes Selene noted wolf body parts raining down before turning to her own job—getting rid of whatever those things were.

As she'd expected, the blobs immediately IDed her as their main threat. They flowed toward her dragon, attempting to make a circle around their enemy. Nope, no circle-forming allowed. Keeping her fingers crossed, she loosed death—she hoped—on the dozen or so blobs below her.

Her dragon breathed fire.

Before the blobs had a moment to react, Selene turned her dragon in a circle, keeping up a searing stream of flames aimed at them. Her tension eased a little when the first one went up in blue flame, making keening sounds as it burned. In seconds there was nothing left. No ashes. Nothing. Except the smell—burnt toast. An almost cozy smell, not one to throw terror into their enemies.

A glance down showed her that Adam was working on his last three wolves. She was tempted to help him, but he obviously didn't need her.

"Impressive display. Now I'll have to give birth to more children. Delivery pains are a bitch. You deserve to be punished for that." The voice was female and angry.

Selene swung to face the person behind her. She widened her eyes when she saw who, or *what*, stood there.

A shadow—at least nine feet tall—with a vaguely humanoid shape, loomed over her. She forced down her instinctual panic. *Think.* She needed a weapon. But this . . . being would kill her before she could act. She was toast—bad metaphor—just like the thing's kids down below.

The shadow hissed at her. "Even immortals can be destroyed by one more powerful than them. You're lucky our leader wants you brought to him alive."

Then it, or she, smiled. Selene didn't know how she knew, she just did.

"But the moment he no longer chooses to protect you, I'll be waiting." The shadow moved to glance over the edge of the roof. "It's Fin's beast I intend to kill before we leave. He'll return to rescue you. His human emotions will be his death."

Selene had never felt so disrespected. This monster thought she was so weak it could look away from her without danger of being attacked; that because her dragon was still down on the street it was safe up here. *Wrong, witch.*

She might not have time to recall her essence from her dragon, but that didn't mean she was helpless. Selene used the shadow's momentary distraction to attempt something she rarely tried—forming a completely different creature while still maintaining her first one. This would drain her essence to a dangerous level, but she'd use every drop if it saved Adam.

She reached for her next creation, a swarm of alien insects with a piercing whine guaranteed to leave ears ringing for days. Added to that, their spit could eat through metal and was foul-smelling enough to make you vomit. The outraged alien mama was still peering at her destroyed children when the insects hit her.

Selene didn't pause to enjoy watching the shadow dance and swat at the highly motivated swarm. She turned to run.

Suddenly, Adam was beside her. She hadn't seen or heard him coming. Back in human form, he wore his vampire face. His fangs were on full display. Splattered with wolf blood, he made even Selene shiver.

He grabbed her hand and then raced away, dragging her behind him. She barely had time to take back her essence from the dragon. Moving at preternatural speed, he was already at the far side of the next roof and leaping to the ground before the shadow noticed Selene was gone. Selene held back a scream as they plummeted. Right before impact, Adam slowed his freefall, and they landed in one piece.

Once on the ground, they kept running. Or, rather, Adam ran and she flew behind him like a car caught in the slipstream of an eighteen-wheeler.

Finally, they reached the Italian restaurant with Dave parked in front of it. They piled into the back seat of the SUV. Adam wasn't breathing hard. She was. Quickly,

Selene collected her essence from the swarm. Almost whole again, except for that small space Meg had left.

Adam checked to see if they were being followed. Once satisfied they were safe, he leaned toward Dave. "Go."

Dave wasn't happy. "I didn't get to crack any skulls." He watched a bunch of police cars speed past. "Looks like you guys had all the fun." He pulled away from the curb with barely restrained violence.

Adam finally relaxed enough to lean back in his seat, but he didn't put on his seat belt. He glanced at Selene. "I showed up just in time to hear that creepy shadow thing sneering at human emotions. It's lucky I didn't bring any of them to her party." He still wore his vampire face to go along with his vampire speed. "I hate big-ass shadows with inflated egos." He held her gaze. "Oh, and never assume anything about me. The human me couldn't jump from the top floor of that building, but as you saw, the vampire me nailed the landing."

She had no answer for that. Luckily, Adam got distracted as they heard more sirens and saw what looked like military helicopters heading toward the apartment building. A bunch of ambulances screamed past. "Who called in the military?"

"I mental-messaged Fin. He contacted the lieutenant general. I don't think the thing that was threatening you will stick around since all her fighters are dead. What was it anyway?" Adam peered out the back window to check for any tails.

She shrugged. "Must be one of Zero's numbers the Eleven didn't get to. She underestimated us today. I don't think she'll make that mistake a second time." Selene hoped she wouldn't have to face the shadow again. Or her children. "So, what did our great and glorious leader have to say?" Maybe she didn't want to know.

"He's ticked. Said we'd better find someplace to lie low and wait for orders or else he'll give us more than a juiced-up shadow to worry about. He's monitoring the apartments of the rest of the Eleven. Everyone else followed directions." He glanced at her. "Meg and Tor are safe."

Selene released the breath she hadn't known she was holding. Meg might no longer be connected to her, but she would always be Selene's sister.

Adam continued, "But Zero's forces destroyed all the apartments. Humans died. Attacks are happening around the world. It'll let up a little when the sun rises. But once day is gone and night falls again, it'll be twice as bad. Zero's heavy-hitters hunt in the dark." He paused and then smiled. "But so do ours."

She digested the news before speaking. "Where are we headed?" Selene figured with his vampire connections he'd have a safe place in mind.

"Vampire headquarters. Even if Zero knows about it, chances are he won't waste his people on the off chance we might be there. Now that the world knows it's under attack, he'll need his fighters elsewhere." He pulled his hood up as the dawn grew marginally brighter.

Selene looked out the window as Dave braked at a traffic-clogged intersection.

Their driver did some creative cursing, banging his fist on the steering wheel to emphasize each one. "It's six in the morning, and it's an anthill out there. Who kicked it?"

"Dave, people are scared. Attacks are happening all over the city. Sirens, explosions, and things like that tend to get people out of bed. They're trying to escape. Then there're all the police, ambulances, and firefighters trying to get through." Selene shared Dave's frustration, though. It was gridlock.

Adam decided. "Time to move faster. Taxis aren't out today. Too dangerous. And no raptor. People will be trigger happy right now. I don't want to be dodging bullets." He pulled her out of the car and then scooped her into his arms. "Carrying you is easier than dragging you behind me." He glanced back at Dave. "When you get through this, meet us at vampire headquarters." Then he ran.

By the time they reached the condo, Selene swore she had wind-burn. His preternatural speed had sucked the air from her lungs and left her hair with a trendy Medusa style minus the snakes.

There were no guards at the condo. If they were smart, they'd all gone to ground for the day. Tonight, they would fight.

Adam set her down once they were inside while he locked the door of the condo. Then he nodded toward the master bedroom. "That's the safest place."

She didn't know why it would be so safe until she watched him pick up a remote from the bedside table and hit a button. A steel panel slid from the wall to cover the bank of windows.

"There's more." He pulled open the closet door and kicked aside a rug. Then he punched another button. A trap door opened, exposing steps that led into darkness. "We have a safe room. Fully stocked. Food, clothes, weapons, and an escape tunnel down through the building's walls and under the road into the store across the street."

Selene stood dumbly watching as he closed the closet door and returned to the middle of the room. He yanked off his boots, pulled off his hoodie, and then tugged his shirt over his head. His pants followed close behind. *Completely bare.* Absolutely. Nothing. Else. He was all taut skin and gleaming muscle.

He turned to her. "Are you tired?" His gaze smoldered, suggesting that he hoped she still had some life in her. "I need time to unwind after a fight. Pretty soon the dawn will drag me down. I don't have to sleep all day, but I'm a lot more ready for battle if I have some rest. Right now, though, the adrenaline is still pumping."

She slid her tongue across her lower lip and felt something low in her stomach tighten as his heated gaze followed her action. "Vampires sure don't have many inhibitions."

Adam grinned a big-bad-raptor smile. "Forget vampires. My dino soul doesn't give a damn about much. It wants what it wants."

"What does it want?"

"You."

CHAPTER THIRTY-THREE

WELL, THAT WAS DIRECT. SHE lifted her chin. "Maybe I don't want to be your cooldown period."

He blinked, and suddenly he was *her* Adam—not raptor, not vampire, maybe not all human. She sort of liked the slightly ambiguous nature of him. Then he really smiled at her, no smoldering, no raptor smile, just a wow smile.

"Never a cooldown, Selene. You're my flash fire, heating me all the way through." Then he turned away. "I need a shower."

He strode away, leaving her to come to terms with being a flash fire. She bit her bottom lip as she considered it. Then she smiled, and she was certain it smoldered. After she took her shower, she might expend some of her own lingering adrenaline.

Her smile faded. This wasn't a time for smiling or for thoughts of pleasure. She didn't know if she would be around to enjoy another sunrise. All the more reason to do lots of smiling now. She might not get another chance. Selene quickly shed her clothes.

When he came out of the bathroom, he brought steam and heat with him. He hadn't bothered with a towel. Beads of water still clung to his damp skin. She controlled the need to close the distance between them and then carefully, sensuously, *hungrily* lick those drops from every inch of his body.

Meanwhile, Adam stood frozen, his unblinking gaze riveted on her. He studied her lips. She hoped they were pouty enough. Then his attention dropped to her bare breasts. Perky enough? She drew in her breath and straightened her back. He continued his journey, down, down until . . . Selene felt his stare as a physical touch. She spread her legs slightly. *Yes.* Right *there.*

His appreciative murmur was completely human male. Her glance drifted down to admire proof of exactly how pumped he was. Oh, yes, she'd absolutely love to help him wind down.

Love. She allowed her thoughts to linger on the word. Selene knew what these brief moments before the battle swallowed them would mean to her. What did they mean to him? Better to not speculate. Just enjoy her time with him and then store the memory away. Later, if she survived, perhaps on some desolate planet while she waited for another battle, she'd take the memory out and . . . She shook her head. Now wasn't the time to go all maudlin.

Selene forced her attention back to right now. She smiled and waved as she headed for her own shower. If this was their last chance together, she wouldn't come to him smelling of toasted blobs.

A few minutes later, she emerged, still as bare as he was. Adam stood in front of the open closet. Selene took a moment to admire all the physical temptations of the man—broad shoulders tapering down to a perfect butt. Strong thighs and legs, both necessary to maintain a thrust that . . . Wait, why was he standing in front of the closet with the remote in his hand?

As though hearing her question, he turned. "We'll be sleeping in the safe room. I don't think any of Zero's people will show up here, but I'm not taking any chances.

Bring your clothes down with you in case we have to use the tunnel."

Selene cast a last sad glance at the bed she'd hoped to make love in. King-sized. Thick mattress piled high with a warm comforter and fluffy pillows. Sighing, she grabbed her stuff and followed him down to the safe room.

She stopped at the bottom of the steps to stare open-mouthed. "What is *that*?"

He sighed. "That is the original Adam's bed. He wanted something unique, fitting for a vampire lord. No coffins for him. This was his favorite room. He only rested in the one upstairs when visitors were staying, and he didn't want them to know about the safe room."

The bed was every human's vision of where a vampire lord would rest after draining his nightly quota of helpless virgins. Huge, with a dark world of demons and other nightmare creatures carved into the massive headboard that reached to the ceiling. Thick posts carved into the shapes of dragons supported a heavy, red velvet curtain. She figured they'd be drawn during his daytime resting hours.

It was all too much, and yet there was something so blatantly sensual in a scary kind of way, that her already thrumming heartbeat quickened even more. There would never again be a bed like this, and their lovemaking would have to rise to the occasion.

Selene scanned what she could see of the room. It was in shadows other than the recessed light above the bed.

Adam gave her a quick rundown. "There's a couch and a few chairs, a bureau in the corner, and a small kitchenette. The bathroom door is on the far wall."

She watched him click the remote again. Above the room, she heard the closet door close along with the trapdoor.

"No one gets down here without my permission. The

rest of the clan knows not to touch the closet door. They think I have valuables stored inside. If anyone tries to open the door, they'll be expelled from the condo. In pieces. A camera feeds me visuals, so we won't be surprised." He walked over and turned down the red velvet spread. Then he just stared at the bed.

"Is there a problem?" She shivered. Naked might be sexy, but it was chilly down here. Selene eyed the spread. She could also present a sensual look wrapped in red velvet.

"Inner conflict." He glanced at her. "My body knows this bed, has slept in this bed, has done lots of things in this bed. My soul has none of those memories, though. The bed is a stranger." He smiled. "Any psychological thoughts on the matter?"

"Of course. Let's get under the covers and give your soul some memories to warm it on cold nights."

"Sounds like a winner." He lay down and then beckoned to her.

Selene's boldness of a moment ago deserted her. Making love with him meant too much to her. She couldn't even pretend to take it lightly. She walked to the other side of the bed and slid under the covers.

He dimmed the light with his remote and then set it on the bedside table.

Silence wrapped around her, bringing with it a lifetime of broken promises and unfulfilled dreams. Would this be one more? And what about her revelation that Meg wasn't her sister in the normal sense of the word? Would that drive a wedge between them? Thoughts on top of thoughts whirled in her head.

"Let it go, Selene. Whatever is bothering you has no place here." He turned on his side to face her.

Selene opened her mouth to deny his words, but then closed it again. No more lies between them. She rolled onto her side. "Help me."

He reached out, wrapping his arms around her and pulling her to him. He buried his face in the hollow of her neck. She sucked in her breath as he kissed the spot where her pulse beat faster and faster.

She reached around to run her fingers through his hair where it grew long in the back. Selene closed her eyes, enjoying the soft slide of the strands. "Your hair is so soft."

"And that's a good thing?" He kissed a path from her throat, along her jaw to her lips.

"Definitely. You're a hard man, Adam. I treasure your soft spots." She reached down between their bodies and wrapped her hand around his cock. "See? Hard."

He moaned against her lips. "You're killing me, woman."

"Not yet, but I'll get there." She laughed.

Adam covered her mouth, stopping all thoughts of laughter. His lips were soft, and she'd have to tell him about Meg when her wits returned. Because they'd run away, leaving her with an empty mind filled only with sensations.

She couldn't resist those lips. Selene slid her tongue across his full lower one, and when he urged her, she opened her mouth to him.

Her senses were exploding too fast for her to catalogue. Fangs, hard and pointy. Tongue soft and insistent. Mouth, warm and tasting of mint from his toothpaste. His scent? Nothing she could compare it to. His scent was his own, and she was convinced his pheromones were legion. She'd recognize his scent among a thousand other men. It sang to her.

When he broke the kiss, she gasped to get her breath back.

"Okay, talking done." Selene ran her hand over his chest, spending a moment teasing his nipples. Soft to hard in two seconds. She reveled in her power.

Not to be outdone, Adam closed his lips over her nipple, running his tongue around it before flicking it until she was panting with the pleasure-pain. And when he sucked gently, she bit her tongue to keep the groans back.

Selene raked her nails down his arms, a signal that soft was over and hard was taking its turn.

Her heart threatened to pound its way free as he flung the covers aside before kissing a path over her stomach. Then he nudged her legs apart so he could glide his tongue along the inside of her thigh.

"Can't wait any longer. Skip the rest of it." Would they ever come together with anything less than this frenzy? She hoped not.

Selene didn't even try to silence her groans as he kissed right *there*. And when his tongue delved deep and slid back and forth, back and forth over that one sensitive spot, she came off the bed. "Now, damn it!" Was that savage snarl really hers?

She thought she heard him chuckle. *Chuckle?* How could he have a chuckle in him when she was going crazy here? He needed a lesson in approved sounds for moments of deep passion.

Adam wasn't expecting it when she shoved him. Before the last chuckle left his lips, he was on his back and she was kneeling between his thighs. His gorgeous muscled thighs. Even in vengeance mode she noticed them. She would enjoy this.

"You chuckled at me. No one does that. Time to pay for your mistake."

"Terror fills my heart." His eyes were dark with arousal.

He bit his bottom lip as he watched her. The tip of his fangs just showed. Selene wondered how those tips could be cute and sexy as hell at the same time. Then he released his lip. The damp shine of it almost made her groan. Oh, the temptation. Quickly, she shifted her gaze from his lips to much lower.

Bending over him, she kissed a path along his ridged stomach and down to her target area. His stomach muscles clenched. Selene clenched a few muscles herself, only a bit lower. How long could she hold everything together before her personal Mt. Helen blew its sensual top?

She cupped each sac, running the tip of her nail in a slow tease over each one. His gasp told her she was on the right track. She moved upward.

Selene swirled her tongue around the head of his cock. She closed her eyes and stopped thinking, allowing the sensations of heat, smooth skin, along with the scent of aroused male to wash over her.

Adam grabbed her hair and hung on as he made sounds meant to encourage her. A random thought: she would allow her hair to grow so she could torture him as it trailed across his bare body.

Then she slid her mouth over him and began the up and down rhythm of sex. She lost herself to everything except this man and the moment until he shuddered. He gave a strangled cry as he tightened his grip on her hair and drew her off him.

She knelt above him, memorizing the sight of his sweat sheened chest, the rise and fall of it as he gasped for breath, and the glazed hunger in his eyes.

Selene smiled. "*Now*, I'm killing you." She was also killing herself.

He didn't speak. Adam put his hands on her hips and lifted her over his arousal.

She took the hint.

Selene didn't lower herself gently. She took a firm grip on his cock before driving down on him. He cried out as she took all of him, pressing down to make sure he filled every empty spot, every tiny pocket of love and hope still alive inside her.

Then they moved. Not a gentle rising and falling. This was a battle, a clawing up a mountain to see who would reach the peak first. Rise and fall, screaming frustration as the goal drew closer. Not quite there. Almost, almost! She heard moans, felt his straining as those glorious thighs drove him into her. Deeper and deeper.

Finally! She shouted her triumph as she reached the peak. Clenched around the moment. Stopped breathing. And just *felt*. She was vaguely aware that his cries joined hers. Amazing.

Slowly, the moment passed and she was able to think in complete sentences again. Tension rolled away, and she slid off him to lay on her back staring at the ceiling. Selene smiled as she watched the shadows that had stalked her for so long drift away. There was sunlight behind them. She turned her head to look at her personal sunbeam. He'd hate her calling him that, so she didn't.

He was watching her, and she knew no man had ever looked at her with that particular emotion in his eyes.

"I love you, Selene."

Simple, heartfelt, sincere. She didn't try to hide the tear that slid over her cheek. "I love you, too, raptor." Selene felt it was right to call him by his soul, the way she'd seen him for the first time at the zoo.

Tension left him as he visibly relaxed. But not completely. "I want to marry you." For the first time, he glanced away. "Before you answer, know that there is a ceremony the Eleven observe when they promise themselves to the one they love."

"Yes. Whatever it is, I'll do it." Didn't he know she'd crawl over glass shards to be with him?

Adam reached out to slide a strand of hair away from her face. "Don't say yes too quickly. During the ceremony, you'll walk into the heart of my beast. You'll see . . . things. About my past. Not pleasant things."

"Magic?"

He nodded. "When you reach my heart, you'll have a choice." His finger trailed over her cheek. It trembled.

"You can walk away, or you can accept a piece of my soul. If you accept me, we will be together always."

Selene understood the concept of "always." An unbreakable bond. And she wanted it with a fierceness that was almost pain. "Absolutely, positively, yes."

With an inarticulate sound, he rose over her and covered her mouth with his. And while she lost herself in his drugging kiss, her memory whispered. *You have to tell him.*

No, no, no! She couldn't ruin this magic moment. *But you have to start your lives together with honesty on both sides.* Selene hated her conscience.

She broke the kiss and watched as he studied her.

"Is there something wrong?"

Selene glanced away. She might have to tell him, but she didn't have to see the disappointment in his eyes when she did. "I have something to confess. I—"

"No." His voice was fierce.

"What?"

"I don't want to hear any confessions now. This moment is for happiness, and you can't ruin it. Whatever you have to say will keep until after the battle."

Left unsaid was, "If we both survive."

Selene wanted to listen to him, wanted to use his words as a balm for her conscience. After all, she'd tried to tell him. Her conscience wasn't having any of it. Sighing, she prepared to override his order.

Suddenly, a loud beep broke the silence. Adam groped for his remote. He glanced at the screen.

With a muttered curse, he crawled out of bed. "Q and Dave are upstairs. I have to talk to them. I'll be back." With that promise, he threw on his clothes and was gone.

Exhaustion was setting in as she watched him disappear up the steps. She wanted to go with him, but it was hard to concentrate on anything as she drifted toward sleep.

Selene hated the relief she felt. She soothed the angry

shouts of her conscience with promises and more promises. As soon as humanity was safe, she'd tell him about
Meg, and she'd explain why she'd kept it a secret from
him for so long. Problem. Right now, she couldn't think
of a good excuse. The truth? She'd kept Meg, a sentient
being with a mind of her own, a virtual prisoner, tied
to her creator because said creator didn't want to be
alone. Selene had kept it from him because she knew he
wouldn't approve. *Not* a good excuse.

The battle with her conscience ended abruptly when
Adam charged back down the steps followed closely by
Dave and Q.

She sat up, yanking the covers around her. "What's
wrong?" Selene didn't for a minute doubt something dire
had happened for Adam to bring them with him. Wrapping the sheet around her, she scrambled out of bed.

Adam hit the remote, and the trap door slid shut. "Zero
has set your father and his troops loose on the city. Guess
he figures he can overwhelm us with sheer numbers."

Q dropped into a chair. "If Zero can take out the
Eleven, he'll cripple Fin. The boss won't be able to fight
Zero mentally as well as controlling the war worldwide
if he has to step in to fight for the city."

Dave nodded as he studied a gun mounted on the wall.
"Just so far a super-brain can stretch before it snaps." He
turned to Adam. "Mind if I borrow the gun?"

"Help yourself." Adam busied himself with finishing
dressing and retrieving some weapons of his own from
the closet."

Selene grabbed her clothes and ducked into the bathroom. A quick washup and she was ready to hold her
exhaustion at bay long enough to ruin her father's day.
Too bad she didn't have a change of clothes. Not really
important. She'd only get blood on them anyway.

Once out of the bathroom, Selene pointed at Dave and

Q. "Why're you guys here? Why didn't Fin contact us directly?"

Dave offered her his be-patient-with-the-idiot look. "What part of the Great Mind is busy saving the world didn't you catch? Fin doesn't have time to issue orders right now. He trusts you guys to handle things in the city until he has a moment free. We're on our own."

Adam glared at Dave. "Cut the sarcasm."

Selene had been about to say the same thing, only with stronger language. Adam opened a door tucked into the corner and kicked aside a pile of boxes. Another trapdoor.

"We'll use the emergency exit in case anyone is watching the building." And then he disappeared into the darkness.

Selene followed the others down an endless staircase, through a dark tunnel, and finally entered the storage room of the store across from their condo building. Their safe room must've been soundproofed because they emerged into chaos. Screams, gunfire, explosions, along with other unidentifiable sounds blasted them once they stepped outside.

Dave led them into the overcast day. In the distance, Selene saw smoke and the glow of fires coloring the clouds with spots of color. A polka-dot sky. A memorable day to die. Or not. She had the best incentive in the world to survive. And he walked beside her.

CHAPTER THIRTY-FOUR

IT RAINED BLOOD AND DEATH for three days and two nights. On the third night, it snowed. A great lead-in for future memorials, if there were any. "It snowed the night Earth died." Because from what Adam had seen of the carnage on both sides, there wouldn't be much left of the planet when this night was done.

As darkness fell, Adam stared out the window of the abandoned house they'd crashed in. After days of killing, they'd needed a breather.

Only a few hours until the end of Winter Solstice, along with the battle for his world. *His* world? Yes, he claimed it, along with the woman sleeping on the couch behind him.

The muted sounds of distant explosions and screams shattered any illusion of a peaceful night. The humans weren't going quietly.

Adam's musings ended at the sudden sense of mental intrusion. Familiar. Unwelcome.

"Go away." Selene's sleepy growl assured him the boss was in her head too.

Fin ignored her. *"You'll have to fight your way to the bridge. Start as soon as your team arrives. I'll be there with the rest of the Eleven to help."*

Adam heard Selene climbing from the couch where she'd collapsed fully-clothed only two hours ago. He wasn't so tired he didn't regret the fully-clothed part.

"Are you listening, Rap?"

Fin's use of his original name grabbed Adam's attention, as the boss knew it would. Adam missed Rap. "Yeah. Question. Why even bother with the bridge or Six? All we have to do is wait a few minutes until eleven-eleven strikes. Zero and the rest of his numbers—and that includes Six—will be kicked off the planet. Problem solved." Okay, not completely. He wasn't sure about Selene's father and what was left of his mercenaries. And would Earth's nonhumans continue their attacks even after their leader was gone?

"It will all end there. You have to be at that bridge to fulfill my vision. So I have seen, and so it will be."

When Fin turned on his prophet voice, it always weirded Adam out. "Wait. What? Is there something you haven't told us? Explain." No reply. Fin was gone.

"Well, that sounded ominous." Selene moved to his side. She stroked his arm as she stared out the window with him. "The end of what, though—humans, nonhumans, us, them? Everything?" Her fingers trailed a path from his arm to beneath his shirt. "I hope Zero doesn't intend to play the asteroid card again."

Her touch heated his blood, melting the ice that had formed around his soul as he thought about what might happen tonight. "Three days of hell, and it'll all come down to the next few hours." He wrapped his arm around her waist and pulled her close. "We'll survive. Zero won't win." Adam would make sure of that even if he had to hunt the bastard down by himself and rip his head from his immortal shoulders.

She didn't comment on their survival chances as she stared at the falling snow. "A cold and beautiful blanket. Not what you'd expect from San Diego. But now? It fits. I hope it falls long enough to cover the memory of what Zero has done to this city and the people who lived here."

Adam didn't think ten feet of the white stuff could do that. "It doesn't feel natural. Probably Fin or Zero flexing his virtual muscles." But then, he didn't know what was real or not anymore.

"How long have you been awake?" Selene's voice was still soft with sleep.

"Not long. The night woke me." *Along with the ghosts of millions dead.* The thought startled him. Adam's raptor figured a million dead was a nice round number. His vampire shrugged its shoulders. A million dead was no biggie. But his human . . . His human would have nightmares for years to come. There was a revelation waiting to ambush him, but not now. Later.

"My father is out there somewhere. Slaughtering people. Earning his blood money."

Selene's father. He heard the anger and sorrow in her voice. What would he do if he met good old dad? Kill him? *Sorrow in her voice.* His beast's bloodlust warred with his humanity. Adam hoped he wouldn't have to make that choice.

The silence between them filled with all that needed saying.

Then someone pounded on the front door. Not an enemy. Zero's fighters didn't knock. Probably the team Fin had mentioned.

While Selene quickly gathered up their few belongings, Adam strode to the door. He could hear Utah's voice outside, so he didn't hesitate to fling it open.

His brothers and Ty along with Lia, Kelly, and Meg rushed in on a gust of cold air.

"Dammit, close the door. No heat in this place. It's already freezing." He joined them in the living room.

Utah punched Adam's arm and grinned. "Oh, I bet you

managed to keep your ass warm while you waited for us." He slid his gaze to Selene and winked.

She didn't wink back. "I took the couch. Only room for one ass there. Adam slept on the floor. This was the only defensible room."

Lia elbowed her mate. "Leave them alone. We don't have time to play."

"There's always time to play." Utah's sulky response was drowned out by Ty.

"Okay, listen up. I don't foresee heavy opposition on our way to Fin's musical bridge. What's left of the enemy forces seem headed there too. Zero must've passed on the same message as Fin did. Stapleton's fighters are mopping up any strays left behind. Who would've guessed humans could be so deadly? Fin owes them an apology."

Tor glanced at the others. "Who made the T. rex king?"

Utah shrugged. "Ty doesn't understand. Fin finally saw the light." He pointed at his brothers. "We're pack again, and we fight as pack. Nothing can stand against us." He nodded at Ty. "The big guy is an official pack member for the night. We go first, and he can tromp along behind us roaring and looking scary."

Ty snorted his opinion of that. "What he really means is that I'll go ahead of you guys and take out the enemy. Then your 'pack' can prance along behind and make squeaking noises to scare away any mice left behind."

Adam wasn't paying much attention to the banter. He watched Selene rush to her sister. She was too upset to lower her voice. "What're you doing here?"

Meg stood tall. It didn't look as though she intended to back down.

"Everyone goes to battle with their mate tonight. We ride as one."

Selene pointed at the other women. "Lia is a vampire. Kelly has power from her piece of Ty's soul. I have skills.

How will you protect yourself?" She didn't pause to give Meg a chance to answer. "I forbid you to go."

Kelly winced as she glanced at Ty. "Uh oh. Poor word choices. They never worked on me."

Ty didn't deny it.

Meg looked as though Selene had slapped her. "I don't answer to *forbid* anymore."

Selene sucked in her breath. That hurt. But Meg was right. "Okay, no forbidding." That didn't mean she'd abandon the fight. "But how will you stay alive? You'll endanger Tor or me if we're distracted trying to keep you safe." She watched Meg narrow her eyes. Selene glanced around. Not good. Everyone had stopped talking to watch them.

"No need to worry. Tor and I have mated. I carry a piece of his soul now. I can take care of myself." Meg's eyes widened, as though she hadn't meant to blurt that out in front of everyone.

Selene's world shrank. It was only herself and this woman she thought she knew so well. Memories tumbled around her, revealing the real world, not the one she'd tried to hide behind for so long. Meg wasn't her real sister. She was a flesh-and-blood construct born of Selene's mind, power, and need for a friend. Meg had no duty to her maker now that she was free.

Meg started to reach for Selene, but then stopped. "It's not what you're thinking."

"You didn't want me there." *Idiot.* The world could end in a few hours, and she was indulging in hurt feelings. *It's more than hurt feelings, and you know it.*

Meg threw up her hands. "Of course, I wanted you there. But—"

She didn't get a chance to finish because Adam pushed past her to confront Tor.

"You married Meg without inviting us? What's that

about?" Adam slammed his fist against his chest. "I'm your brother."

Lia nudged Selene. "Time to deescalate. We have some-place to be."

She was right. Selene tucked her pain away for the greater good. She walked to Adam's side and touched his clenched fist. "We can discuss this later. Fin wants us at the bridge."

Meg wasn't having any of it, though. "No, I have to explain now. I won't go into a battle we might not sur-vive with a misunderstanding." She drew Tor to her and then clasped his hand. "You guys were off somewhere in Iceland fighting evil elves or something. Tor wanted to wait for you, but I was afraid. I wanted us to be joined before that last day came. Tor gave me what I wanted." Her gaze was defiant as she met Selene's stare. "I didn't want to be alone. You understand that feeling."

Her words challenged Selene. She sighed. "Yes, I know what it's like." She tugged at Adam's hand. "Let's get moving."

Adam still looked angry, but he allowed her to draw him away. "Sure. We'll take care of Zero, and then I want a real explanation, not a weak one." He glared at Tor. "Fin could've had us back in a second. Why didn't you ask him?"

Ty spoke. "He asked Fin. But Fin said the evil elves needed a bitch-slapping. He'd bring you home when the job was done." He shrugged. "I didn't agree with him, but he's the boss."

No one said anything more as they quietly left the house. Selene watched Utah and Tor take their raptor forms as Ty transformed into his T. rex. The sheer enor-mity of Ty kept her silent while Kelly, Lia, and Meg climbed atop them.

Adam spoke softly. "I didn't get to see either of my brothers bond with their mates." He glanced at her. "Am

I being stupid for allowing that to upset me when more important things will happen tonight? After all, what'll it mean if tonight is all we have?"

"No." Selene was fierce in her response. "Tonight will *not* be all we have. You might not have been there to see their bondings, but they *will* be there for yours. That's a promise."

His eyes widened at the same moment Selene realized what she'd revealed. She grew still, not even daring to breathe. Yes, he'd said he loved her, but what if he'd changed his mind? What if—?

She didn't finish the thought as he pulled her into his arms and covered her mouth with his. Selene wrapped herself in the completeness of his kiss—the heat of it, the promise of what they would share in a future she was determined to see happen. She slipped her hand beneath his shirt and pressed her palm to his chest. His racing heartbeat matched her own. This then would be a memory tucked away in a corner of her mind, one that would warm future cold nights, one to share with him as they sat before a fire. She completed the memory with the scent of clean winter air and the touch of snowflakes on her upturned face. Perfect.

A shove shattered her bliss. Selene turned and came face to nose with an irritated raptor. Meg leaned from Tor's back. "We need to get going if we expect to reach the bridge in time."

Selene simply nodded. When she turned back to Adam, he was in his raptor form. She sighed. No long talks by firelight until afterwards, whatever that might look like. She scrambled onto his back.

The trek across town took on a surreal quality. No enemies leaped from between buildings to attack them. The streets were empty as the snow fell steadily, relentlessly covering up the city's scars.

The pure nothingness of everything lulled Selene into

a sense of safety. Not good. She had to hone her mental alertness, ready to fling whatever creature was needed into the coming battle. There would be no safety so long as Zero was still around. Eleven-eleven couldn't come too soon. She'd wave as he and his killers faded back into the cosmos. *You were one of them. Will you fade too?* Selene refused to consider that. Adam would wrap his love around her and keep her earthbound.

Shouts and the sounds of gunfire snapped her back to reality. Ty turned onto a narrow street and ran.

Selene felt Adam's frustration with their pace. She could almost hear his mantra of *faster, faster.* Ty might play his huge-and-menacing part well, but he wasn't too quick on his feet. His speed was a constant earth-shaking boom, boom, boom, interspersed with roars that shattered glass. She knew Adam wanted to race around him to reach the battle, but he contented himself with angry screams as he urged Ty to get moving.

Selene tried not to glance across at Meg. She didn't want to act the overprotective sister anymore. But finally, she gave into temptation, and met Meg's gaze. Meg grinned and gave her a thumb's up. Selene returned her smile. She had to allow Meg space to find herself, even if inside she chewed her nails down to nubs.

They rounded a final corner. The street opened into a large square. Once there had been a park in its center with trees and benches. Now the park was only churned mud and bodies locked in bloody struggles. Cries of dying and triumph echoed off the deserted and broken buildings.

Selene slipped from her raptor before he could object. Staying together would endanger both of them. Adam didn't need the distraction of trying to keep his rider safe. He might be almost impossible to kill in his present form, but that didn't mean he couldn't be hurt. And no way could she stay seated once he began fighting.

Getting tossed from his back into a crowd of predators would earn her some serious pain.

He turned his head to object, but she waved him away. "I can take care of myself. Keep your head in the game, raptor." She pointed toward a pack of wolves with murder in their eyes headed toward the brothers.

With a scream of rage Selene figured was aimed not only at the enemy but at his frustration with her, he leaped on the nearest wolf.

She ran in the opposite direction, looking for a calm spot where she could identify her targets and release a suitable nightmare on them.

A momentary break in the mob gave her a view she wasn't expecting. Selene froze. Adam had left a path of mangled wolves behind him and was now facing a new enemy.

Her father.

Too far away. There would be no popping out of a closet with a gun to stop what was about to happen this time. Her father had lost his sword somewhere, and he looked shaken. Perfect prey for a raptor's teeth and talons. One strike and it would be over. Is this what she wanted?

No. He was still her father. And in what might be the last moment of his life, Selene *remembered*. The head. That bloody mangled head of her father's greatest enemy. He'd given it to her for her birthday. He'd claimed it was an honor fitting for his warrior daughter. She'd raced to the bathroom and lost everything in her stomach. Afterwards, she'd yelled at him for giving her something so gruesome. Selene's reaction disappointed her father. Neither had understood the other.

But life's most intense moments sometimes revealed truths hiding in plain sight. Like now.

Her father wasn't a good man. In that instance, though, he'd tried to please her in his own way. Yes, he'd used her so many times. But he'd also stayed with her. Selene's mother had left. Some revelations came way too late, though. She watched, ignoring the battles around her. They couldn't compete with what was happening in her heart.

Adam loomed over the man he hated. Selene refused to look away. Then . . . the raptor turned from her father to seek another victim.

She wanted to plop onto the muddy ground and just shake for at least an hour. Wasn't going to happen. Any minute an enemy would notice her standing there seemingly helpless. Selene took a deep breath.

"Thank you." Adam couldn't hear her, but she needed to say it. "I love you."

Then she focused on the battle. She scanned the square. There were plenty of vampires and shifters, along with a few humans, demons, and some nonhumans she couldn't ID. Other than the vampires, humans, and maybe some of the demons, it was tough to tell who were the good guys.

Then she sucked in her breath. There, only a few feet away, rose the shadow figure she'd battled only days ago. It was still massive, still featureless, but something about its shape had changed.

It saw her. Selene didn't know how she knew, but she was sure its gaze was locked on her. The shadow drifted closer. She wanted to run. She didn't. But that didn't mean she wasn't breaking out in a cold sweat as it neared.

The shadow leaned toward her. "We meet again. When I've dined on all our enemies here, I'll finally be able to collect you for our leader. Don't die."

Selene narrowed her eyes. "Please do die."

The shadow laughed as she placed a hand over where her stomach would be. "I'm sorry to disappoint you, but I most certainly won't die. I can't. I'm carrying the next generation. And they're ravenous. This is a wonderful spot for feeding." She waved at Selene as she drifted away.

Selene watched the shadow engulf a struggling vampire. Once she'd passed through him, he was simply gone.

Pregnant? Selene watched in horrified fascination as a second shadow rose on the other side of the park. This must be the proud papa. Larger than the female, it engulfed those around it at a frightening pace.

A glance showed her Adam laying waste to a dozen strange creatures. Not from Earth, so probably some of her father's mercenaries. Tor and Utah joined in to help. Meg and the other women were engaged in demon destruction. Ty was too big to miss. He was stomping and chomping his way across the square.

No one dared to engage the two shadows. Anyone near them fled. She steadied herself. It was time for her dragon to make a cameo appearance. And while the dragon was engaging the female shadow, Selene would introduce the male to the insects that had been more than effective with his mate. She knew the danger. Giving up so much of her essence to two creations at the same time would weaken her dangerously. But someone had to stop the shadows.

She drew on her power, pictured what she wanted, and made it real. With a thought, she guided the dragon and her insects to their targets and watched them go to work.

She saw immediately that her dragon would have a problem. The female shadow knew what he could do. She was already hiding herself behind the good guys. The dragon had no way of searing her with fire without killing friends.

Selene would try to solve that issue after she took care of the male shadow. Selene fought her way through the blood-drenched mud, trying to keep her balance as she wound her way around the fighters. Bodies pushed and shoved at her.

She had to get across the park to where the male shadow batted at the swarm. The insects wouldn't keep him busy long. By the time she reached him, she'd have to come up with a different attack.

Selene was so focused on the male shadow she didn't see the lion that slammed into her back. It drove her into the mud before leaping over her to pursue its chosen prey. Damn shifters. She tried to rise, at the same time wiping mud from her face. Pain stabbed her back. The lion must've gotten her with its claws. She ignored the coppery scent of her own blood. She could move, so she could still fight.

Beside her, a decapitated vampire head grinned at her in its death rictus. She shoved it away. A body fell on her. She squirmed from beneath it, trying to push back against the panic rising, threatening to freeze her. When she fought for her father, she usually stayed safely on the sidelines while her creations took the fight to her targets.

Selene scrambled to her feet, half blind as she scraped cold mud from her eyes. She stumbled toward the far side of the park.

The snow still fell, muffling the sounds of battle. She passed a human soldier. He was firing into a pack of werewolves. He must have the right bullets because they were all falling or running away. Good man. Who said humans were useless?

She only knew she'd reached her goal when the mud gave way to a paved sidewalk. Selene looked up. Her heart stuttered and then began pounding at triple time.

No! Birch stood nearby. He was playing his pipe, oblivious to everything around him. Didn't he see the male shadow turning towards him?

Selene screamed, trying to be heard above the other sounds. "Birch. Run!"

He merely blinked at her and kept playing.

She made frantic motions for him to look behind him. "Danger! Behind you."

She ran, gasping for breath as she raced with death.

Frantically, she searched for a creation to stop the shadow. Selene could only think of one thing. She pulled the essence she'd used for the insects back to her and then poured all her power into the dragon. The dragon turned. It spotted the male shadow.

Then everything happened at once.

The shadow closed the short distance between him and Birch.

The dragon released a stream of fire that arced across the square.

Selene put on a last spurt of speed. Gods, what else could she do to help the fairy?

The shadow reached Birch. He engulfed the fairy.

The dragon's fire exploded around the shadow.

The shadow disappeared.

Only Birch's pipe remained.

CHAPTER THIRTY-FIVE

S ELENE SANK TO THE GROUND, exhausted from her last-ditch effort to incinerate Birch's attacker. Her clawed back throbbed. The pain kept things real.

She stared at the black patch of earth where Birch had stood. The snow was covering the final evidence he had ever existed. Except for his pipe. That still bore witness for him.

She clenched her fists, aching to pound someone, *anyone* into the rapidly freezing ground. There must've been a way she could've saved Birch. But she'd expended too much power on her dragon. She had nothing left. Wearily, she recalled her essence and watched the dragon disappear.

Adam, back in human form, dropped down beside her. He put his arm across her shoulders and pulled her close. "No one could've saved him. I tried, but I was too late."

Selene shook her head before stumbling to her feet and walking over to retrieve Birch's pipe. She scooped up the instrument and then turned to find the square empty except for their team and the dead.

Ty voiced her concern. "Where is everyone?"

Meg scraped some mud off her jacket. "While you guys were going all prehistoric on the enemy, Fin and Zero were putting out mental calls for everyone to get their butts to the bridge."

Selene wasn't paying attention. She stared at Adam.

He stood facing the street leading into the square, his gaze fixed, seeing something the rest of them didn't. "He's coming. Dangerous. Enraged." Then he blinked and shrugged as he noted all the stares. "Old Adam's vampire power. I randomly see the near future. Remember?"

Before Adam could explain whether "he" was friend or enemy, a brilliant flash of light exploded from the street he was facing.

Selene threw her arm across her eyes even as she reached for whatever was left of her power.

"Kione." Adam's tone sent a clear oh-crap message.

Selene dropped her arm to peer into the fading light that revealed the fairy prince. But this was a Kione she'd never seen. He glowed, caught somewhere between his human form and a figure of light and fury.

He didn't have his hood pulled up. But for a change, she didn't have to look away from his eyes for fear of drowning in the sexual compulsion he could infect everyone with—even here, even surrounded by death. Because Kione's other emotions for once canceled out his power—horror, desperation, and yes, fear.

"I felt him die." He flung his hands out, lightning arcing between his fingers. The ground shook with his anger. "All of Faery felt him die."

Lia started to speak, but Kione interrupted her. "His song called me. I came . . ." He raised his face to the leaden night sky. "Too damn slow!" Thunder rumbled.

Selene narrowed her eyes, studying the prince. She'd never gotten the feeling Birch and Kione were close, but there was something more in his expression than merely shock and anger at the loss of a casual friend. "What did he mean to you?"

The prince speared her with a hard gaze. She could see him gathering himself, calling on at least an outer calm.

Kione raked his fingers through his hair. "He was my half-brother."

Shock silenced them all for the moment it took the prince to continue.

Kione bent his head, his dark hair falling around his face, shielding his expression. "We were not close. He was young and arrogant. He should've had time to mature, to fulfill his destiny."

"And what was that?" Lia's voice was warm, sympathetic.

"King of the Unseelie Court." Kione didn't wait for them to make the connection. "Queen Mab will mourn her favorite son, and then she will come for vengeance. She does not discriminate between friend and foe when rage takes her." Fear again surfaced. "Neither Earth nor Faery is ready for the destruction the Queen will visit on everyone when her thirst for blood overcomes her reason."

Selene followed the logic trail. "Is she your mother, too?"

"Yes."

Selene knew she should be concentrating on Mab's coming attack—the most important part of Kione's message—but she had to know. "You were older than Birch. Why wouldn't you be Mab's heir?"

"Because I'm *not* her favorite son."

Selene didn't miss the bitterness in his voice.

"How long do we have before the queen mobilizes her forces?"

Adam's tone echoed the concern they all felt.

"Not enough time for you to prepare. I'll return to Faery now. I make no promises, but I'll try to stall Mab so you can rally some sort of defense."

Selene didn't miss Kione's good-luck-with-that expression. "Thanks." There was nothing left to say. She watched the prince disappear in a flash of light. By the time she turned back to Adam, he'd already freed his soul. Selene mounted her raptor, and they sped toward the bridge.

She could feel Adam's frustration with Ty's lumbering pace compared to his own. At least the snow had dropped off to flurries. And in a few minutes, they should be able to hear the sounds of battle.

Except they didn't.

They drew closer and closer to the bridge, but still heard nothing. No explosions, no shouts, no sounds of dying.

Ty stopped and then returned to human form. "Something's not right. Too quiet."

Kelly nodded her agreement. "We'd be a lot less obvious if we all went in as humans." She wrapped her arm around Ty as she smiled up at him. "Not that you don't make a glorious first impression as our one-and-only T. rex.

The raptors tucked their souls away without comment. Adam led them as they hugged the buildings, becoming one with the shadows there. Right behind him, Selene could admire the way he moved. A predator—all fluid motion and deadly grace. Adam's prey would only see him in the moment before they died. He might hate the vampire part of him, but it definitely gave him added skills.

As they came to the corner of the last building before the bridge, Adam held up his hand. He turned to the rest crowded behind him. "Take a look. Weird stuff is going on out there."

Selene edged around him and stared. Luckily, a pale light hung over everything, allowing her a good view of the bridge and the empty highway that ran beneath it. The city had no power, but she didn't question the light, no doubt created by either Fin or Zero. "Okay, I don't get it. Zero is standing at the far end of the bridge and

Fin is at this end. Just staring at each other. Seir is in the middle. And it looks as though there's a pile of weapons or something behind Fin."

Utah frowned. "What's with the mobs behind the two leaders?"

Meg had moved up beside Selene. "That must be what's left of the two armies that were fighting in the city."

"That's all?" Jenna crept closer to Utah. "There can't be more than a few hundred on each side."

Selene couldn't help it, she scanned Zero's people for her father. She tried to deny her sigh of relief when she spotted him. She wanted to hate him, but she couldn't. She'd spent her childhood hoping for his hugs. But she was a weapon to him, and he didn't hug his weapons. Instead, he rewarded her with the heads of dead enemies. *He's still your father.* She couldn't rip that stupid whisper from her mind, from her heart.

Her father must've sensed her staring and turned to lock eyes with her. Then he nodded and offered her a small smile along with a brief salute. She returned his nod. Probably the last time she'd ever see him. Still apart. Always apart. She looked away.

"All of the Eleven are there. In human form. I wonder why no one's fighting?" Adam narrowed his gaze. "I see some of the vampires. Jude's there. More humans than I'd expect. Our lieutenant general made it. Thank the gods, most of San Diego's ordinary people escaped the city when the fighting started." He shook his head. "When did I start worrying about ordinary people?"

Utah punched his arm. "Becoming human, brother. Definitely, becoming human."

Selene was still checking out the remainder of Zero's forces. She spotted Octopus Guy. But she stopped searching when she saw the two shadows standing together. No! The male shadow had escaped her fire. She almost lost it and called forth her dragon to finish the job.

Adam clasped her hand. "Don't. Wait. Their time is almost up. They'll all be banished from Earth then."

Almost time. And just like that, all thoughts except one deserted her. *She hadn't told him.* Selene had meant to, so many times. But it had never seemed like the *right* time. Well, she'd run out of "time." What now? Blurt out, "Hey, just wanted you to know that I've been keeping this secret about Meg from you because, well, I didn't want you to think bad of me. So, since we all might die, I'll tell you now." She closed her eyes. *Now* still wasn't the right time. Selene had to believe they'd live through this and *then* she'd tell him."

Tor started to push past Adam. "Let's join our guys."

Adam grabbed his brother's arm. "Whoa. Better find out what's going on first." Something wasn't right. Fin should've been in his mind by now, wanting to know where he'd been, filling him in about the situation. But there was nothing in his head except questions.

"I can tell you that."

Adam swung to face the newcomer emerging from the shadows. Ace. He watched Selene hug the kid. Yeah, he was relieved to see Ace, too. He might not be certain which side the boy favored, but he still liked him.

Ace moved closer. "Fin and Zero are negotiating. Zero knows the game's lost. Less than a half hour until eleven-eleven, and too many of the human race still survive."

Selene peered around at the silhouettes of destroyed buildings. "Yes, but if the rest of the world is like what I see here, there won't be enough humans left to try to rebuild their civilization."

Ace didn't react to her comment, but kept talking. "Zero is about to send your dad and what's left of his fighters away from the planet, Selene. I know all of Fin's people hate Zero, but the guy was just doing his job. He's not about killing for its own sake."

"Could've fooled me." Ty's quiet murmur said it for all of them.

Ace continued to talk, but Adam tuned out. Fin finally was in his head.

"Why didn't you heed my orders, Adam?"

Fin's tone made Adam uneasy. If he didn't know better, he'd say the boss was way beyond tense. What was going on? Adam didn't waste time as he told Fin about Birch's death and the imminent arrival of Mab with her whole court.

Fin cursed. A unique response from their leader, who never seemed to lose his cool.

"I want Selene and her sister on the bridge. It's almost time for her to fulfill my vision. You and the others with you will join the rest of the Eleven."

Then he was gone from Adam's head. What? The boss hadn't even begun to answer all the questions he had lined up. He glanced around. Everyone was still listening to Ace. Why hadn't Fin spoken to everyone? Probably saving his power in case he had to battle Zero. There was only one way to get the answers he wanted. Action. "Fin just spoke to me. Selene, he wants you and Meg on the bridge. Says you still have to fulfill his vision. Don't ask me why. He didn't share with me. The rest of us are to join the others behind him."

It wasn't going to happen. No way would he allow Selene to go off without him. Adam watched the others make their way toward the rest of the Eleven. Except for Selene and Meg.

Selene must've seen him glance at Meg, because she explained. "Remember, the tune is a palindrome. It plays the same melody from both sides of the bridge. That means there are two rails that play the identical sixth note. I need someone to strike the second note while I take care of the first."

"I can hit it. Meg can go with the others. It'll probably

be safer." Even as he offered himself, Selene glanced away.

"It should be Meg. Twins, remember? We share the same blood." Selene shrugged. "That might be important to Fin's vision."

Made sense, but something felt wrong.

Selene reached up to draw his head down to her. She covered his mouth in a long drugging kiss. "Don't worry, I'll be back to get you."

Then she turned to Ace. "I'll stall as long as I can, Ace. If I can hold off long enough, you'll be safe." She frowned. "Or not. I hope you won't be banished with the others at eleven-eleven. Anyway, I don't want to take the chance that you're Six."

Adam didn't hear whatever Selene said next, because without warning, his vision blurred.

No! Not again. He recognized the symptoms. Another one of his vampire visions of the near future was about to hit him. No way to stop it. Between one blink and the next, he was standing in almost the same place. What the . . .? But the scene on the bridge had changed. Selene held a thin pipe raised to strike the bridge, but her gaze was on him. Horror twisted her features, and fear had leached all the color from her face.

That quickly, the vision was over. He was back in the present. What did it all mean? He needed time to think.

Selene stared at him strangely. "You were gone for a moment. The future?"

He nodded but didn't explain what he'd seen. No need to worry her right now.

Selene didn't press him for details. She simply nodded and then started toward the bridge with Meg beside her. Ace remained behind in the shadows.

Adam grabbed her hand before she was out of reach. Selene only looked surprised for a second and then she smiled. "Couldn't stand to be away from me, could you?"

He grinned. "You got it."

Fin turned. He transferred his glare from Zero to Adam. "Stay where you are Adam. Just the two women on the bridge." He must've sensed Adam's decision to ignore him, because he added a mental threat. *"Don't make me freeze you in place. It wouldn't be a good look for either of us."*

Adam wanted to defy his boss but knew it would be wasted effort. Reluctantly, he gave Selene's hand an encouraging squeeze before releasing her. He was primed and ready, though, if she needed him.

Selene strode onto the bridge. Meg lagged behind. She didn't seem too enthused with her part in the coming scene. The silence was so complete Adam could hear their footsteps.

The two women stopped in front of Fin. Adam glanced at Zero. Why was he just standing there? Adam caught movement out of the corner of his eye. Behind Zero, Selene's father was skulking away followed by what was left of his fighters. Not many. Although Adam didn't doubt that a lot of them were still scattered over distant parts of the world.

Selene broke the silence. "When should I do it?"

Adam switched his attention to Fin. The boss looked exhausted. He tried to imagine what it must've felt like to fight a mental battle day after day with someone of Zero's power. Fin probably had a killer of a migraine.

The boss didn't waste words. "Now." He handed her a thin metal pipe.

She nodded. "Meg will need one too. She'll take the other note."

Fin frowned. "She was in my vision, but she didn't have a pipe. That means it will all be up to you." He didn't attempt to explain away why Meg would even be in his vision.

Adam spoke before his boss could turn a thumbs down on Meg. "Selene reminded me. A palindrome. Two rails with the same note. How will she know which one works?" He took it to a logical conclusion. "Both notes probably have to be hit together." Adam shrugged. "Meg fills the bill, though. She's Selene's sister. Same blood."

Fin muttered an oath before shaking his head. "No. My vision showed *only* Selene holding a pipe. So it must be."

"Don't you hate it when he rolls out the so-it-must-be crap?" Seir had moved closer. "Fin's the family seer. He gets all prickly when someone messes with his futures. He's forgotten what happened in other cities. Jenna was supposed to ring the bell in Philly, but she gave Utah the pleasure. Then in Houston, his vision saw Kelly playing her flute. She ended up singing instead."

Family? Even though Adam knew Seir was Fin's brother, he'd never thought of them with parents and siblings. It was just too weird.

Fin turned on his brother. "Yes, and that slight deviation moved our futures in a way we can't see now, but we will eventually."

Selene interjected the voice of reason. "I can only hit one note. Which rail is the right one?"

Impasse. And what a time for it. Hundreds of fighters waited, wanting nothing more than to tear their enemies apart, and Mab headed their way to exact bloody vengeance.

Adam reached for his final attempt at reason. "Look, your visions show only a moment in time. That's all. What happens after that moment in time? Maybe if your Philly vision had lasted a little longer it would've shown Jenna allowing Utah to ring the bell. Your vision showed Jenna because only she would give Utah the chance to do the actual banishing." It made sense. Sort of.

He thought of one more argument to add. "It's eleven o'clock. We have eleven minutes before Zero and his people are banished. I'd also bet Mab is already on her way. Party time. Let's just forget number Six. When eleven-eleven—"

"No!" Fin's voice was the roar of an angry god. "It must be as I saw it or you chance changing the future to one none of us might like. I have not suffered for Earth and its people so that my vision can be tossed aside."

Adam watched Selene tense. She turned to meet his gaze, and something in her expression said Adam wouldn't like what came next.

Selene looked back at Fin. She didn't flinch. "It will be only me." She beckoned to Meg. Selene handed her the pipe and then waved her toward the other end of the bridge. Selene stepped behind Fin to pick another pipe from the pile of weapons. Fin still looked threatening, but he didn't stop her.

"Wait. What?" Adam couldn't remain quiet. Why was she deliberately defying Fin? Without pausing to think, he started towards her shouting, "Are you crazy? You don't pull the tiger's tail."

But then he saw Fin's expression. His boss didn't look mad, he looked as though he'd just had a revelation."

Adam turned to gaze at Selene. She smiled at him, a sad little lifting of her lips. "You've forgotten my power."

Her power? What did that have to do with anything?'

"I can use my essence to create any living thing I've seen. And I've seen Meg in the mirror my whole life." She reached toward him and then dropped her hand. "I was young and lonely. I needed a friend. And so—"

"You *made* one." Adam's voice shook with rage and betrayal. She'd created a copy of herself, one that his brother loved. He didn't try to hide his bitterness. Why did she keep it from him? *Stay calm.* Too much was at stake for him to lose control now. But he hurt, damn it! She hadn't trusted him.

Selene shifted her gaze quickly to Fin. "So, you see, everything will be fine. I'm the only one striking any notes on this bridge."

The full impact finally sank in. Adam abandoned calm. "Like hell it'll be fine!"

She cast a stricken glance at Adam as she lifted her pipe. Then she froze.

Her expression jerked him from his own churning emotions. Horror. Fear. The exact emotions she'd worn a few minutes ago in his vision. *A warning of danger.*

His predator instinct kicked in. He leaped aside. Behind him, the male shadow bore down on him. Where had it come from?

In the instant left to plan, Adam noted the monster's gaze. It was fixed on Selene. So, he wasn't the target. A quick glance showed the female shadow stalking Meg. The shadows didn't want Selene playing any tunes on that bridge. But the path to Selene went through him.

Adam made his decision. He had no weapon to destroy the shadow, but at least he could slow it down long enough for Selene to do what needed doing. He had faith in her.

Adam freed his beast. This would be a good test of Fin's belief that the Eleven would be tough to kill in their dino forms.

The shadow had almost reached him when he heard Fin shout, "Now!"

Adam's raptor crouched, ready to spring. *Now would be perfect, Selene.*

CHAPTER THIRTY-SIX

PANIC FROZE SELENE. FEAR FOR Adam left her mind blank. For only a second, though. How had the monster reached their side of the bridge unseen? The creature's gaze was fixed on her, but it would have to go through Adam first. Her raptor was ready to spring. He'd die. *Die!* The word set up house in her brain and sang its own song of sorrow.

No! Absolutely wasn't going to happen. She had to save Adam. In seconds the man she loved would disappear like Birch had.

Wait. Where was the female? Was Meg safe? Selene started to look toward the other end of the bridge. She stopped. No time.

She needed a distraction. Something that would stop the shadow, even for a few minutes. She still held the pipe. *Do it.*

Selene struck the sixth rail. The note rang out. Clear. Sharp. An arrow of sound that blended with Meg's and immediately sought out its target.

She didn't search the crowds for Six. Selene didn't give a damn about anything except Adam. She turned to see him back in human form staring at—

Amid cries of amazement, the male shadow was putting on a light show for the ages. Starting at where his feet should be, he was breaking up into tiny sparkling bits that drifted away and winked out. The last thing to disappear was his sort-of face with its stunned expression. Hello, number Six. Relief made her legs weak as she checked that both Meg and Adam were safe.

Would Queen Mab turn around and go home when she found out her prey was beyond her reach? From what Kione had said, the answer was no.

She forgot about Mab for the moment as the pregnant female shadow wailed her distress. Selene wanted to assure her she'd be reunited with her lover in a few minutes, but she forgot about the shadow as she locked gazes with Adam.

He knew now that Meg was more than her sister, that she was a part of Selene herself. He'd make assumptions. Meg was her slave. Selene lived through Meg, experiencing everything her creation did and felt. He'd think of Meg with Tor. He'd assume everything bad because . . . She. Hadn't. Told. Him.

He narrowed his eyes. His expression hardened. Anger, but there was hurt and confusion as well. He wasn't the only one suffering, though. Lesson learned: procrastination didn't cancel the pain, it only postponed it, allowed it time to grow and fester. Sometimes loving someone too much led you to make dumb decisions.

He reached her in a few strides, outrage sharpening his features as he treated her to a brief flash of fang. Ah, that was the vampire she loved. Even in his anger, she found him glorious. She'd lost her perspective when it came to all three of him—man, vampire, and raptor.

"You didn't tell me you and Meg were the same. Didn't you think I'd want to know? Didn't you trust me with the truth?" Each word landed with a gavel's force—judging, finding her guilty.

There it was again, the hurt, quickly hidden. It wounded her more than all of his anger. "I always meant to." *Weak, Selene.* "It was just never the right time." *Lacking creativity.*

"Does Tor know we're sharing the same woman?"

That was a stab to her already bleeding heart. "There's no sharing going on. Meg is completely her own person." *Now.* Selene lifted her chin to return his glare. "We're not connected. The essence I used to form her no longer belongs to me. She is free. And I *never* spied on her thoughts or feelings."

"Yes, Tor knows everything. I told him."

Selene jerked. She hadn't noticed when Meg arrived.

"He never told *me.*" Adam didn't try to hide his sense of betrayal.

"It wasn't his right to tell." Meg didn't blink in the face of Adam's vampire stare.

Even in the midst of her emotional crisis, Selene applauded Meg. Blood ran true.

Selene never knew what Adam would've said next, because Seir spoke.

"It's eleven-eleven, folks. Time for some of us to disappear. The suspense leaves me breathless. After all, I'm like a middleman. Will I stay or will I go? The excitement is too much to bear."

In spite of his sarcasm, Selene heard the tension in Seir's voice. Most of the fighters behind Fin and Zero had grown quiet. Waiting. Personally, she was hoping for a fireworks display that would whip Zero and his people away so she could finally celebrate her freedom from fear. *Unless you go with them.* After all, she'd come to Earth as one of Zero's immortals. *Please, no.* She couldn't survive being ripped from Adam.

He grabbed her hand and squeezed, an anchor to this world, to *him.* Always to him.

"You aren't going anywhere, lady. You owe me too many explanations."

The minutes dragged on. Voices called out, asking what was going on. Exactly what Selene wanted to know.

Adam started hauling her off the bridge. "If nothing's

going to happen, we need to get out of here. This is making me nervous. Besides, Mab could show up at any moment. Oh, and if you haven't noticed, the mobs are ready to rip out each other's throats."

He obviously had put aside his anger in favor of saving her. *Hold tight, raptor.* Yes. Raptor. Because he might be living in a borrowed vampire body with its borrowed powers, but she'd always think of him as she'd first seen him at the zoo battling Crow. She missed the good old days.

Just when Selene expected the crowd to explode into violence, Balan materialized from shadows that hadn't been there a moment ago. The crowd quieted again as their attention shifted from each other to the appearance of the black jaguar in the middle of the bridge.

"Just. Freaking. Great." Adam pulled Selene close as he faced the jaguar. "The official observer-and-reporter— in other words, chief spy—for the big kahuna. I always thought he worked for Zero, but I've got the feeling the chain of command goes higher than we knew."

Balan roared and the Earth screamed, a grinding shriek torn from its very center. The world shook. Cracks snaked across the bridge. And beyond the bridge, fissures opened to swallow some of the remaining buildings. Not an earthquake. This was the planet in agony. Selene fought to remain standing.

Balan's full power was on display for the first time. At least she hoped he didn't have more in store. Otherwise, they were all doomed. And from the terrified expressions on the faces of the hardened fighters, they realized it too.

Zero answered Balan's challenge. "What words do you bring, servant of He Who Shapes Worlds?"

Selene leaned into Adam to ask, "Servant of who?"

Adam didn't get a chance to answer.

"You have failed." Balan bared his teeth in a silent snarl.

Selene realized she wasn't hearing Balan's voice in her head as usual. "The cat's talking out loud. Why?"

Adam shrugged as he kept his attention on Balan. "Guess he wants the terrified masses to get his message too." He nodded toward the crowds pushing and shoving to distance themselves from their two leaders. Most of them turned and faded into the night.

"Huracan is disappointed." Balan was using his prepare-to-die voice.

Adam didn't give her a chance to ask. "I've never heard of Huracan."

Silence wrapped around everyone, a quiet filled with foreboding, promising that Huracan's displeasure would fall on all of their heads.

With his unblinking gaze fixed on Zero, the jaguar spelled everything out. "You and yours will never again leave this planet, never again wander the worlds of this plane to carry out His wishes. You are no longer worthy." He turned to encompass Fin and Seir in his condemnation.

Zero glared the length of the bridge at Fin. "This is your fault. If you hadn't played the traitor, we would be done and gone by now."

Selene made the connection. "Traitor? Then that means—"

Adam didn't give her a chance to finish. "Fin worked with Zero to destroy other civilizations. Maybe even my first one."

Uh-oh. Selene could feel Adam's beast battering him, screaming to burst free so it could attack Fin. Not a great idea. The Eleven were savage, but they weren't in Fin's league. "Think. Fin's been on our side since the beginning. He's the only reason we were able to battle Zero to a draw. I mean, without him, you'd have died back in your original time."

Adam didn't look too impressed. "Then why keep his

connection to Zero a secret?" He widened his accusation to include her. "Why is *everyone* keeping secrets?"

Now wasn't the time to talk about hers, but she could guess why Fin had failed to mention his previous employment as Destroyer of Worlds. "He was afraid you guys would react exactly the way you are now." A glance told her Al and a few others of the Eleven had given in to their rage and were stomping around in their dino forms.

Fin ignored those behind him. Instead, he shouted back at Zero. "We were wrong to play gods. *He* was wrong to ask it of us."

He being the mysterious Huracan? Selene had no time to think beyond that before Kione appeared in a flash of light. He wore what she supposed was the fairy equivalent of a panicked expression. She couldn't see his eyes, but his body language shouted, "Be very afraid."

"Mab comes. She's brought her whole court with her. I've only seen her in such a rage once. The Iflingdons angered her thousands of years ago."

Who? Selene's head was about to explode. "What happened to them?"

"They're extinct." Kione turned to face the west. "You have little time." He pointed.

Everyone turned to stare. There. Spread across the entire night horizon was a pale blue glow, and beneath it a rolling avalanche of ice and snow. Selene shivered. Even this far away, she could feel the freezing bite of Mab's anger.

"Fuck."

That word coming from Fin's mouth shocked Selene almost as much as the approaching fairies. Fin was above common language. He didn't indulge in emotional outbursts. He was the cold one, the ice king.

Fin turned to eye how many fighters he still had. His expression said he wasn't impressed. "If you need another weapon, take these." He stepped aside so they could see the pile hidden behind him "Choose only the iron ones. You can kill or at least hurt fairies with them."

As many rushed to arm themselves, Adam asked the important question. "Can we win with the few fighters we have left?"

Ty spoke before Fin could answer. "Bring it, fairy queen. We have this."

Fin looked less certain. "We can win the battle, but when it's over there won't be enough left of Earth to support what remains of human life."

That shut Ty up.

Seir shouted, "Join with me, brothers, *now*." All of his sly sarcasm was gone. Urgency framed every word.

Adam registered the word "brothers" and then put it away for later, when Mab wasn't headed toward them with annihilation on her mind. "What should we do?" He'd also save his mad at Fin for a better time. But right now, survival came first.

"Make sure everyone stays on the bridge. And keep the fairies off it." Then Fin joined Seir in the middle of the bridge.

Zero did the same. He waved the remainder of his own immortals onto the bridge before joining Seir and Fin. Not many of them. Adam recognized the female shadow and Octopus Guy. He didn't take time to study the others.

Everyone waited. Adam kept a tight hold on Selene. He might be ticked off at her, but that didn't mean he didn't love her and wouldn't protect her to his last breath.

The rest of the Eleven and their wives stood close by. Jude and Xavier along with Shen and Greer were also there. It made sense the boss's assistant and chef would do double duty as fighters. Fin didn't hire one dimensional people. Oh, hey, the lieutenant general had stayed to fight. Adam would never again look down on humans. Even Ace had joined them. And at the last minute, Dave huffed and puffed his way onto the bridge. He'd shed all his attitude along the way. Adam couldn't identify the others still standing behind Fin. Not much of an army, considering that the snowball-from-a-frozen-hell rolling toward them probably hid thousands.

Adam scanned the bridge again. Kione had disappeared. Adam didn't blame him. After all, he had to face his queen when this was over.

"That's it." He looked beyond the shadows one more time to make sure no more of their people had stayed to fight. "Guess everyone else checked out the odds then decided to lay down their cards and run."

Selene squeezed his hand. "Don't worry. We have the mega-watt, power triplets in our corner. Oh, and they have you. Can't do better than that."

Say it out loud. You can't count on an afterwards. "I love you."

She stood on tiptoe and kissed his cheek. "I love you, too, raptor. Always."

Not good enough for a possible last kiss. Adam wrapped his arms around her, pulled her close, and covered her mouth with his. Her lips were soft, warm, and filled with promises—that their love would last beyond any battle, that together they could do anything, even stomp a fairy queen into the ground. He deepened the kiss. Adam liked her promises. Finally, as the shouts around them grew louder, he stepped back. "We'll continue this when it's over." Over.

Yes, he'd make it happen. Both of them would be alive at the end of the fight.

The Unseelie Court was almost on top of them when Fin, Seir, and Zero joined hands.

Adam didn't have even a heartbeat to question why before their power struck him along with everyone else on the bridge. It was like someone flung a cement blanket over him. One minute he was standing there wondering what the three would do and the next his butt was flat on the ground. Their power pressed him into the bridge, took his breath away, and scared the crap out of him. Automatically, he reached for Selene. She lay beside him, her eyes wide with shock. She opened her mouth to speak, but nothing came out.

Unable to move and barely able to breathe, he could do nothing but watch everything play out.

"We need more power." Seir swore as he scanned the crowd.

"Ace." Zero's voice held a compulsion no one would ignore. Unlike everyone else, the kid was able to rise and join them.

Zero grabbed his hand. "Hang on, child. Join your power with ours."

Eyes wide and confused, Ace obeyed. Adam knew the boy obeyed because he felt the jolt through his entire body as it happened.

"Look. They're here." Selene gasped between each word.

One glance told Adam all he needed to know. Mab's army of trolls, elves, boggarts and other creatures was about to overrun the bridge from both ends. Meanwhile, Fin and the other three stood frozen with eyes closed.

The four were now lit up like mini suns. Didn't look as though they'd be much help in defending the bridge. Guess that was his job along with all the others flat on their backs right now.

Not for long, though. He closed his eyes and freed his beast. His raptor screamed its joy as it rose from the ground. No amount of power would hold it down. The rest of the Eleven followed his example.

Selene still couldn't rise, but that didn't stop her from calling five flying creatures into being. Snakes. Transparent. He had to squint to even see them. Long and as thin as strings, they slithered through the air. He wondered how they were supposed to do any damage until he watched the first one attack.

The elf had big ears, and it didn't even see the snake dive into one of them. Then the elf's skull lit up from inside, and Adam heard a pop and crackle. By the time the snake exited from the opposite ear, the elf was dead with only wisps of smoke coming from its ears to mark its passing. Adam shuddered. A lust for killing might rule his raptor form, but that didn't mean he was stupid. Good things didn't always come in small packages.

As much as Adam wanted to join the fight to keep Mab and her army off the bridge, he wouldn't leave Selene unprotected. Lowering his head, he gripped her jacket in his jaws and yanked her to her feet.

She managed to move, but haltingly. "Wow, I never felt power like they're putting out. I think the force is weakening a little, though."

Then he crouched so she could scramble onto him. This time she would stay safe on his back instead of running off to fight alone. Selene evidently agreed. Once settled, she drew her iron sword with one hand and her knife with the other.

"Let's get after it, raptor." She hunched over him, still fighting the power surge from Fin and friends. Around them, others slowly recovered and climbed to their feet.

And so began the weirdest battle Adam had ever seen. Everyone moved in slow motion. Nearby, a troll flung itself onto the bridge, its movements sluggish and strained. It was a big, hairy salmon fighting its way upstream.

Adam's raptor leaped, straining every muscle, and met the troll's charge in midair. He stabbed his toe claw into the creature's spine at the same time he closed his jaws around the troll's neck. He tore off its head, glorying in the spray of warm blood.

Three small creatures leaped onto his back. Small, fuzzy, cute, with icepick teeth. They didn't stay there long as

Selene carved them into bite-sized bits with the iron knife Fin had sworn would kill fairies.

He turned to search for more prey as Selene recalled her killer snakes. She instantly replaced them with five copies of Q. Their only Quetzalcoatlus was hard pressed to keep the skies above them fairy-free.

Then everything devolved into a roiling mass of savagery. Utah and Tor joined him. Pack again. Adam's raptor shook with bloodlust. Meg on Tor and Lia on Utah fought atop their men. Splattered with blood, Meg wielded an iron spear while Lia's vampire fangs were on full display.

Somewhere nearby he could hear Ty's roar along with Kelly's scream of defiance.

The battle raged on for years. That's how it felt. During the moments between kills, Adam caught glimpses of bodies littering the bridge. Friends, allies. He didn't have time to ID them. Sorrow would come later. Selene was still safe on his back, and his brothers and their wives still surrounded him. He fought on.

But he was beginning to tire. Coated in blood and hurting from where a Red Cap had gotten him good on the leg—murderous little monster with his cap soaked in the blood of his victims. Adam's wound ached a little less, though, at the memory of the dead fairy with his cap soaked in his own blood for a change.

Atop him, he heard Selene gasp. What? He looked up. And wished he hadn't.

CHAPTER THIRTY-SEVEN

———

THE FIGHTING STOPPED.

Silence. Except for the bass-drumbeat of Selene's heart.

Then the sound of distant pipes. Not the sensual enchantments Birch had played. These? They were the melodies of death—the wails and shrieks of the dying. Meant to freeze their listeners with fear. They worked.

Beneath her, Adam tensed.

They watched as through the darkness and softly falling snow, Mab came.

If the fae queen was going for terrifying beauty, she'd nailed it. She drove an icicle-draped chariot that floated above Highway 94, pulled by a white serpent as long as a jumbo jet. The creature undulated through the air, sinuous and deadly. Its scales gleamed in the light beaming from Fin and the others. Mab's gown was sparkling ice crystals and her hair was windswept snow that streamed behind her. And her eyes . . . Selene shuddered. They were a frozen lake with something dark and wicked moving beneath the surface.

"My mother bears death in both hands."

Surprised, Selene glanced beside her. Kione stood there surrounded by scores of Red Cap bodies—no wounds, no blood. They'd all died smiling. She avoided meeting his gaze.

He laughed. "Bloodlust made them careless. They looked me in the eye. Too much pleasure can kill."

Adam lowered his head, careful to focus on the prince's chest.

Kione answered his unspoken question. "Why did I return?" He gestured towards the fast-approaching Queen of the Winter Court. "My mother never loved me, never called me son. All through the years that I suffered from my curse, she ignored my pain. It was Fin, a stranger, who rescued me. I looked within. Who did I want to be: one who was loyal to Mab or loyal to the person who saved me? I chose, and so I'm here to fight for Fin."

Selene thought about Kione's first comment. "Death in both hands?" She watched Mab's approach. Finally, she noticed what the queen carried. "She has a sword in one hand and a head in the other." Disgusting. But her father would admire the queen's trophy. The face was hidden by a bushy black beard and long tangled hair crusted with frost.

"Her sword has drunk the blood of thousands. The head is that of the king of Iflingdon. You should feel honored. She only wields both when the enemy she plans to destroy is worthy."

He pointed. "Notice the High Fae who escort her. They are beautiful, lethal, heartless, and wear white. Mab is color coordinated in all things."

Not funny. Selene dragged her attention from the queen long enough to notice her guards. Five on each side of her chariot. They were gorgeous killing machines. They rode tall in their saddles with hands on swords made from a material that swirled with colors. Cold and proud, she couldn't imagine any real emotion ever creasing the perfection of those faces. Their white steeds, as beautiful as their riders, cantered through the air.

She compared the guards to Kione. He was as beautiful

and dangerous, but she refused to call him heartless.

"I don't believe this." Jude's voice broke the silence.

Selene found him in the mob. His vampire cool was gone. His fangs dripped blood, the same color as his eyes.

She followed his gaze. Her heart dropped to her stomach and lay there. Behind the chariot strode giants, at least twenty, as tall as the surrounding buildings, if any of them had still stood. What came after the giants was an endless stream of the High Fae that went on as far as she could see.

Jude's laughter rang hollow. "She wore us out fighting the lesser monsters before hitting us with her big guns. We're screwed."

Suddenly, the paralysis the spectacle of Mab had caused shattered, and the fighting continued with renewed savagery.

Selene didn't hesitate. She retrieved her Q wannabees, leaving Q on his own, because she'd need every bit of her essence to help Adam. Selfish? Yes. But he was everything to her. If go down they must, he'd be the last one lost if she had anything to say about it.

The fae creatures attacked with restored energy, knowing their queen was close.

Selene slashed and screamed and killed. Fae blood ran down her sword, down her arm. The grisly head belonging to some nightmare landed in her lap. She grabbed it and tossed it over the side of the bridge. Its dead eyes stared at her until it disappeared.

Selene wanted to create something to help, but she couldn't breathe, couldn't think past the next thrust of her blade, the next wailing creature as it died. She ignored the stings of scrabbling claws as they dug into her. Adam roared as he tore flesh apart in a killing frenzy. Vaguely, she realized he was keeping the worst from her.

She glanced up through a red haze to see Mab's serpent had finally reached the bridge. It rose above them, opened its jaws filled with fangs longer than a man's arm, and spewed venom at them. The poison sizzled as it splattered on the cement, and screams split the night. Frantically, she twisted, searching. Was Meg safe?

The serpent shrieked, its cry ending in a hiss.

The power of that sound knocked Adam back into his human form. Selene was flung to the ground along with everyone else on the bridge.

Before anyone could move, the serpent inhaled and then breathed a cloud of ice shards at them. Selene flung her arm across her face to protect it, even as the ice pierced her arms along with any other exposed skin. She took her hand away to find some of the queen's smaller subjects impaled on the shards. Mab obviously thought they were expendable. Bitch.

She'd barely had a chance to scramble to her feet before the queen spoke.

"Where is the one who killed my son? Release him to me, and you may live."

The queen's voice had a lot in common with her serpent. Behind Selene, Adam moved close, her personal wall of strength.

Kione carefully removed an ice sliver from his neck. "She's lying. No one will leave here alive if she can help it. Mab feels perfectly confident in challenging even those who claim immortality."

Selene decided she was the most qualified to answer the queen.

Adam sensed her intention and clasped her arm. "Don't. You'll make yourself a target."

She stroked his hand. "Someone has to tell her." Selene nodded toward Fin and the other shining three. "They aren't going to help."

She shouted to Mab before Adam could mount another argument. "The killer is gone. I banished him from this planet. He can never return."

"Noooo!"

Mab's cry was an icepick to her brain. Selene clamped her hands over her ears. When she finally took her palms away, blood smeared them. Everything about Mab was a destructive force.

"Ripping my son's murderer apart and bathing in his blood was *my* right. You've cheated me of my vengeance. I will take all your lives as payment for your insult."

Chaos erupted.

Mab's creatures that still lived made a dive for safety off the bridge. At the same time, Mab levitated into the air, waving her sword and the revolting head above her. "Kill, kill, kill!" The giants and High Fae behind her echoed her call.

The serpent stood upright in the air, a nightmare version of a snake charmer's cobra. It hovered over the bridge, poised to impose Mab's wrath on them.

No time to run, no way to keep everyone alive, unless . . . Selene sucked in her breath. She couldn't. But with death hanging above them, she had no choice. She closed her eyes, and called forth the deadliest creature she'd ever encountered, the one she'd sworn never to loose on even her worst enemy, the one she kept hidden in the darkest recesses of her mind where she'd never have to think about it.

As the abomination materialized, she pleaded with any gods that might be monitoring the battle that she'd have the power to control her weapon.

Selene's pounding heart wasn't loud enough to drown out the sibilant whisper in her mind. *"Finally."* No! She didn't hear that. This was *her* creation, born of her memory and made real by her essence. Hers. It would obey *her*. The soft chuckle mocked that belief.

"What the hell!" Adam's shout jerked her back to the here and now.

She looked up. And there it was. Her own personal

planet eater. Too massive to make out a shape, any more than she could describe the shape of an incoming storm front. It was all roiling darkness, blacker than even the night sky.

Selene blocked out the shouts and screams from thousands of throats, friends and enemies alike. *Concentrate. Control it.* But how did you control a creature that spanned miles not feet, with a mouth big enough to swallow an army in one crunching bite, and an appetite that not even all of Earth could satisfy?

She fell to her knees, weighed down by the power above her, by the loss of her own strength. Any minute now she expected to sink through the concrete to the highway below. "She's too much." Yes, it was a she. "I can't . . ."

Adam wrapped his arms around her, protecting Selene not only from her own stupidity, but also from the panic surrounding them.

"You *can*." His words carried all his faith in her, his conviction that she could do this.

And so, she'd try. Selene gathered her power. She rolled it into a tight ball where her heart beat madly. Then she wrapped heart and power into a casing of steely determination. Ready, aim, *fire*.

Her will pounded the vast winged darkness that filled the sky. She felt its attention focus on her, test her, and then yield. For now. The creature opened her mouth.

"Will you get a look at that? It could swallow half the city!"

Ty's shout was more admiration than horror. Figured. T. rex to the core.

But that's not what caused Mab's army to flee. As the creature turned her attention to the fae, they could see beyond the wide-open jaws into another world. A barren plain with black sand and distant mountains that belched fire into an empty yellow sky. But close to the entrance was something that looked like—

"What the—?" Q flapped down beside Adam as he returned to human form. Q, who had a snarky comment for everything, got no further. Speechless.

Selene finished her thought. "A nest. She has young. Everything living on Earth will feed her and those babies."

"Can we kill—?"

Selene didn't allow Kione to finish. There was no time for useless conjectures. "No, we can't kill her. She's a living portal between worlds. If attacked by what she considered an overwhelming force—which we don't have—she'd simply close her mouth and withdraw from Earth."

Adam asked the pivotal question. "Now that she's scattered Mab's army, can't you just take back your essence?"

She wanted to say yes and then watch all those waiting for her answer sigh their relief. Selene told them the truth. "No. I don't have the strength left to control her beyond what I've done so far. And before you ask, running won't save us. Now that she's started, she won't stop until this planet is bare of life."

"But I thought the creature was just fabricated from your memory. How can it be a real portal with a nest in another world? You didn't create that." Lia seemed outraged at the thought.

"I don't know." Selene's whisper shut everyone down as they all watched the living portal tear Mab's serpent apart to pass on to her hungry family. Selene didn't even notice the spray of blood raining down on them.

Adam broke the silence. "Okay, I'm done with waiting for our shining foursome to wake and save us."

Before Selene could speak, he grabbed her hand, shoved aside any in his path, and strode across the bridge to where Fin and the others still stood. On the way, she chanced a quick glance at her creation, who was now working on the giants. Monster Mom wasn't eating them. One after the other, she gulped them down. They tumbled through Mother's portal where they would feed the babies. Selene made a last effort to reclaim her essence. No deal. Mama wasn't returning to sender.

Adam cuffed Fin's shoulder. "Hey, oh glowing one. We're about to become baby food. Turn off the night light and help save us." He paused for a moment. "Please."

Selene thought Fin wouldn't respond, but then, slowly, he turned his head to stare at Adam.

Selene's gasp joined the other watchers on the bridge. What faced them wasn't Fin. It was—

An explosion and sun-bright flash of light ended her thought.

Suddenly, she *wasn't*. Not anyone. Not anywhere. Blackness. Nothingness. No memory. No body. No past, no future, no *present*. Floating through the timelessness of never-existed.

Wait. Something. A word? She clung to the sound of it in her . . . mind? No, she didn't have a mind. But still, it was *there*. She followed the word as it moved through the blackness.

And when it seemed in danger of escaping her, she opened the mouth she no longer had and screamed.

ADAM!

CHAPTER THIRTY-EIGHT

—◆—

FIN TURNED TO MEET HIS gaze. Adam had only a moment to make sense of what he saw. His beast stirred.

And as the boom and flash of light took him, his raptor broke free.

His soul tumbled and clawed through a universe without light, without meaning, without memory. No. That wasn't right. There was *something*. Just out of reach. It trickled and oozed into the crevices of his soul. Did he have a soul? Yes. *Remember*. Three other times—floating in a sea of nothingness, no body, only his soul remained of what he had once been. What was he? His soul knew. It roared its message of rage, of its need to return to . . . *someone*.

This time would be different. No one-way trips without his okay. *Remember*.

A whisper. *Adam*. He knew the name. *His*. He knew the voice. It was the one he'd return to, damn what anyone else wanted.

He had no body, no senses, but he had his will. And that will turned his soul around. Adam was going back. He fought against something thick and sticky that tried to hold him. Not real. He had no senses. He pushed aside whispers that fogged his thoughts with words demanding he stay away. Nope, wasn't going to work this time. He battled the compulsion. Nothing would stop him from finding *her. Selene.*

"Selene!" Her name was a joyous shout as he catapulted onto the bridge and back into his human form. He landed on his butt. Again.

But it was worth it as Selene landed beside him. She shouted his name and wrapped her arms around him. Their reunion ended quickly.

What was going on? Nausea churned in his gut. The planet was spinning. Day became night in seconds and then back to day again. Beside him, Selene pressed her hand to her mouth. Things changed even as he blinked. Blink, that house was rubble. Blink, the house was whole and untouched. Blink, destroyed vehicles cluttered the highway. Blink, the highway was empty. Then there were the seasons. Blink, snow. Blink, heat. Blink, flowers bloomed. He closed his eyes. "This isn't happening."

It would only be a matter of seconds before he had to crawl to the edge of the bridge and empty his stomach.

Suddenly, everything stopped. Cautiously, he opened his eyes. First thing he noticed? Everyone else was still down except for Fin and friends. He climbed to his feet and pulled Selene up with him. "Are you okay?"

She nodded. "Probably. My stomach is still in orbit, though."

Adam narrowed his eyes as Fin approached. This was the man he knew. No, not man. What he'd seen right before his joy ride into hell hadn't been even close to human.

Fin's smile was more of a grimace. "I tried to keep all of your souls away until we'd finished. You would've spared yourselves some discomfort."

Adam knew his smile was just as insincere as Fin's. "I'm all about truth in advertising. You hijacked my soul three times before without explaining. From the original me to dinosaur to human to vampire. Wasn't going to get away with it a fourth time. I need a destination ticket from now on before I go anywhere."

Selene brushed her hair away from her face as the cool breeze picked up. "What happened?" She frowned. "And was that the real you I saw right before the world came apart?"

Fin ignored her last question as he swept his arm to encompass their surroundings. "What happened? Look around you."

They looked.

Adam whistled softly. "Time travel?" Everything seemed exactly the way it would've appeared before humanity realized they were in danger. Cars on the highway below them. Buildings all intact. No fae army. He noted that the rest of those on the bridge were now stirring. "Better get Octopus Guy out of sight. I don't think San Diego is ready for him." How had Fin and the others done this? What kind of power could move all of those near him back in time?

Fin smiled. "Returning to an earlier time wouldn't put out the fire. We'd still have to walk into the flames when Zero attacked humanity. Again. I don't believe any of us want that." He glanced to where Zero was speaking to Octopus Guy. "No, something else. I'll explain later." Fin watched the rest of the Eleven struggling to their feet. "You're right about not wanting to draw attention. We don't need the police involved." He started to walk away.

"Wait." Selene ran after him. "I saw your real face right before everything went wrong. What are you? Tell me—"

Fin waved her away. "Later. No time now." He joined Zero in shouting to the others on the bridge. "No questions. We'll talk once we get to a safe place."

Adam noticed the word "we." He figured it was all about brotherly love until the danger was over. Then what?

Seir clarified. "Our safe place is the restaurant." He turned to Zero. "Need directions?"

Zero's laughter mocked the question. "Of course not. I never attacked the place because I wanted to give you a false sense of security."

Fin snorted his opinion of that. "You didn't attack because you couldn't get past my protections."

Zero shrugged. "There was that, too."

Jude interrupted. "It's almost dawn. Will you be teleporting us? I assume with all your godly powers that won't be a problem."

Fin speared Jude with a hard stare. "We used all our 'godly powers' to save your lives. We're all powered out. You can walk for all I care. Just get there." He joined Seir. "I know you drove here. You wouldn't leave your car behind, even for the end of the world."

Seir nodded, and Fin beckoned the other two. "Let's get going." He called over his shoulder as he left, "The rest of you can follow us."

Selene didn't even wait for Fin to walk away. She pointed to where Dave stood. "Our ride. We can squeeze a bunch of us into the SUV."

A short time later, crammed into the vehicle, they were on their way with a few other cars following. No one spoke during the short drive.

Once inside the restaurant, Selene paused to notice that Fin and Zero had chosen seats at opposite ends of the long table. From there, they glared its length at each other. Seir looked bored from his seat in the middle.

She picked the seat across from Seir. Adam dropped into the one next to her. Seir's expression brightened.

"I notice you're a middle-of-the-road kind of guy. Middle of the bridge. Middle of the table. Spreading your loyalties right down the middle." Selene didn't try to hide the accusation in her voice.

Seir showed her his fake offended expression. "You

didn't seem to mind taking half my aid when I offered it." He smiled. "Besides, every battle needs a referee. That's me."

Adam wanted to ask Seir what he and his brothers had done on the bridge. And what about Ace? How did the kid fit into the picture?

The conversation stopped, though, as Octopus Guy lowered himself onto the seat next to Adam. Okay, that wasn't exactly accurate. Actually, he spread himself across the four chairs beside Adam. Even then, he had to curl his arms, tentacles, whatever close for him to fit.

"This fiasco didn't have the optimum outcome for me, but no one can ever say that Bernius doesn't know how to adapt to altered circumstances." His many eyes scoped out the table. "No refreshments? Would it be too much to ask for a few freshly caught fish?"

Adam fought to keep his concentration on Octopus Guy as Selene placed her hand on his thigh. It was scary how easy it was for her to distract him. He covered her hand with his and squeezed, hoping she'd get the message that amazing things would happen once they were free of this place.

"So, you have your future planned?" Seir sounded interested.

Bernius gave his version of an octopus shrug. "I have more intelligence than any other water-dwelling creature, along with vast experience in bending others to my will. It shouldn't take long for me to organize the higher life forms in the sea into a force to be reckoned with. Then, with my ability to exist on land and communicate with both humans and seafolk, I expect to build my empire—"

All talk stopped as Zero stood.

"Now," Selene whispered, "We'll find out what happened on that bridge."

Zero broke the silence. "I'm sure you have questions."

Shouts erupted from all sides of the room.

"What happened at the bridge?"

"Who are you guys?"

"What do we do now?"

"Why was I with you?" Ace still looked shellshocked.

"Are you really brothers?"

"Silence!" Fin's voice dripped threats of death and dismemberment.

The questions were silenced. Zero seemed impressed.

"Thank you, *brother.*" Zero emphasized the word to answer the question about their relationships to each other.

Ace couldn't stay silent. "Not me. You're not my brothers."

Zero cast him a thoughtful glance. "No. Not our brother. Something else." He didn't elaborate, much to Ace's obvious frustration.

Zero continued. "Who are we? The three of us are all sons of Huracan—he whom the Maya worshipped as the god of natural disasters as well as one who had his fingers in the rise and fall of many civilizations. Humans were merely the latest."

Seir broke into Zero's explanation. "Our father believes his press releases. He sees himself as a creation god." He glanced quickly at the ceiling. "Just making sure Dad isn't listening in. Anyway, he doesn't create life. He destroys it so other living things can become ascendent. Then he tears them down when they become too powerful in his estimation." He scanned the room. "As the Eleven know, your original civilization was Earth's first. Not a trace was left for future archeologists to ponder over. It was humanity's turn this time."

Zero glared at Fin. "All would've gone as our father planned if my brother hadn't decided to betray us."

Fin was unrepentant. "The complete destruction of

lifeforms he alone chooses is wrong. I could no longer condone the evil."

Adam didn't like the way Zero was beginning to glow again. Time to change the subject. "I don't care about your family fights. I want to know what happened on that bridge."

Around the table there were rumbles of agreement.

Seir stood. "Let me explain. I'm the youngest and least volatile. While my brothers mentally berate each other, I'll tell you what we did and why."

Selene leaned into Adam. "This better be good."

"We're alive and we're together. That's good enough for me." Adam kissed a spot right behind her ear and she hummed her satisfaction.

"First, we decided time travel wasn't the best solution to our problem. Yes, we could have gone back and saved Birch. Mab wouldn't have waged war on us. But other things would've remained the same. The planet still would've been almost uninhabitable and the human population decimated after my brother was done. Besides, there was no way humans could be wiped out completely in time to meet our father's deadline anyway, so he would still sentence us to forever on this planet. And who wants to live on a world with no fine restaurants or upscale shopping?"

Adam shook his head. "Seir is all heart."

"Get to the point." The male voice came from next to Seir.

There was no one sitting there.

Startled, Seir cursed and then relaxed. He pointed at the empty chair. "Meet Coraven. He would've been Fin's number Three. Invisibility is only one of his talents."

"Okay, who would've been Two?" Selene was checking out the table to see if there were any strangers.

Seir widened his eyes. "Why, you, sweetheart. I wonder how you would've handled that." He grinned.

Selene looked away.

"I'll finish, Seir. We need this done so everyone can get some rest." Fin rubbed his eyes and yawned.

Seir opened his mouth to complain, but then nodded.

Fin stood and looked out over his small army. "I'll make this short. My father isn't a creationist god, although he'd like all to believe it. None of his sons are either. But we do have powers." Fin gestured at Adam. "I've taken his soul four times to keep him safe."

"Is that what you did to us on the bridge?" Mr. Invisible next to Seir sounded as though he was close to taking issue with all the soul-stealing.

Fin nodded. "We took your souls so you'd survive while we . . . solved the problem."

The silence was a tightly stretched guitar string ready to snap if Fin didn't hurry up his explaining. It wouldn't be a winning tune. Adam rubbed his thumb over the pulse point of Selene's wrist as he waited.

"We can't create something that has never existed, but we can recreate. A little like what Selene does only at a much higher level."

"No kidding." Selene's comment was an awed whisper.

"And we don't lose any of our essence in the making. We took every soul on Earth, including the souls of all those who had died since the beginning of humanity's awareness of us—they linger for quite a while after death—and stored them safely while we destroyed the planet."

Fin was faced with open-mouthed disbelief. "I know, impossible, right?" He smiled. No one smiled back. "Then we recreated Earth exactly the way it was on the day before humans first realized our danger to them. And before you ask, that means every living and nonliving thing."

Kione couldn't remain silent. "If you can do that, then

why not just destroy Mab and her army? Why the battle
with her?"

Fin shrugged. "We can't kill humans directly, and the
Fae qualify as intelligent, sentient beings. Anyway, afterwards, we placed the souls into their recreated bodies.
They have no idea we ever existed, but their souls retain
every memory in their lives up until that moment."

Jude shook his head. "I can't wrap my mind around it.
What you describe is impossible."

Zero laughed. "Something is only impossible because
you've never seen it done. You have no idea of the forces
that fill your universe and hundreds of others." His laughter faded. "But I'll admit it was only possible because
we joined our powers." Zero didn't look at his brothers.
"We've never done that before."

Seir held up his hand. "Discussion over for now. Everyone find somewhere to crash. Once we're all rested, we'll
talk about our futures."

No one argued. Adam figured all of them were speechless. Nothing could top what the three sons of Huracan
had just claimed they'd done.

As Selene grabbed his hand, and they stood, Ace
stopped them.

"Please, wait a few minutes, Selene. I have to find out
why I was with them on the bridge." He took a deep
steadying breath. "I don't want to face them alone. You're
my friend. I think I'll need some moral support for this."
Ace looked embarrassed.

Adam was reminded of how young the kid really was.

Selene smiled. "No problem. We'll have your back."

Fin, Seir, and Zero didn't look welcoming as they
approached. But Adam gave Ace credit. He stood tall and
asked his question.

"Why did you choose me to help you? I could feel my
power meshing with yours, but I don't know why."

Ace rushed his words at the end. Adam understood. He'd want to get this over with too, if he was faced with the kind of force pressing on them now. Fin and Seir were sending go-away signals, but Zero wore a satisfied smirk. Adam didn't trust that expression.

Zero tried to look sympathetic. "I chose you because you're family."

Wow! Bombshell. Or not. Fin had suspected that Ace was Zero's son. Adam glanced at Selene who was staring wide-eyed at Zero.

"Family?" Ace's voice shook.

"Your mother couldn't raise you because she was on the move a lot. I took you off her hands because that's the kind of guy I am."

Lots of eyerolling ensued.

"Anyway, I found that wonderful old woman to raise you. Her death was an inconvenience. So, I decided to put you into stasis until the time when I could give you my full attention." Zero made an attempt at a kind and loving expression.

Adam didn't believe it.

"Who am I?" Ace straightened and lifted his chin as he met Zero's gaze. "Am I your son?"

Zero seemed shocked at the thought. "No. You're his." He pointed.

"Fin?" Adam knew he sounded disbelieving. But he couldn't picture his boss—cold, in control, and deadly—losing himself to passion and fathering a child. It just didn't feel right.

"Uh-oh." Selene warned him of bad things to come.

"You bastard!" Fin was no longer Mr. Cool. "I had a son and you kept him from me?" He flung himself at his brother. No fancy powers. Just fists and fury.

Seir tried to get between them but got punched in the face for his trouble.

Selene grabbed Ace's hand. "Let's get out of here. When everyone calms down, I'm sure Fin will want to talk with you."

Ace nodded. He seemed too shocked to say anything. Adam pushed both Selene and Ace from the restaurant. Behind him he could hear the men yelling and cursing. He got a certain satisfaction from the violence. No matter how powerful, all men harbored their own personal beasts waiting to break free. Adam wasn't alone.

CHAPTER THIRTY-NINE

———

THEY DECIDED TO GO TO Fin's condo. Ace needed to talk to his father. When Fin finished working out his rage on his brother, he'd return there.

As soon as they were inside, Ace rubbed his eyes and yawned. He didn't fight Selene when she suggested he sleep until Fin got home. Once he'd left the room, Selene broached the biggest issue on her personal horizon.

"I love you, Adam. So, what are we going to do about it?" She held her breath. Was that too blunt for him? Would he prefer she simper and blush and flutter her eyelashes? Nope, wasn't going to happen. She liked the direct approach. But that didn't stop her from fearing he might just say, "Nothing."

He led her out to the balcony where he drew her down onto a padded bench. Silently, they gazed out over the newly restored city. The air was fresh and crisp as dawn lightened the sky, a fitting beginning to their new life.

Their new life. It had to begin with the truth. No more excuses. "About Meg—"

He placed his finger across her lips as he shook his head. "I understand, Selene. She was your companion, a real sister to you. I was angry because—"

She pushed his finger aside. "You thought I didn't trust you. Maybe it began that way, but in the end, it was all about fear." Selene took a deep breath. "I was afraid once you knew the truth, you'd leave me."

He met her gaze. "Never fear that again. You're stuck with me, lady."

She stroked the side of his face, lingering on his strong jaw. And waited, and waited, and waited. Just when she was ready to scream from impatience, he spoke.

"I want to join with you in our mating ceremony, Selene." He held his hand up to stop her from replying. "No, listen. In case you've forgotten, the ceremony involves you walking into the heart of my beast and taking a piece of my soul. It's not only symbolic but magical. It will fill the empty space where Meg's essence used to be. It binds us forever to each other. During the ceremony you will possibly view things that happened to me in my previous incarnations. Some might be tough to watch. At least that's what Lia, Jenna, and Kelly said happened to them. Will you have me? Forever?" He grinned. "Oh, and I love you, too."

Despite his smile, Selene sensed his tension. Time to put him at ease. "Bring on the ceremony. I'd do it now if we were able."

He exhaled his relief as he lowered her to the bench and buried his face in the curve of her neck. "I want you. And I just might explode like Six if it doesn't happen soon." Adam raised his head. His smile was the hottest thing she'd ever seen.

"Hey, look around, no nosy neighbors." She widened her eyes to show how amazing the idea she'd just had was. "We can celebrate my coming-soon walk into the heart of your beast."

"Now? Here?" His expression was hopeful with a touch of doubt.

"Sure. Why not?" Selene swept her arms wide to encompass the pure perfectness of the setting. "We're too high for anyone except a passing bird to see us. Ace is asleep and Fin's not home. So . . ." She shrugged. "Why not? We made love in a closet. I'm adventuresome when it comes to sex with the man I adore."

Adam didn't have to answer. His gaze was a lit torch to her passion. In moments she'd shed her clothes and was wrapped in his arms. Selene thrummed with anticipation. "Show me the best you have, raptor, because this is our first day in a brand-new world."

And he did.

———

Floating in a sea of glorious fulfillment, she almost didn't hear the front door open. "Oh, no." She shook Adam, who had floated a lot further from shore than she had. "I think Fin is home."

"Damn."

He scrambled for his clothes as she did the same. By the time Fin joined them on the balcony, they were sort of dressed. Hopefully, he wouldn't notice if they looked a little wild. They still wore the blood from the battle, so they could blame the fight for the way they looked.

From his expression as he dropped down on the bench beside them, they could've been naked and he wouldn't have noticed.

"My son?" Fin leaned back and closed his eyes.

"Sleeping." Selene took note of a bruise on Fin's jaw along with skinned knuckles. "Do you want me to wake him?"

Fin shook his head as he opened his eyes. "No, let him sleep. He expended a lot of power on that bridge." He offered her a half smile. "Besides, I have to figure out what to say to him. My parent skills atrophied from lack of use long ago."

Selene reached out to place her hand over Fin's in a comforting gesture. "It'll come. You're both dealing with tons of confusion right now." Her voice softened. "Does he know his mother?" Left unsaid was, "Do *you* know his mother?"

Fin exhaled deeply, but he didn't shrug off Selene's hand or her offer of sympathy. That surprised Adam. He'd always felt one kinship with his boss: neither of them liked to show weakness to others.

"My . . . son thinks of the woman that raised him as his parent." He raked his fingers through his hair. "But you would know his mother, Selene, if you'd been working with Zero when he was in Oregon. And Adam would also have known her if his soul hadn't been elsewhere at the time."

What? Adam leaned forward.

"She was Number Seven to us. Lia banished her from Earth back in Portland. I had a relationship with her a long time ago." He cast them a side glance. "I neglected to mention that."

Adam opened his mouth to condemn Fin, but closed it again on second thought. They all had secrets. Why should his boss be any different? Of course, Fin probably had more secrets than the rest of the Eleven combined.

Fin was upset. His eyes reflected a world of hurt. That shocked Adam. For as long as Adam had known him, his boss could've posed for a statue of Mr. Stoic. Nothing ever seemed to move his mood out of neutral. But this time his sorrow was on full display.

Selene patted Fin's hand. "Things will get better. Ace will be thrilled to know his real dad. You have the rest of your lives to bond. And your son can't blame you for anything when you didn't even know he existed. All the blame goes to his mother and Zero."

"I can't believe my brother kept me from my son for all those years as revenge for me choosing life over death."

Selene's narrowed eyes said exactly what she thought of Zero.

What about Ace's mother? Why didn't she ever tell Fin

about his son? After all, she'd been with him a short while ago in Portland. Adam chose to remain silent. Fin's decision to save the lives of the Eleven and defy his father's orders had cost him his son. Adam could only offer him a little relief from his sadness by changing the subject.

"While you're waiting for him to wake up, can you help us plan the mating ritual?" Adam allowed a moment of silence for Fin to digest the request.

Selene spoke first. "Adam and I love each other. We want to start our life together on Earth as soon as possible."

Fin blinked, and he was back in control. His eyes were cool with a hint of humor, all the sorrow pushed aside. Or at least covered with a veneer of what everyone expected to see. "I figured that announcement would be coming soon. We should do this before the rest of the Eleven get involved elsewhere."

Adam frowned. "Elsewhere?"

"You didn't think they'd all hang around San Diego, did you? Now that the current threat of destruction is over, it's time to move on."

Adam didn't believe a word of that, but for now it suited his purpose to agree. "Sure. So how soon?"

Fin glanced at his watch. "How about in two hours? That's enough time for me to call everyone back, Greer to whip up a suitable feast, you to take showers, and Shen to find clean clothes for both of you.

Dazed, Adam and Selene followed Fin back inside where Shen took over. Adam decided if he were the kind to keep a journal, this day would take up a whole book.

CHAPTER FORTY

———◆———

A FEW HOURS AGO, SELENE HAD been focused only on Fin's balcony. Now, she was able to appreciate the wonder of Fin's luxury penthouse. She met Adam at the door leading to the vast open space that included the living and dining areas. A soaring ceiling and enough space to almost double as a football field assured her Adam's raptor would fit in here. A floor to ceiling wall of windows spanned three sides of the room. All the better to admire the amazing views. The sun was shining and all was right with Selene's world. Today she'd bond with the man she loved. Forever. Yes, forever had a nice ring to it.

Adam pulled her close as she started to enter. "Before we perform the ritual, Selene, I have to make sure you understand what you'll be undergoing. It won't be fun, and it could be dangerous. I don't—"

She put her finger against his mouth. "Shush. If you're trying to wiggle out of this, it won't work. You're mine, and I'm going into that room to make it official." Then she pulled his head down for a deep, drugging kiss. "That's what I'm talking about."

Adam visibly relaxed. He grinned at her. "Let's do it, lady."

Selene stepped into the room and then stopped. "Whoa! Color me impressed."

The long dining table was set for the coming feast. The

other furniture in the area had been pushed to the side. Most of the remaining space was taken by the rest of the Eleven. Dressed in tuxes, they faced each other, forming an aisle.

In the background, she could see others, but only one was important. Meg waved and mouthed, "You look beautiful."

Selene blinked away tears as the turned back to Adam.

He whispered to her, "You can always run to me if you feel threatened."

She met his gaze. "The only thing that could threaten me is the chance of losing you."

"It'll never happen." And then he was gone.

Fin moved from where he stood beside Ace and took Adam's place. "I assume our raptor has filled you in on all the possible dangers, and you've told him he's worth it."

She smiled up at him. "You bet."

Fin returned her smile. It was one of his rare real ones. "Then allow me to escort you to your chosen mate." He offered her his arm.

She took his offer, and as they paced slowly down the aisle, the Eleven chanted. Their voices rose and fell, rhythmic and mesmerizing, in a language she'd never heard before. The chant was joyous, and even though she couldn't understand the words, she knew they were filled with hope.

As they drew close to the end of the aisle, Fin released her. She raised her gaze.

Adam waited for her in his raptor form; filling the room, her vision, her heart.

Selene walked. And when she drew near, she refused to close her eyes. Selene didn't have one doubt that she would be able to enter the heart of him.

The moment was magical. One moment her raptor was there and then he wasn't. But what waited wasn't what she'd expected. Selene had spoken to the other three wives and Meg to find out what they'd experienced. This wasn't it. No prehistoric scene with roving dinosaurs. No vision of Adam's first life and the horror that had destroyed it.

She was standing in a huge room. Above her, a domed ceiling disappeared into shadows. The floor was gold. She peered more closely. It looked like the real thing. Around the perimeter of the room were too many statues to count. All of the same person. There was only one door.

Then she looked up. There he was. The model for all those statues. Sitting on a throne that perched on a high dais. Gold. What else? This was feeling more and more like a bad movie.

The man stood. No, not human. He watched her—tall and regal, with long silver hair, overly large silver eyes with no whites but with a vertical pupil like a cat, and cheekbones too sharp for any human. He looked very much like Fin during the moment she'd seen his true form.

Huracan. "Your sons send their love. Okay, they don't, but I'm sure they would if they weren't so mad at you." She forced her hands to remain still. *Don't shake, don't shake.*

He didn't laugh, and she didn't think her snark had amused him.

He stepped down from the dais, one intimidating step at a time, until he stood in front of her. He was as tall as his sons.

"I am Huracan, and you are nothing but a messenger for me. I could send back your body as a warning, or perhaps have Balan return to them, but I decided a living you would make a more impressive bearer for me."

He smiled and coated every cell in her body with dread. *Don't let him know how terrified you are.* "A wise decision. And your message is?"

His expression hardened. "Don't anger me. Those who don't respect me, don't live."

He didn't have to explain. She nodded.

"Tell my sons that it isn't over. Perhaps I'll come myself next time since I have fathered two failures and a traitor. Or maybe I'll discover something more entertaining that doesn't require my presence. After all, I'm a god of wind, storm, and fire as well as creation. It may happen in a year or a thousand years. Time means nothing to me."

Wisely, she decided not to call him on his creation god claim. *Bet you can't kill humans directly any more than your sons can, pompous jerk. So, you'll still need minions.* She drew in a deep breath of courage. "Right. Got it." Selene dared to ask one question. "Where are we?"

His smile was slow and cruel. "We're in the time of the Maya. I am their god and this is my temple. They understand the power of a god and the consequence of failing one. You have yet to learn that lesson."

Time travel. Selene's heart was beating so hard she was surprised the sound wasn't echoing off the temple's walls. "How do I get back?"

Huracan waved her away. "Find your own way." Then he turned his back on her and returned to his throne.

Selene didn't waste time. She raced for the only door she could see, yanked it open, and flung herself through before he could change his mind, almost knocking over a supplicant heading inside.

Then, nothing. Mist descended, blotting out everything. She spun in a circle, panicking. *Run.* Selene listened to her instinct. She took off into the fog. Reason tried to assert itself. If Huracan wanted her to relay a message to his sons, he wouldn't make it impossible to return to her time.

She kept running, Adam's name a mantra as she pictured Fin's condo, pictured the Eleven lined up to form an aisle, pictured her raptor waiting for her.

The fog thinned. Suddenly, she was stumbling through
a city street, one littered with debris and lined with
destroyed buildings. Screams and explosions spurred her
on. Panicked people rushed everywhere. Not humans
as she recognized them, but close enough to realize this
must've been the world Adam and his brothers had origi-
nally lost to Zero. Because ahead of her was a small group
of people gathered around some who had fallen. Dead.
Her attention zeroed in on one male who crouched over
a female sprawled in that loose-limbed way the dead had.
He raised his head to meet Selene's gaze. *Adam.* No matter what body he hid within, she'd always know him. His
face was twisted in sorrow.

She wanted to stop, to comfort him, but she didn't. It
wasn't their time yet. She couldn't help him.

She raced into the future. The fog engulfed her again,
but she ran on, whispering his name over and over.

Once again, the mist lifted. Selene got a brief view of
tall grass, rocks, a few trees, and a stream. An animal in
the distance told her all she needed to know. A dinosaur. Not a time period she wanted to visit. She pushed
herself to her limit. Off to her right, she spotted three
raptors. Selene knew exactly what they were because she
had Adam's beast as her model. And the one in the middle was *her* raptor. No matter what guise he took, she'd
always know him.

The three raptors looked interested. Uh-oh. Not good.
Ahead, she saw the fog forming. Now, it was a race for
survival. If she ended up a meal in Adam's past, she'd
never forgive him.

Selene swore she could feel the raptors' breaths on her
neck when she finally flung herself into the fog. The raptors' screams of frustration followed her.

She was almost too exhausted to remain on her feet,
but she staggered on. Selene once again pulled up the

image of Adam waiting for her, held it there, and allowed nothing else to distract her.

Something tugged at her. "Adam, Adam, Adam." The pull grew stronger. She followed it, not worrying if there might be something in her path. "Adam, Adam, Adam." Her entire body vibrated with the power of whatever was drawing her.

Finally, through the fading mist, she *saw* him. He waited for her in his human form. He still stood where she'd left him. Sobbing unashamedly, she threw herself into his open arms. As she calmed, he spoke. But the words sounded strange, not the way he would normally speak.

"You touch my soul, Selene. You touch what I am, what I once was, and what I will be."

Somehow the words sounded right to her. She didn't question her response. "I accept what you share with me today—your love, your soul. I give my love and my soul in return." Not her words, but the *right* words.

He traced her lips with his fingertip before kissing her lightly. There was nothing light about the emotion flowing from him. It wrapped her in warmth she never wanted to leave.

Adam spoke the last words of the ceremony. "Take what is mine, and let it join us forever."

She rested her head against his chest, the enormity of what they'd just done finally washing over her. Selene could feel the part of his essence he'd given her. She was once again whole; the empty space Meg had left filled. Selene wanted nothing more than to find whatever room Fin had assigned them and make love all night with him.

But that wasn't to be, just yet. "I have a message for Huracan's sons."

Adam tensed. He said nothing as he led her back down the aisle through the throng of cheering friends.

Fin waited for them. "What did you experience?"

Selene told him. When she'd finished, he merely nodded. "I'll pass on the message to the others."

Fin gazed into the distance, his expression hard. "Make a token visit to the feast so everyone can congratulate you and then you can make your escape. You're in the green room."

Adam took that as a dismissal. He didn't hurry over to the table. Instead, he drew her into a corner. "What do you think?"

"I think Huracan isn't finished with us, but we can't live our lives worrying about him. Some of Zero's people will probably cause trouble too. Octopus Guy seems bent on world domination." She smiled as she looked up at him. "But you know what? This is our time. I intend to enjoy every moment of it."

"Absolutely. First, I'm Rap from now on. I don't have to be Adam anymore. I might own the vampire's body and talents, but I choose my humanity. Second, let's grab a plate of food and take a long look at the green room."

The green room was never the same.

AUTHOR BIO

Nina Bangs is the New York Times and USA Today bestselling author of more than twenty-six paranormal romances. She lives in a Texas condo with a water view. When not reading or writing, she dreams of investigating old castles in hopes of meeting a few resident ghosts.

OTHER BOOKS BY NINA BANGS

GODS OF THE NIGHT SERIES
Eternal Pleasure
Eternal Craving
Eternal Prey

THE CASTLE OF DARK DREAMS SERIES
Wicked Nights
Wicked Pleasure
Wicked Fantasy
My Wicked Vampire
Wicked Edge
Wicked Whispers
Wicked Memories

THE MACKENZIE VAMPIRE SERIES
Master of Ecstasy
Night Bites
A Taste of Darkness
One Bite Stand

Made in the USA
Las Vegas, NV
11 October 2022

57026411R00245